P9-ASA-492

GOOD FORTUNE

A NOVEL

GOOD FORTUNE

C. K. Chau

HARPERVIA

An Imprint of HarperCollins*Publishers*

This is a work of fiction. Names, characters, places, and incidents are products of the author's imagination or are used fictitiously and are not to be construed as real. Any resemblance to actual events, locales, organizations, or persons, living or dead, is entirely coincidental.

HarperCollins books may be purchased for educational, business, or sales promotional use. For information, please email the Special Markets Department at SPsales@harpercollins.com.

FIRST EDITION

Designed by Yvonne Chan

Art by Sandra Chiu

Library of Congress Cataloging-in-Publication Data has been applied for.

ISBN 978-0-06-329376-2

23 24 25 26 27 LBC 5 4 3 2 1

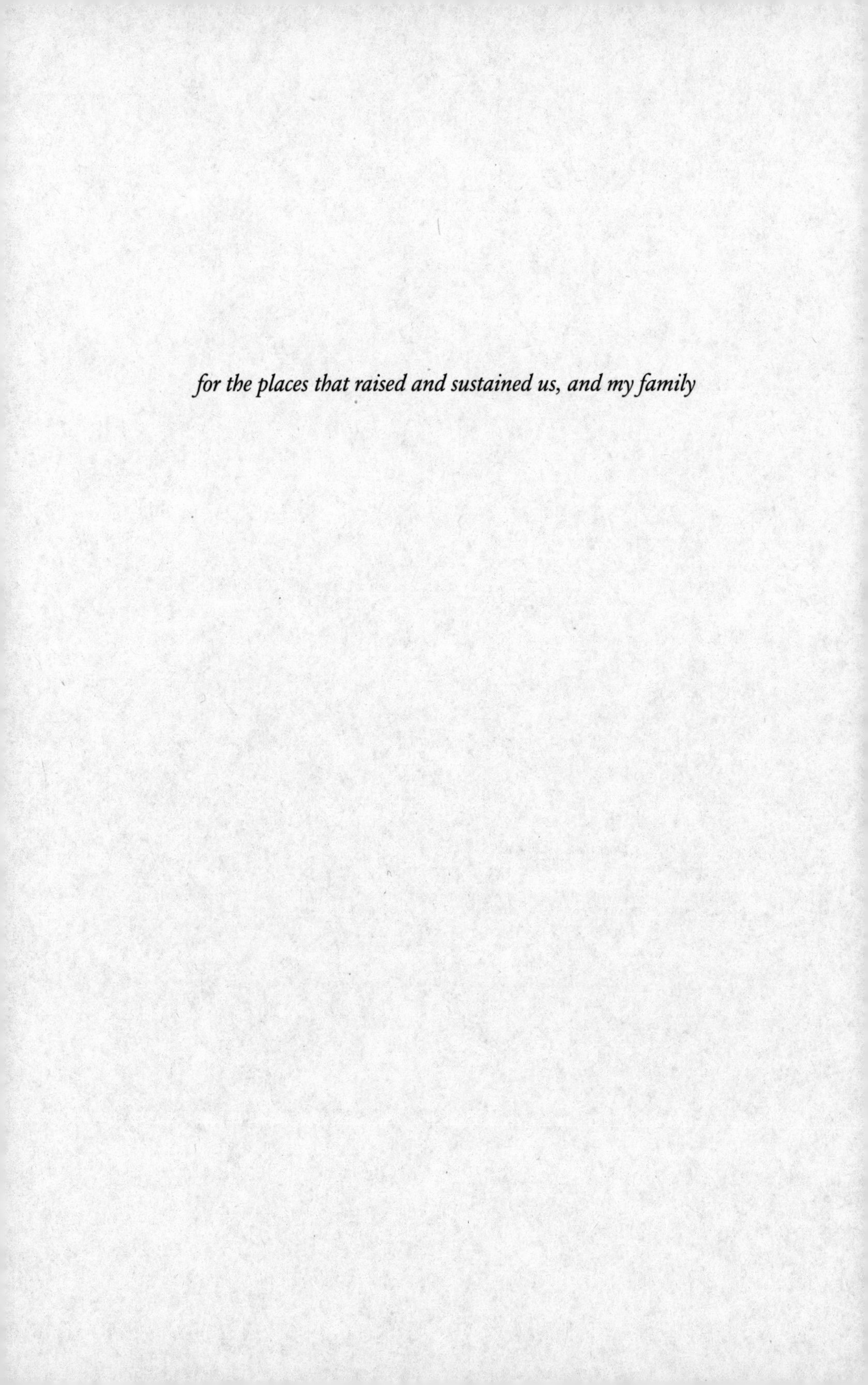

for the places that raised and sustained us, and my family

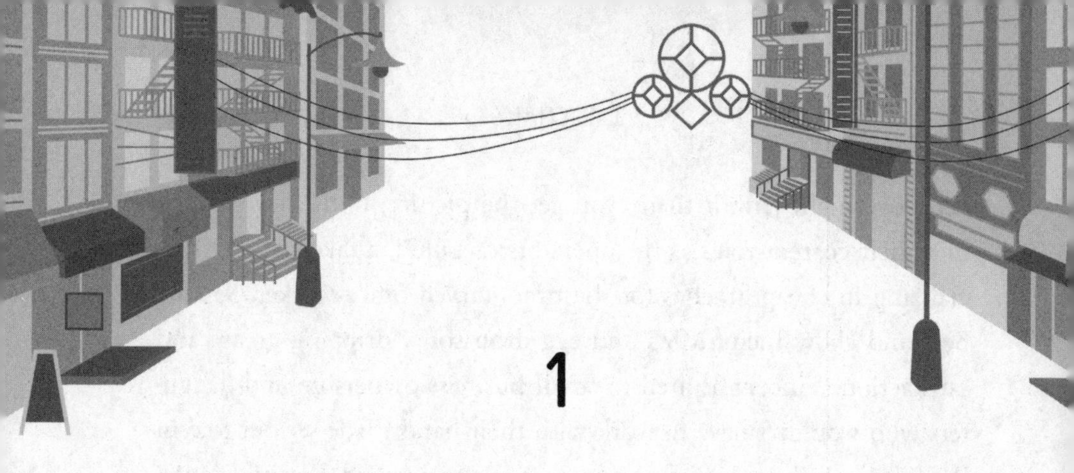

1

Presenting the Chens of Essex Street—of Chinatown, of Manhattan, of the city so nice they named it twice, of gold mountain, of the italicized, of the hyphenated, of *mei gwok*, of *zung gwok*, of the center of the world to the center of the world. Call it America. Call it the neighborhood. Call it around the turn of the millennium, give or take a few years. They came by way of two parents, Jade and Vincent—not their natural names, but the useful ones—in the usual fashion and the standard cadence. They came with similar teasing, small eyes, raffish black hair, and pert mouths; they came with red faces and squalling voices; they came easily, laboriously, frantically, lazily, and in the middle of the night, and landed in New York Presbyterian. There were five of them and what bad luck, all of them girls—Jane, the loveliest, the sweetest, the Goat (the Ram, the Sheep); then Elizabeth, sharpminded and sharper tongued (the Monkey); Mary (the Ox); Kitty (the Rabbit); and Lydia (the Dragon)—who became, collectively and in short, the Chen girls.

Their parents survived as many in the neighborhood did—hand to mouth and on odd jobs, by the skin of their teeth. Relief seamstress here, overnight janitor there, you get the picture, until they stepped into their current roles as the operators of Lulu's, a takeout joint specializing in cheap lunches for the time-starved office worker. Sesame beef and chow mein, MSG and egg drop soup, dripping grease and satisfaction. Vincent aspired to small business ownership and daughters who wouldn't have to work with their hands; Jade set out to win the lottery. Neither achieved success. So Jade pursued a realty license, Vincent ran somebody else's restaurant, and they called it an American dream.

They came for a better life, for opportunity, for the *e pluribus unum* of potential earnings. They ended up with seven in a two-bedroom in a fourth-floor walk-up with leaking pipes, flaking paint, inconsistent heat, quarrelsome neighbors, and a landlord who remembered them only when the rent was due. Better than many, they admitted, and better than before, but not quite what they imagined. Seven hundred square feet among seven people—little to go around. Little space, little privacy, and little peace. What they had, they shared; what they shared, they resented. Jade and Vincent in one bedroom, and four girls in the other, split across two sets of bunk beds, with a rotating fifth on the sofa—trying to imagine anything else besides bills and student loans and the rent due, and the fruit of their dreams yet to bear.

And what burdens those dreams were! Money, success, happiness, and Chinese husbands, to name a few, doctorates and devoted daughterhood, but most of all, the ends justifying the journey. But as the aunties might warn you, there's no counting on these American girls, these bamboo daughters. For despite their most promising start, the girls remained ungracious, unrefined, ungrateful, and, most unfortunate of all, unemployed and living at home.

Long story short, those aunties considered them unremarkable girls from an unremarkable family, decidedly of the neighborhood. Their achievements were fair, but nothing of distinction. Their Chinese, with its juvenile vocabulary, American inflections, and poor grammar, was worse, if still comprehensible—and please note the Chinese here is, alas, Cantonese, which may be a meaningful distinction in many other places around the country and around the world, if not in downtown Manhattan. Just please don't call it a dialect.

Their lives came with a persistent low-balance warning.

Lately, their troubles took the shape of a once-beloved, currently down-on-its-luck, or what the myopic might call derelict, community space on Forsyth and Canal. In 1993, it proudly launched itself as The Greater Chinatown Neighborhood Youth Recreational Center. The decade since hadn't been kind. Now, fading away under graffiti tags, tax liens, aggressive mold, and years of skipped maintenance, the building listed itself as ripe with potential, if desperate for the attentions of a Jade Chen type to rescue it from certain condemnation. Lucky, then, for the neighborhood that there was a Jade Chen, who muscled her way to brokering any property no other agent would touch and received little for her efforts but ingratitude, indigestion, chronic migraines, asthma, heart palpitations, and acid reflux. Had the owner heeded Jade's many kind, if unsolicited, warnings and hints as to how to get it into selling shape? No. Had he taken her up on any of her generous offers to oversee the listing for a steal of a fee at 5.5 percent? Of course not. Some people couldn't ever see the forest for the trees—or, in this case, the entrepreneurial genius in stirrup pants—just because of some paperwork. But no longer. After years of neglect and weeks of Jade's psychological disintegration, prosperity loomed on the horizon. Realtor license or not, nothing changed minds faster than hearing *all cash*.

"Girls," she cried, shouldering her way past the front door of their apartment, groceries in hand. "You won't believe it! You won't believe what your mama did!"

Four girls, in various collapsing postures and states of undress, blinked at her from across the room.

At five foot three and undisclosed weight, with gossamer inches layered on by the perm of her hair, Jade Chen resembled many of the unassuming grandmothers around the block, at least until she opened her mouth. Nothing could be said, if not said loudly; nothing could be done without fanfare or frustration; and nothing ever happened without her first hearing about it. Two days' worth of groceries swung wide from her clenched fists.

Kitty leaned back on the sofa while Lydia flipped through TV channels with a yawn. "Did what, Mother?"

Elizabeth took the groceries from her mother's hands and unpacked damp bags of gai lan and radish onto the counter. "Destroy Chinatown."

"LB *aaaa*," Jade whined, clicking her tongue. "*Neih gong matyeh, aaaaa*?"

Don't be alarmed—this is no clerical error or wail of sudden calamity, no wrathful god striking Jade suddenly unable to speak. An *aa* can be worth thousands of words. Whining or flat, long or short, rising or falling, it's a punch of seasoning on a complaint or a question, a musical interjection, and an all-season accessory to highlight how you might really feel.

Elizabeth rolled her eyes. "*Mou je aa*," she conceded.

Of course, no one speaks italics, and if they did, they wouldn't speak it at home. That's for you. All the better to dodge the thorny consonants and yowling vowels of Chinese, the jagged edges of its rises and falls, the traps of vocabulary. Show a little gratitude. What they spoke might be called Chinese, though their parents would dispute that classification, threaded with English, but it was in all other ways the usual bullshit—sibling rivalries and spending money, test scores and expectations, ressentiments of daughterhood.

When the girls were young, Jade and Vincent often fretted about their daughters and their tongues, anxious for them to escape the cruelty of scrutiny. They had long avoided English in public unless absolutely necessary, and in the event of emergency, called a daughter. Jane and Elizabeth preferably, Kitty and Lydia in a pinch, Mary as last resort. They left their daughters to grow into their hollowed Chinese, plugging English into whatever sprang a leak, stumbling on the wrong sounds, chasing intelligibility—but as Jade insisted, at least their English was beyond reproach. No trace of an accent, no problem. A hallmark of their success. A hallmark of their loss.

What the girls couldn't have told their parents was how much they longed to choose for themselves. Each time they opened their mouths, they felt compromised by their parents' decision, marking them for one culture over the other, for this life over that one, standing apart rather than with their parents and grandparents. They wanted both. Instead, they found themselves half in and half out in a pidgin of their own making. So let's kill the italics and do as Jane and Elizabeth did at their joint elementary school parent-teacher conference—translate poorly. Follow along or make the most of it.

Jade harrumphed, rustling through her purse for her apartment keys.

"All I'm saying," Elizabeth replied, "is that the neighborhood *means* something."

"You are being very dra-ma-tic," Jade said, striking the hard consonants of English for emphasis. She relished the contrast of a sharp English syllable against the melodic rises and falls of Chinese.

"Kitty," Elizabeth called. "Get off your ass and help."

Lydia's leg fired at an angle to boot Kitty off of the sofa. "You heard her."

Kitty rolled her eyes, flinging her Tamagotchi at Lydia's arm. "You could get up too, you know."

"Your aim sucks," Lydia replied.

"Kitty!" Elizabeth called, and Kitty came, feet dragging on the hems of her pajama pants.

"LB, you're so unfair," Kitty replied, dutifully sinking her hands into another plastic bag and retrieving a head of cabbage. "Jane never talks to me this way."

Lydia rolled her eyes. "Jane babies you."

"Says the baby," Kitty snapped.

"Jane's at the library, and I'm asking you to help me, okay?" Elizabeth said.

"Why me? It's always me! You never ask Lydia to do *anything*. And Mary's just sitting there!"

"I'm *studying*," Mary retorted.

"V. C. Andrews?" Kitty replied.

"Unpack the bag," Elizabeth said.

Lydia cackled in triumph.

Jade threw her handbag onto one of the kitchen chairs. "No one is going to ask me what I did?"

In unison, the three girls intoned, "The rec."

Jade stretched a finger high into the air. "The rec!"

Practical and austere, dependable and dull, The Greater Chinatown Neighborhood Youth Recreational Center had once been a brave new world of city funding and dedicated resources, only to fade into old age as the rest of the neighborhood did. The brick dirtied, the signage shedding letters in vandalism or neglect until it came to resemble its neighbors: a little haggard, a little hardened, but not unwelcoming.

The unimaginative and unsophisticated might look at it and see unpaid property taxes and urban decay, a sign of the troubles from the last decade, but in the right light at the right angle, it could be opportunity for the cunning and quick. Jade saw a sizable commission for an intrepid upstart; the girls saw another victim of the changing city, waiting to be cannibalized into cupcake shops and coffee shops in the circle of life; but Elizabeth felt it as a keen loss, a passing of the heart of the neighborhood and the joys of her schoolyard days.

"Your mama doesn't even have her license yet, but she is closing big, big deals."

The girls mumbled half-hearted congratulations.

"You're helping them turn the city into a strip mall," Elizabeth said.

Jade shuddered an aggrieved sigh. Some children come as gifts from heaven, dutiful and compliant, quiet and sweet; some are karmic punishments. Jade considered Elizabeth, on occasion, a karmic punishment. It wasn't that she ignored every single bit of well-meaning advice (though she did); or that despite Jade's many pleas for her to study something profitable, she'd chosen communications and photography (at a median income of forty thousand dollars!); or that she insisted on working dead-end jobs (destroying her hands!) until she could make her own way rather than pumping any of Jade's connections. She supposed she knew so much, and couldn't admit that her mother might know things she didn't. "I am investing in the neighborhood. I am *raising* the property values."

"Mother, what values? We don't own this apartment."

"Elizabeth, what kind of daughter can't be happy for her mother, aa?" Jade replied.

"I'm happy!"

Jade preened. "When I told your friend Alexa at the store, she congratulated me right there."

Kitty crumpled a plastic bag between her hands.

"Good for her," Elizabeth said.

"Alexa said that she was going to teach me how to drive," Lydia said, rising to join them in the kitchen. "Did you get any snacks?"

Kitty whipped a bag of baby carrots at her chest.

"Kitty!" Lydia cried. "Ow!"

"How's my aim now?"

"Girls, stop fighting," Jade said. "Dinner soon."

"Alexa's not going to teach you how to drive," Elizabeth said.

"Shows what you know," Lydia replied. "We're friends now."

Jade answered with a sly smile, "She has an ad at the pay phone on Canal Street. Did you see it?"

"No," Elizabeth said. "I don't go scanning phone booths for Alexa Hu."

"You should," Lydia replied, tearing into the bag and crunching a carrot between her teeth. "She's everywhere."

Jade lifted a threatening finger. "What did I say, Lydia? Dinner soon. Start the rice."

Lydia rolled her eyes. "I'm meeting Chester."

"What, again?" Elizabeth said. "You have a shift tonight."

"Kitty's taking it."

"What? No, I'm not."

"You're taking it, Kitty. You said, aa."

"I *didn't*. Like I don't have a life?"

Lydia snorted. "You *don't*."

Jade sighed. "Ai, giving birth to a slab of roast pork would have been more useful than you, LB. Why don't you find a good, well-paying job like that Alexa?"

"I'm doing okay," Elizabeth replied.

Jade snorted. "Opening doors and delivering food . . ."

"Helping our neighbors," Elizabeth said, talking over her. "And enough to help with the groceries, which is more than I can say for *some* people around here . . ."

Mary raised her book to cover her face.

"Why do you insist on being stupid?" Jade sighed. "You are not a social worker. You have a college degree, and you're wasting . . ."

"Mother, she's a weather girl for Channel 5. I'm not desperate."

"You're not finding anything either," Jade replied, jabbing her in the chest with the sharp end of a nail.

"Service jobs don't look very good on a résumé," Mary replied.

"And when was the last time *you* chipped in without being asked first?" Elizabeth replied.

Lydia crunched another carrot. Wet orange flesh speckled her large teeth. "Alexa could get you a job, LB."

"I'm not asking Alexa for a job."

"Why not?" Lydia said. "What's the point of knowing people if you aren't going to take advantage?"

Jade slapped Lydia hard on the shoulder in agreement. "Your baby sister knows better than you."

Elizabeth narrowed her eyes. "Why don't you start the rice?"

"Why don't you, big mouth?"

"Girls, girls!" Jade clucked. "Don't you want to know how your mama did it?"

They groaned in chorus.

Elizabeth couldn't think of anything she'd want to hear less. Climbing over the groceries gathered on the floor, she shoveled loose notebooks and a bulky laptop into the large pocket of her black JanSport and slung the strap onto her shoulder.

"And where are you going?" Jade said.

"Lulu's," Elizabeth said. "It's *quieter* there."

"Great! You can cover for me," Lydia replied.

Elizabeth glared at her and rushed out.

Jade collapsed into one of the kitchen seats with a loud sigh. "Nobody in this family ever appreciates what I do."

Kitty set a hand on her shoulder. "Mommy, we *do*," she said. "We just don't want to hear about it, that's all."

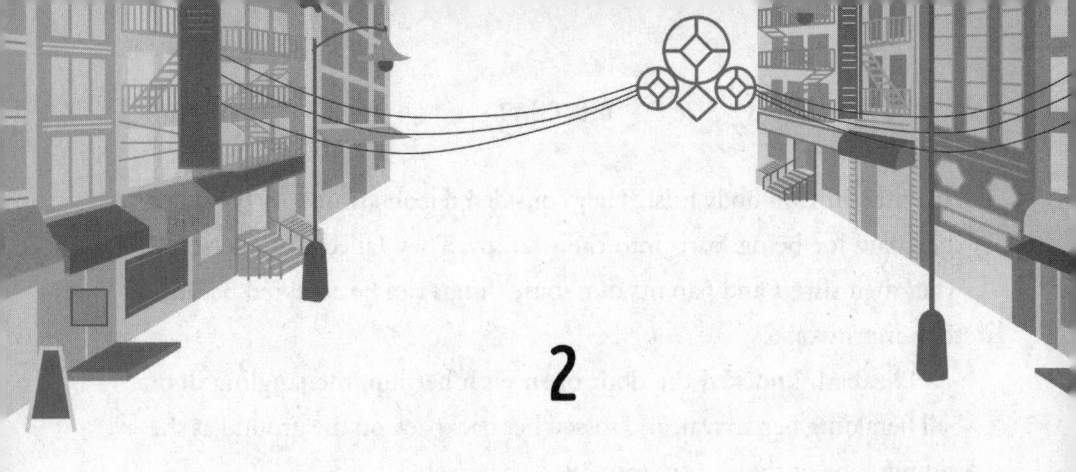

2

Every block in the city has its own peculiar landmark that comes recommended with a disclaimer—the laundromat with a mysterious and miraculous free dryer when you need it that only runs short cycles; the liquor store that closes and opens at random; the wandering dumpling cart that only takes cash. Lulu's was theirs. Drunk after 1 a.m.? Stuck without food on a national holiday? Broke? You already know. The neon sign had long stopped working, though electricity still hissed through it; the paper menu bled ink; the tabletops were sticky and populated with unfilled salt and pepper shakers; and the only people who might be found eating there were employees. But ten dollars for an egg roll, soda, rice, and entrée—what more could you want?—and if you want more, best go elsewhere.

For the last ten years, Vincent (mostly) and family (sometimes) operated Lulu's. Operated, as in didn't own. He didn't complain. A paycheck was a paycheck, and a life was a life. He could learn to chop broccoli and deep-fry chicken just as he'd learned how to read. The youngest Chens dissented. They couldn't bear the toil or the time, and definitely not the smell—that *eau de* fry grease that couldn't be smothered under cucumber-melon body mist. They considered it an affront, the penance they paid for being born into their family. They failed to understand what their sisters and parents did: some things can be accepted because they aren't worse.

Elizabeth knocked the door open with her hip, the jangling door bell heralding her arrival, and tossed her backpack on the ground as she slid into one of the empty seats. "Ba," she greeted.

"Floor's dirty," he said, without glancing up from the newspaper.

It would be easy, if unwise, to mistake Vincent Chen for a serious man given his looks—thick square bifocals, button-down shirt, slight frame, thinning hair, and ratty sweater. Many often did. It was known he didn't gamble, didn't gossip, and rarely chose to leave home. But with a wife like Jade and daughters like Kitty and Lydia, aa, who couldn't understand a need for peace and quiet? But blink and you might miss the twist of humor in his expression, the slight pout of his lips as he laughed without laughing.

Elizabeth lifted her backpack and dropped it onto an adjacent seat. "Happy?"

"I figured you might be coming," he said, licking his finger and turning a page of his newspaper. "Your mother seemed very excited when I talked to her."

Excitement, he left to his wife and daughters.

She unpacked her old laptop onto the table and shoved the Ethernet card into the slot. It whirred and spat dust as it tried to spin its drives to life. "She finally offloaded the rec."

Vincent's jaw dropped. "*Waaa*, already?" he said. "She must have put the nails to the Chieng brothers."

"The screws, Dad," Elizabeth corrected.

"Nails, screws, same thing," he said.

"She's practically counting the commission," Elizabeth said. "Never mind what happens to the rec."

Vincent tucked his newspaper under an arm and joined her at the table with a cold dish of noodles. "Don't let her hear you say that," he said.

Elizabeth sunk back into a chair. "All it needs is . . ."

"Fresh paint?"

She rolled her eyes. "Some money. Someone who cares about it. Then it can go back to what it used to be."

"Instead of Old Lady Tang's personal gambling hall?" Off her unamused look, he sighed, poking at the wet mass of noodles with his chopsticks. "Ai ya, LB. Things change. Nothing you can do. Try not to worry, la." He punctuated the thought with a loud slurp of noodles before holding out his chopsticks to her in offer.

She shoveled a large bite into her mouth.

He nodded slowly at her. "Not hungry?"

She rolled her eyes in answer.

"How's the job hunt going?" he said, retreating to his position behind the counter. "Any offers?"

The bell rang again, saving her from fumbling for a lie. Jade and Vincent might be called easygoing when compared to other parents on the block, but that didn't mean they understood. Ask the older daughters in your area and they won't tell you: the truth might set you free, but lying keeps everybody happy. Elizabeth lied about her smoking and drinking, about late nights and dates, about grades, and now, about work. Finding a job seemed so simple—submit résumé, submit to interview, submit to boss—but turned out harder to land in practice. Call it another unspoken rule of the city: from dates to doctor appointments, job interviews to restaurant reservations, nobody ever called back.

A piercing squeal punctuated the silence. "Eeeee, Lizzie! How *are* you!"

An easy question to answer; she wasn't—a Lizzie, that is. For the uninitiated and unfamiliar, she might be Elizabeth; for her family and close friends, she was LB; for her parents in fits of pique, she could also be known as 慧欣; or, simply, scathingly, daughter. But a Lizzie? Never. Except to neighborhood darling, Channel Five meteorologist, and Elizabeth's long-standing personal nightmare Alexa Hu. She was a pale, small-pored, five-foot, and size-zero terror in a Lord & Taylor suit. Her career trajectory, like her hair, her manners, and her accent, betrayed no flaw. For years, her accomplishments bullied every Chinese American girl between Centre and Clinton; now, she was the first of their class of Chinese daughters to marry, triggering a thousand leading questions at a thousand family dim sums.

"It's *so funny* to run into you here," she said, clapping Elizabeth in a short hug.

"At my parents' restaurant?" Elizabeth replied, lightly returning the embrace.

If Alexa heard, she didn't understand. "I've been so busy I haven't been able to breathe, but I *had to* catch up with you. You're impossible to get hold of, you know." When she spoke, her voice rose and fell with a trembling whine like erhu.

"I'm always around," Elizabeth said. "How's everything with the wedding?"

Her glossy curtain of hair rippled with discontent. "Everything's *horrible*. And Bryan, I love him, but he's so checked out, you know what I mean? Playing basketball with his friends, and whatever else men do." She yanked her cell phone roughly from the belt loop of her pants, the exterior almost fully covered in hot-glued rhinestones that sparkled weakly under the dim lights. A small jade Buddha charm dangled from the corner.

She flipped it open and scanned the screen, heaving a large sigh. "He's unbelievable."

Elizabeth leaned her laptop shut. "Isn't your mom helping out?"

"You would think, right?" she said, flicking her phone shut. Walking around the side of the counter, she greeted Vincent politely before rattling off her order in breathless Chinese.

Elizabeth waved her father into the back. "I'll ring it up," she said, heading behind the counter towards the register.

The burner fired up with a click, followed by the familiar clang and scramble of the metal spatula scraping down the wok.

Alexa simpered, clicking her tongue. "God, you're so sweet," she said. "Your parents must be lost without you, right? Anyway, Bryan has all of these people—*school chums* or something—coming from Hong Kong. Last minute, of course, and we don't know if we'll have enough space at the reception. I'm like, *honey*, can you *help* instead of making things harder? But you know how it is."

She didn't. Her last boyfriend had been a five-month, live-work affair, and the high point had been trying to deduct the expenses from her taxes.

She punched the subtotal, and the register trilled.

Alexa fished a Coach wallet from her stiff Louis Vuitton handbag, thumbing three crisp twenties and holding it out for her to take. "I am *telling you*, Lizzie, if you ever get married—*when*, when you get married—you must, must, must call a wedding planner. Don't try to do it yourself like I did. No matter how on top of things you think you are, it's too much for anyone! Even me!"

Elizabeth slowly counted out change. "I'll keep that in mind." Behind her, she heard the rustle of paper and plastic bags, the quick snap of plastic lids.

Alexa snatched the change out of her hand before she could finish counting it, and threw loose coins into the soup container for tips. "It was so good to see you. Tell Lydia it's so sweet of her to call and check on me *every day*, but we can talk after the wedding. And come, come, come—I'll *make sure* that you're in the running for the bouquet." Grabbing the two full plastic bags of food on the counter, Alexa trotted for the door. "But no cheating, though! Yum cha soon, okay? Bye, Uncle!"

As she opened the door, a figure passing through slowed and hugged her in greeting.

"My gosh," Alexa squealed. "It's been *so* long, I almost didn't recognize you!"

Jane hovered in the doorway, pulling the hood of her sweatshirt down from her head. "Congratulations," she said. "We're so happy for you and Bryan."

Alexa puckered her mouth in a show of an air kiss. "Chens, you're so *sweet*!" she said. "But I've got to run this over to my aunty before she has a heart attack. Bye-bye, la!"

Elizabeth waved again, exhaling once Alexa cleared the block.

Jane greeted them both with a yawn, switching off her Walkman and setting it on the table.

"What are you doing here?" Elizabeth said. "I thought you were paying rent to the computer lab."

"Lydia said she needed someone to cover," Jane said, sinking into a seat and tossing her backpack onto another chair. Folding her arms on the table, she leaned her head against them and shut her eyes.

"Lydia says whatever she has to so she doesn't have to show up."

Jane groaned. "Leave her alone."

Elizabeth had long accepted that loving her sisters didn't mean understanding them. What they wanted, what they chose, who they were. They were familiar strangers, colleagues, and partners who knew each other too well and drove each other crazy. That is, except for Jane.

To her had gone the sweet and docile temperament their parents once hoped they'd all inherit. There was no one more patient, more kind, or more loving than her older sister; with no one else did Elizabeth ever feel as comfortable. While Elizabeth loved all of her sisters, only one seemed to truly understand her.

"What are you doing here?" Jane said. "I thought you were at home with the others."

Elizabeth clicked her tongue. "I couldn't get anything done."

"Did anyone call you back?"

She shook her head.

"Alexa was telling LB she'd have a good spot for catching the bouquet," Vincent said. "Beat all the other girls away."

"If I can't find a real job, I can always marry rich."

Jane hummed in sympathy.

"Well, don't worry, la," Vincent said, squeezing her shoulder. "Until your time comes, we're more than happy to have you at the apartment."

"Thanks, Dad."

"Until we die and the landlord evicts you," he replied. "But there's still time for your life to turn around before then."

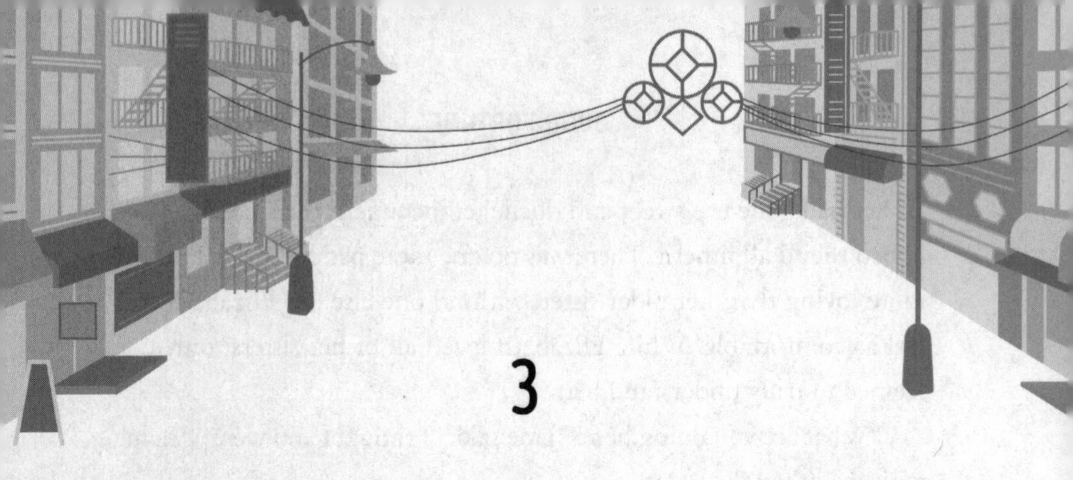

3

Three weeks later, Alexa Hu married Bryan Wei in front of the entire neighborhood. Nothing unites a block like a common grievance or a wedding, and everyone got their cut of both joys: the mothers discussed and lamented the strength of the menu and the quality of the food; the local girls labored over finding the right dress and the best way to sneak themselves drinks; the gossips scrutinized the guest list for who might have been scrupulously ignored or forgotten; but no one relished the occasion more than the aunties. They picked and pecked for loose tongues, old scandals, new gossip, and borrowed grief.

As they entered the banquet hall, the Chen girls closed ranks against potential assault, nodding and smiling vacantly at the chattering neighbors, aunts, and uncles around them as they made their way to their assigned table. Wasn't it sad what happened to Bridget Li? Did they keep in touch with Annette Chan since she moved? What were they studying? How were their grades? What were they doing, where were their cousins, and why hadn't they been seen around this or that recently? They zigged and zagged, deflected and kept moving.

Hadn't Elizabeth already graduated? *Yes, Aunty*. But Mrs. Ng said she wasn't working? *I'm doing odd jobs for now, Aunty, and helping out at the restaurant.* Waa, what was the world coming to if a brilliant and beautiful girl like her couldn't find anything? But Aunty hoped she might find something soon. *Me too.* Wasn't Alexa's wedding beautiful? *It was, Uncle.* Didn't she want to get married soon? *Not yet, Uncle.* Ah, but girls like her were always saying that. Didn't her father come? *He didn't feel well.* Did she have any boyfriends? *Not yet, Aunty.* Such a beautiful girl like her? *It's true, Aunty.* If she wanted an introduction, Aunty could help arrange it, because she wouldn't be so young and pretty forever. *Thank you, but I'm focused on other things right now.* Oh, only joking, only joking! Don't take offense, la.

The aunties fussed over them, fawning over their dresses, their manners, their hair, their makeup—*such beautiful girls, such politeness, such grace*—but they knew how they looked: severe, conservative, unflattering. Five girls in stiff cheongsam in a range of jewel tones like a collectible Precious Moments tableau. If Kitty could have disappeared through the window, she might have tried it.

Lydia peeled off for the bar once they found their table, hoping for a server who might be swayed to "forget" to card. Mary plucked the menu ticket for something to read only to find the entire thing in Chinese. Jade tried to kidnap the photographer for her own personal use. ("Quality prints, aa!") Elizabeth resigned herself to the inevitable chaos of the rest of the evening, and hoped to avoid any more questions about her own future.

A rattling hum of clinking glass filled the room as the bride and groom made their way towards their banquet table. Jade giggled, tapping the edge of her water glass with the tines of her fork. "Such a beautiful couple," she sighed. With a pointed look at her daughters, she added, "A great job and married, buying a house. Taking care of her parents . . ."

Elizabeth looked at Jane, who said nothing. Kitty rolled her eyes.

"If this is what it takes, I'm never getting married," Mary said.

"Won't your online boyfriend be disappointed?" Kitty said.

Alexa grinned and kissed her husband to a round of applause. Jade cooed with delight.

Lydia barreled into the table, champagne splashing out of the glasses in her hands and onto the tablecloth. "Party time!"

Kitty reached for a glass, but Lydia pushed her aside.

"Way more FOBs here tonight than I thought," she said, downing the first glass.

"Lydia!" Jane cried.

Kitty looked near tears, batting at Lydia's arm. "Mommy, can *I* have champagne? Tell Lydia to give me the other one . . ."

"Lydia, sit down and be quiet," Elizabeth added. "You can't say things like that."

Jade waved her off with a mild laugh. "LB, let her have her fun."

"Can I—" Kitty tried. "Mommy . . ."

"Ai ya, Kitty, have whatever you want."

"Oh, please," Lydia said, sliding into her seat. "It's, like, a compliment. It means that they actually *got* here, didn't they?"

Mary sniffed. "Fresh off the boat is a pejorative—"

"People can hear you," Elizabeth interrupted. "Remember where you are, please."

Lydia mocked her with a quick raise of the eyebrows and rolled her eyes. "Yeah," she said, draining the second flute. "I'm at my *friend's* wedding. You're lucky you were even invited."

"Your manners, Lydia."

Lydia waved her off. "Chill, would you? Try and remember what it's like to have fun."

"Or you ought to try and have less," Mary replied.

Lydia jabbed her thumb against the tip of her nose, oinking at her in response.

"Lydia," Jade sighed. "Who taught you to do that? You look so ugly."

"She started it."

Apart from their squabbles and Lydia's insistence on abandoning sobriety, the reception otherwise passed in an orderly procession of courses and easy conversation. They watched the bride and groom pour tea for each other's parents, slice and shove wedding cake into each other's faces, and dance the first dance. Jade burned through a stack of Pizza Hut napkins ferreted from her purse as she cried through the toasts, and the Chen girls all learned how many people their mother seemed to know (and how many people seemed to know something about the five of them). As they picked at the last of their cake, they splintered into the usual factions: Mary sullen at the table, Lydia and Kitty unrestrained at the bar, and Jane and Elizabeth on the dance floor, trying to make each other laugh.

When she'd had enough of the crowd, Elizabeth returned to their table to see Kitty and Lydia pushing their way through to the floor. They draped their arms over one another, bony hips jerking side to side as they whooped and pouted in exaggerated sensuality. Performing for cameras that weren't there. One day they might learn to admire people other than the Hilton sisters, but for now, they were the stars of their own reality show, too glamorous for their neighborhood by far and too busy to be bothered.

Mary grunted in greeting, sliding Lydia's untouched glass of water from across the table.

Elizabeth sank onto her seat, toeing off her heels and flexing her aching feet. Jade had howled in complaint any time she'd even looked at her camera case that evening—not that it would have fit in her purse—but she couldn't imagine a better time for pictures. The aunties and uncles this side of drunk, the kids losing themselves to the music on the dance floor, and no one paying attention to what she was doing. It wouldn't be hard to find some shots—the uncles gambling on cards; the waiters loitering by the galley, smoking behind the kitchen. Jade thought it a waste of time, hiding behind a camera instead of taking center stage, but she didn't understand the appeal of things that didn't make money. Elizabeth liked to look. It taught her to slow down, to notice the details. It taught her how to be in the world.

Jane slid into the free seat beside her. "What's on your mind?"

Elizabeth created a frame with her thumbs and index fingers and centered Jane. "Snap."

"So you're bored."

"Who could be bored at a wedding?" Elizabeth said with a wave of the hand. "Did you see Kitty or Lydia? Are they still conscious?"

Mary gravely shook her head. "The kind of attention seeking they do won't earn them the response that they're looking for."

Elizabeth laughed. "Not the response *you're* looking for, but I think they get something out of it."

Mary sniffed, turning back towards her reading. "It's *so* inappropriate."

"What's appropriate for you, Mary?"

Mary didn't answer in time. A rumble of discontent rippled from the center of the dance floor, the thick mesh of bodies parting to reveal a figure marching through with short, rapid-fire steps. No one else could move with such singular intent and focus, such predatorial precision. No one else would have a crisis at someone else's wedding. But Jade Chen was not anyone.

The pulsing beats of "Waiting for Tonight" blasted, and Elizabeth took a gulp of her champagne, steeling herself for the landing.

Jade crashed against the table midsentence, white-knuckling the back of Jane's chair as she tried to catch her breath. "Didn't know," she gasped, "knew the family, but Aunt Pippa didn't say, horrible, and I, *ai ya, why is he at Alexa Hu's wedding*, and she told me . . ."

Elizabeth pushed one of the water glasses towards her. "Mother. Breathe."

She took a bracing breath. "You'll never believe who came tonight."

Jane and Elizabeth glanced at each other and shrugged. Mary didn't even glance up from the wedding program.

"Our *angel* investor!" she cried. "He's come for the wedding, would you believe it, with *friends*, and he's *so excited* to meet you, Jane." There could be no denying her conviction. If she believed it, it was as good as destined. Verification was for the weak-willed and nonbelieving like Elizabeth, who doubted that the investor remembered anything about Jade's life, never mind wanting to meet her daughters.

"And you too, LB. I'm sure there's lots of . . . politics to talk to you about. They're smart, you know. And single," she said. And there it was—the urgency of the occasion. "He and Bryan are good friends."

Among the neighborhood, there were certain golden sons, long-awaited, much-anticipated, and over-appreciated. But with great prestige came great expectation—academic achievement, professional acceleration, Chinese wives, and Chinese sons all their own—and apprehension. Fattened as they were on endless praise, minor liberties, and their mothers' devoted attention, they often wasted what freedom they earned. Bryan, Mr. Alexa himself, fell among that lauded group, shaping his life out of what his parents wanted: piano lessons, Ivy League, law school, corporate ladder climbing. When she was younger, she had envied those boys for their freedom, but what good was freedom to choose if you never chose anything at all?

Jane elbowed her sister and flashed a cheerful smile at their mother.

"Come on," she said, rising. "It's always nice to meet new people at a wedding."

Elizabeth jammed her feet into her shoes. "Is it?" she hissed. "Is it *always nice* to meet people at a wedding?"

Jade dragged them towards the other side of the room. "Come be friendly, la!"

Elizabeth fell in line.

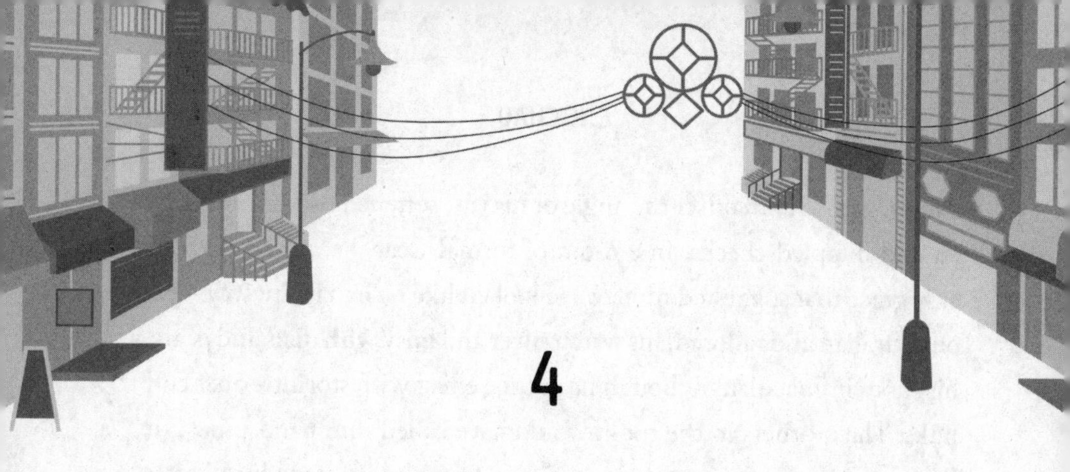

4

Of course Jade didn't make introductions as much as fish—for compliments, gifts, job offers, favors, you name it. At the last neighborhood get-together, there had been Winston, who smoked (only) Winstons, sported a Members Only jacket and a thick mustache, and worked in personal injury law. Would Elizabeth want to go out with him sometime? *No, thank you.* What about working in his supply-closet office in Flushing as a legal assistant? *Not with that commute.* Three weeks after they'd met, she'd caught him on TV, surrounded by showgirls singing the jingle for his law firm. *Get hurt? Can't work? Don't be a jerk! Dial Berk & Bi, Attorneys at Law!* That was the caliber of men Jade considered good for her daughters.

They arrived at the outer edge of a crowd, and Jade tapped one of the men on the shoulder. "Mr. Brendan?"

He turned.

Cue the harps.

This was no middle-aged man but someone nearer their age. Boyish, if pushing thirty. Thick, dark hair swept back from his broad forehead in a floppy wave; fine, long eyelashes framed narrow, lidless eyes; a strong, square chin offset the angle of his jaw, softened by traces of baby fat and dimpled cheeks. In a room of formal wear, he moved with an easy grace that suggested money. He looked like he had it, anyway—his outfit Italian and tailored, his watch silver and busy with dials and gears, his shoes immaculate—though he cut the effect with stormtrooper cuff links. The mothers in the room would have called him handsome, but that wasn't it. He was a golden retriever; friendliness made him better looking.

"Jade!" he said, taking her into his arms and kissing her on both cheeks. A slight accent hung on his words, halfway British and halfway Cantonese, singsong as a playground rhyme. "We thought you'd deserted us!"

On anyone else, the gesture would have looked affected, but he made it look natural.

Jade giggled. Elizabeth hadn't suspected that was a sound her mother could even produce.

"Mr. Brendan!" she said. "You know I wouldn't!"

A laugh rang out among the crowd, and Elizabeth startled to see the mixed company gathered around him. Here were the breeds of rich she recognized—six or seven standing apart from the rest of the room, dripping in diamonds and sleek sophistication, talking to nobody but themselves and thinking themselves all the better for it. No one knew better than her how ridiculous Jade could be, but it was a wedding, she was an elder, and ridiculousness didn't give anyone the right to rudeness—especially not to a stranger. Especially not to her mother.

"I want to introduce my daughters," Jade said. "They've been strong supporters of our little community center. This is my oldest, Jane, who's studying to become a doctor, and Elizabeth, who is . . . graduated from college."

"In a year," Jane added. "Finishing up in another year."

Elizabeth tried a smile. "It's true, I'm a graduate," she said. "Though I forgot to bring my diploma with me."

Jane kicked the back of her foot.

Mr. Brendan returned a smile, showing celebrity teeth, even and bleached white. "Hey, that's awesome," he said. "I don't know if your mother's told you, but we have *so* many ideas for the center. We want to be part of the force to help turn New York around, you know?"

Elizabeth's smile sharpened. "I don't think New York needs to be *turned around*," she replied. "And you know the rec is something like an institution—I mean, Jane and I practically grew up—"

Jade pinched her bicep.

Their new friend didn't notice.

"I'm Brendan," he said. "One of Bryan's cousins of cousins of cousins. You know how it is."

"Brendan . . . ?" Elizabeth said.

"Brendan Lee."

"I'll leave you to get introduced," Jade said with a coy flutter of her hands as she slipped back into the crowd. "Make friendly, la!"

Brendan gestured towards their outfits. "Going traditional, huh?" he said. "That's awesome."

They blushed. "Our mother picked these out," Jane said.

He laughed, air whistling faintly through his teeth, and Elizabeth softened. Anyone with a ridiculous laugh couldn't be too bad, no matter how expensive their clothes. "Jade?" he said. "Right on. I bet Alexa and her parents appreciate it. They're into that kind of thing, you know. Tradition." He glanced down at their empty hands. "Where are your drinks?"

Elizabeth shrugged, but their newfound acquaintance sprang into action. A knight in shining Armani, he returned with two full glasses of champagne.

"Thank you," Jane said. "That's kind of you."

"It's a wedding. It's not right for you not to be at least a little drunk."

"A gentleman and a scholar," Elizabeth cracked.

He didn't seem to hear her. Not when Jane sipped at her champagne, touched his arm, and smiled at him. Not when Jane stood near enough to dazzle. Elizabeth had seen it before—the awestruck look on men's faces, the loss of speech, the way they arched towards her light. It spoke well of his taste. Years later, Jade claimed it was a moment of predestination, red thread unspooling to its natural end, but Elizabeth, shortsighted as she was, considered it her luck to be third-wheeled wherever she went, especially where Jane was concerned. Girls like Jane got the beauty and the popularity; Elizabeth got the jokes.

They made the rounds of acceptable wedding small talk: he was born in Hong Kong, studied in the UK; cycled through LSE, Goldsmiths, and Goldman; and returned home when his father's health declined. He had five sisters of his own, all older, three much older. She supposed he might be the singular kind of golden son—the one trying to make right. He'd never been to New York—shock! horror! treason!—and intended to swing all of the tourist traps in one go. Buying knockoffs, dollar pizza, and chicken and rice plates; seeing Liberty Island, the Brooklyn Bridge, Times Square, Rockefeller Center—everything short of a horse-drawn carriage ride through the park, and only because he didn't have anyone to ride along.

Elizabeth shook her head. "You can't just do the tourist garbage," she said. "Come back to Chinatown. Let us show you around."

Jane nodded. "We'd be happy to give you a tour," she said. "And there's all the museums too!"

"Brendan, *aaaaaaa.*" With a fanfare of floral perfume, a woman grasped at his hand and dragged herself into their circle. Everything about her was long—hair, legs, face—except her dress, which threatened to ride up and reveal her most intimate self. She stood with model posture, shoulders rounded and spine slightly slouched in a show of casual disregard, shedding body glitter and bronzer with every movement. "What are you doing?"

Brendan pulled her in towards them. "Ladies, this is Caroline, my sister."

Elizabeth wouldn't have guessed the relation if they hadn't been told. Brendan rounded his edges where Caroline sharpened hers. Only her voice stayed soft, rolling with a warm purr and touched with a thicker English accent than her brother's. Elizabeth suspected it, like her lipstick, had been overapplied.

"You shouldn't make promises that you can't keep," she said to him. "He doesn't like to stay in one place too long, you know. Like the proverbial dandelion."

"I don't know the proverbial dandelion," Elizabeth replied.

Brendan made their introductions as Jade's daughters.

"That's the woman you've been dealing with?"

"Yeah," he said. "The broker or the owner's representative or something. She wasn't very clear about the whole thing."

"I can imagine," Caroline said, eyes flicking over their outfits.

Elizabeth bristled.

"I suppose he's told you we've never been to New York before," she replied. "I've heard a lot about it, you know, but I don't understand the appeal, la. So dirty, and the noise! And not much special at all." Lowering her voice to a whisper, she hissed, "You know, this morning, we saw . . . rats running in the street."

"They do that," Elizabeth said.

Brendan rolled his eyes. "It's not that bad, Caro."

Caroline exaggerated a shudder, pressing a bony hand to her

sternum. "Well, *I* couldn't stay outside as soon as I saw them. Maybe you can manage."

Jane smiled. "Aside from the rats, how's your stay?"

Caroline whimpered. "Abominable," she said. "But we had the chance to spend some time yesterday on Madison Avenue. You'd expect *more* from a fashion capital like New York, given its reputation—wouldn't you think?—but we couldn't find anything."

"Caroline," laughed Brendan. "You found more than your fair share. I remember the bags."

Caroline gave him a half-hearted shove. "He's always scolding me, aaaa," she sighed. "As if I'm *not* his older sister. So rude with our new friends here too."

"By the way, Brendan," Elizabeth said. "If you have any time, I'd love to hear what you're thinking of doing with the rec now that you're taking over."

"*P-lease* don't make him talk about business," Caroline said, "He and Darcy get into it and it's all I ever hear about. So boring."

Jane pointed at Elizabeth. "I can sympathize."

Caroline simpered, taking her hand in her own limp grip. "Thank you."

"Who's Darcy?" Elizabeth said.

Brendan waved vaguely towards the door. "My business partner."

"I thought you were a sole investor," Elizabeth said.

Caroline scoffed. "In his dreams."

The DJ grunted another unintelligible rally to the crowd, hopping and jerking on the dance floor in a stiff "Macarena." They answered with a weak cheer.

"Come on," Jane said with a pointed look at Elizabeth. "We'll leave Brendan and LB to their business talk, and go dance."

As they watched their sisters disappear, Brendan turned his attention to the dance floor, smiling as Jane twirled and dipped Caroline into the next song. Away from his sister and his other friends, he seemed shyer than she first thought. She wondered if it wasn't all put on for their benefit—the persona of the gracious social butterfly, the easy party acquaintance. Maybe he couldn't think of anywhere else he wanted to be less than the wedding either.

Caroline waved at them from the floor, her tall heels clomping offbeat.

"You look like you have a lot of questions," he said. "But I'm afraid it's Darcy who really knows what he's doing."

She glanced over him. "I see."

"I'm still learning the ropes. Real estate is new for me, and Darcy makes sure my excitement doesn't lead to bad decisions."

"Keeps your eyes from being too big for your stomach?"

His eyes wrinkled with humor. "Or my wallet," he said. "Exactly."

On the floor, Jane shrieked as Caroline accidentally tripped her with a flourish of a kick. Elizabeth loved her sister, but as a dancer, she made up in enthusiasm what she lacked in grace. Better than the aunties, but not by much.

Caroline formed wide shapes with her arms, looking like a flight controller.

"What is she doing?"

Brendan howled. "I think she's trying to vogue."

Elizabeth squinted into the strobing light of the dance floor and tried to see it. "What made you decide to do this anyway?" she said. "The rec?"

He adjusted his cuff links. "I want to do something that helps people."

She flashed him her best salesperson grin. "Then you couldn't have picked a better place! Ask anyone here. With the right kind of attention, I know you can bring it back to what it used to be."

He coughed. "I know a pitch when I hear one."

"I'm part of a community group . . ."

"What, like 'neighborhood watch'?"

She blushed. "More like the tenants association."

"In that case," he said, reaching into his pocket for his wallet. He extended a business card. When she reached to take it, he didn't let go. "Elizabeth. It's great to meet you. Everything that you're saying sounds great and important, but I've had some champagne and so have you. What do you say we celebrate, and talk about it during regular business hours like regular business people?"

She softened, and took the card. "Yes, you're right," she said. "You're right. I'm sorry."

"Besides, that way I can make sure that you're talking to the people who know what they're talking about," he said. "And not the guy that signs the checks."

Leave it to people with money to hate thinking about money.

"Haven't you heard my mom? The guy who signs the checks is the most important."

He bowed, extending a hand towards her. "Then shall we dance, Miss Chen?"

She grinned and nodded.

They made their way out onto the dance floor as the song faded out. An accordion warbled into life then, polka-esque.

I don't want to be a chicken. I don't want to be a duck . . .

Perfect timing.

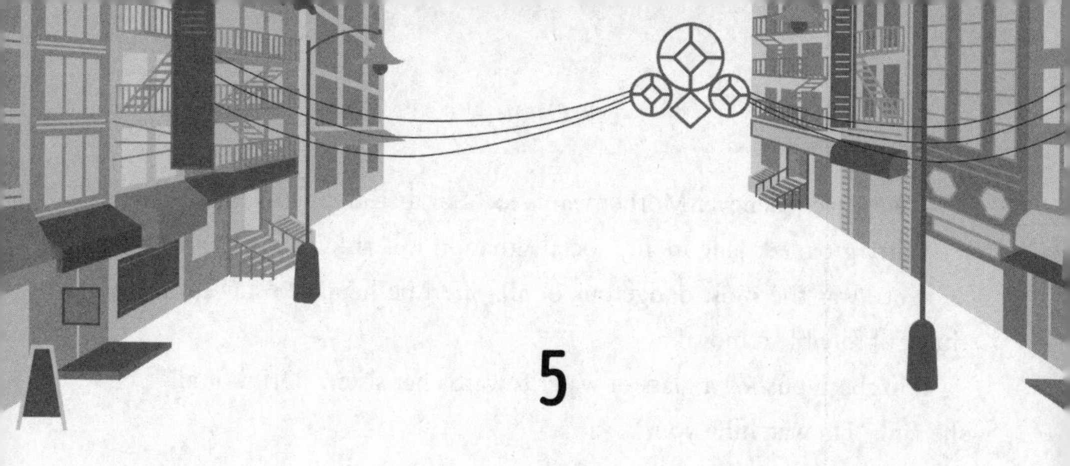

5

Later on, after everyone abandoned their shoes, handbags, and dignity at the table, Elizabeth resigned herself to babysitting duty. Kitty sulked, draining orphaned champagne flutes from nearby tables until she staggered and swayed on her feet. Mary draped herself across four dining chairs, head drooping off of the end as she napped. Lydia, forcibly separated from an indecent dance with one of the waiters, returned to steal another abandoned drink, wave at Brendan in greeting, and disappear into the crowd. From across the room, Jade's shrill voice periodically announced her triumph. "*Fifty thousand over asking!*"

She didn't have to guess at the topic of conversation.

At least Jane seemed to be having a great time. Since Brendan first joined her and Caroline on the dance floor, he hadn't moved more than two feet out of her orbit. Not to dance with anyone else, talk with anyone else, or notice anyone else. Elizabeth would almost resent her for it if she didn't seem so happy.

Kitty laid her head down on her arms. "When can we leave?" she slurred. "I want to go home."

Mary snuffled and rolled onto her side.

"We leave whenever Mother wants to," Elizabeth replied.

Kitty groaned. Jade in any social situation was risky, but a captive audience was the most dangerous of all. She'd be happy to stay until threat of forcible removal.

Elizabeth pushed a glass of water towards her sister. "Drink it all," she said. "I'm watching you."

Kitty whined, taking enough of a sip to wet her lips.

"Drink it," Elizabeth repeated.

Feedback screeched over the AV system, followed by a chorus of loud screams and hoots. Plucky, sensitive strings and piano wailed with feedback through the speakers in a melancholy introduction. A wet, heavy breath sounded into the microphone as the singer waited for their cue. Elizabeth could only watch, open-mouthed and horrified, as her mother stumbled through the first few lines of the song.

An off-rhythm clap sounded as she strained for the notes, voice cracking. Teresa Teng, she was not.

On the floor, Jane didn't notice. She and Brendan only had eyes—and hands and attention—for each other.

With great effort, Brendan managed to tear himself away, whispering something against the shell of Jane's ear before drifting towards the direction of his own table.

Elizabeth had to hand it to him. The man knew how to exploit an opportunity.

Jane slowly fluttered back to their table. "Oh, LB," Jane breathed. "He's so . . . *nice*."

"Yeah, I bet," Elizabeth replied.

"You should dance," Jane said. "I can take over the table."

Elizabeth waved around the room. "Dance with who?" she said. "Somebody's gropey uncle? Besides, I don't know if you've noticed, but

Kitty's passed out, Lydia's probably sick in the bathroom, and Mother's doing her best Vegas act over there."

On cue, Jade screeched a note too close into the microphone, nearly blowing out the speakers.

Jane slicked Kitty's damp hair away from her face. "Poor Kitty."

"Don't feel bad for her," Elizabeth said. "She drank too much."

Kitty answered with a flat snore.

"Okay, I'll check on Lydia," she said. "You stay here and make sure they're okay."

Elizabeth saluted.

After a close standoff, the DJ managed to reclaim control of his own booth, spinning songs for the handful of couples who had the tolerance to remain standing. Anything to keep more over-fifties from doing karaoke. Elizabeth forced another sip of water down Kitty's throat and scanned the room for her mother. She caught Brendan's eye instead, his arms gesturing broad shapes in the air as he shared a story with someone sitting at his table.

When he saw her, he waved.

He would be the type to take care of someone who drank too much, she supposed—until the friend in question turned and stared back in her direction, looking stone-cold sober. This man did not wave. He didn't *smile*. He surveyed their table like a substitute teacher bracing for a field trip. He was blessed with good looks—a broad forehead, carved cheekbones, and a narrow nose that tapered down to the angular point of his chin, which he spoiled with a sulky mouth and an expression that looked both frumpy and constipated. If he claimed he'd had a good time at all in the last few hours, she would have asked for proof. Like Brendan, he wore a tailored, expensive-looking black suit set off with plain cuff links and a paisley pocket square. His dark hair had been combed flat, and a hint of shadow lined his jaw. An elegant pair of thin gold-rimmed glasses finished the look. Nothing about him looked out of place. Distinguished, some might have called him. Prissy, Elizabeth thought.

"Darcy," Brendan howled, clapping him on the shoulder.

So this was Darcy.

She shifted her chair back, the better to hear them with.

"You look like a fucking asshole," Brendan said, laughing. With a thick British accent, he boomed, "*This is supposed to be a happy occasion.*"

Elizabeth draped her arm against the back of a neighboring seat and tried not to look like she was listening.

Darcy scoffed. "It's not *my* wedding," he said. He spoke like she expected—voice honeyed with money, if cut with a buzz of mild offense. His accent sounded more genuinely English than Caroline's. Though condescending, unlike Brendan's. She supposed he was used to giving orders—and only giving them once. "I sat through the ceremony, we were introduced to their parents, we've been here for hours, and now I think I've fulfilled my side of the obligation."

Reaching for a glass from the table, Brendan shoved it into Darcy's hand. "Obligation! Have a drink, dick."

Darcy glanced at it with distaste and set it down. "You don't even know where that's been."

"Would you try and have a good time?" he replied. "It's a party. Have a dance, la."

He sniffed. "There's no one to dance with," came the answer.

"That's why people make introductions," Brendan said. "That's why *aunties* exist."

Darcy laughed. "Is that what you are?"

"You know Jade Chen?"

"The woman who's been announcing our deal details every hour on the hour?" he said. "I think I've overheard her once or twice, yes."

Brendan pushed at his shoulder. "Her family's here and they're nice," he said. "Friendly. Welcoming. Hospitable. Something you might try to be."

"You sound like one of the aunties you hate."

"Come on," he said. Turning towards Elizabeth's table, Brendan brightened. "Look, Elizabeth's over there, and I'm sure she'd love to get another dance in or talk about, I don't know, REITs or something."

"There's a woman who wants to talk about REITs at a wedding, and you're pulling *me* aside?" he said. This time, when he turned, he scanned her face, her outfit, and her snoring, drooling sisters comatose at the table.

She refused to look away first, but her cheeks warmed as if they had caught her listening.

Maybe they had.

She raised a hand to wave, but he had already turned back to Brendan with a brusque shake of the head. "Is that the one you were telling me about?"

"Yeah, boss," he said. "Let me introduce you since you're so hard up."

Darcy raised a hand. "Absolutely not."

"Oh, come on!" he protested. "You didn't even meet the girl."

"It's been a long night, and the last thing I want or need right now is some middle-of-the-road elevator pitch from a girl who's drunk, single, and has nothing better to do at a wedding than to enlighten you with her state-school, intro-poli-sci ideas about how we should do our jobs. No, thank you."

Elizabeth reached for a glass of water and sucked the last dregs of ice into her mouth. If it were any other night, and if it weren't for what her mother might do to her, she would have launched herself out of her chair to tell him exactly what he could do with her middle-of-the-road elevator pitch. Instead, she crunched the ice in the back of her mouth and relished the sting of its cold against her teeth.

Brendan shrugged. "She might try to flirt with you," he said. "It is a wedding after all."

"If you are about to join the ranks of every other aunty in this room set on matchmaking me tonight, thank you, but no thank you, I am not on the market, I am not interested, and if I were, I wouldn't choose the girl whose mother keeps dropping my name as a testimonial to start her own small business."

And there it was, the real problem—not the dancing or the reception or the buzzing annoyances of a wedding, but *them*. The Chens and the Hus and their friends and the neighborhood, as welcome and subtle as fermented fish among the roses. Let him say what he would about them and all of the other *lessers* in the neighborhood, but at least they had better social graces and more pride than to spoil somebody else's big day with petty complaints. Like she hadn't been hit on ten times tonight, like she'd *liked* babysitting her mother and sisters instead of dancing or talking to anyone else, like he could be the only person in the world having a bad time. But people like her didn't have a place in *their* circles, except to make sure that nobody pissed on their doormats or colored outside the lines.

And if this spoiled, whining glutinous rice cake thought he could tell her anything, he needed to look in the mirror first. One of the first things she'd ever learned in the city—in *her* city—was to not dish what you couldn't take; and if it weren't Alexa Hu's wedding and she wasn't an argument with her mother away from being homeless, she would march over in her bare feet, toss somebody else's drink in his face, and teach him a lesson. But it was still Alexa's wedding and she still needed her parents' apartment—so fuck him very much.

Brendan clicked his tongue. "Fine, you baby. Let's get you another drink and see if you can't look a little less . . . you."

As they disappeared towards the far end of the bar, she threw him a finger underneath the table. So this was the all-important business partner, the real estate expert, the man who ran the show! Leave it to her to run into import-export Mr. Monopoly at a family wedding. A man like that deserved to be laughed at publicly and often by as many people as possible.

It was already funny, if she thought about it. It was hilarious. So what if some patronizing, entitled, silver-spoon, private-school Wall Street jackass didn't think she was good enough? Any other time, what he said would have been a compliment. Any other time, she would already be laughing. All she needed to do was figure out the right way to tell the story.

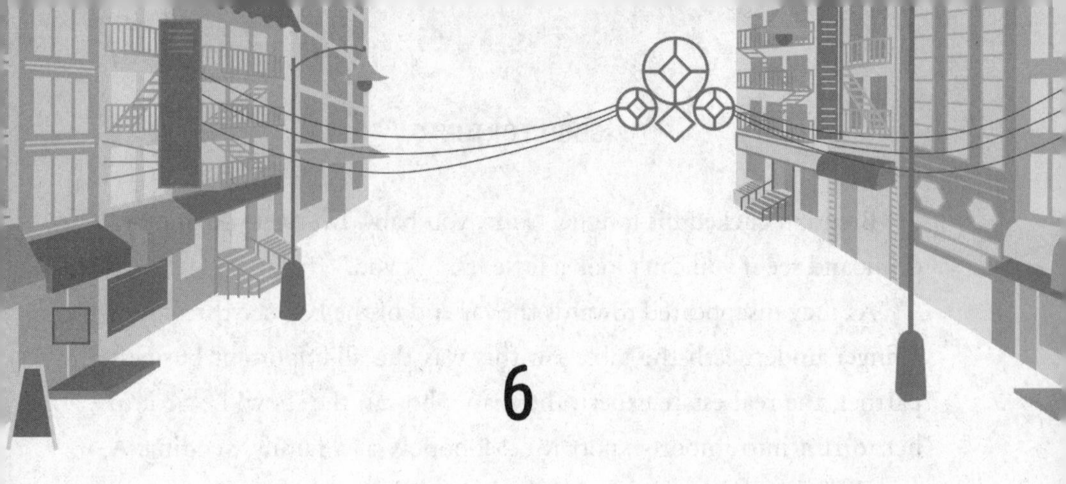

6

Nothing that funny or ridiculous could hurt that long; she wouldn't let it. After twenty-four hours, the sting faded; after forty-eight, she remembered him with a faint twinge of fury; and after a few more days, it became another horse in her stable of party stories. Elizabeth tried it out on her sisters, her mother, her alumni message boards, and anyone passing through Lulu's who was forced by necessity or circumstance to wait more than five minutes for their food. *You think your last date went bad, well, wait until you hear about this . . .* Stand-up comedian, she was not, but grade on the curve—it helped pass the time.

Life after the Hu-Wei wedding returned to its usual routines. No more surprise shopping trips, no more salon visits, no more visits to the dry cleaner that did alterations. Elizabeth crashed back into the weekday scramble: sending out a batch of résumés ahead of a shift at the parking garage or at nearby offices, working Lulu's in the afternoons and evenings, and avoiding her mother at all costs. Weekends were her own time, which usually meant meeting Charlotte—of the Bayard Street Luos—at the rec.

The Luos, being strict and attentive parents and good Christians, allowed their daughters to venture only where there might be scrutinizing adult supervision, preferably under the eye of a judgmental aunty. The Chen girls, bored and stranded at home during summer vacations, didn't take long to annoy their mother into kicking them out of the apartment so they might cause trouble elsewhere. Enter the rec.

Ten-year-old Charlotte might have tackled advanced summer reading under the wandering eye of student volunteers, but Elizabeth had hustled sixth-grade boys out of pocket money on makeshift handball courts. It was only a matter of time before they collided—literally, in this case—when Elizabeth, wrestling a boy into a headlock after he'd stolen Mary's Super Ball, rounded a blind corner and knocked her to the ground. Charlotte cried, Elizabeth lied—*of course she wasn't fighting, Aunty, she would never*—and a friendship was born out of an apology of peach rings.

In the years since, they turned from the rec's scheduled activities to ones of their own—goofing off with the boys behind the building, sneaking smokes in the unused locker room showers. It was there they shared their deepest hopes and secrets, and imagined the shape of the rest of their lives. Everything else might need to be shared with nosy sisters or pushy parents, but the rec had felt like theirs alone.

Elizabeth ran late that morning, as usual—slept late, woke late, left late. By the time she made it to the center, Charlotte was waiting with a book propped open in her lap and an extra coffee cup in hand. As ever, she looked serious and studious, her glasses thick and boots even thicker. She wore a fuzzy, hand-me-down Garfield sweatshirt over dark jeans, her thin hair pulled back into a low ponytail. As Elizabeth walked up, she held the cup out in greeting.

"Is that coffee?" Elizabeth said.

"Take it and find out."

Elizabeth took a seat beside her and pried off the lid, breathing in the steam. She stole a small sip and scalded the tip of her tongue.

"One of these days, you might learn to have more impulse control than a two-year-old."

"Oh, Char," Elizabeth replied, trying another small sip. "You give me too much credit."

"I know. You don't deserve it."

"Did you bring breakfast too?"

Charlotte rummaged in her bag and produced a wax paper bag with a pork bun inside.

Elizabeth snatched it out of her hand and tore off a large chunk with her teeth, chewing noisily.

"Don't eat the paper on the bottom."

Elizabeth grinned, showing off the red flecks of sauced pork. "You love me."

Charlotte leaned back and shook her head. "Hurry up," she said. "Before Geny thinks of more for us to do."

Geny was of the class of the New York lifers—having survived the Reagan and crack years, she'd abandon the city when the rats did. Years of the rec's decline had done nothing to change her devotion. Elizabeth didn't doubt that as long as the place stayed open and Geny stayed standing, they would find her in the small manager's office with its dim lighting, rubber cement smell, and scattered papers, scrambling for an unpaid invoice. She half expected Geny's body to fuse with the building after death.

"I'm going, I'm going." Elizabeth bit off another large chunk of the pork bun and coughed, trying to chew around it.

Charlotte pointed at her face. "Bite off more than you can chew?"

Elizabeth took a sip of the coffee and tried to swallow.

"You don't have to eat *that* fast."

Elizabeth mumbled around the remainder of the bite, "Hungry."

Charlotte tutted. "That's why you'll never find a good husband, laaa."

With such an opportunity, how could she deny her best friend the story?

Charlotte listened and laughed at all the right places. "Poor LB," she sighed. "To be another brilliant mind written off for going to a state school."

Elizabeth shoveled the last bite into her mouth. "Well, you know they only teach you to read at Harvard and Yale. The rest of us sort wooden blocks into shapes."

"Taking it well, I see."

"Don't say anything to my mom either," she said. "She'll probably say I did something to deserve it."

"I'm not sure you didn't. That's what you get for snooping on other people's conversations."

Elizabeth sucked down another gulp of coffee. "I was perfectly well-behaved, I'll have you know. A little debutante."

"Mm-hmm," Charlotte replied. "Was he cute at least?"

"For what?" she said. "For the trouble of being insulted?"

Charlotte shrugged. "Charlene's aunt said he didn't talk to anyone at the wedding that he didn't already know. He barely said a word to the bride."

Elizabeth raised her eyebrows. "What, are you plugged into the aunty mafia now?"

"My mom likes to know what's going on," she said.

Elizabeth crumpled the wax paper wrapper and shoved it into her pocket. "I can't believe you guys didn't go."

"The Luos don't like to go where there aren't Chinese Christians. You know that."

"You mean your mom doesn't like Alexa's mom," she replied.

"Same difference," Charlotte replied. "Don't say anything to Mariah, by the way. She cried all night."

* * *

Like anything intended for public use, the rec divided its funding sources between a pittance from the city and a lot of individual pittances from various donors and contributors. While the building sat in an area of prime real estate—and *location*, as Jade liked to remind them, was everything—that didn't save it from the day-to-day problems of being a building in New York. The roof leaked, ongoing street construction chased vermin into new burrows in their basement, and the chipping stone facade of the building threatened to fall on the soft heads of unsuspecting passersby. As the city whittled down its pittance with each passing budget cycle, the rec depended more and more on whatever people could spare. Having no real money or power, Charlotte and Elizabeth offered what they had—time, hands, and muscle. A few times a month, or whenever they could spare, they paid their dues, which amounted to little more than groundskeeping to help keep away the rats and the Department of Sanitation. Charlotte assumed the mop, Elizabeth the broom, and the two of them patched a Band-Aid over a bullet hole.

"You can't let it get to you, you know," Charlotte said.

Elizabeth banged the old broom twice against the front of the steps, releasing a cloud of chalky dust into the air. A group of pigeons on the fringe of the courtyard eyed her with great suspicion.

As she started sweeping, piles of grit and sand kicked up into the air.

"People like that, all they do is hang out with the same people, go to the same schools. They don't think anyone who hasn't gone through their club is anyone."

"And that's an excuse?"

"It's an explanation," Charlotte said, tossing the dustpan in her direction, a relic from the nearby dollar store. A crack ran nearly halfway up the pan.

She lifted it for inspection. "What good is a dustpan that's cracked?"

Charlotte shrugged. "Do what you can, I guess." The philosophy of the rec, and the motto of their lives.

Elizabeth grumbled and awkwardly swept the garbage into the pan. Little bits of sand dribbled down through the crack as she carried it to the waste bin to empty. "He thinks highly of himself, that's for sure."

Charlotte shrugged. "Why not? He probably went to an Ivy, won all these awards."

Elizabeth shot her a look. "They *pay* for that, Char," she said. "They pay for the training, they pay for the awards, they win things because other people don't have the time or money to play."

"Spoken like a sore loser."

"I am not!" At Charlotte's look, she added, "I am not a *sore* loser. It's just not fair."

Charlotte radiated a smug serenity. "Is it really about fairness, LB, or is it about him insulting you?"

"Please," Elizabeth said, rolling her eyes. "Like he could."

* * *

Like rats and office workers, they started from the bottom and made their way up, tending to the concerns laid out on Geny's thorough and thoroughly impractical list in order of convenience. *Clean up litter on grounds. Empty the trash. Mop the floors. Sort through donation box. Trim overgrowth on planters. Help with filing. Wash the front windows.*

Someone reasonable might expect that, with all the rats, pigeons, dirt, pollution, and car exhaust downtown, that would be a lost cause. Someone reasonable might expect that the cleanliness of the windows had nothing to do with their dwindling number of visitors. Not Geny. To her, dirty windows were the last stand, a sign that the rec might be beyond saving. So once a month, they tackled the grime with cheap rags and Pine-Sol and elbow grease, and hoped it would make a difference. To Geny, if no one else.

Elizabeth ripped into a bag of dollar-store gloves. Large on her small hands, they flopped loose at the elbow, in danger of catching accidental runoff. Pouring a heavy hand of Pine-Sol into the bucket, Elizabeth dropped the rags in to soak and got to work.

November in the city meant temperatures in the low forties on a good day, and Elizabeth felt her fingers shrink from the cold as she wrung out the rags. The scent of pine clawed sharp in her sinuses as she attacked one of the lower windows, scrubbing furiously. Visibility came in bits and pieces, flecks of dried white *something* chipping onto the ground where pigeons would later peck at them in the vain hopes of finding food. The water in the bucket turned dark as she rinsed out the rag.

Charlotte pulled on her own pair of gloves and joined her.

"Welcome to the party," Elizabeth said.

Charlotte pointed at one of the adjacent lower windows. "I'll start that one."

Cleaning the windows was sloppy work. Between the dirty water in the bucket, the exertion of scrubbing at what lurked in the windowpanes, and the deep squats to reach the windows, Elizabeth usually left looking rougher than when she came. She squatted low now, rinsing and wringing out the rag as someone bellowed her name from across the courtyard. With that kind of volume and control at that distance, it could only be one person.

"Elizabeth!" Jade shouted, horrified. "What are you doing?"

She lifted her hands defensively, dripping water across the pavement. Charlotte turned back to her own window with sudden focus.

"Cleaning the windows," she said.

Of course Jade hadn't come alone. A group of five hovered behind her, glancing nervously at the swarms of pigeons and the litter in the street as if they might turn sentient and attack, Brendan, Caroline, and Mr. Monopoly among them.

Caroline whispered something that made them burst into laughter. Brendan smiled. Mr. Monopoly stared.

A corner of Jade's eyebrow twitched with menace. "Elizabeth," she said. "I'm sure you remember the Lees—Brendan, Caroline, and Louisa, their sister—from the wedding. This is Henry, Louisa's husband, and Darcy Wong, one of the investors."

Brendan whispered to Darcy with a wide grin.

"Good morning, everyone," Elizabeth greeted.

A rat darted out from the bushes, and Caroline shrieked, jumping inches into the air.

"That's normal," Elizabeth said. "I'm sure they're . . . returning to the nest."

Caroline whimpered. "The nest?"

Jade hissed at Elizabeth as she passed, "We will talk about this when we get home, LB. I don't know what you think you're doing . . ."

"Community service," Elizabeth replied.

Brendan gave her a thumbs-up.

Jade smiled even larger. "Since you're already here, why don't you and Charlotte join us on our walk-through?" she said. "Elizabeth is very passionate about the center, you know, and I'm sure can offer lots of interesting history on the building."

As if they cared about history. They hadn't come to hear about how bored teenagers battled their popos on the makeshift badminton courts or how Jade once practiced her stilted English in night classes; they wanted to pick out the good bones before they ripped out the bad ones. Their idea of history was a bite-size blurb on a disposable coffee cup—*a beloved neighborhood treasure*, it might say, *vibrant and rich with tradition, steeped in culture.* She could already hear the whine of the zither.

"We should get started," Darcy said. He spoke as she remembered: quiet and pompous, his tone inflected with an undercurrent of displeasure. He probably couldn't wait to break out the sledgehammers.

She waved them on. "Don't let us hold you up."

Brendan smiled as he passed, the others trailing in after him. Only Darcy lingered in the entryway, studying the exterior. Hunting for insurance write-offs, she supposed.

She waited for him to say something—some witty observation or cutting remark—but he remained silent, arms stiff by his sides.

"It's not structurally unsound, if that's what you're worried about," she said. "Trust me. Apart from a piece of cement dropping on my head once when I was a child, it's been perfectly fine."

His eyebrows raised in concern, but Charlotte interjected, "She's joking!" Silence. "She has a twisted sense of humor that way."

Elizabeth squinted up at the facade, trying to follow his line of sight.

"How tall are you?"

She blinked at him. "Excuse me?"

He pointed towards the windows, his eyes flicking over her quickly. "How tall are you?" he repeated. "You can't be more than a meter sixty?"

Charlotte mirrored her look of confusion.

"Is this some kind of test?" she said. "You're going to tell me that the building code says that you have to be this tall"—she gestured over her head—"to clean the windows?"

He sniffed. "You might want to get a ladder," he said. "If you're planning on cleaning the whole thing."

"Oh!" she cried. "Well, I was going to climb on top of Charlotte's shoulders, but now that you put it that way . . ."

Caroline stuck her head out of the doorway, hissing Darcy's name.

He ignored her. "If you don't have the appropriate leverage, I think you can wait for someone else on staff."

"We do this all the time," Elizabeth said.

Caroline, uncertain of being heard, raised her voice. The rec found itself suddenly haunted by a spirit of the upper class.

"We wouldn't want anyone to get hurt on the premises."

Elizabeth nodded. "No reckless endangerment. Understood."

"Darcy!" His name rang out from down the hallway.

Elizabeth batted her eyes at him with a tight smile. "You're being summoned."

He didn't look away from her. "You should take the proper precautions."

"Speaking of safety," Caroline interjected, "Darcy, everyone is asking about you. They thought you might have fallen down a flight of stairs or something."

That caught his attention. "Why would I have fallen down a flight of stairs?" he said. "We're on the first floor."

Caroline feigned a laugh, dragging him in by the hand. "You know how this place is, la."

Elizabeth flung her rag back into the bucket, fuming. First, her ideas hadn't been good enough for him to entertain, and now, she was too stupid to clean a window?

She would show him.

"Where are you going?" Charlotte called, as she marched around the side of the building.

To find a ladder, and prove him wrong.

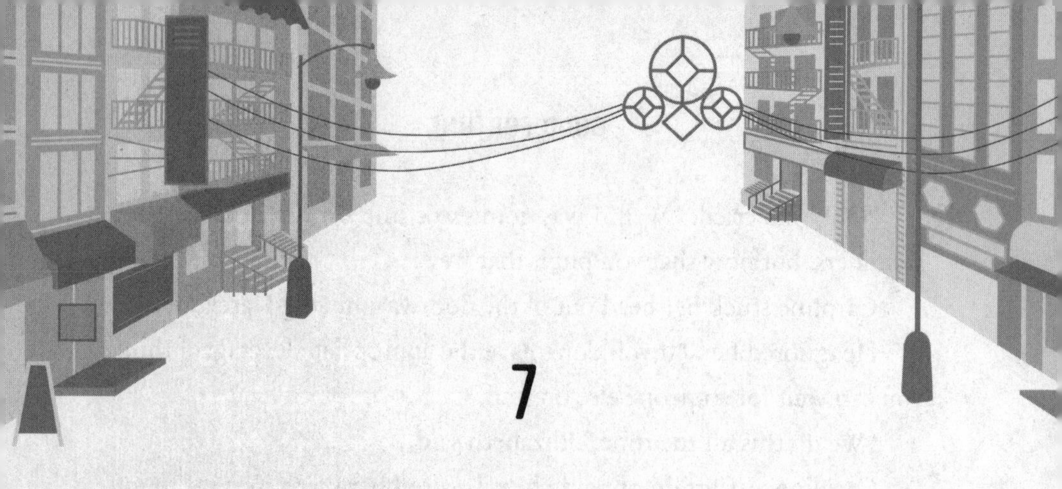

7

After a half hour of fruitless searching, they broke for lunch, hoping to take refuge from their visitors with a sympathetic audience.

No luck.

Not even Lulu's was safe.

Elizabeth shoveled food into her mouth as a precaution against having to make conversation, but Jade filled the silence all on her own. She rattled on about the latest rumors of the neighborhood, sidestepped Vincent's occasional asides, steamrolled any small talk, and baited her audience with pointed questions. Didn't they enjoy the wedding ceremony? Wasn't it a shame about the dryness of the cake? Of course, she'd recommended a different baker than the one they'd chosen, but it didn't matter as long as everyone else enjoyed it. Wasn't Alexa such a sweet bride—and so helpful to her parents! Not everyone knew how lucky they were to have daughters so respectful and so brilliant. "But my Jane is doing her best," she preened. "Going to medical school to make some good money." And with a pointed glance at Elizabeth, she added, "Not a selfish bone in her body, my Jane. Always planning ahead and thinking of the family instead of herself."

Brendan reached for one of the cups of hot tea lined up along the counter. "And Elizabeth?" he asked, politely.

Jade tittered. With a deep sigh, she added, "Elizabeth can be very smart . . . when she tries to be."

All eyes turned towards her, whether in curiosity or contempt. Elizabeth ignored them as she slipped towards the counter to pour fresh cups of tea. "Temping," she said, by way of translation. "Working some odd jobs while I'm interviewing. You know how it goes."

The blank stares told her perhaps not.

Her entire life, she'd been told that, with enough education, she could do anything and be anyone—and learned too late that anything and anyone included only the high-earning. What Jade wanted was a guaranteed return on her investment. Her daughters were meant to climb the ladder, not stick around pulling people up after them. But they had been the ones hanging on the bottom rung once upon a time, and hadn't they once been worth somebody else's time and help? She thought so. She hoped so.

Jade crossed her arms over her chest. "You know, Alexa has very *graciously* offered to help find her something at the TV station, but my Elizabeth always follows her own mind." Vincent lightly cleared his throat, throwing his wife an impatient look.

Darcy approached the counter, reaching for one of the cups she had poured. "Having high standards can be advantageous," he murmured, though whether to himself or to the room, she couldn't tell.

"They aren't *high* standards," she snapped.

Charlotte glared at her from across the room.

"As long as it doesn't blind you to other opportunities."

"Opp-or-tu-ni-ty, yes!" Jade crowed. With a conspiratorial lean in his direction, she added, "You wouldn't happen to know of anything?"

Vincent threw his hands up in the air. Didn't they have other places to go, work to do? Hadn't Jade mentioned an endless number of errands to run?

Back to the center they headed—with all of their new friends in tow.

* * *

While plastic stools could be found in abundance throughout the building, all pastel colored and cheaply made, ladders were harder to come by. After a renewed search, they discovered a relic from the building's earliest days. It looked straight out of Looney Tunes: wooden rungs, slightly uneven legs, and no safety latches in sight. A thin, rusted metal chain hung limply between the legs, offering weak support. Charlotte glanced at it askance, but Elizabeth insisted. They'd done worse in their childhoods—even three years ago!—and with Jane's dexterous, exceptional-med-student pair of hands, it wouldn't take long at all. Teamwork had to make the dream work.

Rust flaked onto her fingers with a loud squeal of metal as she pulled the legs apart. A small chalky puff coughed up from the rungs, the legs tottering as if trying to find their footing.

Charlotte answered with a delicate cough, "Well, it opens."

Elizabeth charged ahead with more confidence than she felt. "Oh, come on, it's easy," she said, breezily. Lifting the ladder from the middle rungs, she carried it towards the front of the building, where it settled with a weary lurch. "See?"

They stared up at the windows uneasily. Six narrow windows on the front side of the building, caked with grime and soot, stretched almost twelve feet in the air. None of them wanted to go up, and none of them wanted to admit to it. Those that could usually called someone in the yellow pages; those that couldn't learned to make do with what they had—and what they had were three girls, their wits, and a ladder of questionable age and stability.

"Uh-huh," Charlotte said.

"If someone stands on the back legs, it won't shake so much."

Charlotte heroically volunteered for that task, leaving Jane or Elizabeth to the climb.

"I can do it," Elizabeth said.

"You're afraid of heights, and you've got shorter arms," Jane replied. "You won't have any leverage. I'll do it."

Score one, perhaps, for the eldest daughters.

They assumed their stations: Charlotte anchored the back of the ladder, Jane climbed, and Elizabeth braced the side rails from behind her sister. For the first few rungs, the three of them watched carefully for any awkward swing of movement, any creak of weakness.

It couldn't be called ideal, but it seemed sturdy enough.

Jane exhaled as she reached the top rung, stretching near to the window. "Hand me the rag, please!"

Easing her weight off of the ladder, Elizabeth jogged towards the bucket and retrieved a rag, reaching it up to Jane's outstretched hand. They fell into a staggered rhythm of handoffs and movements; at a glance, they could have passed for any interpretive dance troupe haunting St. Mark's. First Elizabeth, rinsing the rag in the bucket and returning it, and then Charlotte—one after the other as Jane stayed high on the ladder and scrubbed. It bordered on the ridiculous and the resourceful, the dangerous and the dull—but who cared what anyone called it as long as the job got done? The aunties will tell you—it's the ends that justify the means, the motive, and the opportunity.

Jane whooped in triumph when they finished the first window, chucking the rag down towards the bucket. It missed and landed on the pavement with a wet glop.

Elizabeth clapped her hands. "All right, switch," she said. "I can go up for a while." Toeing away from the ladder, she opened up space for her sister to climb down.

Off to the side, something rustled in the bushes.

Jane gingerly took another step, and the rustle grew louder. A plastic bag, maybe, snarled in the hedges, or an old Little Debbie wrapper torn and fluttering in the breeze. Or, as they discovered, a rat—an oversize, swollen rat, the homegrown downtown New York kind that rivaled the size of their feet—that scampered directly for Charlotte. Nothing moves faster than a rat, except the terrified girl it surprises. Charlotte shrieked, scrambling onto the rear rungs of the ladder and yanking the legs askew.

Weight shifted, center of gravity tilted, and the ladder tipped slowly onto its side—taking the girls with it.

Elizabeth reacted with a shout, sprinting to steady it.

She made it in time to break the fall.

The ladder pitched, its legs collapsing shut, sending Jane tumbling backward towards the ground.

"Jane!"

She landed hard against Elizabeth's chest, knocking them both to the ground in a tangle of limbs. Elizabeth went, as the saying goes, ass over teakettle, head pinging against the loose gravel as her back connected with the pavement.

Jane groaned, rolling her head against her sister's neck.

Elizabeth's mouth slicked with fresh blood. "Ow."

Charlotte screeched towards them, abandoning the ladder on its side. "Oh my god," she cried. "Are you guys okay?"

Her ears rang, her body ached, and her sister felt like she weighed a lot more when all of her pressed against her chest.

Jane shifted on top of her with another groan, rubbing at her head.

"LB, are you all right?" she gasped.

Elizabeth tried to shove her sister off.

"I'm going to go get help!" Charlotte said, racing inside.

At last Jane moved off of her, and Elizabeth stayed prone on the ground, gasping for air. It hurt to breathe and it hurt to move. She prayed the damage was minimal: bruising rather than breaks.

Elizabeth gently probed at her teeth with her tongue. Nothing loose, nothing missing. Great start. Climbing onto her hands and knees, she spat blood against the pavement. Less great, perhaps.

Ever the medical student, Jane poked and massaged various parts of her body—leg, chest, neck—checking her for signs of something serious. "I don't think you broke anything."

"How are you? You were up highest."

Jane exhaled, short and sharp. "I think I'm okay," she said as she climbed to her feet. A sudden cry called her conclusion into doubt.

Elizabeth glanced at Jane resting all of her weight on one foot. "Well, that looks normal."

Jane winced, testing her ankle. "I think I twisted it."

Elizabeth didn't know what she should be looking for. "Can you walk?"

She limped a step. "Probably not without making it worse."

"Oh my god!"

From halfway down the hall, the voice: its sharp soprano of panic, its frenzied cadence, its accusatory howl. Elizabeth steeled herself for the lecture of a lifetime. She tried a grin, and her mother shrieked.

"Your teeth!" she cried. "Elizabeth, what have you done? What did you do?"

"Oh god, are you all right?" Brendan said, rushing towards Jane and poking gamely at her ankle.

"Brendan!" Caroline cried. "You don't know what you're doing."

"And you're getting your pants all dirty, aa," Louisa added.

Brendan carefully scooped Jane into his arms and carried her to a nearby planter, where she braced against the narrow stone edge.

"The ladder slipped when we were cleaning the windows, Aunty," Charlotte said.

Jade moaned, throwing her arms into the air. "Well, aren't you proud of yourself," she clucked. "Always having to get involved. Don't you feel smart now?"

"You were *cleaning the windows*?" Caroline said. "All three of you?"

With a look to Jane for permission, Brendan eased up a leg of her jeans to expose her ankle, already red and swelling.

"Call the hospital," Darcy said.

"No, you can't," Elizabeth said, firmly. "We don't have any insurance."

"It'll be fine," Jane said. "I don't think it's serious."

"It won't be fine," Brendan said, squeezing her exposed calf. "You can't stand."

Jane released a tight exhale, though perhaps not entirely due to the sprain.

"Elizabeth, are you okay?"

Elizabeth rubbed at her jaw. "Don't worry. My face took the fall."

Caroline pointed at her own teeth and whimpered.

Jade shoved a bottle of water into her hands. "Rinse your mouth out," she said. "You look like you've got rabies."

"Rabies makes you *foam* at the mouth, not bleed," Elizabeth grumbled.

Charlotte rolled her eyes. "LB, take it."

Brendan reached for his phone, flinging it open and dialing.

"You can't," Elizabeth begged. "We can't afford it."

Jade continued her litany under her breath, shaking her head. How ungrateful Elizabeth was, how inattentive Elizabeth was, how reckless they were not to consider what might be a better course of action. What had she done to raise such mindless, idiotic girls? What had she done in another life to merit this kind of treatment? And now, they might have to lose a month's wages—or more!—because she hadn't thought about the consequences.

For Jane, at least, Jade was all solicitous concern and comfort.

"This is ridiculous," Brendan said. "If it's a matter of money, *I'll* pay for it."

"Yes!" Caroline cried. "We must do what we can."

"We couldn't possibly," Jade said.

"The building is in our management," Brendan said. "We would have been responsible regardless. Please."

Jane shook her head. "That's not necessary."

"We'll get ourselves checked out," Elizabeth said. "Just not the hospital, please."

"This is absurd. I've already called the paramedics," Darcy said. "You both need to be examined."

Elizabeth groaned. "Not you too. I'm fine."

He looked at her with disbelief. "You are, in fact, bleeding from the mouth."

She twisted the cap off the water bottle and took a big swig, spitting pink into the street. Her mouth stung with open cuts. She tried a placating smile, and split the corners of her lips further. "See?" she said, wincing. "Fine."

Darcy was unmoved. "You might have a concussion."

Brendan shook his head. "I've heard enough. You're both going."

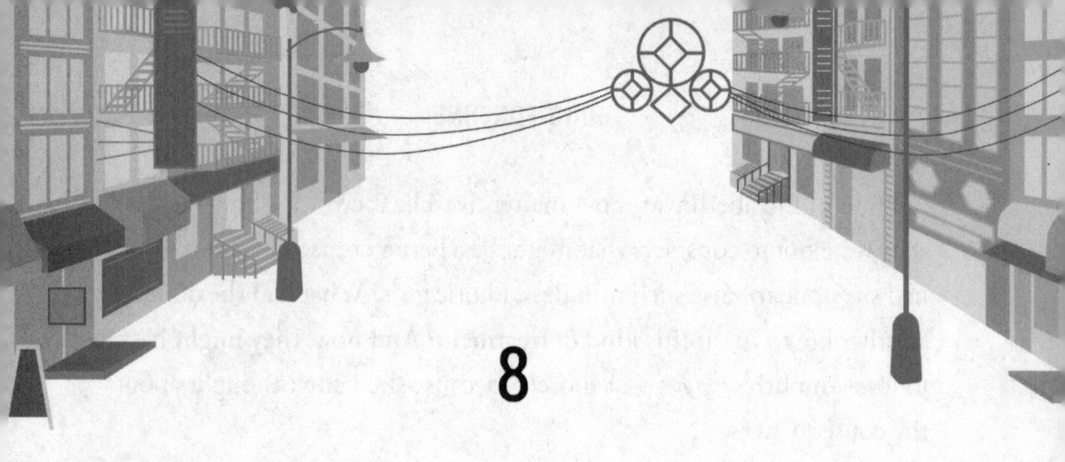

8

Their new friends couldn't have imagined the peculiar thrill and glamour of the American hospital waiting room. The uncomfortable seating, the disinfectant smell, the TVs playing informational health content on a loop, the noise of other people rustling bandages and paper towels and napkins wadded up against cuts or other exposed areas of skin, coughing and sniffling and groaning. Caroline stared straight ahead, purse clutched to her chest with pure terror as if poverty might be some kind of contagion.

The second hour stretched on, the third. They filled out intake forms, complied with the instructions from the dismissive or openly hostile nurses, listened to a loop of top forty, and waited for their names to be called. The time passed in waves of "Mambo No. 5." Any longer in the waiting room, and she might actually remember all their names.

Darcy sat across from her in the waiting room, thumbing through pamphlets. *Hypertension*, *Risk Signs of Type 2 Diabetes*, *Identifying Symptoms of Stroke*, *Common Questions About Alzheimer's*. On a bulletin board behind him, posters for a 9/11 fundraising drive mixed in among the staid stock photos of smiling patients reminding passersby about cholesterol and STD testing.

"You really don't need to stay," she said.

He unfolded one of the brochures. "I wouldn't talk much if I were you," he said. "You might tear those cuts open again."

"Now *you're* a doctor," she said. "You're trying to get me to shut up."

He glanced at her. "Is it working?"

"You'll never get Elizabeth to stop talking," Jade said. "If she's determined, she will. That's how she is. She's a Monkey, you know."

Elizabeth tipped her head into her hands with a muffled groan.

They waited and waited, listening to the slow tick of numbers and names called ahead of them. As it stretched past the third hour and into the fourth, the group thinned its numbers. Charlotte needed to head home but promised a visit; Caroline and Louisa went out in search of food for everyone else; and even Jade needed to return to let everyone know no one had died since she couldn't get through on the phone. Elizabeth expected Darcy to make a break for it as soon as the opportunity presented itself, but he stayed, thumbing through the same four brochures and pretending that he hadn't read them before. Maybe he was trying to play conscientious, she thought, to avoid the risk of a lawsuit. At the least, she hoped she'd done nothing to threaten their relationship with the rec.

After another hour, the nurse came to take Jane for X-rays, and Caroline and Louisa returned with containers full of hot congee and soup. Elizabeth took one of the containers and sipped at soup to fill her stomach. Caroline offered her a plastic spoon, and Elizabeth pretended she hadn't been drinking from the lip of the container.

"Does it hurt very much?" Caroline said.

"All of the cuts in my mouth?" Elizabeth said, blowing on the soup. "Yes, it hurts."

Caroline buzzed with exaggerated concern. "You're so brave," she said. "So devoted. Doing all of this for the community center . . ."

"I'm not brave," Elizabeth said. "We were pretty stupid to use a ladder that old without a safety latch."

"Yes," Darcy said.

"Well, *I* think you're brave," Caroline insisted. "You tried to catch your sister while she fell."

"I wasn't thinking."

"Darcy, aaaa," Caroline said with a coy glance. "You and Brendan *must* renovate that front walkway. We wouldn't want any more accidents."

"Of course not," Darcy said.

"And ladders from this decade," Elizabeth added.

"And licensed workers to use them, yes."

"You don't need a license to use a ladder," Elizabeth replied.

Darcy unfolded his next brochure with a crisp rustle of paper. "Maybe you should."

"Of course, we must start right away," Caroline continued. "The sooner this place can be made presentable, the sooner you'll get partners on board, la."

"Other partners?" Elizabeth said.

Caroline waved her hand. "Retail, silly," she said. "You've got to have a draw, you know—something that makes people want to visit . . ."

Elizabeth straightened in her seat. "People visit when there's things to do," she said. "When they can get the help they need. It's a community center, not a mall."

"Don't worry, la!" Caroline purred. "Darcy's done lots of these kinds of projects before."

That was what worried her.

Caroline turned breathless with awe. "They always turn out so *beautiful*. Lots of gardens and walking space, like something out of a story. Wouldn't that be better than that gloomy little prison building?"

Elizabeth grunted.

"Probably no garden with the cost of land here," Darcy said.

"Brendan?" Caroline called.

He chewed on a fingernail and didn't answer.

"Brendan, you have to do something about all that *concrete*. It's so dangerous, aa, and so *ug-ly*."

"I heard you, Caro," Brendan said. "We're not talking about this right now."

"I mean, I think it's only smart given the accident."

"Ai ya, Caroline," Brendan interjected. "Leave a note or something. Otherwise, please . . ."

"I am trying to make *conversation*," Caroline hissed.

Elizabeth sipped at her soup and tasted blood faintly on the back of her tongue.

"Is Georgiana still working up in New England, Darcy?" Caroline said, opening a container of soup for herself. She split a pair of disposable chopsticks and brushed off splinters, poking at a knot of noodles piled on the bottom of the container without lifting a single bite to her mouth. "Have you eaten yet? Did you want some?"

Darcy shook his head. "She's gone back to school."

Caroline beamed. "I can't wait to see her again. It's been so long, aa, and I miss her very much. But I'm sure she'll want to come for the commencement gala."

"Georgiana likes to concern herself in plenty of things that aren't her business, so I expect she'll be there, yes," Darcy said.

"Georgiana?" Elizabeth said.

"Darcy's younger sister," Caroline said. "A beautiful name, if you ask me."

"I didn't name her," Darcy said. "She came that way."

"She's the one who came up with the idea for the Wongs' first center."

"That makes a lot of sense," Elizabeth said.

His dark brown eyes settled on her, curious. "What does?"

"That your sister roped you into it," she said. "Otherwise, I'd expect you to get into something else—securities or something."

"I'm not a banker," he said. "And she can be rather insistent when she wants to be."

Elizabeth studied him. "She wouldn't let it go, huh?"

Darcy sank lower in his chair. A sulk, the aunties might have called it, if he wasn't such a polite boy, such a respectable boy; god knows only the girls needed to be kept in line.

Caroline nudged the open noodle container towards him. "Darcy, eat something, laaaa."

Elizabeth half expected Caroline to spoon him a bite.

"You know, Darcy is so generous, aa," Caroline said. "He never thinks of himself."

Elizabeth smiled flatly. "I'm sure."

Caroline brushed her free hand along his arm, and he spooked, jerking his elbow back against the seat.

"So what's it like?" Elizabeth asked. "At the centers you run?"

"It's a community center," he said. "We work with our corporate partners to offer classes, athletics, camps, and private events with a focus on revitalizing the neighborhood."

"What does that mean, revitalizing?"

He tossed aside the brochures and removed his glasses, folding them in his hands and looking at her straight on. "Why are you so opposed to what we're doing with the center?"

"Because I know what happens to us after you open. You and your partners talk up your impact on the community and how you want to clean it up and write us off on your taxes. But then what?"

"You think all of our motives are suspect," he huffed. "Just because we want to help . . ."

"Please. You're not saving the rec out of the goodness of your heart. You're making an investment. Maybe that helps us, or you turn it into a mall, I don't know. But once you reach the people that you want or get the money that you want, it's the locals who need the rec the most who get left behind." She crossed her arms over her chest and waited for his answering shot, but it never came. He stayed silent, studying her with that same curious expression, as if no one had ever thought to talk back to him before.

Likely no one had.

He unfolded his glasses and replaced them on his face. The look disappeared, replaced with the same constipated expression he'd worn all day.

"Trust me when I say that we have no desire to change the neighborhood," he said. "It's what drew us here in the first place."

She leveled a glance at him. "And trust *me* when I say that you aren't the first person who's promised that," she said. "Everybody likes the character of a place until there's too much of it or something happens that they don't like. If you're there for the community, then be there for the community. And if you're not, then at least be honest about it."

He opened his mouth to respond, when the nurse stepped out and called her name.

With a nod, Elizabeth stood. "Excuse me."

As she disappeared behind the door, Caroline drew her mouth over her teeth in a derisive sneer. "Have you ever met anyone so hardheaded!"

Her sister crowed in agreement as Brendan sunk his head in his hands. "And the accident with the ladder today!" Louisa said.

"I know!" Caroline cried. "Who even *asked* them to clean those windows? As if they could ever get them clean."

Louisa clicked her tongue. "I'm sure it was her idea."

"Absolutely," Caroline said. "You would never have let your sister do anything so dangerous, Darcy."

"No," Darcy said. "I would not."

"And your sister would never ignore good advice just because she thought she knew better . . ."

"I hope not."

Caroline shifted in her seat. "And, really, not wanting to go to the doctor? How bad could their situation be?"

Brendan worried his lip between his teeth.

"Brendan, if it wasn't for you . . ." Caroline said.

"Caro, I don't want to think about it."

Darcy rubbed at his jaw but said nothing.

"Jane is such a darling—but the family!" Caroline snickered daintily behind her hand.

"I think her family's rather resourceful," Brendan sniffed.

"Please, Jane's the only one going anywhere," Caroline said. "She'll be working to keep them for the rest of her life."

"Something you ought to pick up from them, Caroline," Brendan said.

"And that mother!" she continued. "I'm sure she'll come asking for a favor sooner or later. People like *that* always do."

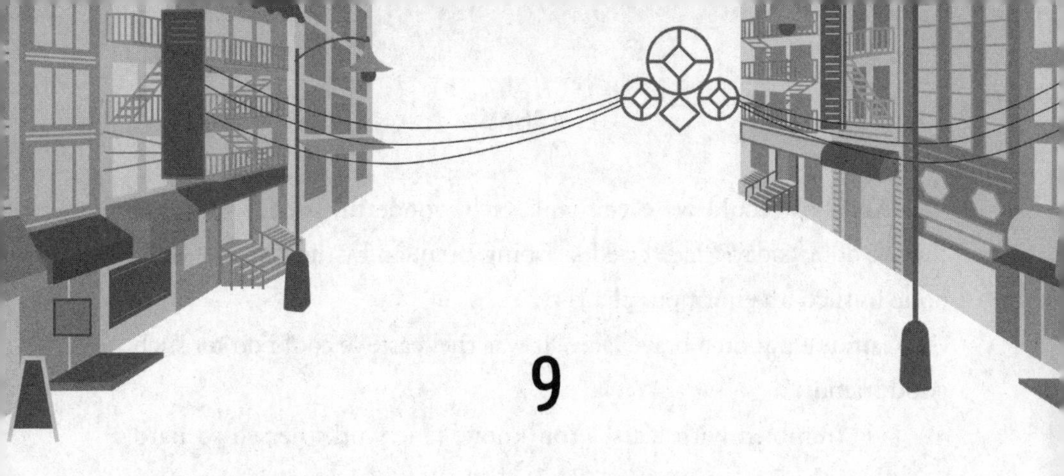

9

Jane and Elizabeth returned with good news from the doctors: no concussions, no breaks, no casts—a heavily bandaged ankle, prescription antiseptic mouthwash, and a few weeks of rest would sort everything out. As they met their friends in the waiting room, they begged for a payment plan, for a chance to split the cost, but Brendan wouldn't hear of it. The Lees wanted to pay for everything, and would. No argument.

As they packed up their things and headed out towards the street, Jade greeted them with a cry of alarm.

"Mother, what are you doing here?" Elizabeth said. "How did you get here?"

Jade pressed a hand to her forehead, overwhelmed with emotion. "My Jane, look at you!"

"Mother, I'm fine."

Elizabeth hovered at her shoulder. "Mother," she repeated. "How did you get here?"

Jade waved her hand vaguely in the air. "They're looking for parking," she said. "On crutches! My beautiful Jane, my poor baby . . ."

"Who's driving?"

"And how could we ever thank such wonderful friends for what they've done today?" Jade cried, clasping Brendan by the arms. "You've done us such an enormous cha-ri-ty."

Caroline put on a brave face. "It was the least we could do for such good friends."

Jade trembled with tears. "You know, Jane works herself so hard and never thinks to complain," she said. "I tell her again and again, *look af-ter your-self*, but she's always thinking about others. Thank you so, so much. I don't know what we would have done without you."

"We have to repay you," Elizabeth said. "It's too much money."

Brendan shook his head. "Absolutely not," he said. "We're friends, and friends take care of each other."

"Please," Elizabeth said.

"It's nothing to us," Brendan said. "And it's everything to you. Why can't you take it?"

That was the problem.

For her entire life, she'd known every major expense to come with a ritual of hand-wringing, desperate pleas at the family altar, and anxiety, but they'd managed. On credit or layaway, haggled or borrowed, by the grace of financial aid, they made lemonade out of rotten fruit. Of course they needed the money—everybody, present company excluded, needed money—but taking it would make them out to be exactly what Caroline suspected. She didn't want to owe them anything, not even gratitude. She wanted to say no.

"There's absolutely no reason to refuse," Darcy said. "You can't afford it on your own. You said it yourself."

Elizabeth felt a flush of shame rise in her cheeks, but nothing could have prepared her for what followed. Wasn't it just like the Chens to always be exceeding expectations? A white delivery van covered in graffiti swerved from the center lane with a blaring honk to double-park outside St. Vincent's driveway, *The Blueprint* blasting through the lowered windows. Passersby lingering by the makeshift 9/11 memorial stared. One even snapped a photo of Kitty leaning half her body nearly out of the passenger-side window.

Caroline laughed nervously. "What is this?"

The rear doors to the van popped open, Mary leaping out like a would-be kidnapper.

The horn wailed. "Get in!"

Brendan exhaled through his teeth, squinting in concern as he passed behind the open rear cargo doors. "I don't think this is legal."

Darcy pursed his lips. "It *absolutely* is not."

"Isn't your sister in *high school*?" Caroline said.

"She has a learner's permit," Elizabeth mumbled.

On cue, Lydia leaned out the driver's side window, the broad brim of a Yankees cap covering her face, her oversize hoop earrings swinging violently as she cursed out another driver trying to squeeze past an idling car on the opposite side. A cacophony of car horns blared as drivers creeping forward blocked half of the intersection.

Elizabeth assessed the seat layout. The van had been built to haul loose sacks of rice and produce, not passengers. A few twenty-pound bags of rice stood in for seat cushions on the cabin floor. No seat belts—or seats—could be seen.

"You've just been released from the hospital," Darcy said. "This isn't safe. It isn't *legal*."

This fell on the less concerning end of the legal spectrum where the Chens were concerned, but she supposed he would find that less reassuring than she did. "Listen, this is fine," Elizabeth said. "We've done this a thousand times."

He stared at her, aghast. "You've done this a *thousand* times?"

"It'll be fine," Elizabeth insisted.

"You barely escaped a concussion," he said. "You're going to sit in the back of a cargo van without a seat belt?"

How many times did he need to hear her say it? "We're going to be fine."

"Just because you repeat it doesn't make it true."

Brendan shook his head. "Darcy's right. We can call a car."

Elizabeth groaned. "It's only a few blocks."

"It is not a few blocks . . ." Darcy began. Brendan laid a hand on his chest and he quieted.

Jade's face lit with a scheme. "Yes, Elizabeth," she said. "There's no use in you getting hurt on the way back. Why don't you go with them to the apartment and make sure they don't get lost?"

Elizabeth whined, "Mother."

But Jade's attentions had already shifted. Snapping her fingers, she pointed for Kitty to step out. "Jane should sit up front. Kitty—"

Kitty rolled her eyes and climbed out. "You don't need to tell me. In the back. Again. Kitty always sits in the back."

"Kitty, help your sister, please. She's injured."

Kitty sighed. "Yes, poor Jane . . ."

She didn't move quickly enough. Brendan, industrious and dutiful, took the crutches and propped them against the van, hoisting Jane up into the passenger seat. Elizabeth half expected him to buckle her in.

Jane covered his hand with her own. "I'm so sorry for all the trouble."

Brendan looked at her nervously. "I didn't hurt you, did I?"

She shook her head.

He rested his forehead against hers and sighed, the picture of relief. "Good," he said. "We'll be right behind you."

"You don't have to worry."

Brendan hopped back onto the sidewalk, heading down the block in search of a cab.

Caroline watched him go with an annoyed cluck of the tongue. "Let's go see how the other half lives."

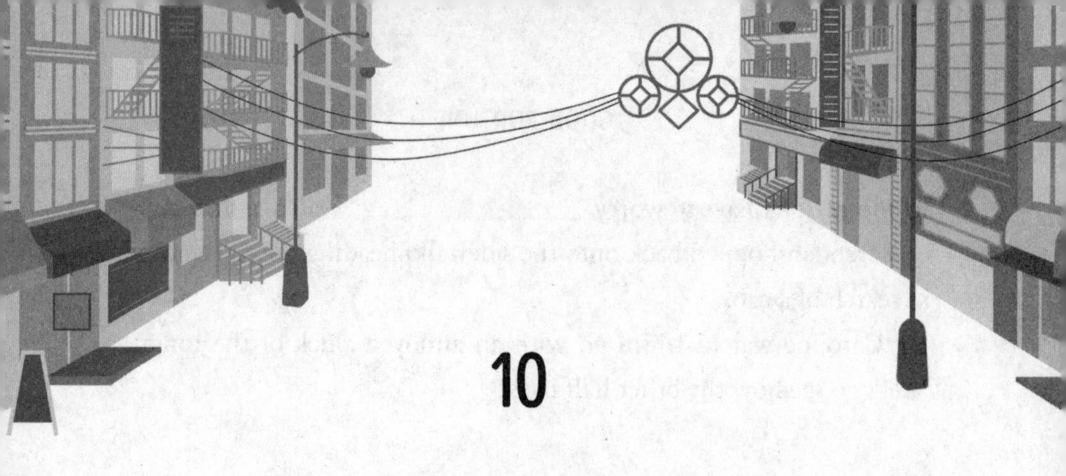

10

An apartment never seems smaller, messier, or dingier than whenever it has people to impress. At least the entryway hadn't smelled too strongly of urine, and they'd remembered to take down all their hand-washed underwear from the shower rod that morning. Small blessings. The cab pulled up outside of the industrial-looking building squeezed between two shuttered and gated storefronts, and their guests arrived. Chez Chen.

On the fourth floor, in their apartment, awaited a homecoming feast: steamed snapper drizzled with oil and sauce, topped with scallions; egg rolls from the restaurant; sautéed long beans; and slices of sponge roll from the corner bakery, filled with airy whipped cream. For the price of a little blood and mutilation, they could eat like kings.

Jade waved them in. "We planned this to wish Jane and Elizabeth home," Jade said. "But please join us."

In space, as in life, the Chens did the most with less. Caroline took in as much as her system would allow: crumpled grocery bags and half-open backpacks piled carelessly along the wall, towers of plastic storage containers threatening to come down on their heads as they passed, old magazines with missing covers or pages lying on almost everything in sight, plastic toys everywhere. It defied taste. It defied order. It broke every law of interior design and skirted the laws of physics.

No wall had been left untouched. An oversize square calendar, gifted from the local Buddhist temple, was covered with a smaller daily calendar, its edges frayed from the imperfect tears of the days preceding. School award certificates and diplomas hung beside Jade's wedding photos and the girls' school photos, five of them looking almost identical in matching mushroom cuts and crocheted sweater vests.

Their new friends moved with the slow deliberation of soldiers on patrol, their eyes scanning for dangers, feet tiptoeing around possible trips and traps. Brendan was the first to the dinner table, sliding onto the kitchen chair with the most intact upholstery. "This is a wonderful home you have."

Caroline squeaked.

Darcy hunched as if worried to make contact with the air. Some people made themselves at home anywhere they went; he was not one of them.

Lydia thundered past them with a loud snort. "Can we move a little faster, please?" she shouted, forcing her way through against the wall.

"Lydia," Jade hissed, whacking her lightly with a rolled-up circular. To the others, she added, "She's just joking, la! Such a funny girl."

As usually happened when they were all together, the apartment descended into a flurry of noise and complaint: Jade fussing over their guests, Jane rummaging through the packed hallway closet for extra plastic stools, Lydia and Mary fighting over use of the computer. Elizabeth tried to figure the odds on someone making a break for it (low but not zero) or hovering by the doorway all night instead of fixing a plate (medium-high) when Darcy pointed towards a framed certificate on the wall and cleared his throat.

At least he didn't raise his hand.

Most days, she walked past it without a second glance, all of the awards and the memorabilia, the photos that tracked them from first grade through graduation—a shrine to their work and their achievements, an offering for future blessings of success.

"In recognition of outstanding performance . . ." he read.

She gestured to the ribbon beside it. "Not that outstanding," she said. "We lost."

"Vice-captain of the debate team?" he said.

She arched a brow. "You look surprised."

He almost seemed to smile at that. "I'm not."

She followed as he continued his way along the wall. Explaining an old report card or school photo would be one thing, baby photos another. If he came after the voluminous bloom of her hair or the look of her CHIP-approved Coke-bottle glasses, she wouldn't be afraid to hit back.

"This must be your grandmother?" he said, pointing to a Polaroid taped to the back of an index card.

Elizabeth from two years ago grinned at her, sporting a regrettable pixie cut, her arm slung around an older Chinese woman in a neon windbreaker.

She shook her head, reaching for the crumpled clipping beside it. "That's Mrs. Ng from across the street," she said. "Her building did everything they could to get her out a few years ago. Turned off her heat, didn't make any repairs, faked eviction notices, everything."

He glanced from the photo to her. "What happened?"

She shrugged. "We fought like hell," she said. "She'd been in the apartment for over twenty years, but you know how it is with new management. They don't care."

He frowned, trying to read the clipping.

"What I meant was . . ."

His eyes met hers, cool and neutral. "I know what you meant," he said. "You think you know what's best for the neighborhood."

Her cheeks heated. "No," she replied. "I just know the people who live in it."

"Everyone!" Jade called, waving her arms. "Please!"

Caroline took a plate and gamely poked at a piece of scallion. "You didn't need to go to all this trouble, Aunty."

"No trouble, no trouble," Jade cried. "After everything you did for us!"

"You would have gone to the doctor, surely," Darcy said.

"Surely," Lydia smirked.

Their kitchen barely had enough seats for all of them on a good day; with guests, they'd brought out the heavy artillery—pastel-colored plastic stools and metal folding chairs to help bolster their numbers—but their guests didn't seem too eager to sit.

"We've been sitting all day," Caroline said. "It's good for us to stretch our legs once in a while."

They fell into the halting silence of eating, exchanging minor remarks on the quality or the value of the food, overly effusive praise on the skill of the preparer, and polite questions about their lives. How were the younger girls finding school? *Boring and endless*, came the answer. Where did Jade learn how to prepare such delicious long beans? *Oh, it was nothing, nothing—very kind of you to say*, she insisted.

Elizabeth served herself a portion of rice from the cooker, picking indecisively among the open containers lined up on the counter.

Darcy stepped up beside her.

Elizabeth set down the serving paddle and moved to the next dish. "Look at you, breaking bread with the underprivileged."

"Instead of torturing Victorian orphans?"

She stopped. She stared. Sauce dripped off the end of her serving spoon. Darcy, learning to joke? Darcy, smiling? Something had gone terribly wrong. It could only be explained as some cosmic disturbance in the Force.

Mary dropped her elbows onto the table, asking what their distinguished guests might be planning for the rest of their trip.

Brendan broke the terrible news. "We're headed back to Hong Kong tomorrow."

Jade, in the middle of serving Brendan an extra egg roll, flung it towards him with sudden force. "Waaa, so soon? You've only just arrived!"

This was nothing less than a tragedy of the highest order, on the level of the passing of Princess Diana, whose photo crowded their actual relatives on the ancestral altar. They might never recover.

Brendan casually slid his plate out of her reach. "Something urgent's come up, I'm afraid," he said. "Some family business I need to attend to."

"I hope everything's all right," Jane said. "Nothing serious?"

Brendan shook his head. "Nothing that should keep me away for long."

"Yes," Darcy said. "We should be back in time to get our staff settled."

Elizabeth dropped a piece of shrimp in the middle of the table. "Staff? For what?"

"Look at that," Vincent said, plucking up the stray. "It's so fresh it's jumping."

Darcy wiped at his mouth with a napkin. "The center is hardly in good condition, and there's a lot of work that needs to be done ahead of any reopening."

"Sure," Elizabeth said. "But it's going to stay open to the community, right?"

Brendan tried to look reassuring. "You can count on us."

Darcy seemed less certain. "We'll evaluate it as a potential option."

Jade, sensing danger, slid her plastic stool beside Brendan, shoving Darcy aside as she squeezed between them. "Your mother must be so happy to have such a dutiful son, la, for you to be going back like this."

Darcy and Caroline snorted.

"I heard that," Brendan said.

Darcy served Brendan a fish cheek. "Dutiful, maybe. But you're a little too quick to drop everything you're doing when somebody says they need you."

Brendan elbowed him in the side. "Thanks for the vote of confidence."

Elizabeth moved to the counter and sliced a piece of sponge roll. "Don't let him talk to you like that," she said, serving Brendan a slice on a fresh plate. "There's nothing wrong with loyalty."

Darcy turned to look at her. "*If* it doesn't overrule good sense."

At the table, the others watched them with a mixture of curiosity and apprehension, dread and glee. Nothing could be more entertaining than a family gathering descending into chaos, and nothing guaranteed chaos faster than Elizabeth provoked. If Darcy had looked anywhere else around the room, he might have caught the telltale signs of warning—Vincent's wry smile, Lydia's and Brendan's broad grins, the nervous flutter of Jade's fingers against the edge of the table—but whatever the reason, he didn't look away from her.

And that provoked her most of all.

She pushed a slice of cake onto the edge of his plate. "Some people don't crunch numbers before deciding whether or not to show up."

"You can't help very many people if the money runs out."

"I don't think it's as much about the helping as it is about the money for *some* people."

Darcy huffed. "Before you can be accountable to other people, you have to be accountable to yourself."

Caroline sighed loudly, nibbling on the edge of a leafy green. "Well, I think you're doing a great job. Not everyone would take on such a big project."

"The rec isn't just some building," Elizabeth replied. "It's a part of people's lives. It's a part of *our* lives. It matters, whatever the numbers are."

"You can't know how to change things if you don't figure out what works and what doesn't."

Elizabeth's jaw tightened. "What works for who? For you and your investors, or for the people who use it?"

Jade hummed nervously. "Now, LB, why don't you sit down and stop bothering our guests . . ."

Any hopes Jade harbored for brokering a peace ended with the next shot. "It's not as if their demands are always reasonable," he replied. "But we're easy to blame, so we're blamed."

Elizabeth slapped a handful of paper napkins onto the table for their guests. "Well, won't someone think of the developers."

Darcy shook his head, slicing into his piece of cake and taking a bite.

Caroline groaned with exaggerated relish as she pushed her nearly full plate towards the center of the table. "Thank you for a lovely meal."

Kitty wordlessly jumped to her feet and served her a piece of cake.

"You're the ones who are being unreasonable," Elizabeth said.

Darcy aimed his fork at her. "And you're not half as clever as you think you are."

Elizabeth could hear the record scratch as Jade drew back in her seat. Jade may have complained every hour on the hour about her own family—and didn't she have the right, having suffered and sacrificed for them, day in and day out?—but she considered that a mother's privilege. From the rest of the city—the world!—she expected nothing less than lavish recognition and praise, envy and awe. Any insult to home, husband, or her daughters was a declaration of war. "My Elizabeth graduated at the *top* of her class. Tracked for gifted right out of kindergarten, and *paid* to attend college. Scholarship, you know," she gushed.

Caroline squealed. "Oh, a scholarship student!"

"And she won some kind of contest with a *beautiful* poem, which they asked her to perform . . ."

"A poem!" Caroline cried, clapping her hands. "Perhaps you can treat us to a reading?"

"Some things should not be held against us, no matter what," Elizabeth said. "High school poetry being one of them."

Brendan tried to be nice. "I'm sure it can't be that bad."

"Believe me, the best part of the poem was the money that came with it."

Darcy nibbled at another few crumbs of cake, and Elizabeth marveled at his commitment to finish something he hated purely for the virtue of finishing it. It'd be admirable if it weren't so stupid.

"You can't please everyone, and you shouldn't try," Darcy added. "Apart from being poor strategy, it's rather irresponsible."

Elizabeth huffed. "So now you think it's irresponsible for people to help each other?"

"Ai ya, LB, why don't you ask our friends if they'd like some more tea?" Jade said, chewing on the edge of a nail. "Stop causing trouble, la."

Reaching for the teapot, Elizabeth began to top up all of the half-empty cups on the table and sprinkled a little more into Brendan's near-full one. After an evening of picking fights, a single turn of good manners would hardly erase all of her earlier faults, but she hoped it might endear Jade to forgiveness in the morning.

With great maturity, she behaved herself—even as she felt Darcy's eyes watching her as she poured.

He deigned to push his teacup towards her, fingers tapping the table as she obliged him in topping it up. She could feel his focus on her fingers, on the way she held the teapot, nitpicking her technique, as usual. Now he could add unsophisticated and clumsy to his growing list of complaints.

But no matter how much he found fault with her—and the feeling most definitely was mutual—nothing would keep them out of each other's lives until the Lees finished their work on the center. He was the best punishment her mother could have crafted. He was her personal purgatory.

And now he was reaching for the teapot.

Mary drained her tea. "All support is about showing up. For yourself, but also for others, whenever needed, and however appropriate."

"Mary," Lydia said, blinking at her. "Thank you."

Elizabeth shook her head. "You shouldn't make people jump through hoops to get you to care."

Darcy's mouth quirked with the hint of a smile as he refilled her tea. Unprompted. "We have different ideas of care."

Elizabeth helped herself to the last word. "Or maybe one of us is a better person."

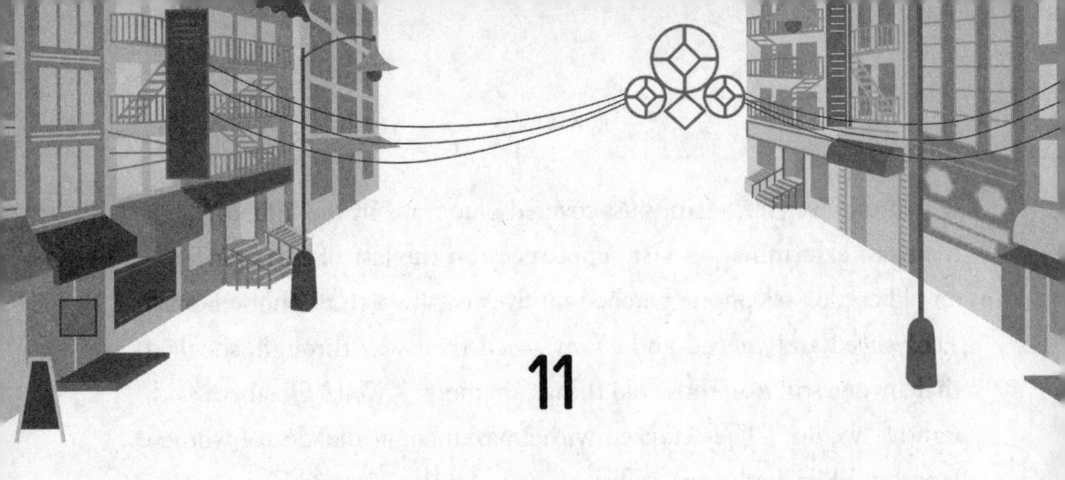

11

Their impromptu visit threatened to mutate into an extended stay. Beg, plead, and pray as their guests might, Jade insisted, Jade wouldn't hear of their leaving so soon after dinner. Besides, aaaaa, any exertion before proper digestion would make them sick—and what kind of host would she be then? So there came dessert and drip coffee, polite conversation, and a quick tour.

Their guests couldn't help but marvel at how they all lived. Nothing could be too small to escape notice or amazement. How well they fit all of their earthly belongings into such a tiny space! How quaint! How incredible! How could anyone live like this! Indeed, the Chens manipulated space like the best of illusionists—storage bins dangling from makeshift hooks on coat hangers, on top of boxes, items nested within items and packed into crevices. Surely they'd seen smaller spaces in Hong Kong, but Caroline assured them she'd *never* and she couldn't *imagine* how she could get by without her necessities. Life without a walk-in closet or king-size bed couldn't be considered living at all. How brave they all were to suffer like this. How noble.

In their apartment was a New York their visitors hadn't seen—and hoped to never see again: dust-covered glue traps in the kitchen from their last extermination visit, appliances on the last of their last legs, an old corded telephone perched on five years' worth of phone books. They *ooh*ed and *aahh*ed and *oh my god*ed their way through, shocked that anyone still *used* those old things anymore. ("Well," Elizabeth said, tightly, "we do.") They clucked with amazement at the idea of women Jane's and Elizabeth's age still sleeping in bunk beds, and jeered at the sight they must make with their legs dangling off the edge.

"Very cozy, aa," Caroline said, walking into the narrow aisle of their bedroom.

Lingerie and handbags dangled from the corner posts of the bunk beds, dirty laundry scattered across the floor. Twin-size bunks anchored each side wall, leaving a gangway of walkable space in the center of the room leading to the window. A squat fourteen-inch TV/VCR set perched on top of the cast-iron radiator in the corner, its power cord stretched taut from the opposite wall like a trip wire.

Lydia rushed past them towards the window, rummaging for a nearly empty tube of lip gloss and swiping a thick coat onto her mouth. "We don't entertain much," she said, smacking her lips. "We prefer to go out."

Kitty didn't dare to follow her lead, instead climbing up to the top bunk on the left side of the room and crawling the length of the mattress to dangle and drop herself on the opposite end of the room.

"Is this how you usually get around?" Brendan said.

Lydia pulled a skinny cotton scarf from where it draped on a bedpost, looping it around her neck twice. "Kitty!"

"I'm coming," Kitty howled, but Lydia had already disappeared out the window and up the fire escape.

"Your sisters are such int-er-est-ing people, aa," Caroline said. "So *active* at their age!"

Brendan peered over his sister's shoulder. "Where are they going?"

"The roof," Elizabeth said. "Shall we go?"

Jane widened her eyes. "LB!"

"I'm always up for an adventure," Brendan said, taking Jane's hand.

Jane colored. "Follow me," she said. Cutting through towards the open window, she climbed over the dresser and out. Brendan followed, the metal steps clanging noisily under his weight.

Caroline looked at the fire escape queasily, but stepped through, heels slipping into the narrow grates.

Darcy hovered in the doorway, carefully studying the walls.

"Are you going to stay here?" Elizabeth said.

He didn't answer, slowly passing down the wall of torn boy-band posters and pages of teen magazines.

Elizabeth pushed past him to a set of plastic drawers stacked beside the radiator. She palmed a camera and lens and slung a camera strap around her neck. "Are you coming or not?"

He pointed at one section of the wall, almost hidden behind a crush of handbags dangling from the top bunk's post. "Did you take these?"

She was surprised he even noticed. A little collage lived in the inches of space between Cindy Crawford and Jessica Alba, packed with little prints and Polaroids. There was the Bowery glistening after a rainstorm at night, blurry reflections of neon in the puddles; produce vendors on Canal hawking their wares; an old man captured spitting into the street—all clustered among the candid moments of their lives. Lydia in her homecoming dress and corsage, Jane studying at Lulu's, Jade's hands pinching dumplings.

He pointed at Mary and Lydia giggling on the Coney Island boardwalk two years ago, a streak of orange light blurring over the tops of their heads. "Are these your photos?"

She nodded. "My mother calls it a waste of time."

"Seems like more than a hobby."

Elizabeth anticipated some critique or passing insult—*this would never be good enough to get you into the Getty*—but nothing else came. Maybe it was a side effect of indigestion or the fact that she rarely had an audience for her photos, but she almost wished he would. She wanted to know if he saw anything in her work, if he thought there might be anything there to see—though, of course, he wouldn't.

"Well?" she said.

He pouted, looking sullen. "You aren't interested in what I think."

She laughed. "Maybe you're right," she said. "But that hasn't stopped you from telling me yet."

He turned back to the photo wall. "There aren't very many pictures of you here."

"Because I'm usually the one taking them," she said.

"Because you're the only one who can, or because you won't let anyone else try?"

She twisted the lens into place on the camera. "Jane tries, sometimes. But the others only think of me when they want something." Through the window, the sun crested behind a neighboring building, casting her in gold and orange light. "Had enough? Want to go up?"

"They're not bad pictures," he said, without moving. "I don't know much about art, really—that's more my sister's domain—but it seems like you're very careful."

"In the way I take pictures?"

"In the way you present people—your subjects." His eyes landed on her, looking her over with careful regard. It wasn't quite like judgment, but it wasn't neutral either; she couldn't figure out what he was trying to read. "It comes through, how you feel."

She shrugged. "I'm an open book."

He shook his head. "No," he said. "You have a strong point of view."

"Try telling that to my mother," she said. Ducking through the window, she waved for him to follow. "Now, hurry up. Before they think we've killed each other."

* * *

Open space in the city, by any other name, was free parking. One way or another, people capitalized on opportunity—camping in the park, chaining their bikes, occupying stoops for conversation. If they could, they did—at least, until cops, landlords, or pigeons came pecking. The roof at Essex Street was claimed as a bootleg backyard, populated with plastic lawn chairs and potted plants—legal and otherwise—and a small pigeon coop.

Loud hip-hop thumped in welcome as they climbed off the fire escape onto the roof, where a group of loitering teenagers greeted them with cheers and a mound of empty beer cans.

Elizabeth sunk onto a plastic lawn chair with a loud groan. "Make yourself at home."

Darcy remained where he stood, arms stiff against his sides. He was like a toy soldier with a Bluetooth headset.

"You can sit down, you know," she called, stretching her arms over her head. "Nothing's going to kill you."

Darcy perched delicately on the edge of an adjacent lawn chair, the plastic squeaking under his weight. "These are yours then?"

She waved her hand vaguely. "Ours," she said. "The building's. Tomato, to-mah-to."

"That isn't very reassuring."

She uncapped the lens of her camera and stole a quick photo of him. The shutter clicked, film whirring a second later.

"Are you taking a photo of me?" he said.

"That's what that sound is," she said. At his silence, she added, "That's a joke."

"You joke a lot."

She shrugged, and raised the camera up to her eye. "Relax. I'm taking a few test shots."

He squirmed in front of the lens. "It isn't going to end up on your wall?"

"You have to qualify for that sort of thing."

He pressed his knees together and angled towards the camera.

"This isn't a school photo," she said, squinting into the viewfinder. "You don't have to pose."

He huffed, glancing from one side of the roof to the other. "I'm *not* posing."

"Just act natural."

She could see him fighting an impulse to roll his eyes as he leveled a flat stare in the center of the frame. She should have expected it would be too much for him to understand what natural meant. He probably emerged from the womb in formal salute.

"Whatever you might think, we're on the same side, you know," he said. "About the center."

She readjusted the focus. "I know what you're trying to do," she said. "But it isn't going to work."

He shifted closer, his face swallowing the lens. "What am I trying to do?"

"Entrapment. Appeasement. Intimidation tactics," she said. "You get my guard down so you can convince me that killing the rec is actually a better idea in the long run."

She took his silence as confirmation.

"But I've never liked being told what to think, so you won't get the honor of showing me the errors of my ways. Sorry," she said. Turning towards the crowd in the distance, she caught Lydia twisting up towards the sky, twirling on her bare feet. The shutter fired.

When she turned back, he was still watching her.

"Do you always assume the worst intentions of everyone you meet?"

She smirked. "Only for those who deserve it."

He shifted closer. "And I deserve it?"

She lowered the camera, fussing with the settings dial. When she looked up, his eyes were still on her, waiting for an answer. She fought the urge to muss his collar, or nudge his glasses just out of place. She wanted to see him unsettled. "Don't you?"

"We wouldn't be making this investment if we didn't believe in what it could do," he said.

"The rec means a lot to the people around here—to me," she said. "I don't know what it means to you. Maybe a lot, maybe a little. But whatever happens, I'm not going to let it go down without a fight."

"I thought as much," he said, softly. Leaning into her space, he tapped the top of her camera with the tip of his finger. "Strong feelings, strong point of view."

"Is that a bad thing?"

"It can blind you to the reality of a situation. It can keep you from seeing what needs to be fixed."

Before, their closeness seemed like sound strategy, an easy way to throw him off-balance and unsettle him. She hadn't realized how close he'd come since. She felt an overwhelming urge to put distance between them now.

She set her shoulders, trying to force more confidence into her voice. "Don't fix what isn't broken."

Slowly, he closed what little distance remained between them, arm ghosting hers. "Don't let your feelings overwhelm your good sense."

"There you two are!" Caroline boomed, bounding towards them

with forced cheer. Elizabeth jumped from her seat, skittering towards the other side of the chair to meet Caroline.

"Darcy, so rude, aa, neglecting your friends like this."

Darcy didn't move. When he spoke, his voice sounded almost dark. "I never promised I would be your chaperone, Caroline."

She winced but tried to hide it. "Not me," she cried. "You're always picking on me, aaaaa!"

"I'm sure that's how he is," Elizabeth said.

"Where's your brother?" Darcy said.

Caroline pointed to the other side of the roof. "Where else? Smoking with the boys." She made a gagging noise.

Elizabeth couldn't pick Brendan out for a few minutes. He stood away from the crowd of teens a few feet down the same wall by the parapet, his arms clipping wide circles as he spoke. Jane leaned into him, her head settling back against his shoulder, giggling at his story.

"Well, I'm determined to be a better friend than Darcy *or* my brother," Caroline said, jerking her forcefully by the hand. "Elizabeth, let's go."

Elizabeth stumbled on her feet. "Where are we going?"

"To go and get Brendan, silly," she said. "How horrible of him to abandon us like this."

Darcy shrugged. "I don't feel abandoned. I'm perfectly fine right here."

"*Daaaaaaaarcy*," she whined. "You should come with us."

Elizabeth tried to lead her away. The more distance, the better. "If we're going, then we should go," she said, but Caroline stayed her with a hand on the arm.

"Yes, go," Darcy said, waving them off. "I'd only get in the way."

Caroline offered her most flirtatious smile and coquettish batting of the eyes. "And just what do you mean by that, sir?"

"He hates to see us go, but he loves to watch us leave," Elizabeth cracked. "Your typical male chauvinist."

Darcy smirked. "Please," he said. "It'd be chauvinistic of me to get involved."

Caroline looked between them, baffled.

Elizabeth didn't need to be told twice. The more time she spent talking to him up here, the more confused she became. Nothing had changed. He still wanted to gut the rec, pushed his unsolicited advice and opinion on everything, and expected the world to bend around him. Maybe he wasn't Damien from *The Omen* as she had expected, but not being the Antichrist was a low bar.

A little polite interest in her photos and she'd almost lost it. Get it together, LB.

Throwing an arm over Caroline's shoulders, Elizabeth hauled her in the direction of Brendan—as fast as Caroline's skinny legs could go.

"We thought we would see what trouble you're up to," Caroline said as they approached.

"Nosy as ever, Caro," Brendan said.

Jane shuffled towards Elizabeth, wrapping her arms around her and burrowing her head against her shoulder. Jane under the influence of anything wasn't much different from Jane in real life—sweet and affectionate, if more prone to public displays.

Elizabeth kissed the top of her head.

"It's so nice of you all to show us around while we're here," Caroline said. "I don't know what we would have done without you."

"Asked the hotel," Brendan replied.

Caroline batted at his arm. "You know what I mean. And if you ever go to Hong Kong, promise you'll call us," she gushed. "So that we can return the favor."

Elizabeth took the last of the joint from Jane and breathed deep.

"I'm sure we'll see you before then," she said, exhaling smoke. "You have so many arrangements with the center."

"Arrangements," Caroline scoffed. "Brendan hasn't organized a thing in his life. He'll probably hire on a management company."

"A management company?" Elizabeth cried. "I thought you were going to be involved!"

Darcy grazed her side as he stepped into their circle, his knuckles brushing against the back of her hand. Elizabeth jolted back, opening up space. "That is involved as far as Brendan's concerned," he said. "What exactly do you think management companies do?"

"I thought you were going to take an active role here, not turn it over to some cronies."

"You're making a lot of assumptions. They're not going to make any major decisions," Darcy replied. "All they'll do is oversee the execution."

Elizabeth rolled her eyes. "And nothing has ever gone wrong from plan to execution."

"I suppose you're looking for a position?" Caroline said.

Elizabeth held out the last of the smoldering joint. "No," she said. "Thank you."

Darcy took it from her with a light shrug of gratitude.

She stared at him in amazement as he lifted it to his lips and took a drag. "You smoke?"

Brendan snickered, shoving his hands in his pockets. "No," he said, flashing him a quick glance. "He doesn't."

Darcy pressed his lips into a thin line. "It's dead, anyway."

Brendan murmured in understanding. "Look, LB, I know it's not what you want to hear, but . . ."

Elizabeth grinned, elbowing Jane. "LB, huh?"

"Yeah," he said, sheepishly. "What I wanted to say is that . . . we're not abandoning the project."

Caroline cooed in agreement. "Definitely not before the opening!" she said. "Wait and see. It'll be the best gala you've ever attended."

"I haven't attended many."

Jane squeezed Brendan's shoulder. "A gala could be a great way to support some of the local businesses around here. They never get to do these kinds of events."

Elizabeth's eyes gleamed with an idea. "Especially if they could be contracted for the catering and the facilities and whatever else you have planned," she said. "Entertainment, decorations . . ."

"And you aren't interested in management?" Darcy said.

Elizabeth colored.

Brendan clapped Darcy on the shoulder. "Don't worry about him. He hates a good time."

Darcy scoffed. "Oh, yes. An overdressed dinner with bad food, bad music, and too many people who feel comfortable asking for favors—that's my idea of a good time."

Locking his arms stiffly at his sides, Brendan swayed in place with a scowl. "This is what you look like."

Elizabeth snapped a quick photo.

"*You* might not care about how you look in public, but other people do, Brendan," Caroline said. "Imagine trying to insult Darcy for his composure, la!"

"I hope I'm never so composed that I forget how to have fun," Elizabeth said, leveling her camera at them.

"A lark is one thing. Not everyone likes to be the butt of a joke," Darcy said, tapping at the underside of her camera. "Or the subject of a photo."

"Everyone needs a little ridiculousness in their life. Except for you, I guess."

"Avoiding public humiliation is sound strategy."

"You're never going to go on *The Bachelor* then?"

"Not if I can help it, no," Darcy said.

Elizabeth nodded with exaggerated understanding. "So there's nothing ridiculous about you at all. You're beyond criticism."

He sighed. "No one is beyond criticism," he said. "I know I have my faults."

"You're stubborn and can't take a joke?" Brendan offered.

"You're *too* generous to your sister," Caroline added.

"Once I make up my mind, I don't usually change it."

"You don't believe in second chances," Elizabeth replied.

"I don't think many people deserve them."

"And you think *that's* fair."

He crossed his arms over his chest. "And should we talk about your faults?"

She laughed. "Don't worry, la. My mother reminds me every day."

A clamor of excited shouts drowned out any possible response as a gang of preteen girls rushed them, a raspberry-scented swarm in Rocawear.

"I think we're being jumped."

Caroline darted behind Brendan.

"LB," Lydia shouted. "Get the fuck over here right now!"

Elizabeth approached the parapet where Lydia sat dangling her feet over the edge. "Why do I have to get the fuck over here right now?"

"Simon's cousins are in from Valley Stream, and we're going to have a dance-off."

Elizabeth waved her to continue. "What does that have to do with me?"

Lydia whined, "I need you to take shots for my modeling portfolio!"

Elizabeth shook her head. "Film's expensive, Lydia, and I'm not wasting shots on bad light. They're going to look like shit."

Lydia had no distinction between wants and needs; anything she wanted was a matter of life and death, and things she didn't want barely registered as reality at all.

Lydia squealed with fake tears. "Not the ones you take!" she cried. "Please, big sister? Please? If you don't help me, I don't know what I'm going to do . . ."

The others hadn't dared to come any closer, preferring to watch from a safe distance. Elizabeth didn't blame them. Like their mother, Lydia turned unpredictable around an audience; it took a steady hand and calm demeanor to try to keep her well-behaved. But knowing her baby sister didn't make it any easier to say no to her. She'd been watching and protecting her from the beginning, and she didn't know how to stop.

"That doesn't work on me, you know."

Lydia practically tackled her. "You're the *best* big sister ever."

Darcy watched them with apprehension, shaking his head.

She gave her sister a light pat on the back.

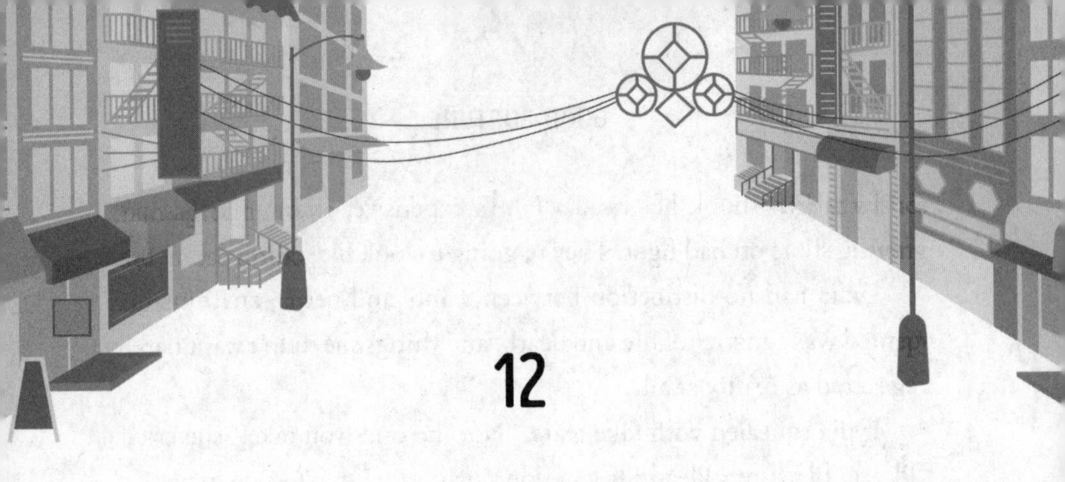

12

A *Vogue* shoot this was not, but Lydia gave her all in a backless silvery halter top and a red plaid miniskirt, pouting at the camera behind thick eyeliner and glazed lips in her best "Blue Steel." As she cycled through all four of the hunching and seductive poses in her repertoire, Elizabeth spent the last shots of her first roll. Not that Lydia cared. Once she set her mind to anything, there was little talking her out of it. If she wanted to go out, it didn't matter if no one else did, if there were no ways to get there, if she didn't have money. Where there was Lydia's will, there would be Lydia's way. Making peace with it was a Chen rite of passage. Elizabeth wouldn't change it for anything, even if she did often wish that her baby sister could be *less* babied.

Lydia's friends cheered and chatted through the shoot, snapping their own shots from sleek digital cameras dangling from their wrists, spritzing her between frames with more body spray and hairspray until a faintly sweet and chemical odor hung over them all.

Even Jane and the others got in on the fun. Elizabeth spent the first frames of her next roll on candids of Jane and Brendan, and even Kitty, sitting in the corner with her knees up against her chest, chewing on her thumbnail and staring out at the skyline. Caroline reveled in it too, stomping in front of the camera to deliver Kate Moss, sucking in her cheeks and angling her shoulders.

"You'll send me some of those, won't you?" Caroline grinned.

"If they're good," Elizabeth replied.

"Don't be so modest, aaaa," Caroline said. "Your mother says you're an expert in everything you do."

"My mom still quotes my kindergarten report card," Elizabeth said. "I don't like to promise more than I can deliver."

Some people might get away with it, but she'd seen firsthand where that could land those like her. A reputation for being unreliable, in the best case; a refusal of payment or a formal complaint, in the worst. Most days, she tried not to think too much about what her life might have been if her parents had the right resources or time to devote to her and her sisters. What if their lives could have been smoother, nicer, a little more polished and a little less coarse? There would be no trading the experience she had gained or any of her skills for the helplessness of girls like Caroline, but there was something to be said for how easily wants and needs could be met in this city—in any city—with the right amount of money and the right people. It made a difference, moving through the world when you believed it could be yours for the taking instead of fighting for every single scrap.

Darcy skulked at the edge of the crowd, pulling at the cuff of his sleeve. He looked almost casual—or what passed for casual where he was concerned. His dinner jacket had finally been abandoned, his collar loosened and the top two buttons of his shirt open.

Caroline popped onto her tiptoes to press a kiss against his cheek. He faced the camera with stoic reserve.

Elizabeth fired off a shot.

"I hardly consented to being a prop in your photo, Caroline."

Caroline giggled. "It's only a picture."

Elizabeth lowered the camera. "I could take some professional headshots for you, if you want," she said. "My going rate is usually a hundred an hour, but for you, two fifty."

He pursed his lips. "A hundred and fifty percent markup?"

"Sticker shock?" she said. "Don't you know that price means quality?" Toeing a few steps to the right, she angled him off-center in the frame. A play of shadows fell across the left side of his face, highlighting the brightness of his eyes, the stark line of his jaw.

He swallowed. "Are you going to put the camera down?"

"Why should I? My services seem to be in high demand tonight."

So much of the force of his personality was rooted in his body, she noticed—the way he carried himself, the severity of his posture, the distance of his gaze—but his face betrayed that delicacy and meanness that she found common in men of a certain income bracket. Strong in features and sulky in mouth. He glanced into the lens, and the shutter clicked and whirred. "Elizabeth."

"Don't look at me," she said, crossing to his other side.

He scoffed. "Then where am I meant to be looking?"

"Caroline," she said. "Anywhere you want."

He sighed, attention shifting to the sleeves of his shirt.

She focused the camera on his hands, watching as he folded the fabric over itself towards his elbow in quick, even movements, the muscles in his forearm flexing lightly with the motion. Too good to push it up like the rest of them, she supposed.

He cleared his throat. "Don't you need a consent form?"

"I'm not publishing these," she said. "But you can buy my silence, if you want."

Caroline laughed. "Where would they even be published, Elizabeth, your *blog*?"

Darcy extended a hand. "May I?"

She lowered the camera and looked at him. "May you what?"

"Use your camera."

Growing up with four sisters had taught her never to lend what couldn't be lost, stolen, or damaged. After all of the hours spent delivering groceries, carrying packages, and sucking up to customers, she rarely let her camera into anyone else's hands. It was her baby. It was her lifeline. It had been the most expensive gift she'd ever given herself.

"I *have* used a camera before," he said.

"If anything happens, he'll be more than happy to replace it," Caroline added. "And besides, everyone's using digital now."

"Thanks," she said. "But I like the one I have."

Unlooping the strap from her neck, she handed it to him. The less time she spent thinking about it, the better.

He crouched low to the ground, raising the camera to his eye and peering through the viewfinder.

"Do you need me to show you how to use it?" she said.

He ignored her. "Do you often take photos of yourself?"

"No."

"No," he repeated. "You like to be the one to set it up." It wasn't a question. It wasn't wrong either.

"I'm not great at posing," she said. As if to prove her point, her shoulders slumped a little further, her gaze slipping past his head towards the high-rise several buildings away.

It was the great power of the camera, reminding any and all that they might be seen. Some embraced it, some ran away from it, but everybody posed. And only the photographer got to see it all.

That was what she loved about it. The distance it offered, the feeling of control.

His finger pressed on the shutter. Two quick shots fired. If he noticed how awkward she looked, she took solace in knowing he'd be too uncomfortable to bring it up.

He lowered the camera and held it out to her. "Just because you see something one way doesn't make it the truth," he said.

She took the camera from him, fingers brushing his as she reached for the neck strap. "Point of view?"

"Point of fact."

"So everyone else has an agenda, but you're the only one who's objective?"

That did it—he rolled his eyes. A lamentable breach of decorum.

"Nobody sees things objectively. You can only try to balance that with as much information and evidence as possible."

"But once you've made up your mind, there's no changing it."

"It takes me a long time to make up my mind," he said. "So I trust my decision."

She stepped towards him, peering up into his face. "And what does your character tell you about me?"

His expression blanked, the gears turning in his head as he searched for a polite response. His jaw tightened. "I haven't made up my mind."

"Final answer?"

He didn't answer.

"You want to know what my character tells me about you?"

"I imagine there's a lot of swearing involved."

She smirked. "I don't think you like anyone at all," she said. "Nobody meets your standards."

"I like the people that I like," he replied. "*You* like to misunderstand me."

"Maybe." When she peered through the viewfinder, his face swallowed the frame, the zoom too close for their short distance. "When you finally make up your mind, tell me how I do."

She thumbed the flash on and fired.

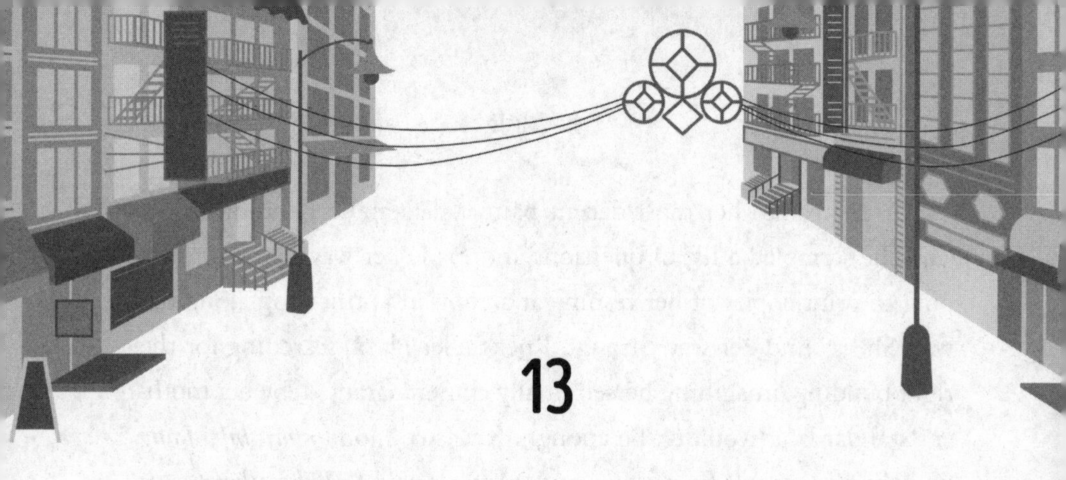

13

Consider it a twist on the old saying—all lucky families might seem alike, but the unlucky ones were each unlucky in their own way. Some turned dutifully to superstition in the hopes of reducing the amount of bad luck; Jade, on the occasion of her fourth daughter's birth and the delivery of her third eviction notice, knew better than to try to beat the odds. Let other families be blessed with their lottery winnings and genius children. Her misfortunes were her own grand tests of character. But on the morning of the Lees' departure from the city, their specific brand of unluckiness struck again. Mary burned her breakfast and set off the smoke alarm, Lydia whined through the chirping, and Jade snapped at each and every noise and misstep until Kitty burst into tears and curled up to sleep watching *Pepper Ann* in the living room. Before the first church bells, Jane left for the library, Vincent left for the sanity of the restaurant, and their neighbors left them endless complaints. Elizabeth wouldn't have called it a good morning at all, except that there had been messages—multiple!—for her on the answering machine: one from Sammy's Three Hour Photo, and the other from the local ACLU.

Jumping into her most decent pair of flats and a hand-me-down suit, she scribbled a list of questions and made her way uptown, stopping to print copies of her résumé at a copy-and-print shop along the way. She wound her way through Rockefeller Plaza, searching for the right building, imagining herself finally chosen. Granted, by her mother's standards, it wouldn't be enough. It wasn't a job (*internship, doing work for other people for nothing*) and it wasn't paid (*helping other people before yourself!*) and there was no guarantee of being hired. But it was a start—a foot in the door and a chance to show up in her sensible flats and navy clearance-rack suits and fight for some good in the world.

The interview took less time than printing the résumés.

She joked, she chatted, she mildly flattered; she emphasized her passion and her skills, her determination and her zeal; and she shook hands as she'd practiced—not too firm, not too loose, confident but not intense—a thousand times.

The interviewer smiled blandly, looking down at her résumé, asked about her greatest strengths, her biggest weaknesses, and her five-year plan, and directed her back towards the lobby. *We'll be in touch*—as honest and reliable as the idea that another train was directly behind this one.

Deflated, but not deterred, she shed the polyester blazer and headed onward and downward—to Chinatown, and her meeting with Sammy himself.

Sammy's sat between two parking garages on a narrow side street, occupied the width of a closet, and reeked of chemicals. It had opened too many years ago for her to remember anything else in its place and hadn't changed since: the water-damaged linoleum tiles squeaking from too many shoe treads and too little cleaning, an ancient cash register parked behind a stubby counter, and ventilation from a single off-brand oscillating desk fan with a grille affixed with masking tape. Developer solution stunk up the interior until it felt like passing the place could give you a contact high. But they were what they advertised: they turned around photos in three hours at cheap enough rates to stay in business. And for $6.25 an hour, fifteen hours a week under the table, and free and unlimited use of the darkroom, she wouldn't complain.

With the swell of his belly and an omnipresent cigar stub in the corner of his mouth, Sammy looked somewhere between forty and seventy years old, a cross of an old uncle and a Buddha. He grunted rather than spoke, spat constantly, and didn't bother with having expectations. Ring up any purchases, develop photos, try not to mix up the names, speak Chinese—did she think that she could do that? Yeah, well enough. If anything broke, spilled, or expired during her shift, or if any customers demanded any refunds, it would be coming out of her pay—did she have any problems with that? Not that she would be willing to admit. Great!—he tossed her the first shift schedule for the week, and told her not to call unless the building was on fire.

Having been down a delivery boy and a cook all day, it was all hands on deck—Jane and Vincent manning four woks, Kitty answering all lines on the phone, and even Mary bagging at the snail's pace she could manage. When Elizabeth walked in, Kitty looked as if she might burst into tears.

"Thank god you're here," she said. "Can you help Mary, please?"

Elizabeth elbowed her sister aside, snapping open the large brown paper bags and stacking quart-size soup containers and small folding packs of rice in quickly. "Jane, should you be working like this so soon after—"

Jane beat her spatula against the side of the wok impatiently. Everyone had their limits. While she didn't usually fold under pressure, she often sounded like a perkier version of their mother when she did. "I'm fine!" she called over the roar of the stove. "Don't *you* get started."

"Mother's in a mood," Mary said, by way of greeting, sliding her the tickets to check against the orders.

"Where's Lydia?"

Kitty gave her a dead stare. "Library." The phone shrilled again and she lifted the receiver to her ear, snapping for the order pad. "Lulu's, what can I get you?"

"At least we don't have to hear her complaining," Mary continued, slowly peeling off a plastic bag from the stack.

"Mary, aaaa," Vincent groaned, sliding a fresh stack of steaming plastic containers onto the counter, "What are you doing? Faster, la! LB, can you please help?"

Elizabeth lifted her hands, clutching handfuls of plastic utensils. "I'm going as fast as I can."

Mary continued as if she hadn't heard, snapping lids onto the containers. "I've told her there's no point in being irrational when she's emotional like this, but she doesn't listen."

"Why is she so upset?" Elizabeth said. "They're coming back, aren't they?"

Vincent set a steaming plate of rice noodles on top of the counter. "Have you eaten?"

Elizabeth sealed a bag, stapling it shut. "Who's running these?"

Vincent pointed towards the end of the counter. "Just leave them there for now."

Kitty reached for a disposable pair of chopsticks, and shoveled a large noodle into her mouth. "Mother thinks they're never going to come back, you know," she said, around her bite. "She thinks they're bailing."

"They already signed the paperwork and paid, didn't they?" Elizabeth said. "What kind of a scam is that?"

"You know how Young Ronny can be. He only gave her the check once the title cleared."

"But she has it now?"

"It's not done until your mama has the money in her hand," Vincent replied. "That's what she tells me."

"I think they'll be back," Jane said. "They said they would, and they will. They just have to handle some business first."

If Caroline was involved, Elizabeth suspected there might be more to their time away than that, but there was no point in worrying Jane.

"They're sending a manager," Kitty said. "That's why Mother's so upset."

"Your mother isn't happy unless she's upset."

"A manager?" Elizabeth said. "They were serious?"

Kitty nodded. Jade had taken the news that morning with all the kindness of an orchestrated coup. *No one ever considers your mother*, she'd cried. *All the work that she's done—wasted!*

Vincent lifted a three-page handout from the counter. "He faxed it," he said.

"He *faxed* it?"

"Mother doesn't have email," Jane said.

Kitty gave a heavy sigh. "I tried to tell her she needs one," she said. "You should get one for the restaurant too, Ba."

Vincent inched his bifocals down the bridge of his nose. "But how will I send the food back?" he said. "Push it into the screen?"

Kitty rolled her eyes. "Forget it."

Elizabeth waved her arms. "What did he fax?"

Vincent tossed the papers to her. "Take it and see," he said. "Your mother already xeroxed twenty-five copies to hand out around the neighborhood."

Manager was an oversell. The Lees' candidate had made his ascent the traditional way—by being acquainted with the family. He had trained in hospitality without working in service, did nothing without first consulting and flattering his supervisors, and had garnered a list of accomplishments without having worked on any projects. Ahead of his visit, their new manager wanted to check in on his itineraries and smooth any ruffled feathers.

> Under the most auspicious guidance of Peony Plum Property LLC and the Lee Family Trust, I take it as the highest honor to help transform this beloved, mismanaged community center into a thriving nexus of interconnectivity. I'm deeply honored and gratified to work with Jade Chen and the staff to develop the building to its fullest potential for all stakeholders and the City of New York. One hears many things about New York—it being the city that "never sleeps" and I too "never sleep," though for work more than play—and I'm excited to become acquainted with all of these things in time. Every place a man lives and works comes to reflect a true aspect of his self in one way or another. I look forward to unearthing that with all of you. Yet no man is an island, and I happily embrace support from all staff in these endeavours. Please find a list of detailed preparation instructions attached for my arrival in a fortnight. 见到您很高兴了.
>
> ---
>
> Geoffrey Collins, BSC Finance and Accounting, AAS Hospitality, TKE
> Sr. Mgr. and Dir. of Logistics, Peony Plum Property LLC
> Founder, Hunsford Principal Ventures
> Special Advisor, Rosings Corporation and Charitable Trust
> Personal Advisor, The Rt. Hon. Lady Catherine Cheung
>
> *"In the midst of chaos, there is also opportunity."* 孫子

Elizabeth wondered how his email signature left any ground for his résumé to cover.

Vincent couldn't wait to meet him.

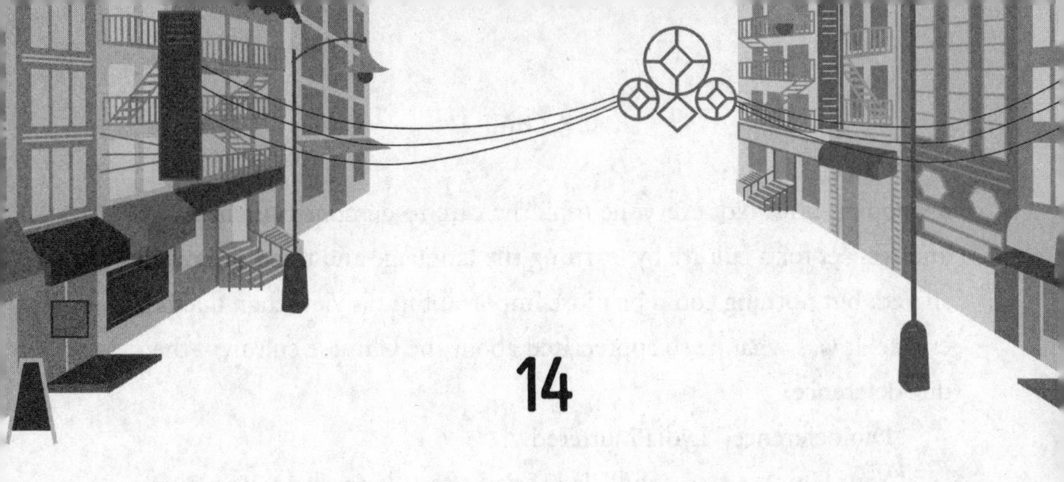

14

No business could be done on an empty stomach, which meant the first order of all business was dinner. Upon his arrival, their guest immediately insisted on meeting with Jade and family as a small gesture of his appreciation. For what, he didn't say—but it didn't matter to Jade, who was flattered enough to soften her grudge at the slight of not being hired. His suggestion took them to a restaurant farther uptown than they liked to go—by way of a recommendation from his mentor, the Right Honourable Lady Catherine Cheung. Geoffrey—and it was a Geoffrey, for he was vehemently "*not* a Geoff"—was a lanky, blond, and sickly looking white man with a patchy goatee. He greeted them three times: first in Mandarin, then in stilted Cantonese, and lastly with officious personal compliments in English. Jade and Vincent thanked him six times by the time they arrived at their table. Jane looked stunned, Lydia didn't bother hiding her laughter, and Vincent could barely stifle his glee—and then they sat down.

Geoffrey, unprompted and without consulting the others on preferences or pricing, ordered for the table in a rehearsed Mandarin delivered to the waiter with a meaningful glance around the table and a stooping bow. Not everyone took the care to demonstrate their love and respect for a culture by learning the language and the customs, he shared, but nothing could be more important in his view than due deference. It was what he so appreciated about the Chinese culture—their due deference.

"Diu deference," Lydia muttered.

"Your Chinese is so good!" Jade cried after a long silence. "So much better than my girls. So nat-u-ral, so flu-ent."

He preened under Jade's effusive praise.

"I'm so happy to be working with you," Jade said. "Though, of course, I *was* told that I would have a large hand in the project, but we can discuss that later."

Elizabeth took the opportunity to gather intelligence. "How did you end up working in this anyway?"

No other conversation would delight him more. While he'd studied hospitality and tourism in school—"A true passion of mine, you see . . ."—he hadn't been able to connect it with the philanthropic and community work he esteemed until he made the venerable acquaintance of the Rt. Hon. Lady Catherine Cheung. No issue could be nearer to her heart than assisting troubled youth. No woman could be more charitable, more benevolent, or more capable in her mission.

With a flourish, he flashed his PalmPilot, impeccably refurbished and a steal from eBay, the screen glowing green with the last few messages, all from the esteemed Lady Catherine with demands of where to go, who to phone, and what to inspect. It seemed she took nothing less than a monastic devotion in the personal and professional growth of her employees. "You see, sir," he began, to Vincent, "no one understands more the role of good management in the modern workplace . . ."

Something started chirping.

Vincent gestured at Geoffrey's pants. "You're going off."

Geoffrey yanked a small pager from his belt loop, squinting at the screen. With an apologetic smile, he excused himself for the hostess desk.

Elizabeth looked at her father. "He can't be serious."

But he was—and returned moments later to his seat with a placid smile. "As I was saying, sir, she really *cares* about her employees."

"Nothing wrong, then?"

Geoffrey shook his head. "A little reminder," he said. "Their fermented black bean sauce is highly recommended."

"So attentive!" Vincent crowed.

Care might be one word for that kind of attention—insanity, another.

Plates of food arrived before Geoffrey could say another word—steamed and fried dumplings, bowls of fluffy white rice, fried whole fish, a platter of glass noodles—and he served himself immediately, scooping several dumplings onto his plate at once and popping one into his mouth.

Fresh from the steamer, it proved too hot for their new friend and he spat it back onto the edge of his plate.

Lydia snorted, covering her face with her hands as Mary elbowed her hard in the side.

"That work sounds so fulfilling, Geoffrey!" Jade gushed. "It's a wonder that you have time for it with all that you do for the company."

Geoffrey sucked the ends of his chopsticks clean. A droplet of soy sauce dangled from the edge of his thin beard. "Of course it's difficult to find the time to invest in my own ventures, but we must all chase the roles that demand *the most* of us. It's the only way that we can grow."

Vincent nodded. "That's what I say to myself when I open up Lulu's every morning."

"Jack Welch has a saying. Or, I think it's Jack Welch. It might be Lee Iacocca."

"I don't think it matters," Elizabeth said.

"True entrepreneurship requires great attention, not only to the *objectives* but to the details, sir. And that's where my background in logistics and hospitality comes in."

"Naturally," Vincent said.

"And Lady Catherine has, of course, served as a mentor to me in the highest capacity," he said. "Without her mentorship, I wouldn't be half as developed as I am. Professionally, I mean. And I find that the best kind of experience is the kind that comes *on the ground*."

"Jane and LB have plenty of experience in that," Lydia muttered.

"Lydia!" Jade snapped.

Lydia reached across the table and lifted one of the lids off the bamboo steamers to find it empty. She sucked her teeth. "Who's been eating *everything*?"

Geoffrey shoveled another dumpling into his mouth.

Jane took one of her dumplings and set it against the edge of Lydia's plate.

"You were saying, sir?" Vincent said.

"Lady Catherine doesn't believe in the coddling that goes on in offices nowadays, you know. *You've got to apply yourself, Collins*, she tells me. *That's the only way to succeed.*"

"Yes!" Jade cried, slapping the table.

"And what advice has she given you about moving here?" Vincent said.

Geoffrey licked his lips, the whiskers of his thin mustache trembling. "She's very concerned about crime, of course," he said. "But I've assured her that I'm quite the expert. A yellow belt in tae kwon do, you know"—as he proceeded to demonstrate a chop against the edge of the table—"and she doesn't need to worry about me."

Lydia snorted. "What do you even have to rob?"

"Is that all she advised you?" Vincent said.

Geoffrey chortled. "Well, as I mentioned, mentorship matters a great deal to Lady Catherine," he said. "Especially in terms of community relations, sir."

Jade perked with interest, nearly upsetting the teacups as she lunged across the table. "Community matters a great deal to us, Mr. Geoffrey. Elizabeth spends nearly every minute at the rec, you know," Jade said. "I mean, when she's not working or studying. She's a diligent and smart girl and looking to make a career in real estate."

Elizabeth growled. "Mother."

"Good for you, Elizabeth," he said. "There are so many young women these days who are afraid of the market."

"Have the Lees shared any of their plans for the rec with you?" Elizabeth asked. "Their plans for the space?"

Jade waved her off. "I told you that already."

"No, you didn't."

"LB, aa," Jade chuckled. "Don't joke. You know I already told you."

"I'm not sure," Geoffrey interjected. "Though I'm sure it has a substantial and a measurable impact."

"As long as it's substantial and measurable," Elizabeth deadpanned.

"It represents a great opportunity for me to distinguish myself in the eyes of the firm," Geoffrey agreed, oblivious to her tone.

Elizabeth balled up her napkin in her hand. "And to support the kids in the neighborhood and give them a place to play and learn . . ."

Geoffrey wiped at his mouth with a napkin. "Absolutely, absolutely! I believe the children are our future. If we teach them well and let them lead the way . . ."

Lydia burst into giggles. "Thanks, Whitney."

"I was planning on getting settled this week," he said. "If it wouldn't be too taxing on your schedule, perhaps Elizabeth might join me." He tried to wink at her, his left cheek seizing up in a twitch.

Jade refilled his teacup. "Of course she will," Jade said. "Nothing would make her happier. Our Elizabeth loves to help. She could show you around the center too. If you have time, of course."

"Mother!" Elizabeth cried. "I'm working."

Jade waved her off. "Oh, a part-time job. Retail, you know," she said. "But we can find a time."

Jane finished off one of the dumplings. "How do you know the Lees?"

"I've had the great honor of working with them over the years," he said. "They're wonderful partners."

Jane sipped her tea. "Have they mentioned anything to you about when they might return?"

Lydia sunk back against her seat with an annoyed sigh. "This is so *boring*," she groaned. "If we aren't getting dessert here, can we go to the Ice Cream Factory?"

Jade glared at her. "We can when we finish."

Geoffrey snapped his fingers for a waiter. "If they'd rather head home, we can call for the check. *Fuwuyuan* . . ."

"Oh no, Geoffrey," Jade said, forcing a laugh. "You know how kids can be. Please go on."

Geoffrey sniffed and turned back to Jane. "Rest assured that gears are always in motion where the Wongs and the Lees are concerned," he said. "Gears are always in motion."

The waiter slid the bill onto the center of the table. Jane and Elizabeth glanced at it, Jade and Vincent glanced at it, and Geoffrey reached for one of the toothpicks, opening it and jabbing at his teeth.

They continued to eat, picking among the plates and chatting, but Geoffrey didn't seem to notice the billfold.

Jade reached for the bill.

He didn't move.

She pulled out a small pile of bills and tucked it into the pocket.

They watched him with bated breath, waiting for the counter. It didn't come.

The waiter slipped past, plucked the bill from the table, and left to ring the charge.

Geoffrey grinned around the toothpick. "You mentioned something about dessert?"

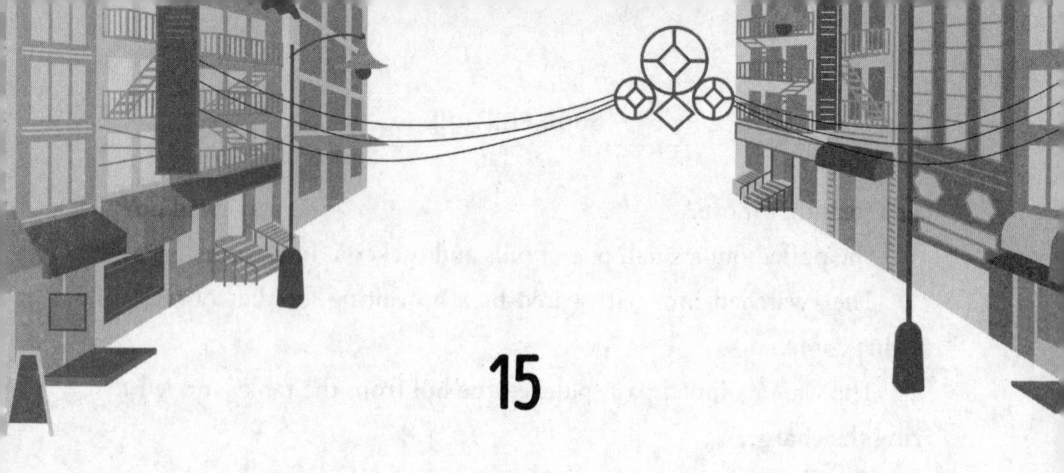

15

Showing Geoffrey around the neighborhood turned out to be the offer she couldn't refuse, no matter how hard she tried. And, oh, did Elizabeth try. Neither Geoffrey nor Jade would be deterred. Every day, he called and left messages on the machine asking about her schedule; every day, he just happened to be near Lulu's and the rec in the hopes of an accidental run-in; every day, Jade wheedled and needled and schemed for her help. It would be the neighborly thing to do, she insisted, since he didn't know his way around and couldn't read a map. It was good karma. It was an easy way to build her network. What would she lose?

Besides hours of her life and a sizable chunk of her dignity? Not much.

But, like Band-Aids, the slower it came off, the worse it hurt—and so Elizabeth relented, delivering the world's quickest tour of the community center. No stopping, no chatting, no bathroom breaks, and no questions—hold everything for the end, and for someone who cared.

It didn't keep him from asking anyway. Was she aware the average median income of the neighborhood was about twenty thousand lower than some of the neighboring neighborhoods? (She was not, but it wasn't surprising.) Had she heard of Robert Moses? (Yes.) Did she know the breed of rats that roamed around downtown? (No, and she would prefer not to know.) He asked about urban blight and dust from 9/11, tax abatements and commercial leases, compliance and charitable write-offs, and the specter of rising crime.

Not that her answers would have mattered. The rec didn't exist to him as anything more than a strip to be developed, a calculation on a spreadsheet, a line item in his eventual pay and promotion schedule. And if it hadn't been for the interest he suddenly took in Elizabeth's life, she doubted it would have been a factor at all.

He shivered as they passed Geny's supply closet of an office. "You don't want to end up in a position like that, Elizabeth," he said, pointing at her office. "And if you stick with me, you won't. There'll be a great deal of opportunity for *enterprising young women* to build their futures here. Trust me."

Elizabeth shook him off. "Geny said you had something you needed me to help with?"

He bowed. "I'm hoping it might be the start of our little partnership."

As they headed down the hallway towards what would be his office, she tried to consider what needed her kind of local touch. Was it permit applications? Questions about the DOB? Canvassing the neighborhood for ideas?

By the looks of his small smile, it hadn't been spontaneous but a planned surprise to cap off their day of walking around.

Plastic floor coverings crumpled noisily as they pushed into the office, the room smelling strongly of dust and mildew. Old furniture, stinking of mothballs and chemical cleaners, sat piled in the corner. A single metal desk and filing cabinet sat underneath the windows, piled with unopened boxes. Geoffrey jerked open the blinds to a dim alley, sending another blast of dust into the air.

Elizabeth coughed. "What is all of this?"

"Supplies." He gestured around the room. "You know, these aren't ideal working conditions."

"Geoffrey," she said. "There are rooms in this building that don't have heat."

He unplugged a dead fax machine and moved it into the hall. "It doesn't seem sensible to have rooms without heat here in the winter. I hear it gets rather cold."

She huffed. "Yes, Geoffrey. In the winter, it does get cold."

"Then it's *most* important that we get started right away!"

Between the two of them—meaning mostly Elizabeth—they carted old furniture into the hallway and slit open the new boxes. Here were all the supplies Geoffrey considered necessary to start his work. *No man is an island*, he liked to tell her, but apparently, a man could be an IKEA showroom.

For all his ambition, Geoffrey was even more useless assembling flat-pack furniture than he was at dinner. For hours, Elizabeth knelt among the various slats and pieces, jamming dowels into preset holes, hammering nails against particleboard, and tried her best not to gut him with the nearest Allen wrench while he talked endlessly of things she couldn't care less about—the Rt. Hon. Lady Catherine Cheung's investments in Singapore, popular architectural styles around the world, and the latest linen and bedding trends in hospitality.

She had no interest in the Rt. Hon. Lady Catherine Cheung, no interest in Singapore, and great interest in all of the work he didn't seem interested in doing. Where was the paperwork for the city, or the plans to review? What was Peony Plum even planning? Geoffrey didn't know—and didn't seem to know what he didn't know.

The more she watched him work, the more she became convinced that the economy thrived on these useless men, the kind who did nothing more than say the right words, charm the right people, and otherwise coast on family connections, family money, and a desire for a name. Like cheap magicians, all they knew was sleight of hand, and as long as they could keep it going, they would.

He leaned in close behind her as she tried to decipher the next page of instructions. "You know, Elizabeth," he said, breath tickling her ear. "You've got great gumption."

"Thanks," she said, scooting away from him. "I don't think it's gotten me very far."

"You would be a credit to any office that you work for."

"If you ask me, I think it's crazy to move halfway around the world without an idea of what you're working on."

"It's not my job to have an idea," he said. "It's my job to *execute*. There's no need to worry. Peony Plum has always elevated the character and value of a place."

Why was it that every time she asked about intention and actions, they talked about character? Buildings didn't have character, and neither did neighborhoods; their character, such as it was, came from the people living there—but their idea of character lived outside the neighborhood. It couldn't be preserved. It had to be invited.

It wasn't the elevation that worried her; it was the altitude sickness.

"Character," she said, glaring at him, "is in the eye of the beholder."

* * *

After another hour and Geoffrey's mildly pointed suggestion that she run out to get his coffee, she clocked out. No more Swedish furniture, no more of Geoffrey rehashing stories of his glory days, no more of

Lady Catherine's words of wisdom. She would try to salvage the rest of her day with a coffee break and the healing powers of a pastry and Charlotte.

"You seem like you're having a great day," Charlotte said, plucking two pineapple buns out of the display case.

Elizabeth dumped a palmful of loose change on the counter with an apologetic smile.

The cashier huffed with annoyance.

"Wait until you meet him," Elizabeth threatened, sliding into a free seat at the end of a long table. "He defies explanation. Mother *loves* him."

Charlotte retrieved their drinks from the counter. "Is that why you're here today?" she said.

Elizabeth removed the lid and took a quick sip. "Playing his guide dog for the day, yeah," she said. "Part of Jade Chen's master plan to fix my life. She thinks that if I play nice, he can get me a real job."

"LB, that's great!"

Elizabeth snatched Charlotte's wrist. "You're not serious."

"Oh, come on," Charlotte said, rolling her eyes. "You're telling me that you're going to turn down a job if he offers? Sammy's is nothing. Isn't this better than nothing?"

Elizabeth touched a hand to her heart, wounded. Sammy's might be a dead end, it might strip her of what brain cells she still had, and it certainly couldn't be called impressive, but it was steady cash and a free darkroom and didn't involve selling pieces of her soul for a little money. Wasn't that worth something?

Charlotte had the nerve to wag her finger. "You always get like this," she said. "Some things aren't about principle. Some things are about money."

"The man is an idiot, Char. He doesn't know anything, doesn't care about anything, and he's only here because he thinks it'll get him promoted."

"You don't have to marry the guy," Charlotte said. "Just take the money and get out. Help your parents with the rent, pay off your loans, and buy some nice things for yourself."

Elizabeth tried not to look as betrayed as she felt.

"I'm on your side," Charlotte softened. "But see this for what it is—a way out."

"After everything the rec did for us, you're happy to let them turn it into boutiques or something?"

"Who does the rec help if it's dead, LB?" Charlotte said. "Don't deliver for everyone else before you deliver for yourself." She sipped at her coffee. "Think about your parents."

"You're joking," Elizabeth said. "All I do is think about my parents."

"If that were true, you'd take the job and you know it," Charlotte replied.

Elizabeth rolled her eyes. "You're not funny."

"I'm being serious."

But Elizabeth knew she couldn't be—no one could commit themselves to having Geoffrey as a boss, no matter how tempting the check. Practicality might be considered a virtue in most immigrant communities, but Elizabeth knew Charlotte would never take her own advice. She couldn't. They weren't those kinds of people.

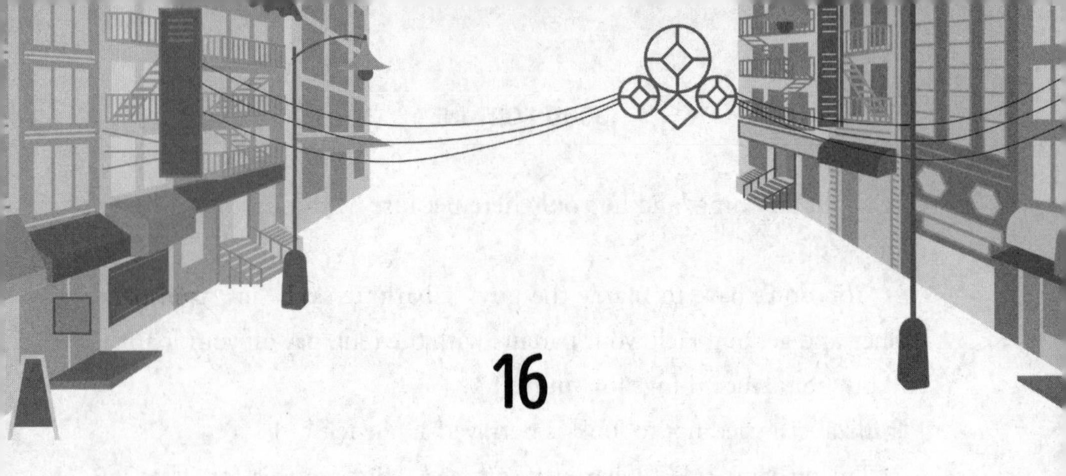

16

Jade may have expected an immediate offer of employment on the powers of Elizabeth's furniture assembly, but Elizabeth knew better than to hinge her hopes on vague promises. And after one week and another, it turned out that she might be right. Like plenty of other men in the city, Geoffrey just wasn't that into her.

Jade cursed and lamented the state of young men these days—their flightiness, their laziness, their carelessness—and blamed their parents, society, and the leeching effects of American culture. Hadn't Brendan told her he would be overseeing the work at the rec? Hadn't he mentioned wanting to be involved? Weren't they business partners, if not friends? And now where was he? Off throwing away his money at casinos in Macau or spending it on scores of meaningless flings with pretty young women? It didn't matter that Brendan wasn't American, that he had other obligations, or that he hadn't made them any promises—until he returned with profuse apologies and small personal gifts to prove his sincerity, men were not to be trusted.

Elizabeth served out her time at Sammy's, breathing in a steady cloud of chemical fumes and fading cigar smoke, picking up neighborhood gossip, and waiting for customers. Most of the aunties and grandmas she recognized, their hair fluffed up towards the ceiling, handing over rolls of film one at a time, asking after her mother and her sisters as she tried to get them to fill out the form for pickup. For the money, it wasn't bad work, even with Sammy bumming her smokes and complaining about her lackluster Chinese.

But nothing mattered as long as it paid. Despite all appearances and accusations, she was still her parents' daughter: if things go wrong, work hard, and if they go better, work harder to keep it. Find a good job, a decent husband, pass go and collect $200 until your body gives out. Elizabeth knew it wasn't that simple, not when opportunities could be a numbers game in their own right. Jade and Vincent did their best, but what did that compare to families with entire arsenals of preparation and spending money at their fingertips? If she was going to shoot for the moon and hope to land among the stars—or, realistically, within the universe of a 401(k)—she might as well try to catch the ones that she wanted. Even if her mother disagreed.

The doorbell jingled with another customer.

Dressed in a pink Lacoste polo with the collar popped, slick designer sunglasses, and rocking a string of puka shells around his neck, whoever it was seemed to have walked into the wrong place in the wrong part of town.

Without a word, he tossed a handful of rolls of film onto the counter.

Elizabeth reached for one of the clipboards under the counter. "Fill this out."

He deigned to lower his sunglasses. "Hey," he said, lazily. "I don't think I've ever seen you around here before."

She stifled a groan and rummaged for a pen. "New," she barked.

He folded his sunglasses and tucked them against his collar, flashing her a wide smile. It must have worked for him all the time, though her knees managed to keep their composure.

Dark hair cropped close to his scalp in a buzz cut, a spray of light brown freckles speckling his right cheek. His small, full mouth teased lightness like a squeeze of lemon in Diet Coke. Maybe it worked on other girls, the confidence he tried on her now, but it left her feeling greasy. The last thing she needed was someone who wouldn't leave her alone on her shift.

"Give it back when you're done."

The pen scratched along the paper as he leaned against the counter. "I'm a student here," he said, glancing up at her from beneath those long eyelashes. "Pratt."

"Is that right."

"You sound like you don't believe me."

"I'm just here to develop the film."

"Three hours, right?" he said.

She sighed. "That's what it says on the sign."

He smirked. "You're cute when you're annoyed."

"Well, you're annoying."

He chuckled, returning to the form. "Spunky," he said. "I like that."

She couldn't care what he liked. She hated the mouthy customers, the ones who wanted anything more than baseline courtesy and competence, and he clearly expected to walk out with something other than his set of prints.

"I'm Ray," he said, sliding the form across the counter to her. "And that's my phone number."

She scoffed and punched the numbers into their system.

"It's nice to meet you," he continued. "And you say?"

The computer beeped. "I can't find you," she replied. "Did you use another name the last time you were here?"

"Try Raymond," he replied. Pressing up on his toes, he leered directly at her chest. "Wu. W-u."

"Do you *mind*?"

"Relax. Trying to read your nametag," he said, tapping at his chest. "*Liza*."

She glared at him. "With a *z*."

"I see that."

She scraped the canisters off of the counter. "These three?"

"Four," he replied.

She found the fourth, rolling near the edge of the counter. "Pratt, huh?"

He shrugged. "I'm up and coming."

She rang up the charges. "Aren't we all," she replied. "Sixty-six thirty-two."

He reached into his front pocket and pulled out the bills. "So when do you get off work?"

She sucked her teeth. "You're not really trying this, are you?"

He laughed. "Trying what?" he said. "You've never had someone ask you out before?"

"This is not asking me out. This is a pickup." She tore the receipt slip and stapled the claim card to it. "Three hours. Don't forget to bring this with you. You can't pick up without it."

"Come on. I'll buy. A drink? A coffee?"

"Three hours," she repeated, flatly.

He grinned. "Nice to meet you, Liza with a *z*."

"I hope I never see you again," she replied.

He pointed at the sign in answer. "See you in three hours."

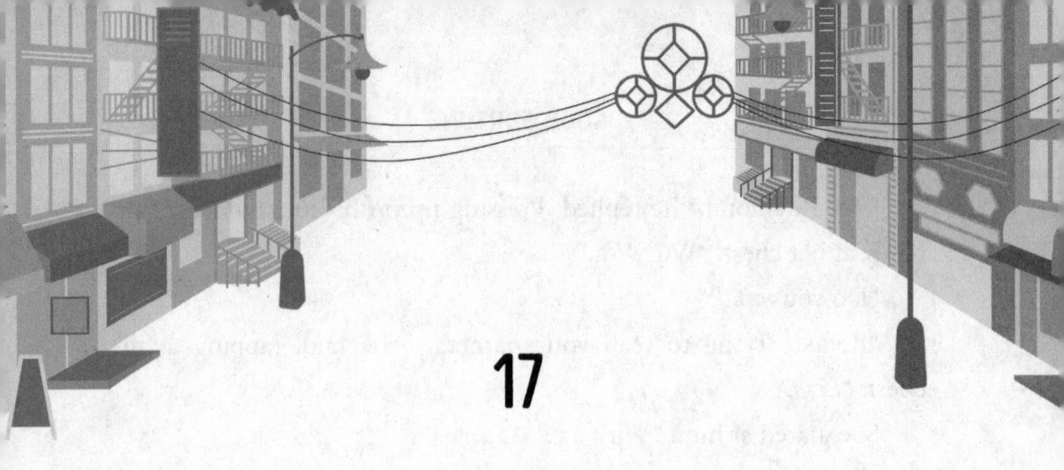

17

Anyone who tried to *love thy neighbor* in this city hadn't met very many of them. From the creeps that filtered into Sammy's and Lulu's to the eccentric neighbors that moved in and out of her building over the years, Elizabeth had seen more than her fair share of equally impassioned and equally deranged individuals. She'd come to recognize them as their own stock background players—the man who wore all white and stood in the center of Sixth Avenue, the woman who ordered the same meal at the same time every day for a year, the C-train saxophonist who could only play "When the Saints Go Marching In." Greatest city in the world, baby.

Nowhere did she meet more of the impassioned and deranged than at her local community board.

Elizabeth once hoped it might be a place to, well, find community and organize solutions for their common problems—the parking, the noise, the rats, the garbage, the rent, the rent, the rent. After all, no struggle was ever so personal, no enemy more reviled. As a girl, Elizabeth heard her parents and neighbors speak of the landlord the way they might otherwise talk about evil spirits. Drop the check in the mail, then turn around three times and spit. As she grew older, she came to understand the world through it—security, labor, worth. Everything, as the theater kids sang, was rent.

In practice, it involved little more than taking confession from hall monitors and self-appointed neighborhood watchmen, each with their own personal axes to grind. All they ever did was review the agenda and argue. There were homeowners concerned about property values, taxes, and the homeless; there were seniors looking to find company for a few hours; there were business owners looking to air grievances; and there were those select few who sought help navigating the serpentine processes of the city and didn't know where to turn. Where they could work together, they tried; and where they couldn't, they fought loudly and bitterly for several hours a month in a building without proper lighting or heating, and called it progress. It was the closest Elizabeth came to working in city government.

There wasn't ever much to learn, but it was free entertainment and potentially useful networking. And sometimes, a free donut and coffee. Tonight, she brought her own snacks. Coming in late from her shift at Sammy's, she met Jane and Charlotte in the last few rows near the rear. Elizabeth cracked open her coffee and sipped at it as the organizing chairwoman droned through the minutes from the last meeting.

"How was work?" Jane whispered, handing her a sheet of dried cuttlefish.

Elizabeth bit off a chunk and chewed.

"That good?"

An older woman two rows ahead of them shushed them.

Elizabeth slunk lower in her seat, sipping at her coffee.

The door clattered as another latecomer scrambled inside. A messenger bag clipped Elizabeth's hand as the person cut through their row, splashing scalding coffee all over the front of her shirt. With a yelp, she handed the cup to Jane, lifting her shirt from her skin with a whine.

"Be quiet!" the woman ahead of them hissed.

Charlotte waved her off. "Why don't you mind your own business?"

Jane layered on tissue-thin napkins against her shirt as if to blot her dry.

"Hey, Liza with a *z*," hissed their new aisle-mate. "Fancy seeing you here."

Elizabeth groaned. "You've got to be kidding me."

He looked the part of a college student this time, the sunglasses chic exchanged for a knit beanie, ripped jeans, and a raglan shirt.

Elizabeth dabbed at the growing wet stain against her chest and shushed him.

He reached across her to extend a hand to Charlotte.

Charlotte took his fingers. "I'm Charlotte. LB didn't introduce *you*."

He gave a teasing smile. "We kind of ran into each other."

Jane shot her a look.

"He had his film developed," she said.

"Oh, did he?" Charlotte replied. "Did you know she was going to be here?"

Ray propped his feet up on the empty seat in front of him. "I think it's important to get out there and hear what's going on."

"Civic duty," Charlotte said. "I see."

An aunty two rows ahead gave them the evil eye. Elizabeth shrugged in apology, Ray swore at her, and the meeting came to order.

Mrs. Delgado wanted to know why no one policed the sidewalk for vagrants outside of P. S. 140 when there were young children, Mr. Aumens was convinced that his water bill couldn't be right because the *Post* wrote an article six years ago about malfunctioning meters, and Manny wanted to know why he couldn't be compensated for the cost of extermination in his store. Ray cracked commentary in low whispers as the community board chattered on with their agenda. Elizabeth tried to focus on the meeting but couldn't help but laugh.

After the meeting, Ray didn't beeline for the exit but looked at the three of them. "So what are you doing after?"

Charlotte smiled. "I have to meet my parents for their church group," she said. "So I guess I'll see you later. Bye, Chens."

Charlotte's knee bumped Elizabeth's hard as she made her way out the other side.

Jane lifted a hand in introduction. "I'm Jane, by the way," she said. "Elizabeth's sister."

Ray grinned. "I hope you'll let me walk you both back," he said. To Elizabeth, he added, "I'm sorry if I didn't make a great impression earlier."

Elizabeth shook her shirt out. "You mean with the coffee, or at Sammy's?"

"Don't tell me you're still mad about *that*," he said. "Let me make it up to you."

"Sure," she said as Jane flashed her a secret thumbs-up. "You can try."

Her new friend had deeper pockets than she thought, springing for a macchiato at the first coffee shop they passed.

"Fancy," she said.

"That's me," he said, paying for her drink. "I'm a fancy guy."

Jane fiddled with the loose sugar packets at the napkin station, looking too excited to be a real third wheel.

"Tell me the truth. What were you really doing down here?" she said.

He bumped her lightly. "A guy can't be interested in what goes on around the neighborhood?"

She snorted. "Not a guy like you."

"What does that mean, 'a guy like me'?"

She pointed at his outfit. "Designer sunglasses, art school," she replied. "A SoHo kid."

"I'm an overseas kid," he said. "And the sunglasses are fakes. Real good ones, though, right?"

She gave an apologetic shrug. "When you assume . . ."

"I won't hold it against you," he said. "I'm new to the neighborhood, and I thought I'd check out the little neighborhood meeting. What happens in Chinatown affects all of us, so that's worth a little time now and then."

She tried not to smile. "So does that mean you'll be a regular?"

Ray bounced on his toes, leaning into her space. "Depends. Will you be there?"

"Maybe."

"Then maybe," he said.

The barista returned with two small paper cups of coffee, snapping the lids on. Elizabeth tossed a bill into the tips jar, and they headed back out onto the street.

They made their way down Allen, slow as tourists, watching as the dive bars and lounges yielded to more sedate red brick buildings. Elizabeth let her attention drift, catching the passing chatter of other pedestrians, of Ray's commentary about his time in the city, his excitement for meeting new friends. This, he added with a pointed glance at her that suggested something more—a move that she was ashamed to admit almost worked.

He was new to the city, one of the dreaded transplants that threatened to overrun the city like some kind of noxious weed. But he wasn't like the others she met, all starry-eyed with dreams of shoebox apartments and endless personal drama. He seemed happy enough to go to class and try to make some kind of art, filling his nights with cheap beer and pilfered copies of *The Village Voice*. He was a dive in a city brimming with boutiques. She knew dive. She liked dive. She started to think she might like him well enough too—popped collar and polo notwithstanding.

The city always felt smaller than it had any right to, and nowhere did she feel it most than when she crossed from one neighborhood to another, from home to somewhere outside of it. Outside of Chinatown, she played and worked, pretended and mythologized. She spun stories of herself outsized and exaggerated, the passing torch of a main character in a place full of them. But as soon as the sidewalks narrowed again, the smell of crushed garbage and rotten fish mingling together in seamy rivulets in the road, so did she. Grand Street would be the border to the unmasking.

Ray did more than talk about himself; he listened and asked questions, fell silent at the appropriate places, and left her space to weigh in. A low bar by most considerations, but outstanding for the kinds of men Elizabeth usually met. He tested his jokes with no expectant pause for laughter, and even managed a question or two about Jane's day. Exemplary, in her experience.

As they continued downtown, restaurants yielded to storefronts, many empty, and tiny galleries with large windows showing off their collections for sale. In all of her years in the neighborhood, she'd rarely seen anyone walk in to shop; instead, they seemed littered with wannabes and hangers-on, art students and tourists looking for free wine and an appreciation for that which they couldn't afford to own. A little piece of culture, even for the passing poor. Ray almost dragged his feet whenever they passed one, eyes lingering on the pieces inside. Paintings he glanced at before moving on; it was the photos he eyed with open envy.

At the next gallery they passed, she stopped. "What is it you're looking for?"

"Trying to see what's getting sold, I guess," he said.

"You want a gallery show someday?"

He shrugged. "Doesn't everybody?"

Some might have called it selling out.

She'd never thought about it. What she liked about photos was the taking of them; the results didn't always deliver as expected. Over the years, with practice, she had learned to shoot better shots, to hedge her bets with lighting and angles, but she had never learned to like looking at her pictures the way some people did. She wasn't an artist—a small gift to her parents, who might not have survived their resulting coronaries—but she took pictures.

"You're telling me you never thought about it?"

"I don't take pictures," she lied. "I just develop them."

He met her eyes and chuckled. "You should," he said, after a moment. "You seem like the type to be good at it."

"At what?"

"Seeing through things."

She couldn't tell if that was meant as a compliment or an insult.

As they hit the intersection at Grand, he stopped in his tracks, turning to make his goodbyes. "Nice walking you."

She grasped his arm. "Walk us across?"

Ray lit up with a grin. "Happy to."

Elizabeth never gave out her number, even when asked, but she couldn't deny wanting to talk to him again. It might be something, or it might be a way to pick up better photography tips; either way, she supposed, she had to try. And besides, he knew he could find her at Sammy's, which was as good as having her number anyway. Turning to Jane, she hissed, "Do you have a pen?"

Jane ransacked her satchel of a handbag and produced a black gel pen. Licorice scented too—a detail Ray would be sure to appreciate.

Elizabeth snatched Ray's hand in her own, jotting down their home phone in big digits across his palm.

Ray smirked. "What's that?"

"A business card," she said.

As she handed him the pen, a passing group of eight forced them off the sidewalk and in front of a parking garage driveway. Voices filtered through from the garage, but Ray didn't seem to have an eye for oncoming traffic or anything other than her. He took her hand in his, running the tip of the pen over her skin in slow strokes, his thumb stroking her knuckle.

"Jane!" someone cried. "Is that you?"

Ray sketched the last round of the 8 on her palm. "I've never been so happy to spill coffee on anyone before."

She ducked her head, desperate to avoid the oncoming blush, when she heard Jane's sharp gasp.

"Brendan!"

Brendan lifted Jane up in a hug, twirling her around.

Jane laughed, a little breathless, as he set her back down. "What are you doing here?"

"LB!" he said, pulling her in for an embrace.

"I thought you were back in Hong Kong!"

Brendan pulled at Jane's wrist. "Obviously we couldn't stay away for long."

Before Elizabeth could think to ask who else was in the *we*, Darcy marched down the block, frowning at a slip of a receipt in his hand.

"Brendan, if you lose that ticket, we'll never be able to get the car back." It took him a minute to recognize them, and another to figure out what to say. "Elizabeth. Jane."

"Darcy," she said. "Nice to see you again."

Wasn't that what people said?

Jane and Brendan looked as if she'd pulled a knife on him.

He stopped short as he caught sight of their new friend. Not one for meeting people who hadn't previously been vetted, Elizabeth thought, although she assumed that he'd been bred for stiff formality and etiquette. Then again, their present company probably didn't rank high enough to merit his good manners—even without the tears in his jeans.

Elizabeth cleared her throat. "Sorry—this is . . . Ray. We ran into him. Ray, this is Darcy. He's working with our mom on redeveloping the neighborhood youth center."

"That's great," Ray chirped.

Darcy barely moved, the bob of his chin a mere suggestion of a human greeting. Grace under social pressure was too much to hope for from a man who couldn't find a good time at a wedding, but this defied even her worst expectations. He clenched his hands, stared into the distance, and avoided any attempt at idle conversation. It bordered on the sociopathic.

Rudeness behind someone else's back was one thing—not polite but, at least, common enough—but to snub someone to their face?

Ray coughed. "Well," he said. "It's nice to meet you."

Darcy grunted in response.

"I'm sorry we didn't call to let you know we were coming. We're not in town for very long, and we didn't want it to get around the neighborhood," Brendan said. "You know how people talk. But let's find time to grab dinner or something while we're here. With the whole family, I mean."

Darcy's hands clenched at his sides. "Brendan."

Brendan almost nuzzled the side of Jane's neck as he leaned in to whisper. "We'll see you there?" Raising his voice, he added, "Both of you?"

Wherever they needed to go, Darcy couldn't stand to keep them any longer. He jerked at the cuff of Brendan's sleeve like an irritable toddler. “In case you’ve forgotten, we’re on a tight schedule,” he said. With a glance at Elizabeth, he added, “I’m sorry that we have to run.”

“No, of course,” she replied. “We’re only going home.”

“Brendan,” Darcy snapped, starting his way down the block. “Christ.”

Brendan shrugged, sprinting after Darcy.

The three of them watched the boys disappear down the next block.

Ray exhaled harshly. “Friends of yours?”

“Friends of my mom,” Elizabeth replied. “Though Jane and Brendan certainly have been friendly.”

Jane blushed. “LB, we were just saying hi.”

“Uh-huh,” Elizabeth said. Turning to Ray, she added, “And what was the matter with you?”

He shook his head. “Save something for next time, Liza. Keep the mystery alive.”

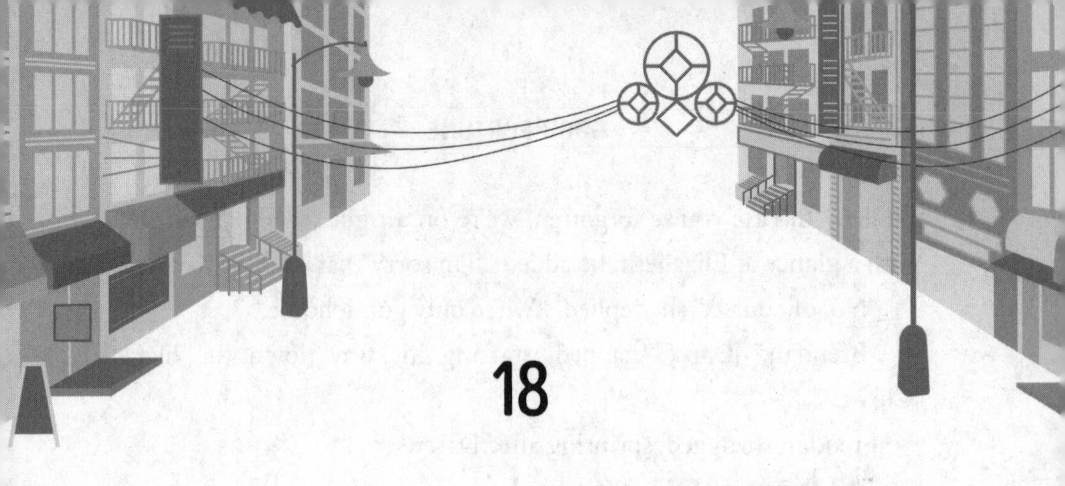

18

He didn't call the first night. Or the next, or the one after that. In fact, he didn't call the first week at all. Another girl might have paced all night wondering about his intentions, or tried to figure out where she may have gone wrong. Another girl might have felt tempted to call him first. Elizabeth did neither; she waited for Sunday.

On Sunday mornings, the religious went to temple and everyone else went to yum cha (or, if you prefer, dim sum). It was a weekly ritual and a gathering, a chance to eat their hearts out and gossip. More than that, it was their version of Marquee—a place to see and be seen. Anyone with ties in the neighborhood ended up in the crowded restaurant lobbies eventually, or found their way in the sights of an aunty who did. If Ray was too busy to tell her why he hadn't been around, somebody else must have seen or heard enough to let her know why.

And, in the meantime, they said their hellos to the families they knew, and the families they knew didn't like them, enjoyed some time thinking about anything besides work, and most important, ate until they could no longer move. Families swelled in the streets and the small lobby, waiting for their tickets to be called; children screamed;

grandmothers fanned themselves; and everybody suffered the misery of smelling the food they couldn't yet eat. Suffering for a little humanity—the most Buddhist they would be all year.

They all had their roles. Jade and Lydia chased the best carts, voices warmed up for shouting inquiries across large sections of the seating area; Vincent paged through the menu to choose among the specialty platters; Jane called the tea; Kitty wiped down the teacups and chopsticks; Elizabeth fielded the well-meaning aunties from the nosy ones and shared only the vaguest updates on their family life; and Mary patiently waited for the food to arrive.

Despite Elizabeth's hopes and her best casual inquiries, no one knew anything of the Wu family, or of a young Raymond. So their LB had finally found someone worthy enough to be her boyfriend, laaaa? What an interesting boy he must be, what a smart character, what a catch! But no, they didn't know him or anything of his family; no, they hadn't heard how he might have found his way to New York from Hong Kong—but they would let her know if they ever had the luck to meet him. Or LB would be making introductions herself soon, aaaa? Wasn't Alexa saying she threw the bouquet her way on purpose?

With nothing to show for it, all Elizabeth could do was smile and make her way back to her own table. There, the food had already arrived, piled and steaming in the center of the table and waiting to be served. Tofu-skin rolls, phoenix talons, shrimp dumplings, chive dumplings, beef tripe, rice-noodle rolls (shrimp, beef), pork neck, radish cake, banana-leaf rice—enough to get started.

Jane poured the tea as soon as she made it back to her seat, and they didn't wait for Lydia and Jade to return before they dived in.

Elizabeth opened a steamer shell, serving Vincent the first of the tofu-skin rolls.

"So respectful," Vincent drawled. "It's not like you."

"I don't like it," she replied. "So you can eat as much of it as you want."

Jade returned, fluttering the menu card in her hand and sliding it back on the tabletop as she glanced at their haul. "No vegetables?" she said with an aggrieved sigh. "No one went to find any vegetables?"

Elizabeth spied Lydia luring one of the waiters behind a decorative folding screen. "I'm sure that's what Lydia must be getting."

Jade took her seat with a sigh, plucking several pieces of tripe onto her plate. "You know, girls, Aunty Pang was saying that Old Ding at the herbalist said that the Lees are back."

Already, the reports were coming in.

"Your Aunty Pippa said Hair Salon Connie heard they were visiting some old uncle or something on East Broadway. And Fat George at the fish market said it's because he owes somebody money. Not that you can ever trust anything that Fat George tells you . . ."

Vincent chewed on a scrap of tofu skin. "I'd go with Fat George. All kinds of people go to the fish market, but who goes to the hair salon?"

"Oh, we already ran into Brendan," Elizabeth replied, snagging one of the chive dumplings and soaking it in sauce.

"There's never enough sweet soy sauce," Kitty groaned, sucking the ends of her chopsticks.

"Stop that, Kitty," Jade said. "People will think I don't raise you properly."

"You can always find more sauce yourself," Vincent said at the same time.

Jade tapped her chopsticks against her plate. "Waa, what do you mean you *already* ran into him?"

Kitty lifted her limp rice noodle. "Mommy, can I take the last one?"

Jade waved her hand. "Whatever, Kitty," she replied.

Lydia crashed into her seat, pulling the plates from the center of the table towards her. "You ate all of the good dishes, you *pigs*," she cried, plucking the last of the dumplings out of their steamers.

"Then maybe you shouldn't be late." Mary sniffed.

"Maybe you should try getting your own food," Lydia replied.

"It wasn't a big deal," Elizabeth said. "We ran into Brendan and Darcy when they were coming out of the garage on their way to some meeting . . ."

Jade gnawed on a radish cake, clucking about its softness. "A meeting! I don't know about any meeting. After everything that we've done for them, to be so horribly cut out like this."

"Don't you mean everything that *you* did?" Vincent said.

"Big Sister Lum says that they've been asking after reception halls in the area."

Vincent unfolded his newspaper at the table. "Probably to run his gambling hall." He split another rice noodle and took half. "Be careful, Jane. He might be looking for dancers."

Jade slurped at her tea. "You joke too much," she chided. "Setting a bad example for the girls."

Elizabeth leaned forward in her seat. "The rec hasn't even started work," she replied. "Why would they need a reception hall?"

"Rec, rec, rec," Jade tutted. "That's all you talk about. What do I know about the rec if no one talks to me about it?"

If there was an answer, the noise of frantic whispers and chopsticks scraping against plates drowned them out. The Lees had apparently entered the building.

Jade stretched past the edge of the table, narrowing her eyes as if to lock Brendan in her sights.

"Jane, you call him," Jade said, bringing her arm up into the air and waving furiously.

A waiter paused by the table in inquiry. She shoved him out of the way.

As the Lees fought their way towards their table, one table after another stopped them to say their hellos or pay their respects. Such a shame to hear about his father, la, but hopefully he might recover soon! How capable he was to step into his father's business like this! How smart! How respectful! So nice to see that they'd come back into town, and hopefully they might stay.

Elizabeth glimpsed Caroline and Brendan walking on either side of an old man hunched in a wheelchair, trailed by five dark-haired attendants that could have been family, friends, or rehearsal pallbearers. It seemed their other friend hadn't showed.

It was almost disappointing.

Their last meeting had been a true return to form—awkward, stilted, and standoffish—and she wanted nothing more than to challenge him for an explanation, assault him with questions, and find out what was really going on. She wanted to hear what he had to say for himself.

After a brief stop to drop off guests at his table, Brendan finally headed their way, sending Jade into a fresh fit of hysterics. Caroline bounced after him.

Elizabeth shifted to make room as Brendan slid between her and Jane, his hand settling against Jane's back. "Sorry to rush this, but we can't stay long . . ." he said.

Caroline flapped her arms in dismay, the menu card flailing in the air. "Brendan, aaaaa," she cried. "What do you think he eats?"

Jade waved for them to take a seat, though none were empty. "Sit down, sit down!" she cried. "Please, you can take some food . . ."

"He forgot his teeth!" Caroline hissed.

"Thank you, Aunty, but we can't stay long," he said. "We're taking my dad's old friend out today."

Jane brushed her hand over his. "You didn't have to come by and see us."

He squeezed her hand. "Just one last bit of business." Reaching into his pocket, he produced a thick cream envelope and laid it on the table beside them.

Elizabeth read the name of the company in calligraphic script. "What is it?"

"An invitation," he said. "To our annual fundraiser."

"You're fundraising?" Elizabeth said.

He grinned at her. "I thought you were supposed to be the expert, LB. Every year we host a little gathering to raise proceeds for all those mentorship programs you're cheerleading. This is our chance to support the programs at the rec."

Jane was breathless with excitement. "And we're invited?"

"Of course you are! All of you!" he said. "You're our community representatives after all."

Caroline sidled up to the table. "We'll be inviting a few other families from the neighborhood too," she said. "People like to see where their money goes."

Jade stretched across the table, pushing aside dishes and steamers as she tried to flag his attention. "You know, Mr. Brendan, we've hosted many beautiful formal gatherings for the block and we'd be happy to help if you need it," she said. "Venue, catering, planning—I know everybody, you know."

"Thank you, Aunty," Caroline said. "But Brendan and I have the planning all handled. You've helped us so much already."

"I don't mind at all. Not at all," Jade cried.

Elizabeth supposed the objection remained solidly on one side.

Caroline slipped past Jade's seat to drape her arm over Jane's shoulder. "It's been *so long* since we've seen you, la," she said, pecking the air in quick bursts.

Elizabeth drained her tea. "We heard you left the country."

Jade forcefully cleared her throat.

Caroline pressed a hand to her chest with affected emotion. "*You* know how it is whenever there's a crisis in the family," she said. "Always running around on errands, pitching in on work—it's been impossible to find a second for myself!"

The only work Caroline might have done was on her face.

Brendan set his head against Jane's shoulder. "You will come, won't you? You know it won't be the same without you," he said, lowering his voice. "All of you."

Jane smiled. "Of course we'll be there."

Elizabeth elbowed him in the side. "You know the Chens never turn down a chance to eat on someone else's dime."

Caroline nervously drummed him on the shoulder. "Congee, do you think?" she said. "I don't know if he can chew . . ."

Brendan straightened himself with an exaggerated groan and snatched the menu card out of her hand. "We'll make sure you're on the list," he said. "Now, if you'll excuse me, duty calls."

Elizabeth pointed to the cart creeping around the edge of the room. "That's the congee."

With a look of gratitude, he jogged after it with a shout.

Jade sank back in her seat with a triumphant huff. "Do you hear that, girls?" she said. "We're on the list! *VIP!*"

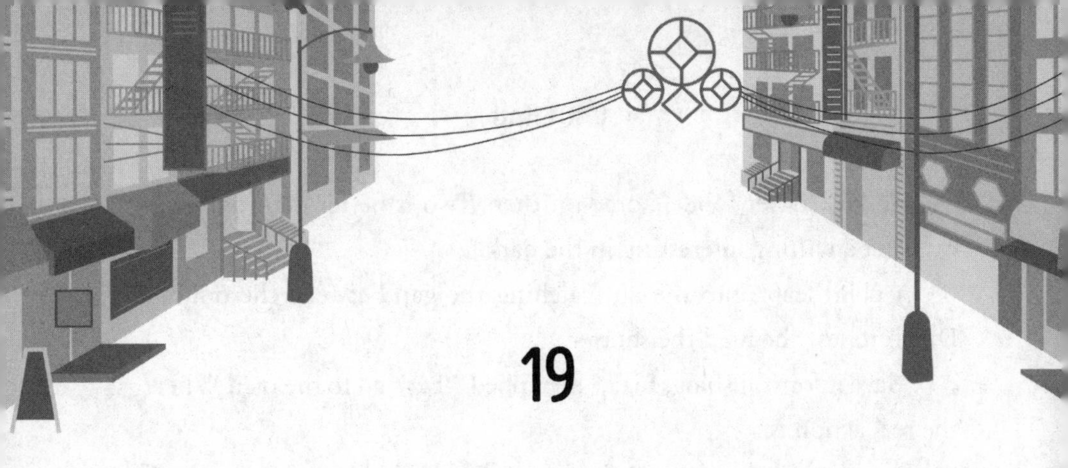

19

There was only so much unbridled joy a New Yorker could take—especially of the ecstatic, ear-piercing kind that Jade preferred. Leaving her mother to her noisy and endless convulsions, Elizabeth went off in pursuit of her own peace with camera in hand. The weekend spoiled her for choice in frames. Mothers stooped over strollers, trying to soothe upset children. Old grandfathers napped against the park benches, their canes resting against the seat beside them, leathery faces upturned towards the sun. The rim of the basketball hoop bent and snapped back into place from the weight of a hanging sixteen-year-old. More than the arch in Washington Square or the span of the Brooklyn Bridge, these were her landmarks, her sights of her city—ordinary people trying to carve out life among the steel and concrete.

"I knew you were the type."

Ray fired a shot off before she realized what he was doing.

"That's not fair," she said. "I can't even see you."

He shrugged. "You'll see it later," he said. "What are you doing?"

She lifted her camera. "Great minds?"

He kicked her foot. “Come on then. Two is better than one. You can’t get anything interesting in the park.”

A child leapt into the air, catching the gap between the double-Dutch ropes. She fired the shutter.

“Save it for your blog, Liza,” he replied. “Let’s go to the pier. Where the real action is.”

She focused the lens on the line of his back. “I need to walk off some shrimp balls anyway.”

He slipped an arm around her waist and tried to pull her close, but she resisted, inching away from his touch.

He pretended not to notice. “Shall we?”

Without traffic from the restaurants, stores, and the park, they felt like the only people on the sidewalk, weaving around each other as they made their way to the water. He never drifted far from her side, grazing against her as he scoped out shots through the viewfinder of his camera. It was casual and accidental, those passing touches—or, at least, it’s what he wanted her to think.

She tried to study his approach as they went, but he didn’t seem to have much of one at all. He fired shots at random, struck by an image or an angle or a feeling, and didn’t set up, didn’t check the light, didn’t compose.

“I thought you were supposed to be the pro around here,” she said. “Teach me something.”

“It’s hard to find something that someone else hasn’t done better than you,” he said, shooting up into the boughs of a tree. “But you can try to capture the mood that you’re feeling, or something new. That’s the interesting shot.”

Elizabeth scoffed. “Sounds like a fortune cookie.”

“And you would know, right?”

Kneeling beside a planter bed of hydrangeas, she checked her light, her focus, and clicked off one shot.

"So what's your philosophy?" he said.

"I try to take good pictures."

As they got closer to the pier, they passed rows of tall umber towers in neat lines. Ray stopped to shoot the sign as they passed the first building, everything faded except for the sign-off from the Housing Authority at the bottom.

He squatted on the curb, angling his camera to capture the sweep and height of the buildings, the shadows they cast. "I almost grew up in a place like this," he said.

Elizabeth dragged the toe of her sneaker against the pavement. "I did."

He sucked in a hard breath. "What?"

She never knew how to answer the stunned looks whenever she mentioned it. No one knew how to take the news, if they should aim to sound touched or inspired or horrified. She didn't know what to make of it either. It took up such a small span of her life, but it happened. Living in the houses hadn't been a full story but a passing fact of life.

"I don't remember much. We were there for a couple years when my parents first came here."

Ray whistled through his teeth, hand grazing the side of her hip as they kept walking. "We might have more in common than I thought."

"Yeah?"

He replaced the cap on his camera lens.

She watched him out of the corner of her eye. "You don't have to tell me if you don't want to." Everyone had skeletons in the closet, but not everyone wanted to share. Childhood sagas and family secrets were the kinds of things you had to earn, no matter how desperately she wanted to know.

And then he said, "Are you close with him?"

If there had been a clue as to who he meant, she must have missed it. "Who?"

He took a steadying breath, trying to read if she could be trusted. "Darcy."

She burst into laughter. "Darcy?" she repeated. "Am I close with *Darcy*?"

It couldn't be a serious question, except that he looked so serious.

"When we ran into him the other—it looked like you were, I don't know, *something*."

"I was trying to figure out how to introduce you! I didn't know that you knew him," she said. "'*Am I close with Darcy?*'"

She couldn't stop laughing.

They burst upon the pier then, the air ringing with the noise of traffic and restless skateboarders testing their daring on the concrete road dividers. Past the broad road waited a long pedestrian walkway and families eating ice cream cones along the green space of the park.

"So there's . . ."

"*Nothing*," she said. "You couldn't find anyone else who likes him less than I do and vice versa. Trust me."

Ray relaxed, pulling her against him as they crossed beneath the overpass. "I know his type."

Whatever his type might be, it definitely didn't include underemployed, bleeding-heart underachievers south of Houston Street—bet on that. He would have preferred thoroughbreds, the kind of women who did cotillion and Model UN, who prepared for their lives as the wives of diplomats and other important men. Elizabeth, on the other hand, reused disposable razors.

Underneath the overpass felt like another world entirely. A little dark, a little dingy, smelling faintly of ocean and strongly of garbage. Anything dangerous felt like freedom, and she imagined it as a magical gateway, where anyone could do whatever they wanted. When she was in middle school, stories floated through of late-night parties and drunken boys shoving each other in shopping cart jousts down by the Pathmark, smoking cigarettes or doing bumps until the sun rose. Elizabeth always wondered what it would have been like to watch the sun coming over the water from the shadow world. The city lit all new, born again.

"Would you believe me if I said that we grew up together?"

She froze, mouth agape in disbelief. "You *grew up* together?"

"We were like brothers," Ray continued.

"What happened?"

What else? Some have; some have not. Ray's father worked for Darcy's for years, a longtime and long-trusted employee become confidant if not quite friend. Nobody could really be friends with anyone on payroll, Elizabeth thought, no matter how much they wanted to believe it. But like fathers, like sons, so they became friends by way of the raggedness of childhood.

"I was supposed to be a lawyer."

She looked at him, dressed down in his ratty jeans, bunched up at the hips, and an old T-shirt that had holes along the belly, and tried to picture him in a suit. It didn't compute.

"My dad wanted me to go to law school and Old Wong—his dad, I mean—agreed to pay my way after my old man died. One last gesture of kindness for a friend," he said. "If he was still alive, I know *he* would have kept his word."

"Darcy didn't?"

"Before his dad turned cold, he called the lawyers. And it turned out that promise he made never made it into the will. Anyone with a heart would have respected his wishes anyway. Not Darcy. He didn't want to give up anything he thought he was owed, even for what his dad wanted. But who cares, right?"

She sucked in a hard breath. "Fuck."

"I didn't think anyone could do that—especially not to someone close enough to be family—but I was wrong."

"I thought he was an asshole, but I didn't realize that he was so *mean*."

Ray shrugged. "That's who he is. Who he tries to pretend he isn't."

Elizabeth shook her head. "I can't believe that Brendan could be friends with someone like that."

"He can impress when he tries," Ray said. "But—"

"There are people that matter and people that don't."

"Exactly," he said. "His partners, his friends, his sister—they all love him. It's only the people who can't stand up to him that he treats like shit."

"Because he knows he'll get away with it," she said, shaking her head. "God, I can't imagine him having a sister. Is she like him? A little Mini-Me?"

He shrugged. "I didn't know her very well. I heard she's in boarding school or something now. He probably wants to keep her as far from him as possible."

For all that Darcy had talked about the merit of his judgment and the weight in which he held it, he turned out to be remarkably full of shit. But that was people for you; they abandoned their principles all the time if it got them closer to what they wanted. She felt a small measure of pride in knowing that she hadn't fallen for it. Not once. One thing about growing up in the city: it honed your ability to spot an asshole or a scam from a mile away. Ding, ding, ding, ding.

"Look, please don't tell anyone," he said. "I don't want this getting out to the aunties or whatever, and him coming after me with his team of lawyers."

"You don't have to worry about me. So what happened?"

They crossed the street and weaved through foot traffic towards the water. Skaters behind them hooted and screamed to a beat of clanging metal. "I didn't have anywhere else to go," he said. "I left Hong Kong and worked for a while. Warehousing, trucking, retail—even ended up in the shelters for a couple months—but I saved where I could and tried to figure out my next move."

"What an asshole," she said. "All of this to save—I mean, it can't be *that* much money to him."

"It's a power trip." He tried a smile. "You think it's because his dad liked me better?"

They slowed as they tracked beside the water, and she took his hand in hers. "You don't have to worry about me," she said. "I won't say a word. But if I can punch him in the face and get away with it . . ."

He grinned. "That's real friendship."

"They've invited us to a gala for their little foundation thing."

"That's one thing about the Wongs and the Lees. They love their parties."

It wasn't right that a man like Ray had to be in hiding from the Wongs—and all for something he never did. He deserved better. He deserved some kind of justice. A room full of photographers and Darcy's public humiliation and a chance to restore everything he was owed—that's the least he deserved. "You should come."

He huffed. "Can you imagine?"

She could. Champagne glasses upended, Caroline surveying her party with baleful horror, the endless cricketing of hundreds of shutters firing at once, Darcy's sour pucker drawing even tighter. It would be perfect.

"You should definitely come. I'm sure I'd get a plus one."

"And is that what I'd be?" he said, raising an eyebrow. "Your plus one?"

She blushed. "Is that a yes? For the price of ruining Darcy's evening?"

Ray tipped his finger underneath her chin, looking into her eyes. "It's a maybe."

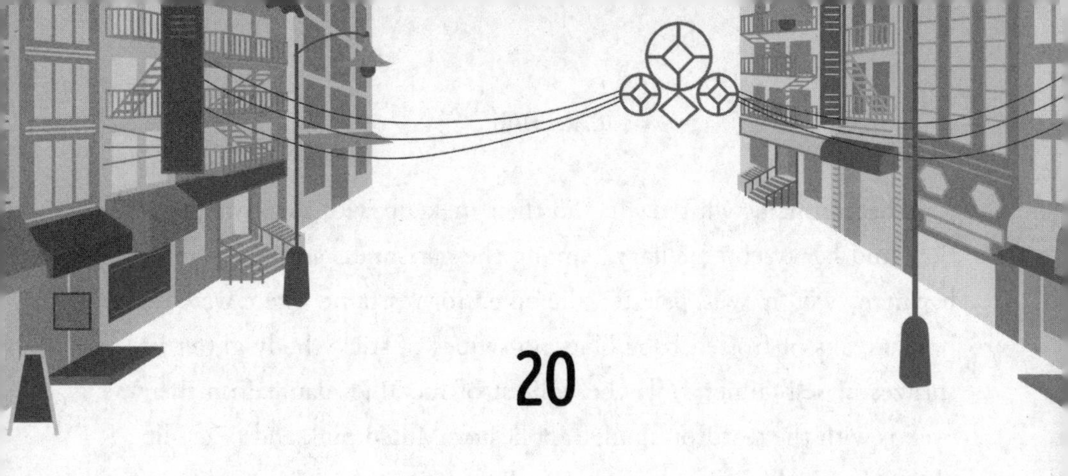

20

Despite being—or, perhaps, due to their status as—honored guests of the hosts, the Chen girls could obviously not be trusted to outfit themselves. Boxes of gowns worth more than their monthly rent came for Jane and Elizabeth to try on and choose between, each with a handwritten note on custom letterhead. Elizabeth hadn't realized custom letterhead still existed, but for Caroline, nothing else would do. At least it wasn't scented. *Flatters your shape*, she suggested, or *To suit your blue tone.*

A thousand dollars for a Caroline Lee was nothing but an outfit while a thousand dollars to an Elizabeth Chen was a month of shelter, a chipping away at her loans, a ward against the future. If she thought about it too long, it made her sick.

Like every homecoming and night out preceding, the Chens readied together, dividing their responsibilities, the medicine cabinet mirror, and shower time like a professional pit crew. Kitty, with the steadiest hand, drew on their eyeliner; Mary, with the sternest distaste, reminded them all of the frivolity and waste of such use of their time. Jane curled their hair, finishing it with enough gel and hair spray that it turned crunchy, while Lydia did their makeup with surprising subtlety and heavy commentary. Among the garishness and diversity of her many wet 'n' wild palettes, she opted for restraint. There were no bold streaks of frosted baby blue, no swipes of sticky body glitter or spritzes of self-tanner, only the lightest of metallics daubed on their eyelids with the teardrop sponge applicator. Muted pink and peach lip glosses finished off their look. *Boring. But I know that's what you like.*

Tyra Banks, eat your heart out.

As soon as the cars arrived, they filed downstairs in a single line, posed for an awkward photo for Vincent in the main stairwell, and headed out. Despite Jade's hard sell to host the gala somewhere in the neighborhood, Brendan's dispatched cars headed uptown and kept going—past Spring, past Fourteenth, and even farther—until they crossed the Rubicon of Times Square and landed outside of Rockefeller Plaza. Brendan whistled at them all as they climbed out of the cars one by one, and nearly jumped when he saw the two of them. "Look at you!" he cried, throwing his arms wide.

In one area, at least, Caroline's taste couldn't be disputed. They'd never looked better. Jane wore a gauzy evening gown of black lace and silk that fluttered and whispered as she moved, drawing over her silhouette with an exaggerated femininity. Elizabeth's dress spoke louder, a deep emerald-green sateen cocktail dress with embroidered gold detailing that softened her broad shoulders and flaunted her strong legs.

Brendan took Jane's hand and led her in a small twirl. "You look beautiful."

She blushed.

"Both of you," he added.

He even made being an afterthought feel like an honor.

"Wait until you see inside. Caro's outdone herself."

The space Caroline had chosen was the Rainbow Room, a place

Elizabeth had only glimpsed in grainy photos in the newspaper. Plenty of things looked stunning in photos just to disappoint in real life, but the ballroom exceeded expectations. Light caught the crystals of the chandelier and made the room sparkle, wide windows showed off the city skyline, and twin staircases trailed down to the dance floor, which looked worn, wooden, and comfortable. Round tables bloomed with centerpieces of peonies and marigolds, and a raised stage parked in between the staircases sat outfitted with a drum kit, amps, and several guitars. Placecards marked each seat, names written in curling calligraphic script and, where applicable, the thick brush of Chinese. With enough money, anyone could have a fairy tale.

Brendan fetched their first glasses of champagne. "Don't mind Caro tonight," Brendan said. "All of this planning goes to her head."

Elizabeth nodded. "It would go to mine too if I had to take care of all of this."

The room looked bare now, but it wouldn't be much longer. An event like this would be packed with people Caroline admired and respected, the kind to write about its success in newsletters dispatched by income bracket and Ivy League affiliation. Brendan shrugged out of his jacket and tossed it on the back of one of the chairs. The place setting read *Ambassador Lo*. "I have to run downstairs to check on something, but you'll be all right up here?"

"We'll see you again later?"

Brendan nodded. "Don't worry," he said, brushing his hand against her bare arm. "I won't abandon you to the wolves."

It wasn't the wolves that made Elizabeth nervous; it was what they thought about the sheep. People in the Lees' circle didn't understand anything of the world, only their expectations of it. They had little interest in learning who Elizabeth was; they wanted to know about her titles, her family, her status, what she had achieved. They wanted to know if she was someone worth knowing—and, by their standards, she never was.

A large poster welcomed visitors into the seating area with a before-and-after photo of the rec—from its original opening in 1993 to a sleek glass-and-chrome rendering of what it might look like in the future. There were all of the usual amenities—landscaping and manicured lawns, tidy brick pathways connecting throughout the small courtyard, conference rooms and offices—with none of the people. *Support the future of The Greater Chinatown Neighborhood Youth Recreational Center!*, it read. BUILDING A BETTER COMMUNITY FROM THE GROUND UP. And there, in the finest print, they were. The *local community liaisons* there to share their stories, motivate, and inspire.

This wasn't a coronation but a roast. And they—the special guests and certain residents—were the ones on the spit.

Jane leaned her weight against her shoulder with a happy sigh. "I can already tell this is going to be a great night."

Elizabeth scoffed. "Wait until Mother gets here."

If they wanted a splash of local color, they couldn't have done any better.

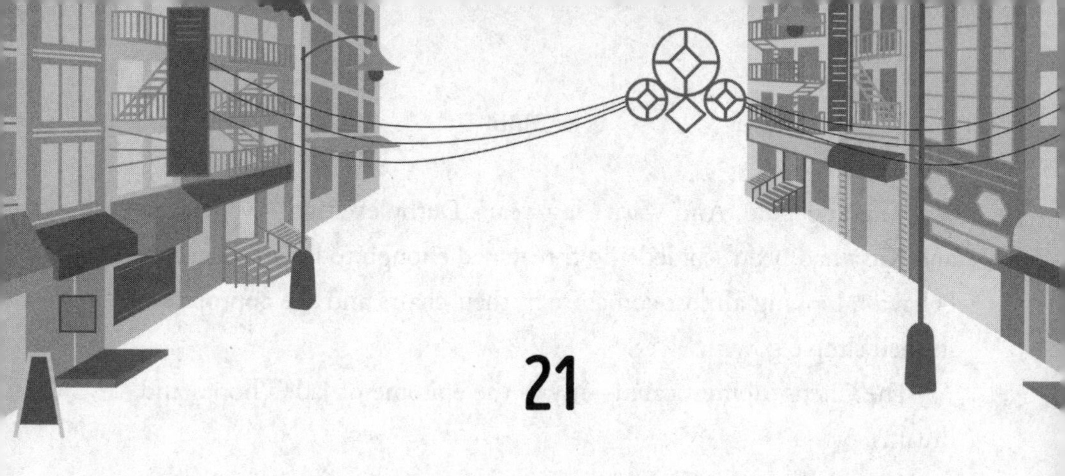

21

Nothing thrilled the wealthy more than the thought of the underprivileged. Not the needy, not the poor, not the homeless, but the underprivileged—with their wide cartoon eyes, tragic life turns, and a mournful backing Sarah McLachlan track. *In the arms of the angel*, indeed. What they wanted were stories of hardships and struggles, of lives and worlds that they could rarely glimpse or understand. They wanted to feel grateful for what they had. Under the scrutiny of Jade's watchful eye, Elizabeth stuck to the script of her college admissions essays: a song, a tap dance, and a reminder of just how far she'd come and how much further she wanted to go. Make the checks out to cash, please.

The night otherwise passed according to Caroline's strict agenda—a full dinner service with punctuating remarks by select members of the foundation, followed by mingling and dancing and pleas for donations. Caroline emceed better than Elizabeth had expected, personable as she cracked jokes, coaxing everyone to open their pocketbooks. After three courses of a formal dinner, Elizabeth considered herself passable enough—if not at choosing the right fork at the right time, then at least in making small talk with men and women whose hobbies included yachting and polo. And wasn't last year's Derby exciting? Even Lydia and Kitty had been scolded and threatened enough to be on their best behavior, looking almost comatose in their chairs and age appropriate in their simple gowns.

The Chens, domesticated—it was the epitome of Jade's hopes and dreams.

At least there was Charlotte.

At least there was an open bar.

And Charlotte, practical Charlotte, dressed in a sapphire evening gown with a beaded shawl worn to a homecoming and prom years ago, rushed to her side as soon as dinner service ended.

"Oh, thank god," Elizabeth said as Charlotte pulled her towards the bar. "If I had to try to talk about lacrosse again, I might have passed out."

Charlotte clucked. "I thought you had grand plans for tonight."

"Ray didn't show."

"Well, at least your other friend's still here."

"My who?"

"Your *friend*," Charlotte said with a suggestive arch of the eyebrows. "Mr. Wong, of the Wongs."

Elizabeth scoffed. "He is *not* my friend." And after everything she had learned from Ray, she would make sure they never would be. To be Darcy's friend would violate every principle she held, every unspoken rule of friendship, and surely certain charters of the Geneva Conventions. But small blessings, at least they hadn't been seated together at dinner.

"Don't you want to mingle?"

Elizabeth stared. "Char."

Charlotte's face slowly split with a wide grin. "You should see your face right now."

Elizabeth shoved hard at her arm. "You shouldn't do that to someone who's emotionally fragile after being stood up."

"Oh, is that what you are?" she said, flagging the bartender and calling for two drinks. "Don't worry. I'm sure you'll bounce back."

Elizabeth scanned the outer edge of the space, watching as the crowd fanned out around the room. So far, so good, no Darcy. Maybe, she thought with undeserved optimism, he chose to bail. Maybe he hated these things more than she did. Maybe she'd suffered enough during dinner that her karma was finally turning around. "So how's your night?"

"I got a couple business cards. It's mostly private banking. Nothing too interesting."

Reaching into her purse, Charlotte fanned them out in her palm—white, off-white, and cream card stocks, embossed and standard type, emptied of personality and full of ego.

Sometimes she forgot how much Charlotte could be like Jade—a prospector always on the hunt for the next whiff of gold, and hoping for a lucky strike. "If you become a banker, I will never speak to you again."

"That's a selling point," she replied. "What did you do, picket the table all night?"

Elizabeth snorted. "I was perfectly well-behaved," she said. "Rave reviews. I should have it laminated so Mother can add it to the wall."

Charlotte draped an arm around her shoulders. "Look at you, suffering for the business."

Getting a drink had seemed like the best idea of the night, had Darcy not chosen that exact moment to stand at his table and glance around the room in search of someone. Brendan or Caroline, she suspected, or Bryan or one of their Ivied friends. Elizabeth shrank back against Charlotte with a gasp, tucking her face into her friend's shoulder as they skirted the edge of the dance floor.

"What's wrong with you?" Charlotte said. "You forgot how to walk?"

She mumbled an answer into the crook of Charlotte's shoulder, peering through the thick of her friend's hair to see if they were being followed.

The house band took to the stage then with the first song of the evening, a pop-rock jam that sounded too close to elevator music for her liking. A few bold guests headed towards the dance floor immediately, others making for the bar in a crush of bodies. She couldn't see anything besides flashes of bare arm and sequins.

Charlotte shoved her off. "He's gone back to his table, you coward," she said. "You can come out now."

Elizabeth lifted her head with a sheepish smile. "Next drink's on me."

Charlotte rolled her eyes. "It's an open bar."

With a wary glance, the bartender set their drinks down on the counter.

Elizabeth tossed a handful of bills down for tip and they took their drinks.

They were halfway to toasting when she heard it.

"Lizzie!"

Geoffrey stumbled forward with a guffaw of greeting, his shirt already wrinkled and dampened with sweat despite the aggressive air-conditioning, his bow tie askew. He snatched her hand in his, all clammy palm and limp grip, and flailed his arm in excitement.

"I would be honored if you would dance with me."

She tried not to splash her drink all over her feet. "Geoff, thank you, but . . ."

He had no interest in hearing her; he'd already decided. With a flirtatious grin, he yanked her forward by the hand, expecting to catch her in his arms. He miscalculated. Her forehead collided against his chin, her drink tipping down the front of her dress, as she tripped and fell into him headfirst. He squealed with pain in an uncanny Chewbacca impression, and ice-cold bourbon pooled between her pushed-up breasts.

There went Caroline's beautiful dress.

Charlotte fought and failed to suppress her laughter.

"Lizzie," he said, rubbing at his jaw with a wince. "You are a *knockout*."

That did it. Charlotte collapsed into giggles, leaving her red-faced and gasping for breath.

"Get it?"

If he meant a mild concussion, then he might be right.

She took a step back, hoping to air-dry and open space between them, but he refused to let go. With one hand strangling hers, he led them onto the dance floor. She surrendered the remains of her drink into Charlotte's grip.

"Isn't this a wonderful party," he shouted into her ear. "Lady Catherine usually thinks they're wasteful and unseemly—except if there's a *social* benefit! And Geoffrey, she says, it would do for you to meet the right people!"

Geoffrey's dancing fell on par with his managerial skills. He didn't listen, didn't lead, and reacted late, his foot slamming down against her toes, his hands pushing lower and lower from their position on her hips. It was more demonic possession than a dance. Elizabeth shoved him back with all the force she could muster, clinging to a single desperate thought: she did not come to the gala to be manhandled by Geoffrey Collins.

"Are you seeing anyone right now?"

"I don't think that's appropriate," she said. "You're my boss."

He tittered. "I'm hardly your boss," he said. "You're a volunteer."

"That's worse."

"I mean that you're at the community center of your own accord," he said. His fingers twitched against her sides.

"You make me sound like a hostage."

He tried to pull her closer, thrusting his hips at her against the beat. Her ears rang, her sinuses burning from the chemical woodsiness of his body spray. She shoved him back with another warning grunt, her knee jamming high against his thigh in threat.

"You're a wonderful dancer, Lizzie," he said. "I'm sorry if I'm not quite at your level."

She squirmed out of his grip.

"Is this a new style?" he shouted. He mimicked her movements as she hopped back and forth on the beat. "Am I doing it right?"

The couples around them stared, not bothering to hide their laughter.

"I hurt myself!" she yelled as the music wound down. "I'm going to sit down!"

He swiped at the sweat on his forehead with his sleeve. "Of course," he panted. "Take all the time you need."

The crowd of other dancers lightly applauded as she made her way off of the floor. Geoffrey took a bow.

At the bar, Elizabeth snatched the remains of her drink out of Charlotte's hand and knocked it back, pounding the empty hard against the bar. "Not a word," she growled.

"Don't worry," Charlotte said, watching Geoffrey's halting attempt at a moonwalk. "If he tries again, I can get him off your back."

Elizabeth waved for another. "You're the best friend a girl could ask for, you know that?" she said. "Always taking one for the team."

Charlotte laughed. "I've never known anyone who needed so many bullets taken."

The bartender slid her a fresh drink with a sympathetic noise.

"Thanks," she said. With a sip, she discovered it was a double. God bless the charitable bartenders.

When she looked up from her drink, there he was again—Darcy, all deer-in-the-headlights in the center of the dance floor, staring in her direction. Tonight, he looked more dressed up than she'd seen him recently—his wireframe glasses absent, his hair slicked back, clean-shaven—but otherwise the same: sulky, annoyed, and definitely bored.

So she'd made a fool of herself at his event. So what? Anyone else might laugh it off as a joke, a little embarrassing incident to kick off the night. Not Darcy. Darcy would hold it against her forever.

He turned towards her with a heavy sigh. Tragedy—in her direction, the bar and more alcohol, but also her.

She raised her eyebrows at him as if in challenge, and he took the bait, charging towards them with purpose. She steeled herself for the curt passing greeting, the recitation of complaints and objections, the condescending questions about what she thought she was doing here—and took a bracing sip of her drink.

He stopped abruptly in front of them. No hellos, no pleasantries, no *can you believe the traffic on Sixth Ave*. Just, "Would you like to dance?"

She choked, alcohol dribbling down her chin.

Charlotte thumped her hard on the back.

He looked at her askance. "Are you—is she all right?"

Charlotte shot her a look. "She's fine."

"Elizabeth, would you like to dance?"

Her brain felt scrambled, from the whiskey, from the lack of oxygen, from her recent head injury, and she found herself nodding along. "I, uh . . . sure?"

Charlotte looked at her like she'd sprouted a second head. Maybe she had. It certainly would be more believable and less embarrassing than agreeing to dance with Mr. Monopoly, the betrayer of last wishes and most unlikable man in lower Manhattan (and that was saying something). Maybe that was her karma for abandoning Charlotte to Geoffrey; when you got rid of one presumptuous man who kept stepping on your toes, it sent you another.

"Fine," he said. "Next song, then."

With no other demands to make of her, Darcy disappeared into the crowd without another word—where she hoped he might be stricken with short-term memory loss and forget all about it.

Charlotte patted her shoulder. "Don't look so down," she said. "The next song might be fast."

Elizabeth sagged against the bar counter with a long wail. "Char."

Charlotte rattled the ice in her glass, finishing her drink. "I can save you from many things, LB, but I can't save you from yourself."

Elizabeth groaned.

"Cheer up," she said. "Try to have fun."

"Fun!" Elizabeth cried. "With the human equivalent of an SAT prep guide."

"Don't make it worse for yourself because you want it to be bad," Charlotte whispered, as Geoffrey marched towards them with a cheerful bounce in his step. "Especially when *you* were the one who said yes."

"Lizzie," Geoffrey said.

"Geoffrey," Charlotte interrupted. "Let's dance." She snatched his hand and pulled him towards the dance floor. "It's one dance, LB. It'll be over before you know it."

Elizabeth bleated in agony.

A dance was never just a dance; middle school had taught her that much. Too much came with it—the closeness, the expectations, the finesse (or lack thereof) of a partner. It led to other things—a conversation, a chance at closing the distance, at a stolen moment out of sight of school chaperones. And with the way her luck was going tonight, she didn't trust her odds.

Darcy sidled up to her with an abrupt clearing of the throat. "Elizabeth."

A deal was a deal.

She took his hand and led them onto the floor.

Despite how curdled he looked every time they met, he relaxed as they danced, steering her around the floor with something approaching ease. Even then there was no hiding the expression of concentration on his face. Nothing about him was effortless; he wouldn't allow it to be. But if she had to suffer through a dance with him, then he might as well suffer through a dance with her.

"Nice turnout tonight, I think," she said.

He looked at her with mild surprise. She hadn't been instructed to speak. "I suppose."

She waited for another remark, but nothing came. They made another easy circle around the dance floor, his hands light against her back. "The rules are clear about this," she said. "I say something, then you say something."

He pulled her closer, angling them between two geriatric couples swaying in place. "I didn't realize we were operating by specific rules. I'll say whatever you want me to say."

She feigned a sigh.

He pushed back against her hands, posture ratcheting straighter. She'd never known anyone whose posture improved the worse they felt. "I think Caroline did a great job."

She glanced around the room. "Do you do a lot of these events with them?"

"With Caroline?"

"With the Lees," she said. "Brendan, I guess."

He almost snorted. "Brendan doesn't plan very many things at all, if that's what you're asking."

"That's why he has you?"

His hand trailed up the plane of her back, all warmth, as he shifted closer. Dancing with him was nothing like dancing with Geoffrey. Darcy was pure ballast, sure in his movements and steady in demeanor. Nothing seemed to crack his shell—and that was all she wanted to do.

"You're kind of an odd couple," she added.

He led her in a careful turn around two other couples. He was a surprisingly good dancer, leading her easily and naturally around the floor. "Brendan and I met in his first year at school," he said. "We were the only Chinese boys in our classes. His English wasn't bad, but you know how fourteen-year-old boys can be."

She'd punched one or two of them in the mouth before, so—no further explanation necessary.

"And what?" she said, stopping abruptly. "You became his grand defender?"

"Don't stop in the middle of the floor," he said, whisking her back into motion. "And no, this isn't a drama . . ."

He trailed off into silence and left it dangling. A man of few words, he never quite finished anything—sentences, stories, details. He always left her with more questions than he answered.

His eyes touched on hers again before looking away.

She focused on what she could see—his posture, his mouth, his hands. He kept time with the music with a tap of his index finger, a brush of his thumb against her spine.

When he spoke again, his voice could barely be heard over the music. "It can be hard to be away from home on your own. Not having anyone or knowing what to do."

She leaned closer, her head almost pressed to his shoulder.

"He needed someone."

She tried to imagine Brendan at Lydia's age, stranded somewhere alien and alone for the first time, looking for something and unsure what. And who else would be there but Darcy, certain in his opinions, stiff in his posture, and absolutely unyielding? An anchor against any rising tides.

She could understand the draw, even if she was skeptical about the source. "And you always put yourself out there for people who need you?"

This time, he was the one who stopped on the dance floor. "Wouldn't you?"

She remembered with faint horror Lydia asleep among the decorative plastic plants in the banquet hall at Alexa's wedding, and having to carry her mother out propped up between herself and Jane. What they suffered for the ones they loved, the ones who needed them.

"It isn't the same," she said. "*We're* not the same."

He slid effortlessly back into formality. "I didn't say that we were."

They fell back into silence, uncomfortable but familiar. She preferred familiar. She preferred to trust the version of him she remembered, all unfortunate manners and underhanded motives, instead of the one who seemed to stand in front of her now. She knew better than to trust a sad story; she'd told enough of them herself tonight.

"How's the photography going?" he said, after a beat. "Have you developed the photos from the roof yet?"

She shook her head. "I haven't had much time to work on my own stuff lately." Biting her lip, she added, "But I was helping a friend with his the other day when we ran into you."

His grip tightened almost painfully around her hand.

"Raymond is so *blessed* to find good friends wherever he goes. Whether or not he can *keep* them is another story."

She lowered her voice. "What happened to being there for your friends when they need you?"

Darcy's jaw tightened as he glanced around the room in search of an out. As if *she'd* been the one to ask him to dance.

If he wanted one, she would be more than happy to oblige. She stepped back, trying to slip away, but he drew her back into hold.

She looked up at his face, as still and implacable as ever.

"We aren't finished. The music's still playing."

She flushed. It hadn't been about her at all, only about avoiding any scene of public embarrassment.

The crowd on the dance floor thinned, and she supposed—or, truthfully, hoped—that he might finally call it, but if there was one thing Darcy would do, it would be to commit to something that gave him no pleasure for the sake of reputation.

"I'm sorry," he said. "I don't remember what we were talking about."

Lying could not be counted among his list of skills. "I don't think we *were* talking," she said. "We shouldn't try. We're not cut out for it."

His mouth flattened into a line. "Something else, then. What books do you like? Or movies?"

"Books and movies?" she cried. "I don't think that'll work unless you have a thing for Silent Bob."

"Silent Bob? Who's . . ."

Too late, she realized this was her chance to confront him about the things that he'd done. To stand up for a new friend and for the neighborhood.

Some small part of her hesitated at the thought of pulling the trigger. She didn't know why.

"You know, I thought you said that once you made up your mind about something, you wouldn't ever change it?"

"I don't see how that relates," he said.

She ignored him.

"So I guess that means you're careful about how you make those decisions?"

His skepticism turned cold. "Yes."

She stood still on the dance floor. "Because if I were the kind of person who made those kinds of judgments about other people, I think it'd be my responsibility to make sure my judgment was sound."

Couples circled around them, eyeing them curiously. "Are you making an appeal?"

A tremor of nerves tingled up her spine. "I'm . . . trying to understand you. I can't figure you out."

He held her gaze, his thumb tracing lines against her fingers. "What's there to figure?"

"It doesn't make any sense," she said. "I hear so many—all the different things I hear about you."

He dropped her hands. "Please. Don't try to piece me together like you do your photos."

She almost missed his warmth. "But I might never have the chance."

The band played out with a rustle of cymbals.

He retreated a step, nodding at her in acknowledgment. "Don't let me stop you. I'll look forward to hearing how I turn out."

Well, that couldn't have gone any better.

Ray hadn't asked her to get involved—but, then again, he hadn't exactly showed up to tell her not to get involved either. He hadn't said much of anything at all. Usually, at this point at any given party when she'd made an ass of herself, she would reach for the nearest jug of whatever and drink as much as she could stomach, grab a friend, and make for the train or the next bar. At least two parts of those seemed doable.

Elizabeth headed off in search of her sister, when Caroline stepped directly into her path.

She braced for impact, but Caroline threw her arms around her and pecked her on both cheeks. "Elizabeth!"

Elizabeth yelped.

"I was looking for you, aa," Caroline said, rosy cheeked with alcohol. "Don't you look beautiful."

One part of that sentence would have been unbelievable enough, never mind both.

"Looking for me?" she said. She tried to peek around Caroline but couldn't see a single face she recognized.

"Your sisters are such lively people, aaaa! They've been telling me all night about a new friend of yours." Her eyes glittered black, watching her face carefully for a reaction. "Raymond Wu?"

Elizabeth's face betrayed nothing.

Caroline draped an arm over her shoulders and pulled her close. "I don't know if you've *heard* about him, but friend to friend, I had to tell you the man is untrustworthy. No use, aa. I don't know the details, but I know he used to work for the Wong family and left them under very suspicious circumstances."

Elizabeth pinked with indignation. "It's incredible how you can know who's to blame without knowing the details."

Caroline forced a laugh. "I know it's hard to hear, Elizabeth, when it's about a man you have a *great* interest in, but if you knew anything about his background, you wouldn't entertain him at all. Better forget about him, la!"

"His background seems to be the only thing that's wrong for you people."

Caroline pressed her hand to her throat. "Well," she said. "Well, well, well. Excuse me for trying to help a friend."

These people didn't make friends; they collected showpieces.

With a dismissive huff, Caroline left to tend to her other guests.

Elizabeth returned to her table and sank into her seat with such force that Jane slid her a full glass in greeting. "You look like you need this more than I do."

Whatever bad mood she nursed didn't stand a chance.

Elizabeth drained the drink.

"Wow," Jane said. "Really bad night."

"What about you?" she said. "How's yours?"

Jane tried for nonchalance, but there was no hiding her glow of contentment.

"That's convincing," Elizabeth deadpanned.

"I saw you dancing earlier," she said. "You looked like you were having a good time."

Elizabeth stole a sip of Jane's drink. "Can I ask you something?" she said. "Has Brendan said anything about Darcy?"

"We don't talk about him much."

"You know what I mean. The kind of person he is?"

"Brendan said that he's like an older brother. He's learned a lot from him."

"What do you think?" Elizabeth said.

Brendan breezed towards their table with a hoot of greeting, grazing Jane's cheek with a kiss. He had long passed sobriety and now spoke louder and laughed more—quite an achievement, given how prone he was to smiling every other time they'd met. His cheeks flushed bright red from the alcohol, his jacket discarded and abandoned.

He glanced down at the empty glasses on the table. "You aren't drinking. You should be drinking."

Jane ruffled his hair with her hand. "I'm fine."

He bit her bare shoulder. "Jane, you're . . . more than fine."

Elizabeth considered flicking him with ice water to cool him down.

"You should sit down before you hurt yourself."

Elizabeth rose from her seat. "I'll go get us some water. You can take mine."

As she left, Elizabeth saw their heads drift closer together in conversation.

Waving at the bartender, she called for a whiskey soda and two glasses of water.

A cackle rang out from an adjacent table, glasses rattling as a pair of hands slapped the tabletop. "What can you say about a good boy like Brendan, aa?" Jade said, voice raised to near shouting.

Her mother couldn't be called quiet in the best of times, but drinking made her abandon all sense of volume control.

"Such a charming young man. So sweet, so devoted. And a hard worker!"

Lilly, Charlotte's mother, sipped at her glass of wine. "These boys, all day long, in front of the TV, the computer, video games, all day."

A smaller group of matrons surrounded them, all dressed in high finery, attentive to the sermon.

Jade sniffed. "Of course, it was so for-tu-nate that I could broker that deal for the center. And I knew that Brendan would be the right kind of man. You know, the kind looking to make an investment, la. To stick around and not zoom, zoom, running away like all the others."

Lilly hooted.

Jade leaned an elbow on the table and whispered into the crowd of women, who answered with bright laughter. Whatever Jade thought, Elizabeth knew these weren't like the aunties at the local bingo hall. They were Caroline's friends, Caroline's acquaintances.

"It's so lucky that Brendan and Jane get along," she continued. "It's so hard to find a good influence for your daughters, you know. And Brendan is such a man of the world! There's no shortage of doors he could open. Imagine!"

Jade basked in the attention. She didn't hear what her daughter did—that they were laughing *at* her, not with her.

Elizabeth cut towards her mother's table, conscious of Caroline and Darcy watching from the opposite side of the room with horrified glee.

"Mother," Elizabeth said. "I think you've had enough."

"And here's my daughter coming to scold me for having a good time. LB, aaaa, what's wrong now?"

One of the donors slapped the table with a dramatic sigh. "At least your daughter still cares about you, laaaa. My girls only think of me when they want to go shopping."

Jade closed her eyes and nodded slowly. "I suppose that is a blessing, sister."

"Mother," Elizabeth said, stooping beside her mother's seat. "It's late, and I think we should go."

"Go!" Jade cried. "But we're having such a great time!"

The crowd of women yelled in protest.

"We don't want to embarrass our hosts," Elizabeth said.

"Embarrass!" Jade cried. Turning towards the host table, she stretched her arms out wide. "Darcy! Caroline!"

"Mother!"

"Ai yaaaa, LB, stop coming up with problems. We're friend-ly, aaaa. Close friends," Jade said. She rose from her seat and pointed at their hosts. "Isn't that right?"

Caroline laughed meanly, shaking her head at their antics, but Darcy's expression remained flat. As if he'd given up on having anything to do with them at all.

All night, she'd played with crossing some kind of line with him. With both of them. But no matter what she wanted to prove—about Ray, about herself and what she considered a worthy cause—none of that was worth the cost to the rec or the neighborhood if she burned all of their bridges. But she'd never been the best at telling a good fight from a winnable one.

Lilly patted Jade's hand. "Listen to your daughter, la," Lilly said.

Before Elizabeth could breathe anything close to a sigh of relief, the band resumed playing over the noise. The opening notes of their song prickled her memory, a sweeping strain of lounge piano that echoed through the emptying dance floor.

Elizabeth froze.

Mary swayed barefoot on the edge of the stage platform, clenching the mic with both hands to hold herself upright.

Lydia careened hard into Elizabeth's side, lipstick smeared across her mouth. "Please tell me that she is *not* . . ." Lydia said. "This is not happening?"

The piano continued its long, melodic introduction.

Lydia keened with humiliation.

Elizabeth stared. "This is *not* happening."

Mary bumped her teeth against the mic. "Every night in my dreams," she whisper-sang. It would still have been humiliating, if survivable, if Mary had been on key. Unfortunate for all involved that Mary considered herself a natural talent but had never taken a lesson in her life—and greatly needed them.

Lydia covered her eyes with her hands. "Maybe no one will know that we're related."

The nervous laughter in the crowd shifted to snickering, but Mary persevered. She was undeterred; she was heartfelt; she was the drunkest Elizabeth had ever seen her and cracking all of the notes. "This is not happening," Elizabeth repeated, but it was—and all of it seemed to be happening at once. Her mother and Lilly haranguing donors into an impromptu hand of poker, cash only; Mary pounding at her chest and wailing; Caroline in danger of losing oxygen to the brain.

A small crowd gathered at the front of the platform stage, lighters flickering back and forth despite the express disapproval of the waitstaff.

Elizabeth rushed the stage and grabbed at her ankle, but Mary kicked her off. "Mary, get off the stage. This is not open mic at Sing Sing."

"You never let me have my moment," Mary whined. Leaping off the stage with microphone in hand, she dragged the equipment down behind her in a crash of feedback. Mary nodded at her older sister as she climbed back to her feet. "I need to find . . . shoes."

At this point, if all of her sisters managed to survive the evening with all of their shoes and teeth, she'd call it a win.

"I don't feel good," Mary said.

"I know," Elizabeth said. "Let's get the others and go home, okay?"

Mary sat down and laid her head down against the table. "Chicken wings," she mumbled, eyes drooping closed.

When the Chens wanted to make an appearance, they showed out. What could she say that she hadn't said a thousand times before? Urge caution? Restraint? What could she do that Jade or Vincent wouldn't immediately excuse? Two elder sisters against a tide of stronger influences didn't leave her much to work with. At least she could say she tried.

Elizabeth sprinted out of the ballroom and into the hallway, following the sound of voices around a corner.

Whatever she had expected to find was not what she found: Brendan and Jane, clinging to each other in the middle of the hallway, blind to the rest of the world. He propped an arm against the wall, boxing her in against him as they kissed. Well, at least someone was having a good time at the party.

Elizabeth whistled sharply.

Brendan pulled away, leaning his head against Jane's with a rueful chuckle. "I think you're being summoned." He kissed her again.

"Sorry to break up the party," Elizabeth called from a safe distance. "But Jane, we have a 911 situation."

Lydia raced into the hallway, shrieking her name. As she rounded the corner, she ran headfirst into the wall in a hard stop.

"Lydia!" Elizabeth cried, as her sister stumbled backward in a daze.

Jane extricated herself from Brendan's arms. "Lydia, what's the matter?"

"Lydia!" Geoffrey cried. "I have your glass of water!"

Lydia nodded weakly and emptied her stomach against the tile.

Elizabeth groaned. Soon, she prayed, it would all be over. The party, the evening, her life—any would do.

"Come on, honey," Jane murmured, helping her sister off the floor. "Let's get you home."

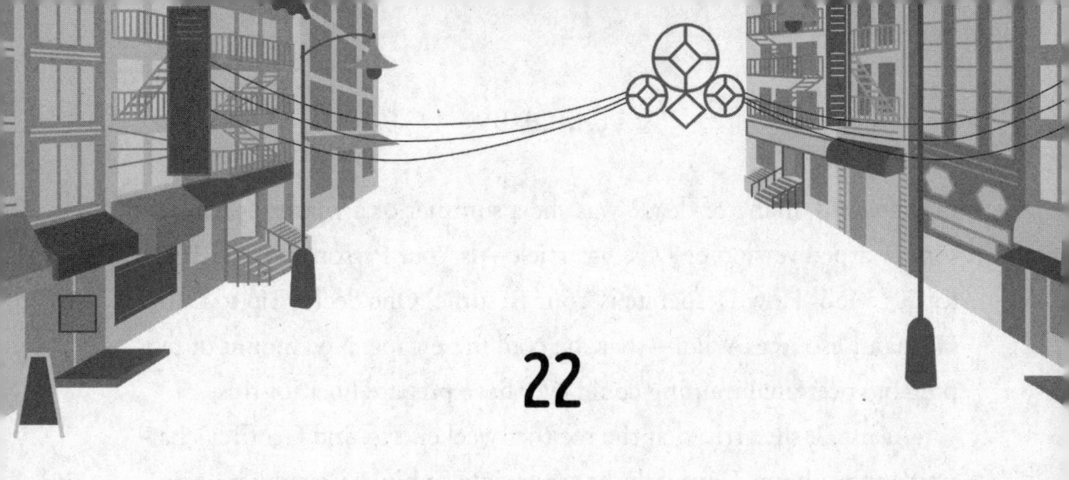

22

At least their long municipal nightmare—one of them, anyway—was coming to an end. With the gala finished, there would be no more donors, no more catered dinners, nothing left to fill the hours except the indignities of paperwork and being kept on hold with the city. That might do for the public servants and the nine-to-fivers of the world, but Geoffrey had dreams and aspirations, and, most important, strings to pull to send him elsewhere. He'd done what he could do, and what he did amounted to little more than redecorating.

Elizabeth hoped they might see less of each other now that his time at the center had an expiration date, but pending absence only made the heart grow fonder. He needed to consult her every thought and opinion, from paint swatches and email subject lines to vetting contractors and brands of hand soap for the women's bathroom. Nothing could be more important, and nothing could be done without her.

Each question he posed seemed more inane than the last. What was better for personal growth, Lizzie, the city or the country? If she could live anywhere in the world, where might she live? What did she consider to be the highest value of real estate? Who did she admire most in the world, living or dead? Was she a summer or a winter? It felt like some warped version of a *Cosmo* article—Is Your Personality Too Toxic to Get a Job? How Desperate is Your Résumé? One Secret Tip to Drive Human Resources Wild!—that she couldn't escape. No amount of test prep or vocational training could ever have prepared her for this.

As usual, she arrived at the rec that weekend to find Geoffrey chatting on the phone. Unusually, he sat upright in his chair, neither dozing with a sandwich in hand nor practicing his putt into a coffee cup. A notepad and pen rested beside him as if he'd been taking notes. Such attention! Such responsibility! Maybe he was finally beginning to take his role seriously.

The speakerphone crackled with bluster. "*Natural* fibers, Geoffrey! What have I told you?"

Maybe not.

There could be no mistaking that shrill bark, that officious drawl. Part stern grandmother, part head of state, the Rt. Hon. Lady Catherine Cheung spoke slowly and crisply, her accented English clipping the consonants short and stretching the vowels long. Every remark became a proclamation, every observation a judgment; nothing could escape her attention—or her steel tongue.

"I do apologize," Geoffrey said. "The man in the shop said—"

"I should have been consulted," she sniffed. "I'm sure you looked like an appliance salesman. Need I remind you that you are a *reflection* of myself and Rosings . . ."

"I will be sure to discuss these decisions with you ahead of the next event."

"As you should have done, Geoffrey," she replied. "But no matter. We must discuss your departure. My nephew has used you for his little side project long enough. A ridiculous enterprise, if you ask me."

"Very ridiculous," he chirped.

"Young people are not in need of *more* recreation," she said. "They loiter and tear up the lawns. Riling each other up. Jumping on skateboards and huffing paint—absolutely terrible for the neighborhood values."

Elizabeth slurped noisily at her coffee.

Geoffrey cringed, waving his arms furiously for her to stop.

"What's that, Geoffrey?" she barked. "You've got a terrible connection."

He banged his hand against the window a few times. "Just some street noise."

She tried to leave him to his call, but Geoffrey signaled her to stay where she was.

Catherine clucked with dismay. "Mayhem on the streets. Pandemonium. I wonder why they considered investing there at all . . ."

"With your support, I'm sure the neighborhood will improve in no time."

She loudly cleared her throat. "Geoffrey, focus. Now, make sure you present the offer exactly as I advised," Catherine said. "Ex-act-ly!"

"Of course, Lady Catherine."

Why he wanted her to stay to listen to his conversation, she didn't know. But every time she tried to duck back out into the hallway, he waved her back in.

A loud cough shook through the phone. "One hates to see an investment wasted, you know."

He waved Elizabeth closer. "You've been so helpful, as always," he said. "I don't know what I would do without you."

"Nothing good, Geoffrey," Catherine answered. And with one last gasp of a reminder about the best method for selecting red ginseng, Catherine ended the call.

"Now," Elizabeth said, "what did you want to see me about?"

Geoffrey set his hands on the table with exaggerated somberness. "There's some good news and some bad news." A long, dramatic pause held in the air. "The bad news is that I've been recalled to one of Rosings's other outposts to oversee one of our other developments. Lady Catherine doesn't believe in wasting time doing nothing, you know."

How that could be true with what she'd seen of Geoffrey's personality, she didn't know. But she'd take her wins where she could get them—and Geoffrey leaving the rec in the hands of more capable management would be an undeniable win.

"We'll be sad to see you go," she lied. "What's the good news?"

He smiled even wider, looking like a ventriloquist's doll.

"In the few short weeks that we have known each other, I've gotten the chance to see the elegant workings of your mind and the mulish devotion you bring to your work."

That didn't sound good.

"Thank you?"

"Mules aren't common in the office, you know." He stepped around the side of his desk, eyeing her as he straightened his nameplate.

She felt an urge to skitter to the other side. "No, I didn't know."

"Let me be direct. Your mother's been telling me about the struggles you've had . . . and I want you to know that I am willing to be used."

"That's okay."

"I have a lot of connections, you know, and I happen to know of a perfect opportunity—"

"Geoffrey, I can tell you now," Elizabeth said. "I'm not selling knives."

"No knives. But how would you feel about a life of intrigue, travel, and personal growth?"

She stammered. What could you even say to that?

"As you know, Lady Catherine feels very strongly about mentorship, and after telling her extensively of your situation, she agrees that you would benefit greatly from her insight," he said. "Out of the generous spirit of her heart, she's decided to offer you a starting role as a collections specialist with the Rosings Corporation."

Like a double-decker tour bus changing lanes in the middle of rush hour, it proved disorienting and inconvenient all at once.

She gaped at him. "Geoffrey, I didn't apply!"

He grinned wide. "This is a formal recruitment," he said. "You would be working under *me*, but it would be a chance for you to *blossom* into the kind of young professional I know you could be. And Lady Catherine has graciously agreed to advance you any relo expenses, which will of course be repaid out of your wages at a very reasonable rate of interest . . ."

Elizabeth widened her eyes. "Relocation expenses?"

"Yes," Geoffrey said. "Very reasonable rates. And you'll be heading to the satellite office in Scranton."

"*Pennsylvania*?" she cried.

Geoffrey clapped his hands. "Excellent geography!" he said. "I knew you were the right choice."

Jade burst into the office with a gleeful shout, carrying a large bouquet of flowers in her hands. "Congratulations, LB!"

This wasn't a job offer; it was an ambush and intervention. Like one of those episodes of *Jenny Jones* where they threatened unruly teens with military school. Scranton was worse.

"I'm not moving to Pennsylvania!"

"You're not *moving* anywhere," Jade said. "They are re-lo-cating you."

"I am not *relocating* to Scranton, Mother," Elizabeth said. "To work in collections?"

"Elizabeth, you are going nowhere right now. Please," Jade replied.

"You have a part-time retail position and stay home bothering me. This is a generous and well-paying job."

Sure—just one far from the limits of anything that might be called civilization.

"I've been applying to jobs *here*, Mother," Elizabeth said. "There's nothing out there for me."

Geoffrey tutted. "A relationship with Lady Catherine can only benefit you if you can impress her, as you have me."

And if she failed to impress, Elizabeth didn't doubt that she'd be out on the street before she could drop to her knees and beg. Taking a job shaking down tenants for a woman like Lady Catherine would be a thankless role—and a favor she would never be allowed to forget.

"I'm not going. You can't make me."

Jade gritted her teeth in silent threat.

"I'm hearing a lot of nos right now," Geoffrey said.

"Thank you, Geoffrey," Elizabeth said. "Thank you for the offer. I'm honored that you would consider me, but I'm not interested."

Geoffrey blinked at her in confusion. "Is this a negotiation tactic?"

"No, listen—"

"Salary will reflect experience and region," he said. "So if you're expecting—"

"I'm not expecting anything," she interrupted. "I will not be taking the job."

"Hardball," Geoffrey said. "I like it. Not enough women negotiate like this these days, and I can tell that you want the job."

Elizabeth shook with irritation. "I don't want anything!" she cried. "Not from you, not from Lady Catherine, not from *rent collections*!"

Jade smacked her in the chest with gerbera daisies. "Elizabeth!" Jade cried. "Think about what you're saying."

Geoffrey shook his head. "I will need to speak to Lady Catherine about this," he said. "She appreciates women who negotiate but not too much. You may be right on the line. But I hope when I return with her counter, you'll find it more agreeable."

"Geoffrey," she said, slowly. "Trust me when I say thank you, but no thank you."

Geoffrey tittered with indignation. "Lizzie," he said. "I certainly want you to be paid everything that you're worth—but a string of dead-end jobs and a degree in *the arts*—"

"Communications—"

"—you can't possibly expect more than what we're offering. I would think long and hard before I make a decision that ruins my future."

Jade pinched hard at Elizabeth's arm. "Of course she will, Mr. Geoffrey! She knows how much Lady Catherine is depending on her." To her, she added, "Why do you want to make things difficult?"

Geoffrey scrubbed at his forehead with his hand, looking troubled. "Lady Catherine has no room on her staff for *difficult* people."

Jade forced a thin laugh. "Joking, aaa! LB's thrilled about the offer, Mr. Geoffrey! She just has a hard time deciding because she does so much for her sisters. But we'll have a big family meeting about it tonight to make sure that she does."

Geoffrey laced his fingers together and nodded. "Certainly it's a lot to think about. But I do hope that you'll say yes."

"Don't worry, Mr. Geoffrey," Jade said, slamming her hand hard against Elizabeth's back. "We will make her see reason."

That was a threat and a promise.

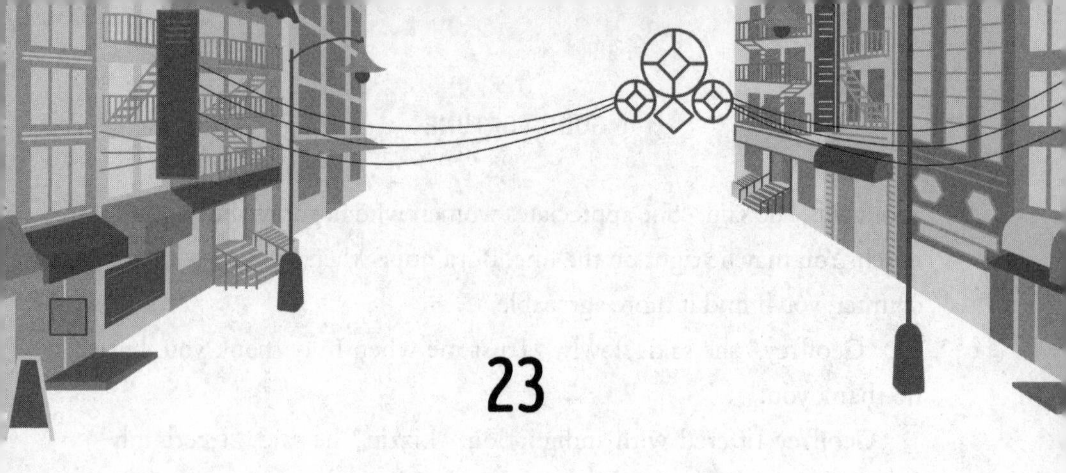

23

No—a single word, a complete sentence, and the worst nightmare of almost every parent around the neighborhood. It might be tolerated in other cities, other homes, other families, but not by Jade Chen. No? What did Elizabeth mean *no*, after years of their suffering and sacrifice, after all of the schooling and the hard work? After everything that Jade and Vincent did for her, and "This is how you repay me!"

Jade ranted, Jade huffed, Jade appealed to Vincent, who turned the page of his newspaper and refused to get involved.

It was a familiar song, and Elizabeth knew all the words. She was careless and ungrateful, selfish and inconsiderate, shortsighted and stupid; nothing she did could ever meet Jade's standards. Her life would never be enough. Not as long as she refused to do exactly as Jade wanted, and live as Jade wanted her to live. "You can't expect me to give up everything I've been working on so you can look better to the aunties in the neighborhood."

"And what do you have?" she cried. "No boyfriend, no career, nothing. What life are you leaving?"

"This isn't about what's best for me," she said. "This is about your reputation."

"Use your brain, LB. God gave it to you for a reason."

The other Chens, scattered around the living room, pretended not to be listening. The chirp of Kitty's Game Boy tinkled in the background.

"I *am* using it. My life is here. You guys are here. The jobs I want are here. Scranton has nothing."

"Nothing at all. Only a paying job," Jade said. "All you do is interview, and then what? No calls, no offers, nothing. More interviews! For jobs that don't pay."

"I'm working!" Elizabeth said. "Sammy's, Lulu's, whatever I can pick up around the neighborhood."

"Do you know how that looks?"

"I don't care how it looks," Elizabeth said. "It's enough for now, and it's *here*."

"Then do whatever you want, I can't tell you anything. See what your life will look like when your dad and I are gone and can't help you. Then you'll be smart, won't you?"

Elizabeth grunted. She loved her mother, though sometimes she wished her mother didn't make that so hard to do. "Why can't I make my own choices?"

"Who said you can't?" she said. "You're so smart. Too smart for me. Go ahead. Don't think about me and your dad—not when I birthed you and raised you and suffered to give you a good life . . ."

"Mother."

She clicked her tongue with disgust. "I don't want to look at you."

If Elizabeth hoped that the situation would resolve with enough time, resistance, or silence, she underestimated her mother. Jade insulted and pleaded, threatened and complained, bargained and bribed. She roped in the other Chen girls. Mary left her a printout comparing the price per square foot in Scranton to New York, Kitty recited prepared remarks while brushing her teeth, and Lydia, committed to the cause, argued that her absence would give them all more space in the apartment. "Think about what *that* would mean for me, personally."

Elizabeth rolled her eyes, tucking a handful of twenties into the envelope for the electric bill. She knew what it meant to the others—a status change, bragging rights, a chance to free up another bed in their apartment—but no one tried to understand what it would mean for her. To abandon every standard she once set for herself and turn into the kind of person who didn't care about anything but themselves, to turn her back on the place that raised her—she couldn't.

She wouldn't.

No.

Like all good American children, when it got to be too much, she tried to run away from home.

She didn't go far.

Like most of the neighborhood, the Luos had heard enough to piece together their own understanding of the events—*Kicked her out, laaaa*, relayed the aunties, *in the middle of the night with nothing! But wasn't that just Jade, aaa, caring about the money over good sense?*—and to doubt the story that went around with it. For now, they might be happy to offer her a couch and a warm bed, but Elizabeth knew any longer than a weekend would strain neighborly relations.

Whenever she needed it, there had always been Charlotte's bedroom—a haven of relative quiet from the chaos of the Chen apartment, small and neat and shared between Charlotte and her younger sister. Split evenly down the middle, Mariah's side still leaned towards childish, a twin bed piled with stuffed animals and knickknacks; Charlotte's looked neat, if noisier, walls decorated with a few punk show posters they'd taped up summers ago and photos of the two of them. At the Luos, everything had its place and its order—even Elizabeth, even the world.

"She won't be happy unless I'm miserable," Elizabeth complained. "All she wants is someone to boss around."

Charlotte pulled back the bedcovers and climbed in. "Don't you think she's just trying to look out for you?"

Elizabeth jerked her hair back roughly to tie it. "I would be stuck in collections for the rest of my life."

"With that can-do attitude?" Charlotte cracked.

Elizabeth crawled in beside her and collapsed against the pillows with a loud sigh. "She wants me to be like her," she said. "Don't care about anything until you get paid first. So what if you're throwing people out on the street?"

"It's not that bad," Charlotte said. "Don't take it so personally."

"Of course it's personal," she said. "I don't want to be harassing people over twenty dollars. It's bad karma."

Charlotte yawned. "Just think about what you could do to change things from the inside."

Elizabeth groaned with relish.

"You and your mom are more alike than you think," she said. "The only way you know how to get things done is with a fight."

Elizabeth socked her lightly with a pillow. "You're supposed to be on my side."

Charlotte wrapped her arms around her and squeezed tight. "Of course I'm on your side," she said, digging her chin into her shoulder. "But so is she."

Elizabeth grumbled under her breath. "Until she decides to ship me back to China for being disobedient."

* * *

Nothing helped to distract from her mother's disapproval like mindless manual labor, and nothing could be more mindless or manual than weekend morning pickup shifts. Elizabeth unloaded fresh deliveries at one of the smaller grocery stores, ran Old Tong his weekly apothecary order, and finished the morning off with a day of photos around the block. The grandfathers playing go in the courtyard, the grandmothers feeding the birds, the delivery boys smoking cigarettes outside their stores. It comforted her, that hum of blood and life in the neighborhood that could never quite be captured on film.

She tried, anyway.

After wandering the block for half an hour, she found her way back outside the rec. Squatting in front of the building, she framed the tall front windows, gleaming in the morning light. With a laugh, she remembered Darcy's horror at the sight of her bloodied teeth.

A shadow passed in front of her lens, blocking the light.

"Hey!" she grumbled, lowering her camera.

"Good morning to you too, sunshine," Ray cracked, sliding his sunglasses down the end of his nose.

She frowned at him. "You're blocking my light."

"Kind of the point," he said. "Can I tell you I'm sorry?"

"For blocking my light, or for ditching me?"

He stooped down to her level, looking into her eyes. "I owe you an explanation."

She nodded. "Yeah, you do."

He tugged at her hand. "Come on, Liza with a *z*. Let's get out of here."

"What are we going to do?"

He shrugged. "Go for a walk," he said. "Talk. Eat. Whatever you want."

He didn't deserve to be forgiven so easily, but it was hard to remember that whenever he smiled at her. A fact he knew and exploited.

A child of the neighborhood, Elizabeth seldom ventured beyond its borders for anything other than a special occasion. Ray hungered to put his feet to pavement in a way that she didn't understand; he considered the city something to claim. From Chinatown, they wound their way uptown. The grandmas and grandpas and metal laundry carts of the neighborhood yielded to the higher-pitched chatter of students and European tourists picking through the weekend sidewalk-table offerings of discount sunglasses, jewelry, and shooting scripts. They passed through without stopping, turning west towards Sixth Ave. and continuing north.

"I'm sorry I abandoned you the other night."

"Especially when I went to all the trouble of adding you to my invite?" she said.

He slid an arm over her shoulders and pulled her close. "I'm sorry, I'm sorry," he said. "I wanted to see you, just not him. Can you forgive me?"

She softened against him. "I don't know."

"I thought it would be better for everyone if we avoided a scene," he said.

"Oh, but I *wanted* you to make a scene," she said. "I could have sold some photos to the tabloids or something."

He shook his head. "I don't think you're the kind of person who likes to see their friends suffer."

She rolled her head against his shoulder. "Is that what we are now?" she said, smiling. "Friends?"

Reaching in his bag, he pressed the hard edge of a plastic case into her hand. In sloppy handwriting, he'd scribbled *DON'T BE MAD LIZA* in Sharpie on the CD and decorated it with crooked stars.

A mix tape—he really did feel bad.

"Just in case," he said.

A deep warmth spread through her chest. She hoped he couldn't see it on her face.

"How was it, by the way?"

"The fundraiser?" she said.

He nodded.

"Self-important and stuffy. What else?" she said. "The Lees love to throw a party. Hopefully some of it makes its way to the rec."

Ray's expression darkened. "I think the Wongs and Lees have a habit of making promises they don't keep."

She pressed her lips together. "I know," she said. "Say whatever it takes to get approval and then pretend like you never said it at all. The developer playbook."

"I have faith in you, though," he said. "You'll keep them honest."

"Yeah, right," she laughed. "I'm the last person they would ever listen to. What do you think they'll do?"

He frowned. "I think Darcy Wong does whatever's best for Darcy Wong."

She set her jaw. "That's what I figured."

The noise of the West Village faded as they crossed Ninth Ave. towards the galleries on Tenth. This far west, foot traffic thinned to a manageable herd, the only noise the squawking of angry drivers caught behind a double-parked car or delivery truck. They fell into a comfortable silence as they crossed into Chelsea, watching other couples on the street.

At the first photo gallery they passed, Ray paused at the window long enough that she dragged him inside. The room smelled like air-conditioning, cool and chemically sweet, and an icy blond woman attended the desk, saying nothing as they entered. Ray studied the photos hanging on the walls with open admiration. Black-and-white prints ranging under a thousand dollars posted for sale—a close-up of a pair of hands performing needlework, joyous Black boys using a large wrench to pry a fire hydrant open, dancers chalking the boxes of their shoes. Here were the kinds of photos liable to earn gallery shows: staged and structured, well lit and balanced, composed. Dishonest, she thought. All silver and no blood.

He lingered longest on the photos of bodies, men and women twisting at odd angles in various states of undress, their muscles highlighted under the lights. It made the bodies look strange and distorted, almost alien. The raw clay of humanity, perforated and scarred, raw and open.

"You still haven't let me see any of your pictures," she said.

He shook his head. "None of them are good enough for you," he said. "They're so basic."

"Let me see and find out."

He knocked her shoulder with his. "You haven't shown me yours either."

"Yeah, but I'm no artist," she said. "I don't go to *Pratt*."

They paused in front of a poster-size print, a naked woman sprawled diagonally across a bare mattress in a SoHo loft, snarling at the camera. Nothing could ever beat female nudity for artistry.

"You never thought about showing your stuff?" he said.

"Selling out, you mean?" she said, smiling. "Sometimes. It'd make my mom happy."

"But you wouldn't want the fame and the fortune? The notoriety?"

She scoffed. "That's why I take pictures," she said. "Because I like being the center of attention."

He shrugged, checking the caption on the wall for the photographer's name.

"I wouldn't want to do anything that didn't end up making a difference," she said. "I thought you didn't either."

He slipped his fingers around hers. "No, of course not," he said. "It's the art that matters."

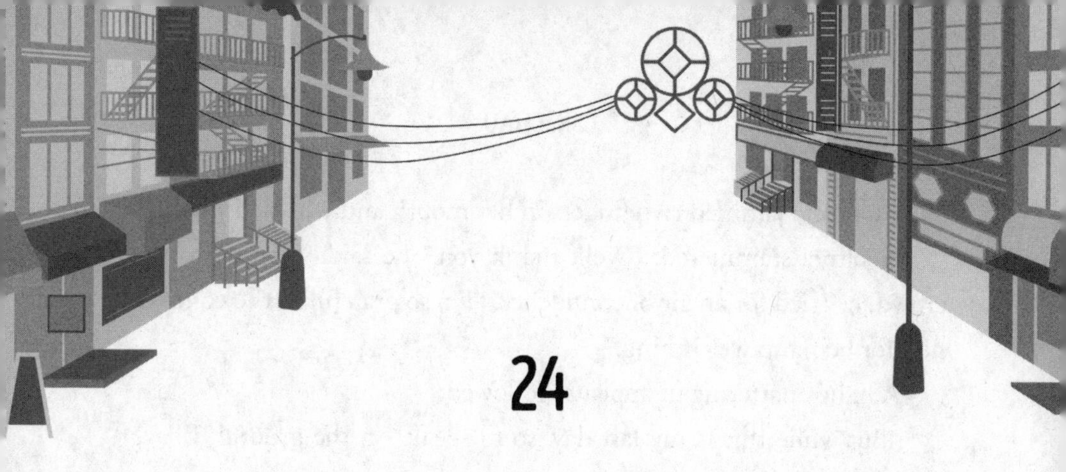

24

As his final triumph, Geoffrey planned his own going-away party in the courtyard of the rec and invited the entire neighborhood. Given his acumen for planning, it had the air of a second-grade pizza party. Party City discounted orange crepe paper looped in crooked lines from tree to tree, table to table. Square boxes of pizza leaked melted cheese through gaps in the cardboard, threatening to topple, beside quarter-filled plastic cups of Hawaiian Punch and iced tea and a lone six-pack of Smirnoff Ice. Folding card tables sat cluttered with party favors and food, which the neighborhood pigeons eyed with great interest. Billy Joel sang staticky through somebody's rescued boom box, and the neighbors gathered and ate and gossiped, and complained about the event between bites of homemade dumplings and noodles.

Elizabeth dished herself a small helping of noodles and tried to avoid Geoffrey's eye.

"If I may," Geoffrey called, tossing his empty plate onto the folding table they used for food service.

The two-dozen neighbors kept chatting among themselves.

"Excuse me," Geoffrey tried again.

Charlotte jammed two fingers in her mouth and whistled sharply.

Geoffrey stammered. "Well, thank you," he said. Turning to the crowd, he tried for an air of confidence. "I'm so grateful to the community for being so welcoming."

A light smattering of applause followed.

"But while this is my last day, so to speak, on the ground, I have some final announcements before I go."

"Hurry up, laaaaaa," one of the neighbors cried.

"Talking too much, the food will get cold," another neighbor muttered.

"I'm happy to announce that Peony Plum will be starting renovations on your beloved community center! The space you love, new and improved! Featuring brand-new retail, luxury housing, and community space, we're proud to introduce *The Fortunata*!"

Elizabeth gasped as the crowd applauded. So after all of their promises about the character of the neighborhood, the new owners would do exactly as they promised they wouldn't—and she knew exactly who to blame. A selfish, rent-seeking corporate shill with no qualms about lying to get what he wanted, who didn't even have the courage to stick around to tell them all himself.

"And while I will be sad to leave you all, I'm happy to report that I will not be going alone. Charlotte Luo will be joining me to fill a new vacant position with the Rosings Corporation!"

Lydia dribbled soda out of her mouth in shock. "No way!" she cried. "That's LB's job!"

Geoffrey cleared his throat. "Charlotte's *graciously* accepted and will be training across Rosings Corporation properties in the Northeast before transitioning to the Scranton office."

To cheer one of their own, the crowd tried to muster more energy, and though Charlotte resisted, Geoffrey pulled her to stand beside him and princess-wave at the crowd.

Elizabeth froze, pizza slice halfway to mouth, dripping grease on the front of her T-shirt. She must have heard incorrectly. She must have misunderstood.

Like the best of all natural predators, Lilly Luo strutted towards the trash can and lay in wait for her prey.

"Lilly, congratulations!" Jade cried, after a long pause. "She's such a bright girl, your Charlotte."

There were no greater fighting words than open compliments.

"Thank you," Lilly said. "We're so proud of her."

Jade lifted her red Solo Cup in toast. "Of course it makes sense that she would receive this offer *after* Elizabeth turned it down."

"But *your* Elizabeth must have much better offers, la. Such a smart girl, and so independent!"

"Yes," Jade said, pressing her lips together in a thin line. "One thing you can say about our LB is how *keen* she is on her independence."

Charlotte fled from Geoffrey's side in a sprint. "Don't be mad."

"Charlotte, you—how? What the fuck?"

Charlotte stiffened, running a hand through her hair. "What, it isn't good enough for you, so it isn't good enough for anyone else?"

Elizabeth softened. "You know that's not what I mean. It's just—after everything we talked about?"

"I know it's a . . . shock since you were the one that he wanted," Charlotte said. "But this is a good offer, and I get to travel."

"Moving to Pennsylvania is *not* traveling."

Charlotte shoved her lightly in the side. "I'm not gone forever, you know. It's not the end of the world."

No, it wasn't the end of the world, but it was the end of a friendship, a childhood, a partnership that saw them through the worst and most awkward years of their lives. The thought of doing anything without Charlotte terrified her.

"You could *try* to be happy for me," Charlotte said.

Elizabeth nearly tackled her in a hug. "I'm *thrilled* for you," she said. "I am. You deserve everything. I just wish it wasn't *this*."

Charlotte rolled her eyes. "LB," she said. "It's just a job."

Elizabeth kissed her on the cheek. "It's not just a job. It's you."

Charlotte punched her arm. "I'm not *dying*."

Elizabeth took her arms, spinning her in a twirl, as the radio blasted the Black Eyed Peas.

The rec had seen them through birthdays and all kinds of firsts, and now the first of their lasts. Now there might be no more adventures, no more explorations, only the two of them driven apart and drifting even further.

"Stop moping," Charlotte said.

Elizabeth looped her arms through Charlotte's with a dramatic sigh. "Sometimes I can still hear your voice."

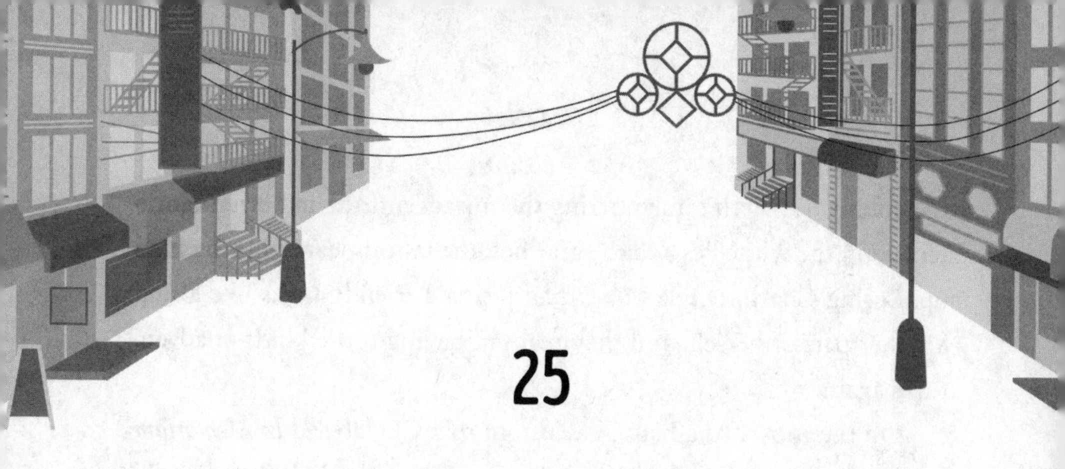

25

They could not send Charlotte off without a proper Chen-girl goodbye—a sleepover masquerading as a night out with questionably cheap booze served out of plastic cups. Charlotte demurred, Charlotte resisted, Charlotte claimed that she couldn't travel hungover when the last time she tried that, she threw up as soon as she deboarded. These were judged to be unsatisfactory arguments; they would eat, drink, and be merry, and if she died, then she died. May she rest in peace in the best city in the world.

Even Jane managed to tear herself away from endless assignments and emails to celebrate. "It's not every day you get a job, Char," Jane said.

"Yeah," Lydia continued. "*And* you're moving out. That's huge."

They went on a tour of greatest hits—slices from Joe's, chicken and rice from the street, dumplings from their favorite B-graded health code violation; cheap vodka from the liquor store that didn't card; candy and soda from the bodega—and sprinted up the fire escape with such force that it rattled as if it might fall down and send them all crashing to Earth. Outside slid from chill to frigid, and they turned frantic with the cold, giddy with remembering the misadventures and misspent afternoons, the white lies and the gray lies, the lessons learned by fucking up. Losing Charlotte felt worse than losing a friend; it was like losing another part of herself, and the dream of having those kinds of adventures again.

On the roof, Lydia blasted a custom mix CD labeled *In Memoriam* as Jane served them all their first drinks. She had a light hand and a weak pour, which made for an excellent start to the evening.

"I can't believe *you're* the first to get out of here, Char," Lydia said. "I mean, no offense and all, but your parents."

Charlotte laughed. "None taken."

Elizabeth hoped Charlotte might miss them all too—the summers and the lazy weekends; the time spent with sisters unlike her own, but sisters all the same; Lydia's big mouth. "To Charlotte," Elizabeth said, raising her cup in toast.

"All right, bitches," Lydia said, downing her first drink. "Let's party." And as Ludacris blasted out of the CD player, she slid and swiveled on her toes into a clumsy pop and lock.

"Don't quit your day job," Kitty heckled, chewing on the lip of her cup.

"Fuck you!" Lydia replied. "LB, get your camera!"

Elizabeth drained her drink and nodded at Charlotte to do the same. "Tonight is not about you, Lyd."

Kitty drummed her hands against the lawn chair. "Shots, shots, shots!"

"No shots," Charlotte insisted. "I'm on duty tomorrow."

"You are not," Elizabeth replied. "You're traveling tomorrow." Though not immediately to Scranton. The Rosings Corporation required a detour for probationary training—though what kind of training was needed to ask people for money, Elizabeth couldn't guess—and she would be serving her time in some town outside of Philadelphia.

Reaching for the handle of vodka, Elizabeth twisted the cap loose and poured a splash into Charlotte's cup and a splash into her own. "For old times."

Lydia cracked glow sticks in her hands and handed them one apiece. "This could be the last time we ever see you," she said with great somberness.

Elizabeth waved the glow stick in front of her face. "Go big or go home, Char."

Charlotte grimaced and downed her shot.

Until the late night hours, they danced and drank on the rooftop, hollering and screaming. Elizabeth poured drinks until the bottles emptied, Charlotte snapping through an entire disposable camera before midnight. The younger girls, overeager and enthusiastic in their drinking, lost stamina, drifting to sleep on the lawn chairs or on the ground, makeup ruined and hair askew.

"Come on," Elizabeth said. "One last run."

Charlotte listed on her feet, looking at her through bleary eyes. Raising a wobbling finger, she tried for stern. "No."

Elizabeth punched her in the arm. "It's your last night, Char! We're going!"

Chinatown after dark never felt like the same place it was during the day. The streets emptied and turned near silent with only the rustle of rats through the garbage and the occasional howl of drunken revelry. Light reflected off of the wet streets, almost glistening in the dark and draping everything else in shadows. As quietly as they could manage, they made their way to the street.

Everywhere she looked, there were signs of a changing city: brand-new realty stickers in windows, gates and shutters over old buildings, scaffolding and construction fencing with beautiful drawings of what was to come. It felt like trying to squeeze into a shrunken sweater, remembering how it used to fit and trying to account for the difference.

At least there was still the old rec—closed, but not yet shuttered; gone, but not yet forgotten. For years, they'd loitered here after dark, watching sketchy pickup games after midnight on the basketball courts or just sharing smokes from the front steps. Close enough to home to feel safe, and far enough away to feel like an escape.

Tonight, they walked the edge of the courtyard, peering into the taped-off basketball courts and playgrounds. Elizabeth remembered how enormous it had felt when she was a kid, the two of them bouncing between jump ropes in the midday heat. Now it just felt small.

Charlotte smiled softly at her. "Remember when you fought Jeremy Chu for my lunch money?"

Elizabeth snorted. "He knocked out my two front teeth," she said. "How could I forget?"

"Oh my god," she said. "Your mother didn't let you out for weeks."

"Look so ug-ly!" she crowed, in her best Jade impression.

Charlotte giggled. "What am I going to do without you to defend me?"

Elizabeth took her hand. "Call me for anything. I'll figure it out."

Charlotte clung on to her with a soft sniffle. "It's going to be so weird without you."

Elizabeth tried to swallow past the lump in her throat. "Yeah," she said. "Now who's going to buy me breakfast on the weekend?"

Their last night together, they split a cigarette and drank cheap canned coffee and waited for the sun to rise. Just like old times.

"Remember that loft that we were going to get together? In the Village?"

Charlotte raised her eyebrows. "It wasn't what you'd call a realistic plan."

"You wanted to be an artist. You wanted to change the world."

"I also wanted to move to Alaska and live in a van."

Elizabeth took the cigarette and breathed a long drag. "It just doesn't feel like you. That's all."

Charlotte exhaled, brushing her hand over her eyes. "Sometimes life can't be exactly what you want."

The sun cracked into the horizon, the clouds around it beginning to lighten. Soon, the air would fill with the noise of impatient car horns and endless talk, the anxious stir of morning.

Charlotte reached for the cigarette.

"I want you to be happy," Elizabeth said, exhaling smoke.

"I'm happy," she said, taking the last drag. "I want you to be happy too."

Elizabeth rested her head against Charlotte's shoulder. What she wanted was to say something poetic and meaningful, something that could capture all of their years of friendship and what they'd meant to each other. What she wanted was a proper goodbye, but she couldn't find the right words, the right thoughts, the right feelings—they all slipped through her fingers, just out of reach. Lost in translation.

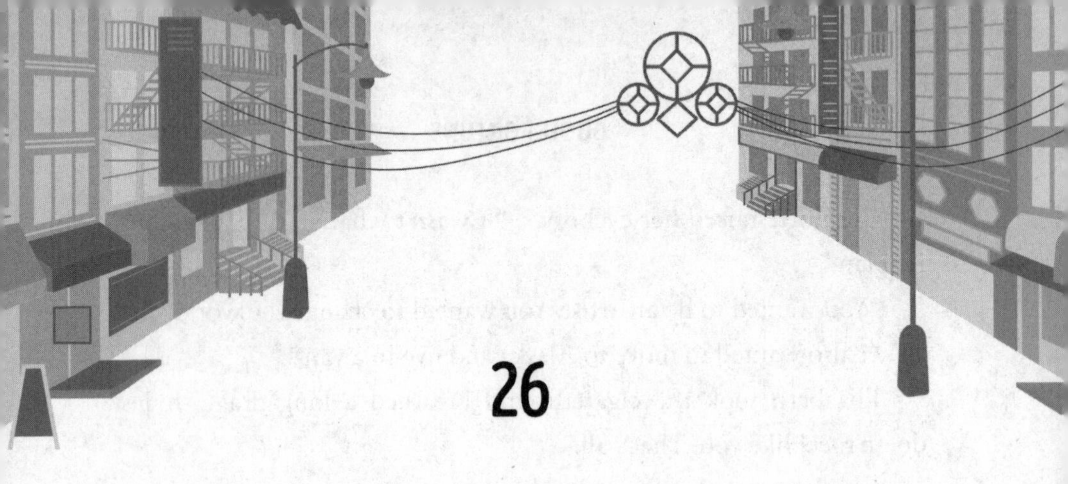

26

Sometimes, when life closed a door, it opened a window—a fact Elizabeth exploited as she tried to shimmy back in through their bedroom window from the fire escape. It was an art form she'd taken years to perfect.

Shoes in hand, she tiptoed through the bedroom and into the kitchen for a glass of water when someone sleeping on the sofa sprang upright.

Elizabeth jumped with a soft yelp, nearly whipping her sandals at the blurry face in the dark.

"And just where were you all night, hmm?"

If it had been anyone else, Elizabeth would have tried a lie. This was not what it looked like. She'd actually been up all night reading Advanced Trig. Something to buy her enough time to brush her teeth and slip into her bed and pretend to fall asleep. But this wasn't just anyone. This was her Aunty Amelia.

All aunties were not created equal: few could be bribed, and even fewer trusted. Unlike the many other aunties Elizabeth knew around the neighborhood, this one she was actually related to, if by marriage and not blood. Amelia was her uncle Randall's wife and an opposite in almost every way to her own mother. Where Jade shouted, Amelia spoke softly; where Jade held a grudge, Amelia mostly forgave and forgot. Amelia was singular: an aunty who could also be called an ally.

Elizabeth wrapped her arms around her aunt. "I didn't know you were coming."

Amelia pressed a finger to her mouth to quiet her, waving her towards the direction of the kitchen. "Don't let your mother smell you like that," she said, rummaging through the cabinets for the coffee filters.

"When did you get in?"

"Last night," Amelia said. "It was supposed to be a surprise, so imagine my surprise when none of you were home."

Elizabeth remembered Lydia and Kitty on the roof last night with a pang of embarrassment.

Amelia didn't miss a beat. "They're sleeping it off," she said, scooping grounds into the Mr. Coffee. "I told your uncle they were probably just tired."

"And he believed you?"

"Of course he did," she said, shrugging. "I'm his wife and I'm never wrong. What were you up to tonight?"

Elizabeth took a seat at the table and dropped her head against her arms. "Out with Charlotte," she said. "She's leaving for her new job."

Amelia flashed her eyebrows. "Oh, the new job."

Of the New Job—or Elizabeth's Folly, or Elizabeth's Defiance, or the worst thing Jade had ever suffered—Amelia had heard plenty. Most of it sandwiched between dramatic sobs and paroxysms of asthma and anxiety with an occasional threat thrown in for variety. Nothing could be done about LB—so reckless, so headstrong—when she insisted on having her own way, no matter what. While the other girls of her class married up and worked their way out, she stuck around, taking nothing jobs and going nowhere, taking *pictures* and not even trying to sell them! All for the sake of her own pride.

Mr. Coffee spluttered in agreement.

Elizabeth moaned. "Do you see what I'm dealing with here?"

Amelia patted her shoulder gently. "Your mother needs a little time," she said. "She isn't good at handling disappointment."

"That is an understatement."

Amelia peered into the bedroom at Jane, practically rolling out of the bottom bunk. "She isn't the only one."

While Amelia wasn't one to snitch, she was hardly immune to the lure of good gossip.

Elizabeth knew when she'd been hooked.

Fetching two mugs from the cabinet, she switched the coffeemaker off and poured them each a full cup. "What are you talking about?"

Amelia's jaw dropped. "You mean you don't *know*?"

A flair for the dramatic ran in the family.

Amelia reached for Elizabeth's laptop, plugged in and charging underneath the table. Opening it up, she turned it to face Elizabeth. "Your sister faced a little disappointment of her own last night."

It had been left on someone's MySpace profile. A row of party photos hovered at the top, the most prominent of a group of four similarly thin, pouty girls in raccoon eyeliner, skimpy slip dresses, and cropped shrugs. And there was Caroline in the middle, flashing peace signs as Brendan and another girl kissed in the background. The caption read: *home is where the heart is <3*.

Elizabeth gasped. "That asshole."

A little disappointment would have been a C on an exam, a meter running out early, a favorite bakery closed for the day. This was nothing short of a disaster of Armageddon proportions—cataclysmic and unbelievable.

That Brendan would hook up with another girl after the way he acted with Jane all summer was bad enough, but to do it with a girl who didn't even crack the Top 8 was even worse. At least let it be someone he actually cared about.

As Elizabeth scrolled through the rest of Caroline's profile, there were no other photos of the mystery girl, and little or nothing of Brendan and Caroline's time back in Hong Kong. If it weren't for the fact that she'd seen the proof herself, she wouldn't have believed it. After all of his sweet words and promises—promises, it seemed, that he never intended to keep—he turned out to be the worst kind of golden son: the unexpected disappointment.

Amelia's eyes lit with curiosity. "So you know him?" she said with deceptive calm.

Elizabeth sketched the details thinly: their meeting at Alexa's wedding, their sudden family friendship because of the community center, Brendan and Jane's hot and heavy summer, and the Lees' immediate return to Hong Kong. Amelia nodded and interjected with indignant noises when appropriate, sympathized with how Jane felt, but refused to assign blame.

"Boys your age don't need any help to be stupid," Amelia offered. "Trust your aunty."

Elizabeth grabbed a cruller from the fridge and shoved half of it into her mouth. "That's true for other people, but not for us. We're too good to suffer by accident."

Amelia handed her a napkin. "I think you're smart enough to know that what people say and what people do rarely turn out to be the same."

The bedroom door creaked open, Jane tiptoeing towards the bathroom in hungover silence.

Amelia shook her head as she watched her go. "Shame it didn't happen to *you*, LB. You'd find a way to laugh about it."

After all, nothing could be funnier than heartbreak.

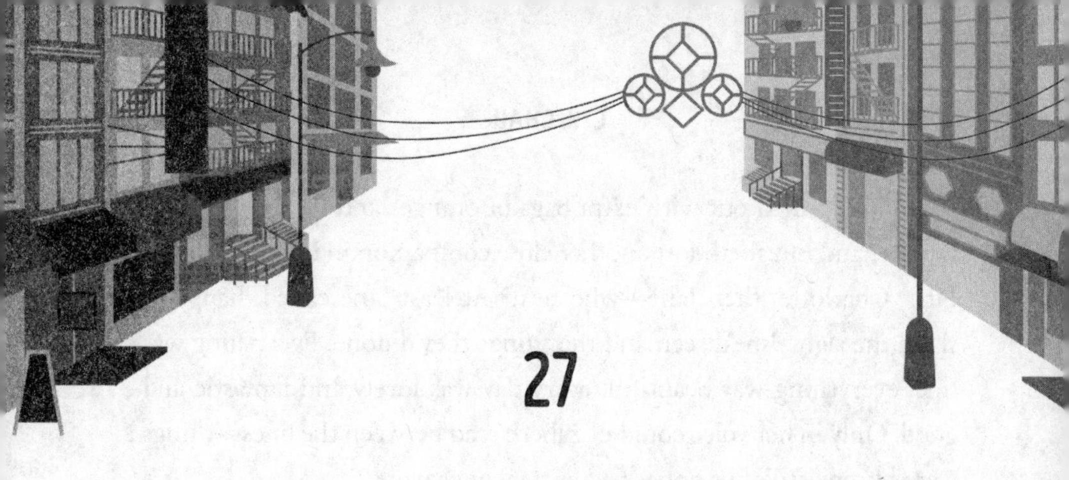

27

No one could get more done than a Chen in denial about her feelings. And, in the days after, Jane worked, Jane cleaned, Jane headed to the library early and stayed at Lulu's late, and never once acted as if anything had happened. She was perfectly fine, perfectly productive, perfectly Jane—even if she barely spoke to anyone or ate anything all day, and *Jagged Little Pill* mysteriously vanished from their shared CD holder.

Whatever Jane might be, it couldn't be called okay.

But there was no point in throwing away time on people who didn't matter, la, and any boy who couldn't see what a catch Jane was definitely didn't matter. And if Amelia couldn't bring the fight to Brendan, that only left them with flight. When the Kous left to return home to New England, they would be taking Jane along, whether she wanted it or not. Jade had no objection, Vincent had no opinion, and the girls were more than happy for more space in the apartment—in short, the Chens were agreed: Jane would go to Massachusetts and get her groove back, and everyone else would cope.

On a gray Sunday morning, they packed up their beat-up Honda sedan and pulled out with extra bags of oranges and lychee and little fanfare, and Elizabeth lost another close companion in under a month. First, Charlotte, then Jane—who next? At least Jane called, happy to share the sights she'd seen and the things they'd done. Everything was fine, everything was beautiful, every day was lovely and fantastic and good. Only in her voice could Elizabeth read between the lines—things were bumpy still, but not as bad as they once were.

And then the unthinkable happened.

A frantic call from Aunty Amelia: "Elizabeth, they're *here*."

They—the villains, Caroline and Brendan—and here, in Boston. Of course they'd needed to do the tourist attractions—what was the point of being a tourist otherwise, aa? historical tours, walking the Green, Harvard Yard—and they'd been window-shopping that day when they stopped at a store with knitted hats. ("Never buy hats, LB. All hat stalls are evil.") As the manager came and asked questions—"And you know Jane doesn't even wear *hats*," Amelia added—*Caroline* walked in.

Of course Brendan wasn't there, the two-timer, the bastard, the son of a bitch. (Amelia loved a swear.) Jane waved, Jane called out, but Caroline brushed her off as if she had no idea who she was. After a second try and a third, Caroline finally stopped and turned to apologize for not being in touch, but she'd been *so* busy and didn't she know that they were scouting new locations for Peony Plum in Boston?

"Brendan's been up to his neck in work," Caroline said. "And every spare second he has, he's with Genevieve." ("And that's how she pronounced it too," Amelia clucked. "*John*-vee-ev. Can you believe it?")

Elizabeth would sooner believe that Caroline decided to give it all up and join the Peace Corps.

Jane asked after her family and her work, but Caroline gave her nothing. Not even one-word answers. They just didn't have time, she said, but they missed her terribly. They thought of her endlessly. They didn't know when they might find themselves back in New York, but whenever they could, they would be sure to visit their good friends. They promised. They swore. They would be in touch.

A few days passed—and nothing.

"I'll kill her," Elizabeth said.

"But wait," Amelia added. "There's more."

The more—that they ran into each other *again* at yum cha because Chinese American circles crowd close together, especially in the Northeast, and Caroline couldn't be bothered to pretend that they knew each other at all. She walked into the dining room without a single glance of acknowledgment.

Elizabeth repeated with greater intent, "I'll. Kill. Her." If she hadn't been prone to dislike and distrust Caroline before, this would have sealed it. How dare anyone treat Jane this way. How dare anyone hurt her sister, the kindest and most generous soul who ever lived. If Brendan had been thoughtless and inconsiderate, this was nothing short of cruel.

Jane reported later, breezily, easily, "It was fine."

And if anyone believed that, the Tappan Zee was for sale.

"I know you, Jane. I can hear when you're lying."

"It's *fine*."

"Jane."

"He never said that we were . . . anything," she said. "He got a little flirty at a few parties, that's all."

She huffed. "Don't let him off the hook like that. He led you on and he played with your feelings."

"I thought it was more serious than it was," Jane admitted. "Caroline tried to warn me. She said he had a whole on-again, off-again—"

"Please, this is what Caroline wanted," Elizabeth replied. "She's never liked us."

"LB, stop it," she said. "If this was what he wanted, they wouldn't have been able to change his mind."

"They don't care about what he wants. They care if he's well connected. You saw how they were at Alexa's wedding."

Jane wouldn't hear it. It must have been something she said, something she did. "There's nobody to blame."

No, there were plenty of people to blame—and they all happened to be related.

"It doesn't matter," Jane said. "Caroline said they're probably not coming back to New York for a while."

"Good," Elizabeth said. "I can't think of a bigger group of snakes."

"LB, please."

"He treated you like shit, Jane. He doesn't deserve you."

"He didn't *do* anything to me, LB."

Elizabeth scoffed. "Yes, he did," she said. "Don't let him get away with it. You're a *human being*, not a consolation prize."

Said one consolation prize to the other. Not that Jane needed to know about it.

In the last few weeks, Elizabeth had seen little of Ray and heard even less. She blamed the usual suspects: a new job, friends, volunteering, school, homework. She blamed Lydia's five-hour monopolies on the internet modem and her sister's nightly telephone heart-to-hearts with every boy in a ten mile radius. She even blamed Darcy and her own cosmic luck. It wasn't until she caught sight of him on the opposite platform at West Fourth, lip-to-lip with a willowy blond, that she got the message.

It would have been worse if they'd been further along, but it had been early if it had been anything; it was like waking up from a schoolyard crush. No harm, no foul, pride goeth before the fall—and there was no point in competing with a girl with a real Chanel bag and Coach sunglasses, no matter how seamless the Canal Street knockoff. She couldn't fault him for believing in trickle-down economics.

All she could do was ready her pitch for the next buyer. *Real designer, luxury, authentic!*

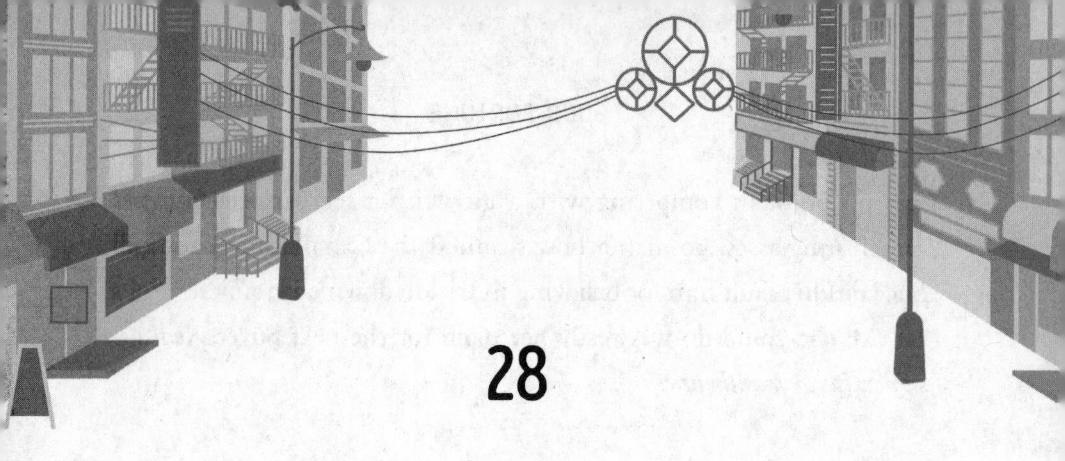

28

The key to pleasing parents was the same as writing a good apartment listing: lying through the teeth. Nothing could be said that couldn't also be spun, and the heavier the spin, the better. Elizabeth hadn't turned down a paying job but focused on a broader array of opportunities. She wasn't still living at home and annoying her mother but forging her own way through the world and supporting her family. Her string of short-term, part-time, entry-level jobs wasn't aimless and undisciplined but a diversification of her skills.

In the weeks since Charlotte's departure, the neighborhood dutifully reported every juicy tidbit and rumor that filtered through from the Luos and the Cheungs and Geoffrey, and the dozens of people between them who'd listened, adapted, and passed on the message. Hadn't they heard, aa, that Rosings didn't just put Charlotte up in company housing but gave her a house of her own? How incredible! How blessed! And didn't they know how much Charlotte's bosses loved her, aa, always trying to help her? Fast track, la! Most definitely!

Jade relished each new miserable piece of information, logging it as another exhibit in her ongoing trial against Elizabeth. That could have been her house, her job, her shortcut to success—and instead, where was she? At home, burning a hole in the sofa. What did she have to say for herself, after hearing how well her friend was doing?

Nothing.

Nothing that she would admit to Jade, anyway.

Because no matter how she tried to spin it, a small part of her wondered if her mother hadn't been right. As rare an occurrence as finding loose change in the pay phone, but not impossible. Maybe she should have held her tongue and gone along with what she'd been told. Maybe she would have been—not better off (that stretched the limits of her imagination)—not miserable. And maybe that could have been enough for her life—to not be miserable. The best future the Chens could hope for.

At least she still had Sammy's and the darkroom.

At least Charlotte called, happy to ask about the rec and the neighborhood as much as talk about her new job.

When Charlotte arranged for her father and sister to come out for a visit—on Rosings's dime, of course—she snuck in an extra ticket for Elizabeth. Would she come?

How soon could she leave?

Charlotte's property listed itself as a *hideaway gem*, *close to downtown Philadelphia*. Elizabeth could speak Realtor: it was nowhere near. It sat in a cul-de-sac about forty-five minutes from the city, a small single-level house styled at the peak of 1970s taste with aluminum siding and a driveway overgrown with weeds. Wind chimes hung from the awning over the porch beside a neglected bird feeder. One of the digits was missing from the house number, though whether stolen or broken, no one knew. It was the very model of a modern fixer-upper.

"*This* is where you're staying?" Mariah said as they pulled up in front of the house. All of fourteen, she showed the social graces of one a few years younger.

Charlotte glanced at her sister in the rearview mirror. "For now."

"I thought you were working for some big-shot company," Mariah said. "They couldn't put you somewhere nice?"

Charlotte smiled. "There's a mall nearby."

Mariah scoffed. "Great. A *mall*."

"And I'm not *that* far from downtown. We can go to Chinatown while you're here, if you want."

"No, thank you," Mariah said. "I didn't come from Chinatown to go to Chinatown."

Inside, Elizabeth called Vincent with a status update in the hopes of dodging more of Jade's helpful reminders or casual threats—arrived alive, met Charlotte, no problems—before joining Charlotte's grand tour: a pull-out bed in the sofa and a futon in the spare room, a coffee table adorned with a single scented candle, and a desk bearing an old telephone and a beaten-up laptop. The walls were old wood paneling, the carpet as downtrodden as the other houses on the block, the screen door's latch broken and temperamental, and all the drains slow. But there was no denying it had its charms—like the thin grass starting to grow on the bare lawn, and its being a hundred miles from the nearest Jade Chen.

They brought in their luggage and Charlotte's groceries from the car in waves, running in and out of her house in an awkward relay. An answering machine perched on a pile of shoeboxes in the middle of the hallway blinked at them.

As Leonard dragged their luggage into the spare room, Elizabeth and Charlotte unpacked the groceries in the small kitchen.

On one side of the room sat a dingy Kenmore refrigerator, a short row of Formica countertops, and a single sink; on the opposite side, a round wooden table and cheap metal folding chairs. Postcards sat taped on the wall, a few photos pinned to the refrigerator with fruit-shaped magnets. One, taken at Elizabeth's twentieth birthday party, showed the two of them pink with liquor, arms thrown around each other. That night, they had made so many promises to each other that Elizabeth couldn't remember half of them. And now Charlotte, tempted by money and security, couldn't be farther from that rooftop, or their city. A price she'd agreed to pay for moving on up and out—even if it was just to Scranton.

Charlotte bumped the fridge door shut. "What are you doing, looking at yourself, you weirdo?"

The piercing squeal of a phone interrupted.

Charlotte pulled a small silver phone from the loop of her belt and flicked it open. "Hello?"

Elizabeth whistled.

"Yes, they just got in," she said. "No, I didn't see—yes, don't worry. I will. Geoffrey, I just told you . . ."

Charlotte drifted into the hallway, voice fading as she tried to get a word in, and Elizabeth turned to the cabinets in search of a rice cooker. Pulling one out from underneath the counter, she shoveled a few cups of dry rice into the bowl to wash.

For all the trouble Charlotte took to arrange their tickets and pick them up, the least Elizabeth could do was manage to start dinner.

After a few more forceful reassurances, Charlotte returned to the kitchen, snapping the phone shut without a goodbye.

"You really must be important," Elizabeth said, shutting the lid on the cooker and switching it on.

Mariah screeched from the hallway, dissolving into tones only dogs could hear. "No way! They gave you a *cell* phone?"

Leonard patted her on the shoulder. "See what you get when you do well in school and get a nice job?"

Charlotte marched past them into the hallway and hit the machine.

A familiar voice crackled through, nearly blasting out the speakers.

"Charlotte," the voice barked. "This is Catherine Cheung. Geoffrey's informed me that your family are scheduled to arrive on the evening bus from New York. If you had the consideration to inform me ahead of time, I might have made a great many recommendations of places to go and things to see. I've been told that I have outstanding taste where these things are concerned, and I'm sure that your family could have benefited greatly from seeing the truly impressive sights . . ."

Elizabeth marveled at how long she seemed to speak without a single breath. What she had left on the machine wasn't a message but oratory—recommendations and advice and reminders on everything from paint brands to what kinds of furniture she might be able to pick up from the junk company Rosings used for evictions. ("Great deals, I assure you," Catherine insisted. "And not a single instance of infestation to date.") Elizabeth was only surprised she hadn't thought to remind Charlotte to brush her teeth and lock the door whenever she left the house—though, of course, she *had* run out of tape.

On the second message, Catherine had much less to say. "You must come to dinner with me. All of you. I insist upon it. A car has been called to pick you up at six. It will be rather relaxed—but no sandals. The last thing anyone needs to see before eating is a bare toe." After a pause, she added, "And do tell Miss Elizabeth how eagerly I await speaking with her."

She'd been called into the principal's office enough times to know a summons when she heard one.

Charlotte deleted the messages with a curious glance in her direction. "I'm sure she just wants to get to know you."

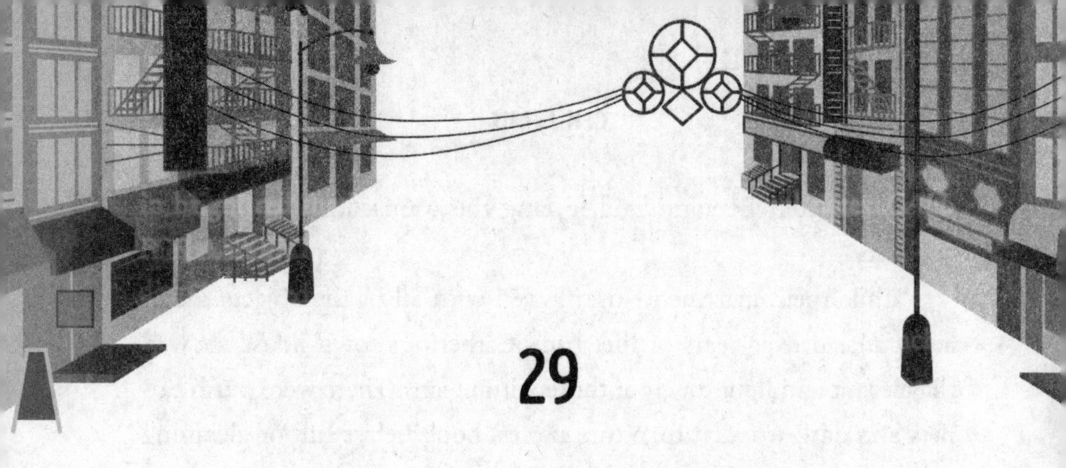

29

Elizabeth didn't know what she had expected—a Chinese banquet hall, perhaps, something traditional, something stuffy, where a golden-brown, perfectly roasted duck might appear center stage—but they didn't stop in Chinatown at all. They drove through it and kept going until they reached a historic-looking town house on a quiet street where Geoffrey met them at the door with an elaborate ritual of formal bows.

Charlotte made the introductions. "Geoffrey, this is my father, Leonard, and my sister, Mariah."

Mariah lifted a hand in a silent wave.

"Oh dear," he said. "Didn't anyone tell you there was a dress code?"

Mariah, dressed in her Delia's best in platform Mary Janes, flushed bright red.

Geoffrey waved it off. "I'm sure Lady Catherine will understand," he said. "She can be quite forgiving of travel difficulties. There's nothing she detests worse than travel."

With a flourish, Geoffrey pulled a small ring of keys from his belt and opened the front door to let them inside.

"Charlotte," Leonard said, eyeing the wainscoting. "This is incredible."

While their apartments overflowed with all of the objects they'd accumulated over years of life, Lady Catherine's town house showed the elegant and light touch of those with means. There were plush carpets and dark wooden furniture pieces, bookshelves full of gleaming volumes of books in English and Chinese, and an assortment of different styles of art hanging on the walls, including several oversize oil paintings of the lady herself. Nothing looked out of place, and nothing looked used; it was a living mausoleum.

Geoffrey preened. "Lady Catherine has the most excellent taste in everything. You won't be disappointed."

They proceeded up to the fourth floor of the house, where a large dining room awaited them, a round table outfitted with place cards for each seat. Elizabeth found herself seated between Leonard and someone else named Anita.

And then they waited.

At exactly six, Lady Catherine made her entrance, swathed in white fur and covered in tasteful jewels. She looked slim to sharpness and older than Elizabeth had expected. Deep streaks of gray twined through her dark hair, and she moved with the slightest duck waddle on the arm of her daughter, Anita. Anita could have been in her thirties if she looked the part, but she drowned in a burgundy evening gown, a pair of thin gold spectacles hung on the end of her nose, and she looked twice that. Elizabeth spied more than a passing resemblance to the Wongs. It was a sullenness of manner, an awareness of their own distinction, an enormous stick up the ass. Their family heirloom.

Geoffrey scrambled to present himself, clasping Catherine's hand in his own. "Ma'am."

And with that, they took their seats.

It turned out that the Rt. Hon. Lady Catherine Cheung was not only a real estate maven and expert in nearly every subject but a gourmand as well. The food was like nothing Elizabeth had ever tasted. There was a rack of lamb and roast chicken, radish salad, tureens of vegetables and potatoes, and a bottle of red wine that required extensive explanation of origin, none of which Elizabeth heard or understood. Leonard, who'd never had a drink in his life, sipped at his glass of wine with a clenched fist.

"The food is incredible, ma'am," Geoffrey said, serving her ahead of himself.

Catherine's lips thinned even further. "I'm glad to see that you enjoy it. Eat as much as you'd like. I'm sure this isn't something you can afford to sample at home."

Elizabeth straightened at the slight as Leonard thanked her repeatedly.

There was nothing they discussed that couldn't be reduced to a personal anecdote or a question of personal taste. Catherine lived and traveled extensively—by which she meant Hong Kong, Western Europe, and occasionally North America—and she understood it like no one else did. She was a PEZ dispenser of little judgments on everything from styles of fashion—"Juicy should never be used to describe anything except fruit, and even then, only on rare occasions"—to etiquette and technology. Britney was an abomination, supersizing the root of most evil, and low-rise pants—here, with a meaningful glance at Mariah—a crime against good taste. Nothing appealed to her because nothing had been chosen or done with her explicit approval.

"Charlotte," Catherine barked. "Have you finished unpacking?"

"I didn't bring much, ma'am, so there wasn't much to unpack."

Catherine dished a helping of green beans for herself with a hum of approval. "Very good, Charlotte. No one likes to contend with excess baggage from a guest. It presumes a long stay." Turning towards Mariah, she said, "And how are you getting on at school?"

Mariah slumped lower in her seat and shrugged.

"Don't slouch," Catherine scolded. "It makes you look like a pygmy. It would behoove you to acquire control of your spine."

Mariah flushed such a deep red that Elizabeth worried she might faint from the blood loss, but she inched her way back up to good posture.

"I've always educated my Anita about the benefits of an iron backbone."

"Yes, ma'am," Mariah mumbled.

"And Elizabeth, I must say I was surprised to hear that you aren't currently employed. Is that correct?"

Elizabeth took a sip of her water. "I'm working some odd jobs right now."

Catherine noisily gnawed on a piece of chicken. "You understand what I mean," she said. "Usually when people decline jobs offered, they have another role they've accepted. I demand an explanation."

"I don't think I owe you an explanation," Elizabeth said. At Charlotte's pleading look and Geoffrey's horrified one, she added, "It wasn't the right opportunity for me. I don't have the right experience . . ."

"Pah!" Catherine interjected. "This would have given you any experience you needed."

"And I didn't want to move far from my family."

Catherine sniffed. "How many are in your family?"

"I have four sisters," Elizabeth said. "And a father and a mother."

"Four?" Catherine trilled. "Good god. How do they feed you all?"

Elizabeth smiled tightly. "We manage a restaurant."

"And it feeds you?"

Elizabeth scraped the tines of her fork against her plate. "We work there."

Catherine squawked in shock. "All of you?" she said. "Like Dickensian orphans?"

"We sometimes let the younger kids out for air."

Catherine shook her head. "It doesn't do for girls your age to be stewing in all of that grease," she said. "It ruins the skin. It ages you. I made sure that Anita stayed far away from those sorts of things."

"You had the means to make sure that was possible."

"Of course," Catherine said. "It's the duty and responsibility of parents to provide for their children, and to avoid *having* children if they can't afford to do so."

Elizabeth speared a piece of chicken.

"Where are your parents from?"

"China," Elizabeth said.

"*Where* in China?"

This was turning out to be a pop quiz—one she was doomed to fail.

"Uh," Elizabeth replied. "My mother's from Hong Kong, and my father's from Guangdong, I think."

Catherine nodded. "And what did their parents do?"

Elizabeth shrugged. "I don't know," she said. "We don't talk about it."

Catherine looked her over with a decisive nod. "Tradespeople."

In the eyes of the Wongs and the Cheungs, nothing could be worse, but Elizabeth considered herself the next in a long line of people who worked to get by. Nothing glamorous, nothing monumental—just enough to build a life.

Charlotte cleared her throat. "This dinner is delicious, Lady Catherine."

Catherine clicked her tongue with disapproval. "If I had known your mother when this happened, I would have given her the most useful advice on what to do with you all. Discipline, that's what you needed."

Elizabeth perked a smile. "I find that there's lots you can learn on the streets of the city that you'd have trouble learning elsewhere."

Catherine harrumphed, giving her the stink eye over the platter of green beans. "You're very free with your opinions," she said. "Rather direct."

Geoffrey leaned towards her. "Very typical attitude in New York, ma'am."

Catherine batted him away. "Yes, I've heard. I suppose this is why people don't like it very much."

Elizabeth wiped at her mouth. "We like it fine."

Slurping the last of the sauce off of her fork, she arched a single eyebrow. "My nephew had a terrible time there," she said. "He said it was far too noisy. Distracting."

Elizabeth wrinkled her brow in confusion. "Your nephew?"

"Darcy Wong."

Elizabeth choked down a sip of her water.

Catherine preened. "So you know him."

"We've run into each other."

Catherine nodded. "He didn't much like it when he visited."

"The city's not for everyone," Elizabeth replied. "Like cruise ships."

Catherine sniffed, aghast. "I certainly would *never* go on a cruise. You meet the most abject people on cruises."

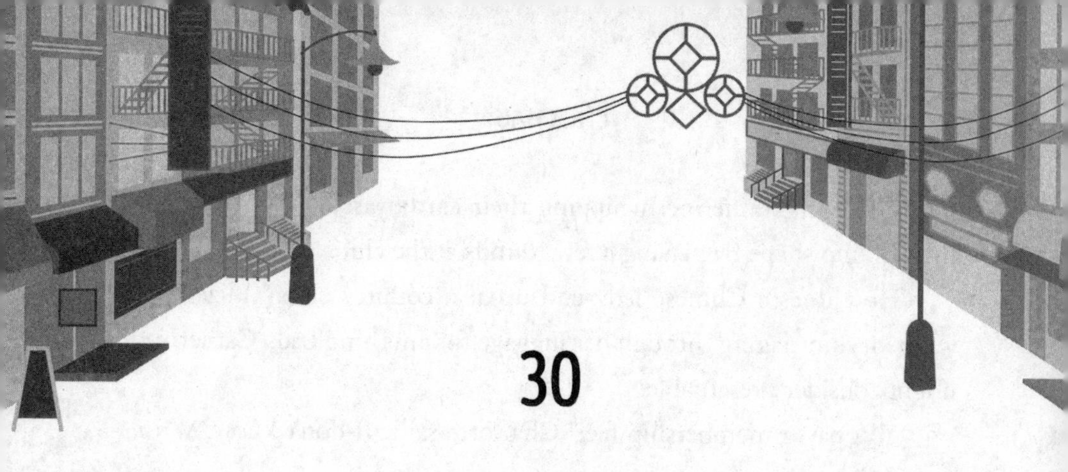

30

Elizabeth learned quickly how seriously Catherine undertook the task of supervising her employees. Like a warden at the prison, she checked in often with dinners and surprise visits, graded every aspect of their stay and their lives, and recommended solutions constantly. She chided Elizabeth on the lack of arch supports in her sneakers and clucked over the sag in Mariah's jeans—"The Gap is the name of the store, not instructions for use"—and argued that Leonard's eyeglasses prescription couldn't be accurate. She insisted on light activity after eating to assist digestion, which she considered the key to all health and happiness in life, and would tolerate no stragglers. Between Jade's frantic calls panicking about a recent notice from the health department ("What does it mean, 'come in compliance'? We have to pay?"), Mariah's daily litany of grievances about their stay, and Lady Catherine's endless check-ins by call, text, and in-person visit, Elizabeth started to feel less like a visitor and more like someone reporting for parole.

Of course, on a sunny weekend morning, none of them could be allowed the luxury of sleeping past seven. They would be spending the morning with Catherine, whipping their cardiovascular systems and their qi into shape by playing a few rounds at the club.

"How does a Chinese lady end up at a country club?" Elizabeth whined, rummaging through her luggage for anything Lady Catherine might consider presentable.

"You pay a membership fee," Charlotte said. "I don't know. Why would I know?"

Elizabeth, having packed nothing for the trip but jeans and inappropriate graphic T-shirts, borrowed a pair of Charlotte's bike shorts for the occasion. "Are you sure they're even going to let me in?" she said, eyeing herself in the mirror. "Aren't women supposed to wear heels and skirts?"

"That would make it hard to golf," Charlotte said.

Elizabeth winced. "Don't tell me you *golf* now like some divorced dad from New Jersey."

Charlotte rolled her eyes. "For all the shit you talk about Lydia, if you stopped being dramatic for one day, your head would fall off."

"You didn't answer the question."

"They're not going to kick you out, you baby," she said. "You might get some looks, but you'd probably get that anyway, what with your sunny disposition and all. And no, I do not *golf* now."

Lady Catherine's car dispatched them directly to the Astor Regency, which turned out to be one of *those* country clubs that prided themselves on their history of tradition and excellence, which meant keeping in with a certain kind of clientele and keeping out everyone else. Upon seeing her outfit, Catherine greeted her with a look of stern disapproval and insisted that she purchase appropriate wear at the club store.

"As my guests, you will be a reflection upon me," she tutted. "So you might try to seem presentable."

It was gym class all over again, ill-fitting uniforms and all.

Elizabeth glanced at the price tag of her new skirt and shook her head. "You can't buy this for me," she said. "That's ridiculous."

"What's ridiculous is you being refused entry because you aren't outfitted properly," Catherine said.

"I can't repay you for this," she said.

"Did you hear anyone ask you for repayment?"

"That isn't right," she said. "This is . . ."

"You're hardly the only one," Catherine said, gesturing towards Mariah, who tried to hide behind a racket display. "It will have to be an entire family affair."

"No shirt, no shoes, no service, Elizabeth," Geoffrey said. "The first rule of hospitality."

Elizabeth gritted her teeth. "Thank you, Geoff."

Nothing would move Lady Catherine from her position. At least Elizabeth managed to keep her own sneakers despite their being "absolutely inappropriate in the club." Walking out of the fitting room with the tags already trimmed off, she wore a new white tennis dress emblazoned with the club's logo, her hair pulled into a tight ponytail and covered with a thin visor. Glancing at herself in the mirror, she cringed. She looked like another prep school asshole.

Catherine practically beamed. "You look—well, except the shoes—rather put together."

It was the closest thing to a compliment she might expect.

Shooing her outside, Lady Catherine turned to her next victim—Mariah.

"Won't they accuse me of shoplifting if I walk out?"

Catherine heaved an exasperated sigh. "Charlotte, please," she said. "I can only manage one child at a time."

"Please don't leave me," Mariah whimpered.

"You'll be fine," Charlotte said, dropping an arm around Elizabeth's shoulders and leading her out.

Elizabeth baked under the morning sun, trying to think of how she could get out of having to golf in front of other people. The only golf she'd ever done was mini, and that had been during the height of Lydia's laser-tag addiction.

Charlotte slathered her bare arms in sunscreen.

"You think Mariah will make it out alive?"

Charlotte slapped her arm. "Please," she said. "She's not that bad."

Elizabeth scraped excess sunscreen off Charlotte's hand. "You didn't answer the question." Closing her eyes, she applied it to her face, slowly working it in.

"Oh my god."

Charlotte's voice had screeched up an octave.

"Char, what the fuck?"

"Charlotte. Hello."

Elizabeth froze.

The voice, she recognized—though she didn't trust what she'd heard. The last place he would've wanted to be was anywhere near this part of the world. Anywhere near her.

"Elizabeth."

She lowered her hands from her eyes. "Darcy."

For once, he looked relatively normal, dressed down in a white T-shirt and navy athletic shorts, a duffel bag slung over one shoulder. A pair of square black sunglasses almost made him look stylish. "You're the last person I'd expect to see at a country club."

She scowled. "I thought you were halfway around the world."

"Obviously not."

"Right," she said. "Okay."

A man beside him slapped him hard on the back. "No manners," he said, extending a hand. "I'm Cas." He looked older than them by a few years, if in better shape. His arms and legs flexed with bands of muscle, his skin glowing a deep copper in the daylight. A small cluster of pockmarks and a half-moon scar textured the lower section of his right cheek, and a diamond stud glittered in one ear. Lydia would have needed six weeks to recover from the warm growl of his voice, low and rich and English.

She took his hand. "Elizabeth."

Lady Catherine burst out of the store, dragging a chastened Mariah behind her. "They're horribly inefficient," she said, by way of greeting. "Oh, Darcy, Caspian, I was wondering when you'd get here."

Elizabeth stared. "Caspian?"

He shook his head. "Cas."

"Hello, Aunty," Darcy said.

"Aunty," Cas echoed.

Catherine clicked her tongue with irritation. "Caspian, why are you always dressed like a vagrant?"

He grinned. "That's just how I look, Aunty."

"Yes, that's precisely my problem," Catherine sighed, donning a thin pair of sunglasses. "Boys, do help your cousin with her clubs. You know how Anita struggles."

With that, she pushed ahead down one of the trails.

"Carpe diem!" she cried. "Time and tide, boys."

Darcy and Cas hoisted several bags of sports equipment between them and ran after her.

Charlotte swung her bag over her shoulder as the others followed behind them. "Looks like someone made a special trip just to see you."

She scoffed. "Oh, please. He just . . ."

Charlotte batted her eyes innocently. "Came running to aunty as soon as he heard you were here? Such a dutiful boy, aa."

Elizabeth swatted her lightly. "Please get a reality check."

"I'm not so sure I'm the one who needs it."

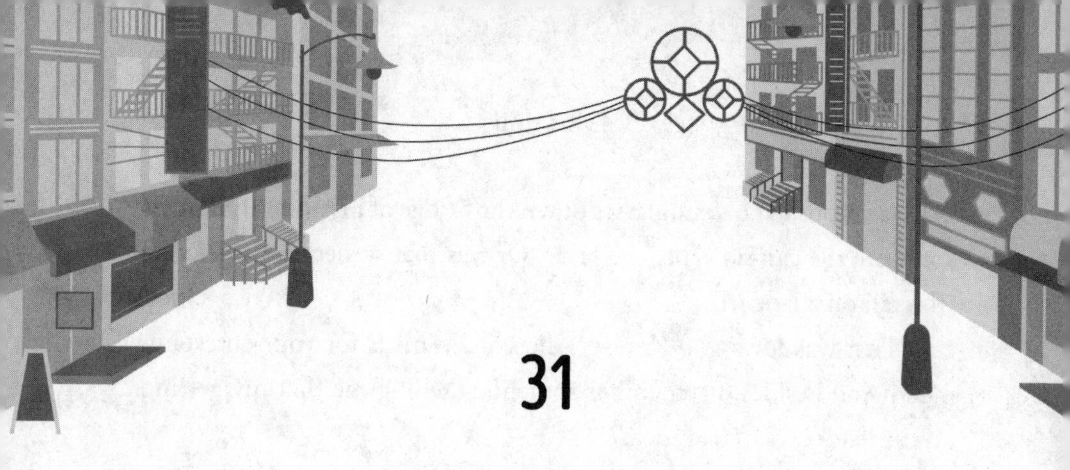

31

Golf was one thing—boring, embarrassing, and full of rules she didn't know or understand—but tennis was another. Tennis involved running, sweating, *exertion*. Tennis demanded a baseline effort. Catherine considered herself beyond the age of playing herself but was more than happy to assign herself the position of line judge. Barking for a staff member to shield her from the sun with a large golf umbrella, she positioned herself on the sideline as they fanned out around the court.

If Elizabeth hoped her crossing to the opposite side would put some distance between herself and the others, she was mistaken. Darcy followed, tossing his gym bag against the fence as he moved to sit beside her.

Catherine narrowed her eyes, tracking them with great interest. "Elizabeth!" she called. "Shall you take first?"

Elizabeth shook her head frantically. "I'm okay with watching for now." She'd come to Philadelphia to see Charlotte, not to subject herself to the agonies of a high school gym class. Changing into a uniform had been mortifying enough. The last thing she wanted was a public showing of her terrible hand-eye coordination.

Darcy pushed his sunglasses down the bridge of his nose. "I thought you were the can-do type," he said. "Or was that someone else I knew who fell off a ladder?"

"That was for a good cause," she said. "This is for your entertainment. And besides, I remember somebody telling me that my getting on the ladder was a bad idea."

When he smiled, it seemed almost genuine, almost as if he was trying to fight a laugh. But that was impossible. Darcy never laughed, and certainly never in open company. It was undignified. It was tawdry. It overexerted the face muscles.

"Anything for the rec, you mean," he said. "Up to and including public embarrassment."

It even sounded like he was trying to make small talk. With her!

Inconceivable!

No Wong could ever debase himself to associate with someone so uncouth and unserious, so lacking in motor skills, as Elizabeth. But maybe he'd finally given up on trying to change her. Maybe, like her mother, he'd learned that Elizabeth would never be anything other than Elizabeth, and resigned himself to the many, many problems of her personality. Because she couldn't hear a trace of the usual criticism or judgment in his voice, and she didn't see any signs of demonic possession.

"Darcy," Catherine called. "You're a *fair* player. Why don't you take the first?"

He fetched his racket and a few balls from his bag and walked onto the court. "Elizabeth?"

"Charlotte!" Catherine shouted. "I hear she rather enjoys the game."

Elizabeth cringed as Charlotte took the opposite corner point. "Good luck," she called. He would need it.

Cas stole Darcy's seat as soon as he left. "Hi."

She leaned back against the fence, ignoring Darcy's curious glance in their direction. "Won't we be yelled at for talking?"

Cas winked at her. "Don't worry. I'll protect you."

It didn't take long for him to reveal his true motives. He wanted to know everything about her. How long she had been in town, what her plans were, how she knew their aunt Catherine. Like Darcy, he also spoke with an accent, though theirs sounded nothing alike. Darcy's floated smooth through his sentences, even in cadence and tone, while Cas undulated through beats and pitches, rising and falling as Chinese did.

Caspian glanced at her out of the corner of his eye. "You're not the kind of person I'd ever expect to see around my aunt. Or Darcy."

She laughed. "I'm Charlotte's friend."

On the court, Charlotte served with a loud grunt, sending the ball into the center of the court.

Darcy flailed as he ran after it, lobbing a soft return.

It arced high into the air, dropping near the baseline where she beat it back for an easy point.

Elizabeth whooped cheers from the sideline, earning herself a glare from both aunt and nephew. The resemblance was uncanny.

"Fifteen-love, Darcy," Catherine said. "Look sharp."

Darcy swore under his breath.

Elizabeth tucked her chin against her raised knees. "I think we're talking too loud."

"You're practically whispering," Cas said.

"They're looking at us."

Darcy retreated to the corner for the next serve.

"You're not invisible."

Cas shook his head. "So how do you two know each other? Are you in real estate too?"

Darcy turned towards them, halfway to responding when Charlotte and Catherine both shouted for him to take his position.

"I'm from the other side of things, the community advocacy side," she said. "He invested in an old community center on my block. That's how we met."

"When we came for Bryan's wedding," Darcy gasped, knocking back a volley.

Caspian waved him off. "Wasn't asking you."

Elizabeth turned back to the game.

Charlotte barely broke a sweat as she ran from one end to the other, whipping back returns. By the sound of Darcy's heavy breathing and the squeal of his shoes, he could barely keep up.

"And you work for the center?"

"No," Darcy huffed, smashing the tennis ball directly into the net. "She just thinks she does."

All of that money and equipment and time, and he still didn't have the skill to best Charlotte. Wasn't that a shame?

"Poor form, Darcy," Catherine chided. "Your focus was lacking."

Darcy panted for breath, dripping sweat against the court as he eyed her and Cas along the fence. He looked miserable, pink-faced and twitchy with irritation.

Cas clapped her on the shoulder. "Well, anything that gives Darce a pain in the ass is all right by me."

"Darcy!" Catherine shouted. "Did you hear me?"

He waved his arm. "I'm fine, Aunt!"

"Good! The last thing we need is for you to be dragged off the premises like some dozy housewife."

Charlotte ran up to the net and waved her racket at him, checking to see if he could still move.

"How are you doing, Darcy?"

He grimaced as he climbed back to standing, swearing under his breath. "Good, good. You've got . . . tremendous footwork. Very . . . nimble."

Charlotte chuckled.

"So what do you do?" Elizabeth asked. "Besides wait for an inheritance?"

Cas laughed, a warm and booming noise. "Not much of an inheritance," he said. "That's for the current wife and kids—not the former."

"It's not so bad, working for a living," she said. "I promise."

Slowly, Darcy moved back towards the line. It was almost unsettling how his eyes seemed to track them no matter his position on the court. Blaming them for his eventual loss, she assumed. For talking too loud or blocking his light, or being there in the first place. For daring to get acquainted without him.

"I haven't been doing much of anything at all," Cas said. "I'm taking some time to sort my head out."

"I get it. It's hard enough trying to figure out what you want to do without people breathing down your neck."

"Much wisdom you have," Cas croaked in a Yoda voice, "young Padawan."

She shoved him lightly. "Nerd."

Charlotte launched another rocket of a serve, and Darcy whiffed the ball as it bounced out.

"*Forty-fifteen*, Darcy," Catherine said. "You are at *game point*."

"Thank you, Aunt," he forced out, swiping at his forehead with his arm and limping back into place on the line.

Elizabeth almost felt bad.

On the last serve, he made one last desperate push, racing for the sideline and swinging hard at a return.

Cas clicked his tongue as the ball slammed into the net. "That's game."

Darcy rattled the fence as he pried himself off.

Elizabeth tried—and failed, if his answering look was any clue—to hide her laugh.

"Please don't let me interrupt."

Catherine clucked. "What *are* you talking about over there, Caspian?"

"The Spice Girls."

"What?" Catherine howled.

"Nothing!" he cried.

Catherine crooked a finger and beckoned them over. "Have some backbone, Caspian! That looks like a lot of chatter for nothing."

Caspian approached the sideline where Catherine sat in a plastic folding chair, hidden from the sun beneath a wide umbrella. Small circular sunglasses sat on her nose. "I was telling Elizabeth about my difficulties in finding work."

Catherine huffed. "Birds of a feather! Though I'm sure you wouldn't do anything so foolish as to decline an opportunity without any other offer." She fanned herself with furious effort. "I must say, Charlotte is performing exceptionally."

"It wasn't the right fit for me."

Catherine gave a dry laugh. "You thought it beneath you."

In situations like these, she'd learned long ago that the best answer was to say nothing at all. Let Lady Catherine draw her own conclusions.

"Of course she turned it down," Darcy said simply.

Four heads turned to stare at him.

"Elizabeth can only ever agree to things when they suit her sense of justice in the world."

Cas clucked with affected concern. "How awful."

Something, Elizabeth thought, staring at Darcy, had gone terribly wrong. The condescending, silent, and stuffy party guest she'd once met had been replaced with someone else entirely—someone who made jokes, who moved with ease through the conversation, who only mildly criticized. Someone almost normal.

"Who's next?" Darcy said with an idle swing of his racket.

"Elizabeth, you play," Catherine said with a sly smile. "How's that for justice?"

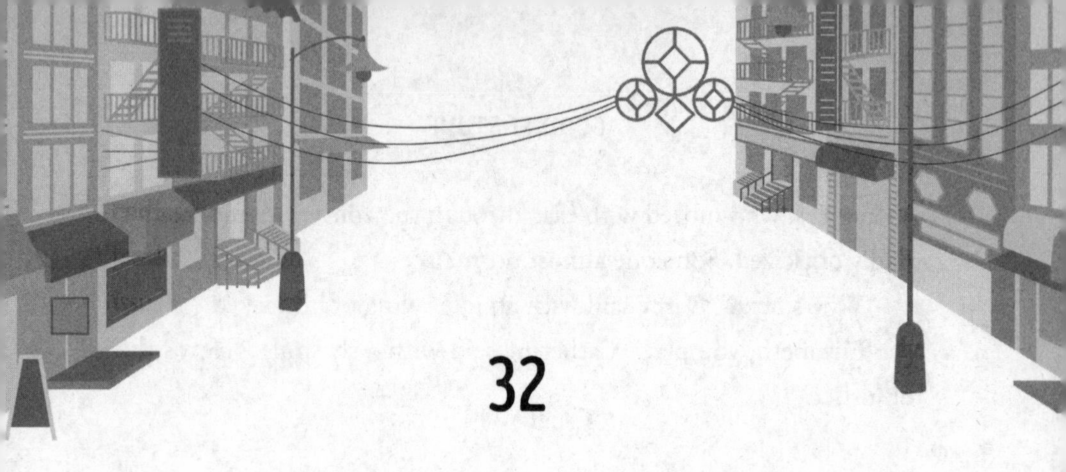

32

Forcing her to play against Charlotte qualified as a crime against humanity. But despite her many pleas and complaints, despite her years of avoiding gym class and her monastic devotion to a sedentary and nonathletic lifestyle, neither Catherine nor Charlotte would accept her refusal to play.

Elizabeth retreated into position on the court with her head hanging.

Darcy took her vacated seat by the fence, wrestling a water bottle out of his bag.

"Please remember that I barely know the rules."

Charlotte cackled. "You're not going to get a pity win out of me, LB."

In one quick serve, the ball struck the corner of the court, pinging with force against the fence as Elizabeth ducked for cover. "What happened to taking it easy?"

Charlotte yanked her ponytail tighter. "That was a baby serve, Chen," she said. "Wake up."

Elizabeth raised her racket in threat. "If you hit a ball in my face, I'm going to kill you."

"If I hit a ball in your face, your anger is going to be the least of your problems."

Catherine tapped her fan against the edge of her seat. "Unsportsmanlike! Unsportsmanlike!"

Charlotte tossed the ball and served again, and this time, Elizabeth stepped up to bat and swung for a return—and missed. The ball sailed behind her to earn another easy point. Darcy audibly scoffed.

Elizabeth trailed after the ball as it rolled to the edge of the fence, shooting Darcy a wary look as she picked it up and tucked it in her pocket. "If you're trying to scare me, it's not going to work."

Darcy squeezed water over the top of his head. "Why would I want to scare you?"

"Psych me out."

He shrugged, leaning back against the fence. Water soaked into his clothes, the fabric of his T-shirt clinging to the hard lines of his chest and shoulders. "I think you're losing fine on your own."

She scoffed, giving the racket another light swing as Charlotte fired obscene gestures at her from across the court.

"Believe it or not," he called, "I don't spend the bulk of my days plotting for your downfall. If anything, I have a great deal of respect for you."

Elizabeth tripped against the court. "Excuse me?"

He drained another gulp of water. "I don't think your decisions are very sound, but that doesn't mean I don't respect the sense of principle behind them."

An occasional wisecrack, a one-off compliment—strange and unexpected, but something she could attribute to the environment. This was going too far. Somewhere, Ashton Kutcher was laughing into his trucker hat, waiting for her to throw a racket.

Charlotte flagged her with a wave of the arms. "Are we playing or what?"

She retreated to her corner with a grimace.

Cas whistled her on. "Go, Lizzie!"

"Not Lizzie!" she yelled.

Charlotte served a slice, sending the ball right against the line. Elizabeth swung hard, and the ball bounced and ricocheted off the rear fence.

"Forty-love," Catherine announced. "Miss Luo, you are turning out to be quite the surprise."

"*Lizzie*," Charlotte shouted. "You're not going to let me shut you out like this, are you?"

Elizabeth threw her a finger.

"Unsportsmanlike!" Lady Catherine bleated.

Before Charlotte could interject, Darcy waved his arms in a time-out motion, jogging towards Elizabeth on the court.

"This is unbelievable," Charlotte said. "Coaching is against the rules!"

"You might want to try hitting the ball," Darcy said.

What insights men could offer.

"Thank you. I had no idea that's what this racket was for."

The corner of his mouth curled but didn't quite lift in a smile. Looking as serious as ever, he circled her, assessing the stoop of her shoulders, the slouch of her hip, the distribution of her weight on her feet. He reached for her racket. "May I?"

She handed it over.

He dragged his fingers against the strings. "You shouldn't use a borrowed racket unless you have no choice."

"I don't play tennis."

"I can see that," he said, handing the racket back. "Show me how you hold it."

She gripped it loosely in her right hand. Subjecting herself to Lady

Catherine's scrutiny had been a necessary evil of the trip, but this was a lapse in sanity.

Across the court, Charlotte looked as if she was barely holding it together.

He wasn't even helping.

All he was doing was looking at her.

That was the problem.

He traced a line from the neck of the racket to the joint of her knuckle, touch featherlight against her skin.

"You want to adjust your grip for more balance," he said, spreading her fingers wider against the handle.

She exhaled. "That's definitely why I'm losing. My fingers."

He chuckled low in his throat. "They're certainly not helping. As for your other issues . . ."

She waved the racket. "Be nice to the girl holding a blunt object."

"I'm not afraid of you," he replied. He made another slow circle around her, pausing at her right shoulder. "Give it a swing."

"What?"

He retreated several steps as if remembering that she didn't like him. "Swing the racket."

She eyed him over her shoulder and circled it wide.

"May I?" he said.

She dropped her arm. "May you *what*?"

"Show you," he said. "Your form is terrible."

She cut another swing with the racket and he hopped to the side to avoid being struck. "How can you tell?" she said. "I haven't hit anything."

She could feel the faint heat of his body behind her as he stepped closer. The light scent of his cologne hung in the air. Subtle, and simpler than she would have expected from someone like him.

"May I?" he repeated.

She ignored the quick jump of her pulse in her throat. "Whatever."

His hand landed on her bare shoulder, thumb pushing against the divot of her neck to reset her posture. She expected something like the brute correction of the women who gave massages at the nail salon, but he was almost gentle. There was no trace of work in those hands, the fingers long and smooth, almost delicate. When he applied pressure, it was as gradual and slow as water building into a wave.

She squeaked, her neck arching back against his hand.

"Stop tensing," he said.

She might, if he didn't make her so tense. "Hurry up."

"Relax," he murmured. "Keep your neck flexible and you won't run the risk of injuring yourself."

He caught her right arm then, his hand trailing down her bare bicep to catch her elbow.

"Think of the racket as an extension of your arm," he said. He drew her elbow back in a wide arc. "The greater the range of motion, the more spin and power on the ball." With his hand on her arm, he led her through another simulated swing.

"This is big talk coming from someone who *also* lost to Charlotte Luo."

His hands ghosted her waist, the lightest pressure resetting the angle of her hips to correct her stance. "Always ground at center," he said.

Cas and Charlotte watched them with matching, manic smiles, and she felt a flush of heat in her cheeks.

Darcy only had eyes for her swing. "First, react," he said, steering her towards center. "Then think."

She shifted away from him, shaking her shoulders out. "Okay. Easy."

His hands yanked her shoulders back. Core muscles she hadn't considered in years jostled back awake. "And stand up straight."

"You sound like my mother."

"God forbid."

His hands lingered on her shoulders, solid and warm.

She shrugged him off. "If I don't take the shot, Charlotte will kill me."

He dropped his hands and stepped back to the fence.

"Are you ready now?" Charlotte cried. "*Lizzie*?"

"Go!"

Charlotte served, the ball cutting a sharp line down the center of the court. Elizabeth leapt forward, squaring her shoulders and strangling the racket between her hands as she swung. Racket connected with ball, force vibrating up her arms as she knocked it out of the park—the ball high and wide over the net, past the lines of the court to slam against the fence. Home run.

"Out," Catherine called. "Game—Charlotte."

"Elizabeth, I have to say, that was the most incredible game of tennis I've ever seen," Cas deadpanned, clapping his hands.

"You can't embarrass me," she said. "I know exactly how well I play. Expert help or not."

Darcy rubbed at the back of his neck.

"Now that you've humiliated yourself, tell me everything," Cas said, flinging a stray tennis ball at Darcy. "How horrible was he?"

Darcy chucked the ball into an open bag. "*Caspian*."

Caspian grinned. "Darce."

Elizabeth chugged a gulp of water. With a sly glance at Darcy, she said, "Do you want me to lie?"

He scoffed. "I wouldn't want you to compromise your principles."

"We met at a wedding."

"I thought you weren't going to lie."

Cas raised both eyebrows, looking between them.

Elizabeth took another gulp of water, pouring a splash of it down the back of her neck. "Well, we weren't introduced," she said. "But I heard about you. It counts."

Darcy shifted away from the fence. "What do you mean you heard about me?"

Cas waved him off. "So what happened?"

"What happened," she said, kicking at Darcy's impeccably white sneaker. "Did he get sloppy and dance badly like the rest of us? No. He never left the people he came with, didn't talk to anyone, and had a perfectly miserable time."

"Sounds like Darce."

"I didn't know anyone else!"

Elizabeth pouted. "Right, and no one can ever introduce you at a Chinese wedding where a third of the room is aunties."

"And what were you doing?" Darcy said. "I don't remember seeing you on the dance floor."

"You don't remember me at all."

He extended a hand to help her up. "I remember you," he said. "Your younger sisters were *very* drunk, and you kept trying to get them back to the table. One of them fell in a fern."

Ah, Lydia.

She pulled herself up to her feet in one quick movement. But he held on.

"Darcy!" Lady Catherine shouted.

Elizabeth slipped her hand free.

"Anita is growing tired, as am I. Our bags, please."

He sprinted towards the pile of sports equipment gathered on Lady Catherine's side of the court and took several bags on his shoulder.

"A shame Anita doesn't feel well," Lady Catherine said. "Her tennis game is rather impeccable."

Caspian followed after him, picking up two other bags. "You've got to learn to loosen up, cuz," he said.

Elizabeth caught up with them both, zipping a remaining bag shut and slinging it over her shoulder. "I should take you to the batting cages."

"You play baseball?" Darcy said.

"I hit things," she said. "It's therapeutic for me to hit things. You need to hit things."

Darcy reached to take her bag, but she dodged him, darting off to the side.

"I don't think that's the solution," he said.

"It's *a* solution."

"Only if you manage to actually hit them."

Elizabeth clicked her tongue. "Unsportsmanlike."

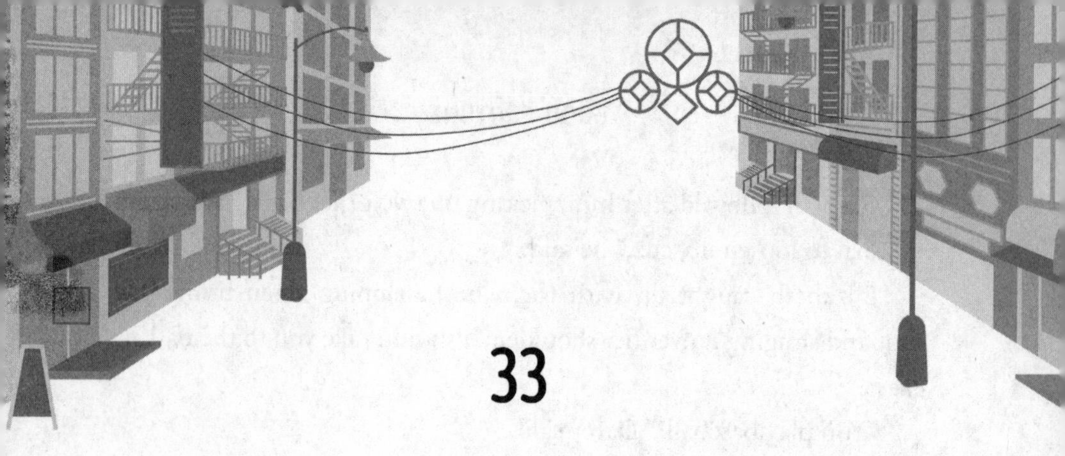

33

Elizabeth learned an afternoon of business at the club was nothing more than an excuse for a day off. Golf followed tennis, lunch followed golf, and then they headed for the spa. The spas she knew were the kinds that came with clip-art coupons and Comic Sans gift certificates, ratty massage chairs and nature sounds CDs. The spa at the club was no amateur hour Magic Fingers kiosk at the mall; this was a steam, a slap, and a soak in front of dozens of other naked older women. Undressing in front of Charlotte and Mariah would be bad enough, but Lady Catherine? Not without substantial compensation for the accompanying years of therapy.

"What can you mean by this?" Catherine said.

"I'm not the spa type," she said. "A walk will do me good."

Catherine looked her over. "It's always discouraging to see sensitivity in one so young," she clucked. "A weakness of the spleen, Miss Elizabeth."

Elizabeth nodded along. What could anyone do about their spleen?

Lady Catherine waved an admonishing finger in her face. "It's from all that grease," she said. "I'll refer you to my herbalist. She performs *miracles*."

By the sound of it, Catherine seemed to think she needed more than one kind of saving.

Charlotte took Catherine's hand and patted it lightly. "Let's go on ahead," she said. "Mariah and I will go with you."

"I suppose you'll wait for us here then? In *exactly* ninety minutes?"

She nodded.

"I do not *tolerate* lateness."

Elizabeth forced a smile. "I won't put myself in a position to be tolerated then."

As they set off in the direction of the spa facilities, Elizabeth took the path leading in the opposite direction. Being at the club was like stepping into a dream of a lawn commercial; green and rolling hills stretched out in every direction, surrounded by neat hedges and flower beds, with walking paths winding throughout the campus. She wound along the dining area, listening to the muffled noise of FM radio piped in over the PA system, and followed the edge of the course to a shaded grove where a few employees loitered and smoked, eyeing her with suspicion. To the rich went fresh air and nature and beautiful things; to the rest of them, the maintenance.

As she passed them, the path cut around the side of another building to a wraparound wooden deck, a few scattered chaises the only seats. Wide glass doors looked into a ballroom-type space, noisy with chatter and the clink of food service. Elizabeth walked up the side steps and onto the deck. It was pretty enough, she thought, looking out at the green. She could almost understand paying for it.

"Elizabeth."

Darcy, freshly changed into shorts and a T-shirt, walked up to join her. Gone was the easy demeanor of Darcy on the courts; this man looked itchy to be wearing anything that wasn't *at least* a polo. Here was the Darcy she recognized, at last—but instead of overwhelming relief, she felt only the slightest disappointment. She'd liked being surprised.

"I thought you would be with the others."

"The spa's not really my thing."

"Right," he said. He looked at her a moment, as if trying to decide if it would be ruder to stay or to go. After another pause, he added, "How has it been so far? Your stay?"

So it was either the baths with Lady Catherine or small talk with her nephew; it was the vacation that kept on giving. "We haven't had the chance to go out."

"Anything in particular you want to see?"

What was there in Pennsylvania? Cheesesteaks and the Amish? "I don't know. I came to see Char."

"Right."

At the rate they were going, they might get through another four pleasantries by the time the others finished.

She considered returning the favor, but everything she might ask felt off-limits, too dangerous to approach without third-party mediation. Who knew what they'd get up to without any supervision?

He leaned his arms against the balustrade. "Just because you came to see her, that doesn't mean you can't do something for yourself while you're here. Not everything has to be for the benefit of someone else."

She snorted. "You *would* say that." Sometimes she wondered if he understood what it meant to do anything unconditionally—to do something for the sake of someone else's happiness, someone else's pleasure, rather than any expected return.

He watched her out of the corner of his eye, looking wary.

Maybe it wasn't the right time to try to explain it.

In the last day or so, they'd managed to find some kind of equilibrium, enough to get along. She could wait to spoil that.

"I didn't know you were going to be here," she said.

He chuckled. "Or you wouldn't have come?"

She looked at him. "You and Brendan left so quickly after the gala, I figured that there was a lot to do."

"That's just Brendan," he said with an annoyed huff. Fond exasperation cut across his features, an expression so familiar that Elizabeth almost laughed at the resemblance to her mother.

"Places to go, people to see?" she said, keeping her tone neutral.

He met her gaze, his eyes narrowing as he tried to read her. "Something like that." Neither a confirmation nor a denial—and no sign of guilt.

"It doesn't seem like he plans on following through on anything that he promised."

Darcy's lips thinned into a line as he glanced back towards the sky. Now he had nothing to say.

"You're alike in that way."

He grunted. "I'm not his keeper."

"No, but he listens to you," she said. "He relies on you."

"A little too much," Darcy said. His arm brushed lightly against hers, a tease of a touch. His voice remained soft as he spoke, so quiet it felt as if she was listening in on a secret. "You should know better than anyone what that's like—to always need to come in and fix things, to be called to clean up the mess."

Was that how he saw Jane? The recreational center?

Her jaw tightened. "Is that what you think of us?"

He stammered for an answer. "No, of course—"

"After everything you said about the community, about investing in the people there, all that matters to you is the bottom line," she said. "Cleaning up Brendan's mess."

He gave a frustrated sigh. "That's not what I said, and you know it."

"So you aren't turning it into luxury condos and stores?" she said. "Geoffrey was wrong?"

Faint color spread in his cheeks.

She nodded. "That's what I thought."

"We can't just ignore the financial realities because it makes us feel better . . ."

She rolled her eyes. "Right, we have no idea what it means to live with financial realities . . ."

"Some things just can't be forced through," he cried. "No matter what you or your mother think."

She shouldn't have expected anything different. It was always her, her family, her mother, her block, her neighborhood; it was never them.

For a gala or for their friends, for something that would benefit the people he knew, it wouldn't take a second thought. For anyone else, he couldn't bring himself to care, no matter how many people it helped. "Brendan calls you, or your aunt calls you, and you're flying halfway around the world, no questions asked," she said. "But for something that helps thousands of people . . ."

"Elizabeth . . ."

"I thought your word meant something," she said.

He huffed a sigh, jaw tightening. "It isn't just about the short term," he said. "Can't you see that?"

She'd seen more than enough. No matter what they were promised or sold, they would end up selling out the neighborhood if it got them what they wanted. People weren't anything other than numbers on a spreadsheet.

"I mean, look at Charlotte," he said.

She turned to him, confused. "What about Charlotte?"

"She took the job in Scranton because she knew what it could do for her."

"Char's the best," she said. "She'd be better off somewhere she could be making a difference."

His hands tightened at his sides. "But what she has is helping her to get there. It's the same with the center."

She turned back towards the green without another word, hoping he would take the cue to go.

Of course he stayed.

He could never pick up a hint unless she beat him over the head with it. And she was starting to consider beating him over the head with other things—golf clubs, to start.

"You're always thinking about what other people need, what the center needs—what about you?" he said. "What is it that you're looking for?"

"Why does it matter to you?"

He pursed his lips with a grunt. "Call it curiosity."

She didn't answer. The last thing she wanted to give him was more proof of her supposed faults.

"Something close to home, I take it?" he prompted.

"Not *too* close to home."

Maybe he imagined her flighty like Brendan, or thought her to be above her station as Geoffrey and Lady Catherine did. Maybe he thought nothing of her at all, given her history with Ray.

He could think whatever he liked.

They lapsed into another stretch of silence, watching the sun disappear behind a passing cloud. Elizabeth wished she'd thought to bring her camera along. Without it, she fell to the mercy of these small moments, too aware of being seen and too wary of being caught looking. She missed its familiar weight around her neck, the protection it offered from having to be with other people.

She could still feel his eyes on her.

"You haven't sent me those shots," he said. "From the roof."

"I haven't printed them yet. You want to make sure you don't look ridiculous?"

His voice dropped to a whisper. "I want to see how you turned out."

A shout came from the distance as Charlotte and Mariah marched over, glowing from exfoliates and shiatsu massage.

Mariah charged towards the deck, halfway through a sentence as she arrived. "And LB, can you believe they wouldn't let me bring my CD player into the sauna?"

Charlotte shook her head. "Come on, LB. We're already late. You know Lady Catherine will be *seriously* displeased." Spying Darcy beside her, she blushed a bright red. "Elizabeth, you didn't tell me *your friend* was here."

"He's not *my friend*," Elizabeth said as Darcy stepped back from the railing. "We ran into each other."

Darcy paled. Making his excuses, he disappeared down an adjoining path towards the men's lockers.

Charlotte turned to her with a smug smile. "And you say that you have a hard time making friends."

Mariah blinked at them, confused. "What are you guys talking about?"

Elizabeth ran down the steps to join them. "Nothing. Your sister's full of shit, and we're going to be late. And you know Her Highness can't *tolerate* lateness."

Mariah didn't even wait for the two of them before breaking into a full sprint.

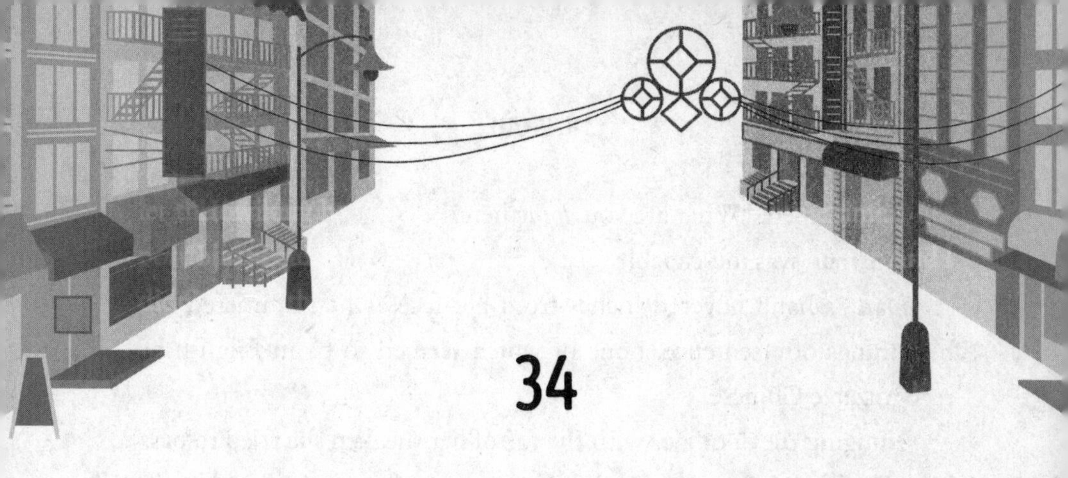

34

From that afternoon, a plague descended on her house—Charlotte's house, anyway—for the remaining week. No matter where they went or what they did, she had the misfortune of running into Darcy. In the parking lot at the grocery store, at the park, at dinner with Lady Catherine, at the mall. Like chickenpox in a kindergarten class, he moved quickly and sporadically, and reappeared whenever she least expected it. It would be enough to make any Chinese daughter reconsider the likelihood of karmic debt.

And when they weren't running into each other, there were always reasons for a visit. Dinner with Lady Catherine and Geoffrey, or brief appointments to inspect apartments or review tenant paperwork. She'd gone two hours out of the city to see Charlotte and instead found herself shadowing the worst of the Peony Plum crew. Enough was enough.

At eight in the morning, with Mariah and Leonard still snoring away in the spare bedroom, Elizabeth finished washing last night's dishes and said her goodbyes, hands still dripping water as she opened the front door—only to be greeted with a yelp of surprise.

She groaned. "What are you *doing* here?"

The man was inescapable.

Darcy's hand hovered inches from her face as he stammered the beginnings of a sentence, none of which seemed to be in English or recognizable Chinese.

Nudging the door ajar with the toe of her sneaker, she tried to pass him, but he didn't move. He didn't seem to understand what she was trying to do—he never did—and he blocked her only way out.

He was definitely some kind of karmic punishment.

Caspian jogged up behind his cousin, tucking his chin against Darcy's shoulder to beam at her. "Good morning to you too."

Darcy shrugged him off.

"We're here at Aunt Catherine's instruction," Cas said.

"We're dropping something off for Charlotte," Darcy added. He lifted a small package in his hand—two packets of unopened smoke detectors. "They're for the house on North Franklin."

Charlotte poked her head out from the kitchen. "What's for me?"

Elizabeth snatched the package and shook it. "Smoke detectors," she said. "You want me to run them over and put them in?"

Charlotte waved her off. "Just leave it," she said. "It's not important."

Elizabeth bounced on her toes. "I'm heading out anyway," she said. "Just tell me where to go."

Cas glanced her over. "Aren't you a little helper," he cracked. "Hot date?"

"Just getting some air."

"Forget that," Caspian replied. "Let's get breakfast."

"What are we talking about?" Charlotte said, tossing the package of smoke detectors onto the sofa.

"Breakfast," Cas said. "Elizabeth was about to tell us that she couldn't possibly, and we were going to make her go anyway. You should come too."

Charlotte, the traitor, snagged her house keys. "It's on you, right?" she said. "Since you're inviting?"

The boys looked at each other silently.

"Or since she schooled you in tennis?" Elizabeth tried.

"Time and tide, boys," Charlotte said, pushing her feet into her old sneakers. "Time and tide."

* * *

They trickled into a place where the signage looked faded, stale coffee parked on burners, and senior citizens loitered en masse at the counter to pick their teeth and slowly make their way through the Soup of the Day. It was called Family Restaurant—though whether run by a family or to serve families, Elizabeth didn't know.

They came, they saw an open and clean-enough booth, took a stack of menus, and settled in. A dour waitress poured them hot coffee as they sat down.

Elizabeth glanced through the menu as a courtesy. What she wanted was a classic American breakfast, something hearty and chemical, all the better to overwhelm her senses and her brain cells with enough sugars and fats to satisfy. Pancakes, bacon, margarine on white toast, hash browns—and all the salt and saturated fats a body could handle. Part of a balanced breakfast.

Darcy stared at his menu with increasing desperation, paging back and forth.

"They're not going to have anything that meets your standards," Elizabeth said.

He glared. "How do you know what my standards are?"

She flicked the lapel of his jacket with a laugh.

"Haven't you ever been to a place like this before, cuz?" Cas said, stretching an arm against the back of the booth.

"Not sober," he replied.

"You can't go wrong with fried food."

"It's not even ten in the morning," he said.

Elizabeth opened her menu again, giving it a quick scan. "You could get a burger."

"It's not even ten *in the morning*."

"Live a little," she said. "Get the freedom fries."

He frowned and turned to the next page.

For all the time the four of them had spent together in the last few days, they'd spent little of it talking about anything besides family and planned futures. Cas drilled them with questions about life in New York (Was it as glamorous, as dangerous, as cool as it looked in the movies? Where was their neighborhood and how was their upbringing, and how exactly had they crossed paths with Darcy and Brendan? How many times had they been mugged?) and they played Spot the Difference with their lives.

Cas, with no siblings of his own, couldn't understand how anyone could be expected to share a room from birth; Charlotte, having never lived away from home, didn't know how anyone could send small children off to live at school by themselves.

"It's not that strange," Darcy said. "Like a long school trip."

"It's hard to leave home," Charlotte said, stealing a wedge of hash browns from Elizabeth's plate. "I've never been away from my parents for so long."

"You've got to make up for lost time," Elizabeth said. "Party every night and trash the place."

Charlotte rolled her eyes. "It's not *my* house."

Cas swallowed a toast triangle near whole. "Are you excited to head out to Scranton?"

"Who's excited to go to Scranton?" Elizabeth said.

Charlotte drained the last of her coffee. "It's nice to try it out for a while."

Darcy speared a wet piece of egg and eyed it with suspicion. "It'll bring you back to New York sooner or later," he said. "Real estate is a precious commodity there."

"It's a commodity everywhere," Elizabeth said. Finishing the last of her toast, she pushed her plate in towards the center of the table. "We'll miss you, though."

Charlotte rolled her eyes. "I'm not *dying*, LB."

Darcy glanced between the two of them, taking a slow sip of his coffee. "Why do they call you that?"

Elizabeth glanced up. "What? LB?"

He nodded.

"Lydia," Elizabeth said. "When she was little, she couldn't say my name, no matter how hard she tried. The closest she got was LB, and it stuck."

"LB," Darcy repeated, slowly.

"That's cute," Cas said.

Of all the times she felt publicly embarrassed by her sisters, she never would have imagined feeling it most when none of them were around. Not that it mattered—Darcy and Caspian wouldn't see much of her or her family after this, if at all, if Darcy had his way—but the story felt too open, too personal, to share like one of her drank-too-much-out-all-night epics.

"The things we do for little sisters," Elizabeth said.

Cas turned to Darcy with a devilish smile. "How many times did G make you watch *Beauty and the Beast* again?"

Elizabeth nearly choked on her coffee. With a sister so much younger, she thought he'd push her off to boarding school at the first chance. She couldn't imagine him subjecting himself to the fashion experiments of a sister ten years younger, pulling his hair into a dozen little ponytails while Belle sang about adventure in the great, wide somewhere.

Darcy wiped at his mouth stiffly and tossed the napkin over his plate. "She didn't make me," he said. "She asked, and I agreed."

"This is your sister?" Charlotte said.

He nodded. "Georgiana," he said. "She's about Lydia's age now."

Elizabeth whistled. "Just wait," she said. "You'll miss those days."

His tone darkened. "I don't think so," he said. "I've seen that movie too many times."

She drained the last of her coffee.

"The things we do for little sisters," Darcy repeated.

For once, they seemed to agree on something. As Catherine might say, *perish the thought.*

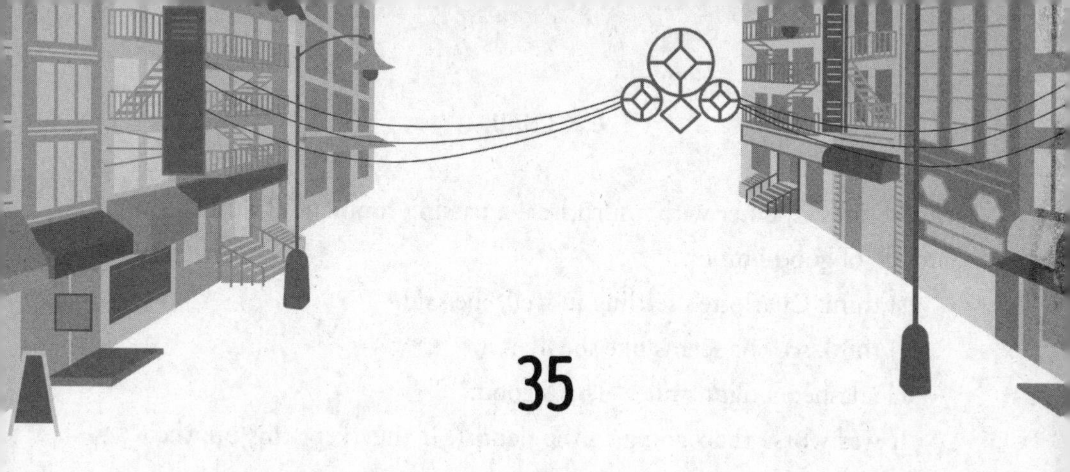

35

As if breakfast hadn't been bad enough, Charlotte and Caspian decided to head off together to bring the car around, leaving the two of them to foot the bill. She wondered if they didn't expect them to tear each other apart for sport.

She hoped he didn't expect her to fight him for it; she'd left her wallet at home.

Darcy tried to flag the waitress for their check with a weak wave of the hand, worse than a tourist fighting for a cab.

The waitress turned to another table.

They were left to their own devices.

Bad things happened when the small talk dried up. And they'd run through it all—his family and her family, the Lees and other common acquaintances, business and school, plans for the weekend. The only things left to them now were current events and celebrity gossip—and she didn't imagine he would have much to say about Hilary Duff.

Though maybe he would.

Even after all the time they'd spent together, she didn't have any idea what kind of a person he was. Every time she imagined she did, he would sideswipe her with a surprise—a passing moment of humanity, a touch of good humor.

"I think Charlotte's settling in well," he said.

"I think so. She seems like she likes it."

He flashed a tight smile. "That's good."

It was worse than going to the dentist. If they kept this up, their next attempt at conversation might last longer than thirty seconds.

The waitress came and scribbled a mystical loop on their guest check, tearing it off and setting it beside Darcy.

Darcy squinted at the mark. "I have no idea what this is supposed to be."

She took the check and marched towards the cashier counter, Darcy following behind her.

He drifted close beside her as the waitress rang them up. Close enough to bump her arm as he reached for his wallet.

"It's a good opportunity for her," he said, laying the bills on the counter. "Even if it wasn't what she wanted."

She could read between the lines. "I'm not ready to jump on the first offer I get just because somebody made it."

He huffed and took his change. "All I'm suggesting . . ."

She didn't want to hear any more friendly reminders, tips, or suggestions. It had been the only thing she'd heard for weeks, from her mother, from Lady Catherine, from nosy and well-meaning aunties. She didn't want help; she wanted the right to make her own choices.

She gestured towards the door. "Meet you outside."

In the parking lot, no sign of Caspian, Charlotte, or car.

Elizabeth swung around the opposite side of the walkway to take a seat on the concrete parking block in front of the diner.

Darcy looked at the ground with apprehension before leaning one of his feet against it instead. His shoes shone with polish. "What are you afraid of?"

She glared at him. "Excuse me?"

"You're smart, you're capable, you're certainly not shy," he said. "What are you afraid of?"

Of course he thought it was her fault—a lack of courage, a lack of daring. It never would have occurred to him that some people had other responsibilities to consider, other obligations. Some people couldn't just abandon their siblings to boarding school and hope for the best. Some people had to think about more than just themselves.

He didn't understand what it meant to have other people depending on him. Not like she and Jane did. Their parents may have earned and handled the money, but it was the two of them that handled everything else. They were the supports whenever there was indecipherable paperwork or intimidating bureaucracy. They were the ones who translated when there were no other options. They were the ones who watched and cared for their younger sisters. They managed when no one else could.

It was how things were.

And if she left, she didn't know what her family would do without her—or who she'd be without them. Together, they were the Chen girls; alone, she would be only Elizabeth.

"I like my neighborhood," she said. "I like the people in it. That's where I want to work. That's who I want to work for."

"It's still going to be there when you get back," he said.

She shook her head. "You don't understand. They need me."

"Do they, or are you afraid to find out they don't?"

She rose to her feet and stepped towards him, her hands tightening into fists. "Don't say shit to me about my family."

He looked as calm and implacable as ever, his hands sliding into his pockets as he watched her. He didn't seem to notice the angry twist of her mouth and the tension in her posture. He didn't care. "I'm not saying anything about your family. I'm talking about you," he said. "Don't limit yourself from the opportunities that are out there out of some misguided sense of loyalty."

She scoffed. "Since when do you care about my opportunities?"

He leaned closer, his eyes scanning her face. "Come on," he said softly. "I'm sure they'll be here soon."

The last thing she wanted was to wait anywhere near him.

She charged ahead, marching furiously to the edge of the parking lot. Where did he get off trying to say he understood anything about her and her family? As if he could know anything about her life.

She sped blindly ahead, ignoring his increasing grumbles of discontent behind her, ignoring anything at all besides the heat of her own anger—and stepped directly into a pothole. She caught herself too late, yelping as she lost her balance.

He caught the side of her arm, his grip tight as he braced her up on her feet.

She swallowed a quick breath and righted herself, glancing at the street for any sight of Caspian's car. "It's fine," she said.

There were worse things in life than skinned knees.

"There are opportunities for you," he said, dropping his hand. "But they might not look like what you expect."

She'd grown used to his many looks since their first meeting: the disapproving frown, the childish pout, the judgmental leer. This was a new one. No judgment, no impatience, no restlessness—his eyes were steady and clear as they held on hers, and darker than she'd realized.

A horn wailed in their direction, piercing and flat, and Elizabeth startled.

Caspian leaned on the horn, staring at them out of the driver's side window. "Sorry, cuz," he said as they made their way to the car. "Forgot where we parked."

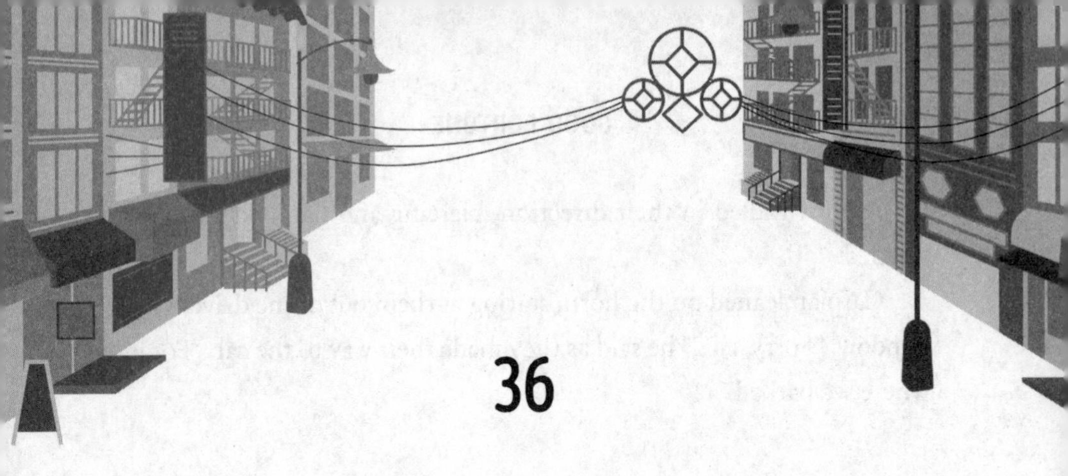

36

Caspian drove in silence, eyeing her in the rearview mirror as she stared out the window and ignored Charlotte's pointed coughs. They'd forgotten where they parked the car, they said, and resorted to finding it with echolocation by the chirp of the car alarm.

Elizabeth wished they'd leave the lying to the professionals.

They might have continued in silence for the rest of the ride home if it hadn't been for a high-pitched ring from Charlotte's bag. Saved by the relentless neediness of a woman pushing retirement.

It was nothing short of mayhem and disaster. A roof alarm at one of the downtown properties had malfunctioned. The superintendent was on vacation, the tenants absolute cavemen—"They wouldn't know how to open a door without a diagram!"—and time was of the essence; in short, Charlotte to the rescue.

Elizabeth leaned forward against Charlotte's headrest. "I'll go with you. We can figure it out."

Charlotte shook her head. "You should go back to the house. Make sure Mariah didn't burn it down trying to make breakfast."

"They'll be fine," Elizabeth said. "Besides, you might need help."

Charlotte turned to glance at the two of them in the back seat. "Darcy can come with me."

"Him?" Elizabeth cried as Darcy furrowed his brow with a noise of protest.

"Catherine insists," Charlotte replied. With a sharp smile, she turned to meet Elizabeth's eyes. "Still want to come?"

Elizabeth slunk down in her seat. "I'll meet you back at the house."

* * *

After a brief stop to drop off Darcy and Charlotte, they turned back the way they came. Without the chatter of the others, Cas seemed restless, fidgeting with the radio dial and the Buddha necklace hanging from the rearview mirror.

"Thanks for making an extra trip."

He slowed to a stop at a light, reaching for the pack of cigarettes packed into the cupholder. "This happens all the time with Aunty," he said, slipping one between his lips. "Everything's a crisis."

As Jade Chen's daughter, crises were the only things they faced—all earth-shattering, all urgent, all the time. She'd learned to react on a moment's notice, changing her plans to suit whatever imagined fire needed extinguishing first.

The light turned, and he sped back down the street.

"I'm surprised you guys are still in town," she said.

Cas mumbled in agreement, "So am I. I'm waiting on fucking Darcy. He's not ready or something, I don't know."

"So, what? If he doesn't want to go, you don't go?"

Cas shrugged. "He's the boss."

"He's too used to having his own way," she replied. "He doesn't even ask you when he knows it affects you too."

"It's what he's used to," Cas said. "That's what happens when you have the money."

She snorted.

Jade liked to say that money was wasted on the rich, and Elizabeth suspected she was right. With all of the resources in the world at their disposal, they still couldn't be satisfied. She liked it more when she didn't know any of them personally, when they existed in her mind like the idea of millipedes. Sure, they were around; sure, she knew they had their place in the circle of life, but they had nothing to do with each other. If she saw one, she might crush it with her shoe and move on.

She folded her arms over her chest. "I thought he had business to take care of," she said. "Investments, family, whatever."

He shrugged. "We were supposed to swing a visit to see G, but I don't know if we'll have time now."

"She must give you a lot of trouble."

He fumbled to light his cigarette. "She's a good kid," he said, rolling down the window and exhaling smoke. "People just talk all kinds of bullshit."

Consider it another unwritten rule: for every golden son, there might be a middling, controversial daughter—sometimes spoken of, oftentimes not. Elizabeth found herself wondering again about what Darcy's sister would be like. Smug, pretentious, self-involved, Ray said, but what else? One of those girls obsessed with Disney, even into college? A runaway? She couldn't imagine any Wong throwing themselves into scandal—not the straitlaced Wongs who couldn't bear improper etiquette and nonclassical music. But people always did treat their daughters differently than their sons.

"I only heard good things from Caroline Lee," she said. "She said she was a sweet girl."

Cas drummed his hands against the steering wheel, banking a

sharp turn. "I've heard a lot about the Lees. Still haven't met them though."

"Brendan's nice," she said. "But I think Darcy likes to babysit him."

He scoffed. "Seems like he needs one from what I hear."

Goosebumps prickled the back of her neck. "What do you mean?"

They swerved into another lane. "Brendan follows him around for everything," Cas said. "Asking him advice on all kinds of things."

Elizabeth sank back against her seat, hoping she didn't look as embarrassed as she felt.

"And he still needed Darcy to bail him out," he said.

"You're worse than an aunty," she said, rolling her eyes. "Bail him out of what?"

"Some kind of a scam," he said as they pulled up outside Charlotte's house. "Some girl in New York out for his money. The whole family was losing their minds about it because he didn't have a clue."

Her stomach rose up into her throat, all acid. "Some girl in New York?"

He pulled up to the curb, shifting the car into park. "Yeah. You might even know her," he laughed.

She was almost certain she did.

With shaking hands, she unbuckled her seat belt but didn't move to get out of the car.

"You all right?"

"Yeah," she said. "It's just—doesn't Brendan get to decide for himself?"

"Brendan asked for his help," Cas said. "And honestly, it sounds like he stopped him from making a huge mistake."

"He doesn't know that," she cried. "He could be wrong."

Cas took another long drag off his cigarette, shrugging. "I don't know," he said. "But I trust Darcy."

And wasn't that the root of all of their problems?

Pulling the handle, she climbed out of the car, her hands clenched so hard they were shaking.

He waved at her before pulling the car into reverse to turn back the way he came, disappearing down the end of the street.

So now she had her answer. It hadn't been Genevieve or Brendan's flightiness, but Darcy and Caroline, determined to keep him from settling. For anyone to think that Jane could be a gold digger! *Jane!* Sweet, sensible, and softhearted Jane, who wouldn't even sneak snacks into the movie theater, reduced to a scheming party girl out for his wallet. Did it matter that it wasn't Darcy's life or Darcy's business? Did it matter that Jane might have made Brendan happy? No—as always, what mattered were Darcy's feelings, Darcy's read of the situation, Darcy's opinions.

He did it because he could. Because he didn't think they were good enough, and they never could be; because they were beneath his understanding, beneath his respect, and undeserving of his notice. Because they dared to consider themselves their equals. And it meant that Jane—kind, understanding Jane, who always gave him the benefit of the doubt—suffered.

And so what if they'd been a little too loud at parties, a little familiar? So what if her mother liked to talk and her sisters liked attention? Everyone had branches of the family tree that cast a little shadow. But that didn't matter to him. No, what he cared about was himself; he couldn't stand the personal embarrassment, even if it meant ruining his friend's life. Even if it made his friend happy.

Nothing mattered at all except getting his own way.

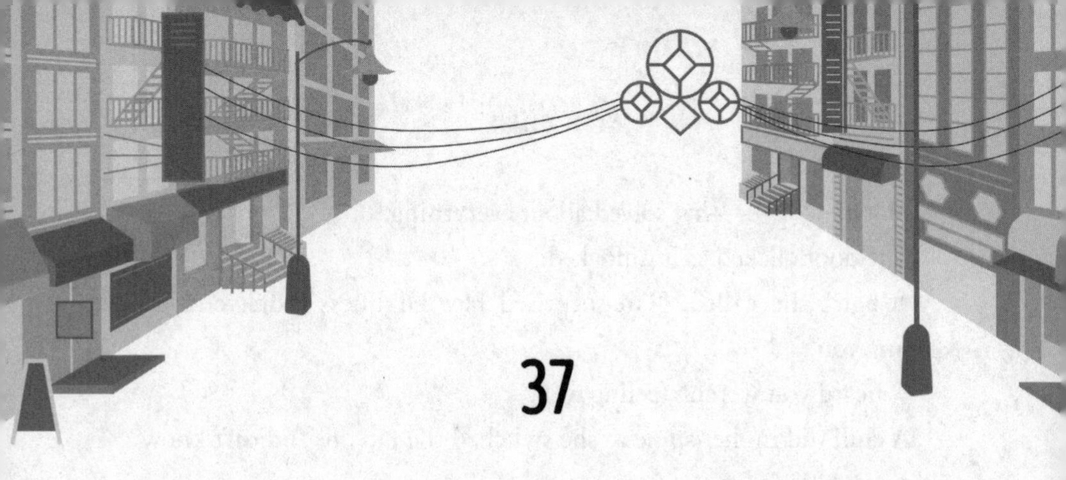

37

The events of the afternoon, coupled with a hysterical call from her mother about a malfunctioning office printer and a substantial lack of food and coffee, left her with a persistent headache and an inability to concentrate. As excuses went, Lady Catherine thought it unmannered and a sign of a flagging constitution—"Too much damp, Miss Elizabeth!"—but Charlotte made her excuses and refused to send her out sick. For once, she could have a night off. Charlotte left her the best of the takeout menus, her Blockbuster membership card, and some aspirin; took the phone off the hook; and told her to get some sleep.

It didn't help.

She couldn't concentrate on anything else besides Jane, besides what Darcy had done. She couldn't stop trying to understand *why*. No one could look at Jane and Brendan and see anything other than what she saw. They had been sickening to witness, insufferable to be around. No one could doubt how they felt about each other.

With a sigh, she climbed out of bed and padded into the living room. Switching on the TV, she let the evening news drone in the background and tiptoed into the kitchen.

Hot chocolate—that solved about everything.

The door clicked as it unlocked.

"Char?" she called. "I'm surprised Her Highness didn't end up keeping you . . ."

"I heard you weren't feeling well."

A chill slid up her spine as she switched the tap off. "I didn't know you had a key."

Turning, she found not Charlotte but Darcy, looking at her through the doorway from the hall. He looked worse than she felt—the circles under his eyes a heavy shadow, clothing rumpled, and a deep sag in his posture, like he hadn't slept in at least a night or, at least, slept well. Good, she thought. He didn't deserve it. She cursed him with a thousand more sleepless nights.

"Charlotte lent me hers."

She switched one of the burners on. It lit with a huff. "Of course she did," she muttered.

He stepped carefully into the kitchen. "How are you doing? Objections to my aunt aside."

She set the pot on the burner. "I didn't know it was you," she said. "Otherwise . . ."

"You'd have had more tact?"

She crossed her arms over her chest, willing the pot to boil faster. Anything to get him to leave. "You could have said something."

"Aunt Catherine asked me to bring you some soup," he said, sliding a bagged container onto the kitchen table.

"Thanks."

Plastic crinkled as he worked the knot loose. "Do you have a rice bowl?"

In the low yellow light of the kitchen, she watched a play of shadows cut across his face. "Just leave it."

He pried the lid off. "How are you feeling?"

"I'm fine," she said. "You don't need to stay."

His eyes scanned her face. "You should eat."

"You sound like my mother."

"It's the best thing to do if you aren't feeling well."

"I'm *fine*."

He drifted towards her, the back of his hand touching the swell of her cheek.

She took a sharp breath, startling out of his touch. "What are you doing?"

He cleared his throat. "You don't feel warm."

"It's my head," she said.

He caught her arm, fingers brushing against her bare skin. "You should see a neurologist."

She stared. "It's just a headache. I took some aspirin and I'll sleep it off."

"They can be serious, you know."

"I'll keep that in mind. Is that all?"

He huffed, rifling a hand through his hair. "No," he said. With renewed focus, he turned back towards the open container, jabbing at the contents with a plastic spoon. "Have some soup."

It was strange to see him suddenly restless when he'd always been so still, so immovable. Now he fussed with the edge of the plastic bag; now he stood; now he sat; now he repositioned the container on the counter. His fingers moved from one task to another mindlessly, but his eyes stayed sharp, focused on whatever it was he was thinking.

She rolled her eyes, reaching for the container. "You're worse than the aunties, you know that?"

He glanced at her askance. "You're going to eat from the container?"

"That's how I eat. Straight from the trough."

"Fine," he muttered, pacing towards the other side of the room. "Do as you like."

"Usually do."

He took her place against the kitchen counter and watched as if he didn't trust her to eat it without supervision.

"You don't have to stay," she repeated.

He scoffed with irritation, looking every bit the harried mother. "You're unbelievable. Have some soup, please."

She dipped the spoon into the gelatinous mix of fungus and beans, and shoved a bite into her mouth. All she tasted was bitterness and salt. "There," she mumbled, swallowing it down. She held up the empty spoon for his appraisal. "Happy?"

If it were anyone else, she might imagine it to be warmth in his expression. If it were anyone else, she could have mistaken his showing up for care.

But this wasn't anyone else. This was Darcy.

And Darcy wasn't looking away.

"I hope you're not expecting a thank-you note."

Again, that little scoff like clearing a blockage at the back of his throat. "Elizabeth."

He looked annoyed, exasperated, his forehead wrinkling with the force of his composure, but it didn't reach his eyes. His eyes were as she remembered in the parking lot, dark and inviting, less guarded. It was like the careful lowering of a veil.

She swallowed hard, squaring her shoulders. If he wanted to fight, they could fight, headache or not. "What?"

He didn't answer.

She waved the spoon at him, hoping to shake him out of whatever mental trap he'd fallen into, but he stared straight ahead, stared through her, and didn't say another word.

He didn't even seem to blink.

"If that's all . . ." she said.

"Elizabeth," he interrupted, his voice dropping low.

She stopped, her breath caught in her throat. Whatever he was thinking, whatever might have come out of his mouth after that, it most definitely was not going to be anything she wanted to hear.

"LB."

And before she could ask him what exactly he meant by *that*, he crossed towards her in two quick strides, cupped her face in his hands, and kissed her.

Kissed! With his mouth!

Gravity took over. Her fingers relaxed in shock, spoon crashing to floor, arms dropping to sides, sky generally falling. Darcy—kissing her! She would never be able to look at that infuriating twist of his mouth without remembering this, the softness of his lips, the gentle pressure of his hands against her arms.

She must be hallucinating. She must have overdone it with the Robitussin. Despite believing that she was conscious and standing in the kitchen, she must be lying in bed, feverish, delirious, and experiencing some kind of psychotic nightmare. How did anybody provoke themselves to wake up from a dream?

His nose nudged hers as he leaned forward for another.

Call it instinct, call it shock, call it a mental breakdown, but she may even have leaned forward to meet him.

This kiss, he meant.

This kiss, premeditated. Unforgivable.

She kissed him back.

And whatever might have remained of her sanity or his sense of decorum went out the window.

He drew her close, her body melting into his as he deepened the kiss. He was better than she would have guessed—not that *this* had been something she'd ever thought about, *ever*—a little desperate, a little rough. Demanding, as always. He tasted like coffee and he smelled like fine things—fancy cologne and clean linen, the sweet cleanness of a mall—and none of this should have been happening and somehow was. It was almost dizzying how off-balance she felt, but he held on to her, keeping her on her toes. Keeping her upright.

She gasped when her back hit the wall, her hands roughing into his hair as he pulled away with a light smile.

And there it was—the shock of cold water, the recognition, the horror of what they had been doing, her mind reentering her body—and the bastard had the audacity to smile. "Come work for me."

Robitussin could not get away with this.

She pushed him away. "What the fuck."

He tried again. Different words, better words, words that could make sense. "What I mean—what I'm trying to say . . ." he said, glancing at her mouth. "LB, I like you."

That wasn't any better.

This couldn't be him. He wasn't thinking straight. He wasn't speaking like he usually did. Somehow, somewhere, when she wasn't looking, he'd been replaced by an evil twin—one who whispered when he spoke, one who said things like this, one who looked at her the way that he did.

She shivered. "I need—I need to sit down."

Her legs couldn't move.

"I like you," he repeated, more firmly. "You can't believe how much. *I* can't believe how much."

Nervous laughter bubbled out of her.

His hand cupped her jaw, brushing her hair away from her face. "I can't stop thinking about you."

She exhaled through her teeth. "What . . . ?"

"It's hard for me to find the words," he said. "I like you. I have feelings for you. I'm only in town because I heard that you were here, and I knew I needed to tell you before I left." His hands slid down the line of her neck, warming her to distraction, but he kept talking somehow.

His words slid over her as his fingers traced the hollow of her throat. And he kept talking. He really liked nothing so much as he liked talking—and she found she didn't mind the sound of his voice. The longer he spoke, the more convincing he sounded—though the search of his fingers didn't seem to imply she still needed much convincing. "I know it doesn't make any sense. Long distance never works, and you and I have never agreed on anything. You're the last person in the world I would have expected to like, but no matter how hard I tried, I couldn't forget you. And I tried."

She stared at him, a faint whistling echoing between her ears. She'd been beneath his notice from the first day they met, and if that hadn't been enough of a mark against her, he'd had to deal with her family. The more she considered it, the more ludicrous it all sounded. It was impossible for him to like her. She'd been nothing but a thorn in his side from the start, fighting to save something he couldn't care less about. She'd bristled and annoyed and frustrated him, and now he'd confused that irritation for something else.

Setting him straight would almost make her feel bad, if any of this were happening.

And he was *still* talking!

"You seem willing to leave New York only on pain of death, for some reason, and have no real ambitions and no plans for your future, as far as I can tell. You're wasting away in dead-end jobs because of some vague idea of principles, and I have no idea what a future with you would even *look* like apart from your mother trying to rope me into some kind of pyramid scheme, your sisters asking me for money, and my paying for everything . . ."

She squeaked in disbelief. Here he was! The man she knew and recognized, the man she once despised! A man so tactless, so condescending, that his own feelings couldn't keep him from reminding her of how little she had to offer, and of how much she stood to gain from being with him. But he assumed that gold digging ran in the family. He thought she would come cheap.

"But I know my life doesn't make sense without you in it. I don't want to do anything if you're not there to do it with me. I don't want to go through the world without hearing every single unsolicited thought that you decide to share. I don't want to miss any of the fights that you pick, though I'll never understand why you pick fights you have no chance of winning. And if that means bearing with your family and your . . . situation, then I will. For you. And I know that's a lot to take in, but I can only hope . . . that you feel the same way."

Her jaw dropped. "Oh my god."

The pot behind her hissed and spat in answer, the water boiling over to burn against the range top.

"Is everything all right?" he said.

She rushed to the stove and switched off the burner. "Sorry. You surprised me."

He leaned against the wall, waiting for her to respond. Waiting for her to jump into his arms, thrilled at the honor of his attentions. "Is that all you have to say?"

"Look, this hasn't happened to me a lot," she started. "The, um, the—what you said, not the pot. And usually, when something like this happens, I think the usual line is 'We can still be friends,' but I don't think I can do that."

His cheeks pinked, mouth pulling into its usual expression of distaste. This, she could handle. This Darcy, she could recognize; not the other one standing there, making overtures about how much she compelled him to speak about his feelings.

"Look, we're not friends," she said. "We were never friends. I never cared what you thought about me, mostly because I knew none of it was good, and you've never cared about telling me anyway. And what you're saying is *insane*. You don't *actually* like me. You've just . . . talked yourself into it."

"No, I . . ."

She shook her head. "I don't like you either. I can't. I'm sorry to hurt your feelings, if that's even possible, but I don't. And I think it's best if we pretend that this never happened."

His jaw tightened, lips nearly whitening with the force of it. He sounded as calm as he didn't look. "That's all you have to say to me?"

"What do you *want* me to say?"

His laugh was bitter. "You fucking kissed me back!"

"You surprised me! It was . . ."

"If it wouldn't *trouble you* too much, maybe you can tell me how *exactly* I've offended you when all I've done is make myself a resource to you and your family."

"We don't fucking owe you anything," she hissed. "You offered!"

He resumed his pacing, his shoulders drawing tighter in towards his body as he doubled back and forth.

"And I don't owe you an explanation because you feel like you deserve one!" she continued. "But if you want to know, then you might ask why I should be *flattered* by you telling me that you like me even though I'm not good enough for you? Even though my family's after your money?"

He rolled his eyes. "Your hot water."

"Fuck the hot water," she replied. "Do you think I could care about anything you have to say after everything you pulled with the rec? Promising one thing, doing another, and then coming here to offer me a job? Are you kidding?"

He clenched his hands at his sides, drawing himself up to his usual height. "I offered you the job because it seemed like the only one you had any interest in taking!"

For so long, she hadn't touched the wellspring of anger she'd carried for fear of what it would mean for her mother, for her family, for the future of the rec—but what did she have to lose? Nothing except his good opinion, and the sooner she could be rid of that, the better. She would torch it herself if she had to—though, judging by the look on his face, she wouldn't have to do much more to reduce it all to ashes.

"I know this isn't anything you can understand, but some people actually want to make a difference and give back," she said. "Not that you've cared if it goes against what you want."

He chuckled. "You seem to know a lot about what *I* want."

"Which is to say nothing of what you did to my sister!"

He colored but didn't say anything.

"Does *that* justify it for you?"

His voice was cold. "You don't need to justify anything."

But he'd pried open Pandora's box, and now she couldn't stop. Every comment she'd stifled, every instance of injured pride or passing offense bubbled out of her now. If he wanted an itemized list of everything he'd done wrong, she could do that too.

"Because she wasn't good enough for *you*. Because even though she made your best friend happy, she couldn't have liked him for anything other than his money, right? Because you think that the only thing we could possibly care about is a payout."

He stared at her in disbelief. "You caught me," he said finally, turning away to open a cabinet and peering inside. When he didn't find what he was looking for, he continued down the line, opening and closing each door in succession with a loud slam. "I admit it! I was trying to look out for my friend. I did better by him than I did for myself!"

She shook her head. "And even if you hadn't broken Jane's heart, do you think I could take you seriously after what you did to Ray?"

The cabinet door slammed shut. "Oh, Ray! How could I forget," he said coldly, "that you were so *invested* in his affairs."

"Who *wouldn't* be after hearing about what you put him through?"

The cabinet hinge squealed as he yanked another door open and glanced inside. "What *I* put him through!" he cried. "God, I've put him through *so much*."

"You cut him off when he needed you, and took away any chance he had at a normal life after everything he and his dad did for you and your family! But I guess they aren't people to you."

He neared the end of the row of cabinets and opened the last set of doors. "And that's what you think of me!" he cried. "Thank you for clearing it all up."

"This isn't your house!" she said. "What the fuck are you doing?"

He slammed a ceramic mug on the counter in front of her. "Here."

She tore open the Swiss Miss packet on the counter, her shaking hands dusting instant cocoa powder and dried mini marshmallows everywhere.

He returned to the table, replacing the lid on the soup container with a hard snap. "You wouldn't have minded if I told you what you wanted to hear. Maybe I should have said that I didn't have any doubts, that nothing stood in the way of my feelings, but I don't like to lie to people, and I didn't want to lie to you. And if you want me to stand here and lie to you now and tell you that I'm ashamed of what I said, I won't."

She poured the steaming water into the mug and watched the

powder puff into a mushroom cloud. Clumps of cocoa floated on the water. "You're fucking unbelievable."

"You want to know the truth, Elizabeth?" he said. "I'm proud of what I've done. I admit it. I've gone to the best schools in the world. I've traveled, I've worked *incredibly* hard to get to where I am, and I have a lot of money because of it—and I'm not ashamed of that. Why should I be?"

She took a fresh spoon from the drawer and stirred her drink frantically.

"Can you honestly tell me that your family *wouldn't* get involved? That your mother wouldn't try to use my name or connections? That your sisters wouldn't ask for money or favors?"

She dropped the spoon in the cup with a soft clink. "It has nothing to do with how you said it, and everything to do with what you said," she said. "Don't try to twist things around."

"Don't lie to yourself," he hissed. "You kissed me back."

She stepped towards him. "Nothing you said changes the facts, and the fact is that I don't like you. I don't feel the same way. I couldn't. I can't. From the first time we met, you showed me exactly who you are and what you think about everyone else. You're arrogant, conceited, and *rude*, and you don't give a shit about anyone. You've never cared about hurting anyone else's feelings, so don't lie and say that you care about mine. And you're the *last* person in the world that I could *ever* . . ."

He waved her off. "Thank you," he said. "I've brought you your soup, you've made your point, and I've had about enough for tonight. This never happened. Good night."

She waited for the slam of the door in the jamb, but it never came.

Tiptoeing into the living room, she glanced at the shut door and burst into tears.

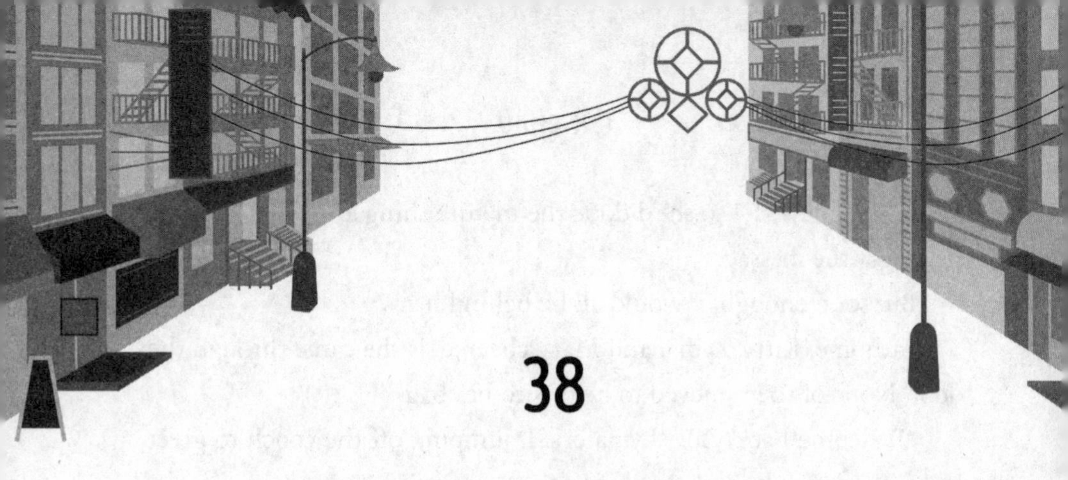

38

Home sweet Holland Tunnel. For the last twenty minutes, they crawled in stop-and-go traffic, breathing in the collected exhaust fumes and watching the slow drip of things unknown from the ceiling. No sight could have made her happier. After the events of the last week, it was comfort enough to know that she might soon be home, fielding arguments between her sisters and smelling Sammy's foul cigar smoke, far from Lady Catherine and the Wongs and all of the inconvenient things they needed to say at inconvenient times.

Catherine couldn't send her off without one last screed of judgments, criticizing everything from her outfit to her lack of plans and future prospects to the problems of her entire generation—a little gift for the trip home. She'd also given Elizabeth a single business card and a lukewarm invitation to apply for any openings of interest.

Elizabeth doubted she would ever be interested.

Not that a lack of interest seemed to matter to anyone in their family.

Darcy had left one last message on Charlotte's machine, asking to speak with her alone before she left town—hoping to plead his case again, she guessed—so she'd done the mature thing and pretended she never got the message.

But soon enough, it would all be behind her.

At home, Kitty, Lydia, and Mary cheered as she came through the door. None of them moved to help with her bags.

"Welcome back, LB!" Lydia cried, jumping off the couch to greet her with a short hug. "Can I have twenty bucks?"

Elizabeth tossed her duffel bag on top of Lydia's bare feet. "Hello to you too," she said. "What do you need the money for?"

Lydia didn't even blink. "Books."

"Bullshit," Elizabeth said.

Kitty munched on a corn chip. "It's almost summer," she said. "We need new bathing suits."

"Why do you need new suits if you're not going anywhere?" Elizabeth said.

"LB," Lydia whined. "It's going to happen this year. I have a plan."

Oh, the familiar saga: suffering and going without might do for Jane and LB, but times had changed. Kitty and Lydia had big dreams and bigger schemes for their vacation; they wanted MTV glitz and Juicy glamour, the thrills and televised ecstasies of a good time. They'd been smothered under the thick smog of frying oil and burning garlic for most of the year, smiling through awkward run-ins with leering security guards and construction workers who cracked the same jailbait jokes and tried the same tired lines, and now they were determined to make their getaway, whether by borrowing, pleading, or stealing.

"It's never going to happen," Elizabeth said, filling a glass with water from the tap.

On the fridge, pinned beneath a promotional magnet from State Farm, was the notice from the health department, sections of it circled in bright red marker and covered with Jane's additional notes. *CALL FOR APPOINTMENT*, Jane had scribbled in the corner.

She pulled it loose and tossed it on the kitchen table.

Mary lifted a finger in agreement. "You know Dad hates the beach."

"Dad hates fun," Lydia groused. "I don't understand why we can't get a house at the shore like normal people."

"Because we don't have shore-house money," Elizabeth said, collapsing into a free seat at the end of the sofa.

"We could totally afford it. He's just cheap," Lydia said.

"He's cheap because we don't have any money."

Lydia bared her teeth in a sneer. "Ugh, you're so annoying."

Elizabeth closed her eyes with a sigh. Impossible now to remember what she thought she missed about home. They chattered at her nonstop, wanting to tell her about what they'd done in her absence, quizzing her about Charlotte and Pennsylvania, about whether she flirted with anyone while she was there, and whether or not she liked it more compared to New York. It didn't matter that she couldn't get a word in edgewise, that they didn't seem to listen to whatever she said; they were happiest hearing themselves talk.

Lydia thumped her hard on the shoulder. "By the way, you're taking up all the space on the answering machine," she said.

She opened an eye. "Me?"

"Uh, yeah," Lydia said. "They're all from that guy, *Liza with a* z, so can you delete them off the machine before I miss an important message?"

"What could be so important for you?" she said.

Lydia pressed a hand to her heart. "I'll have you know your sister is an up-and-coming modeling *professional*, okay?"

"Whatever, Lyd."

While her sisters were prone to exaggeration, they weren't far off when it came to Ray's messages. One after another, they played on the answering machine, ranging from the playful to the faintly harassing. *I'm sorry I didn't call, but it's been a while, Liza with a z. Call me?*

Where have you been hiding out? Taking lots of good pictures? You haven't been at Sammy's, and you know no one can handle my delicate negatives but you.

So you're clearly on another planet. ET, phone home whenever you get this.

("God," Lydia interjected. "Please tell me you aren't *that* lame.")

Elizabeth, at least tell me why you're avoiding me. Can we talk?

No, thank you. She had learned her lesson. The last thing she needed was a repeat with someone who brushed her off as a second choice only to come back with his tail between his legs. And it was impossible to think about Ray without dragging Darcy into it—what Darcy had done to ruin his life, how Darcy had reacted to her defense of him. They were like a package deal—to think of one meant thinking of what had happened to the other.

She erased the messages on the machine, called and left a message with the health department, and checked her email.

Her inbox chimed and pinged with a frenzy, cluttered with spam emails and paranoid chain letters and basic form rejections from the last round of internships and jobs she'd applied to. She clicked among her inbox, deleting most and ignoring the rest, when she spied an email from an unknown sender. *An explanation* promised the subject line.

She certainly had mail—and she didn't have to guess from whom. She only wondered if it was worth opening. (Did curiosity kill the cat? Of course she did.)

Forgive me for resorting to this, but you refused to hear me out otherwise. (And could he blame her?) I don't blame you (a likely story), but you accused me of a few things that I want to clear up in the interest of my character, if nothing else. (Of course he only cared about his reputation.) The first—that I broke up Brendan and Jane; the second—that I kept Ray from his rightful inheritance. If I should say anything that offends you in explaining myself, I apologize, but I stand by my judgment and my actions. (And where did he get off judging anybody?)

On Jane—of course I noticed that Brendan liked your sister after they met at Bryan's wedding. I'm not blind. As you may have noticed, Brendan likes everyone—a fact that others have taken advantage of in the past. (As if Jane would ever!) Whatever you might think, we always planned on returning to Hong Kong after the fundraiser; even if we hadn't, the health of Brendan's father would have necessitated it. But his sisters were concerned he might try to extend his stay for her. You know your sister better than I do, but by all appearances, she didn't seem to like him as seriously as he liked her. Apart from flirting with him at parties, she treated him the same as anyone else. Maybe I saw what I wanted to see (of course he did), but you should know well enough that I aim to be objective about these things. I didn't want her to be indifferent. I only saw that she was. And even if she hadn't seemed indifferent, the way your mother and sisters talked about him was more than enough to convince me of other motives at play. (This she uneasily conceded.) I don't say any of this to upset you. None of us are responsible for our families, and their behavior doesn't reflect on you or Jane as people. You're both the best of your family, and I've found you to be passionate, brilliant, and candid (She refused to be swayed by easy flattery.)—though sometimes perhaps too candid. (That didn't take long.) Brendan is like a brother to me, and you can't blame me for wanting to protect him, especially if I was led to assume her intentions were driven by other factors. (Anyone who believed Jane capable of "other intentions" was looking to find them in the first place. She did *not* forgive him.) Would you have done any differently if it had been your sister? (She pleaded the fifth.)

Despite what you may think, no one held him at gunpoint to keep him from leaving. All I did was tell him how I felt, and let him draw his own conclusions. I only recommended that he avoid coming back to New York until he could sort out how he felt. (Poor Brendan. Ruined by those who thought they were looking out for him.) But I do regret lying to him about your sister. We were in Boston at the same time that she was, but he never knew. Caroline thought it too soon, and I agreed. I'm sure you think that's beneath me (No, it seemed perfectly within his character.), but it's all over now and I can't change anything about the past.

As for Raymond—I don't know what he's told you about me, and I don't care. Here are the facts. (An underhanded attempt at making his argument.) It's true that Ray was related to one of the administrators that worked for my father, and that my father was his godfather. It's true that my father supported him generously, paying for his education, making introductions, and involving him in programs that I also joined. My father was a man of high expectations, and he demanded excellence from both of us. After my father died, his estate allotted Ray an annual allowance of about eighty thousand dollars so long as he completed a law degree. After his own father died, he came to tell me that he had only been in it to please his father and didn't think the law suited him. (His prerogative.) The funds had been set in an account specifically for education costs and couldn't legally be moved. Out of loyalty to our fathers, I agreed to settle it with him personally. Instead of the annuity, he accepted a lump sum of a quarter of a million dollars. (Jesus Christ. She couldn't imagine Ray having that kind of money. Not when he could barely scrape together loose change for coffee.) He told me he would use it to start his business. I admit that I wanted to believe him more than I actually did, and we left it there.

I didn't hear from him again for three years. You can imagine my surprise when I finally did. The man has a way with excuses. He told me he'd run into difficulties with his investors and asked to be restored to the original terms of the will. You can't blame me for refusing.

Elizabeth, this next point I tell you in the strictest confidence. (How dramatic.) I believe I can trust you not to repeat this, and I hope that my trust in you is not misplaced. As you may recall, Georgiana is ten years younger than me, and her guardianship came into my and Caspian's care after my father passed. A year ago, she came to me with plans for a summer study program in Paris with one of the conservatories. My work schedule didn't permit six months away, and I could hardly let her go alone, so I hired someone to stay with her for the duration of the semester. Ray found his way there around the same time. (So what?) They hadn't spent much time together when he still lived with us, but Georgiana remembered him, and he quickly became one of her only friends in Paris. Ray, as I'm sure you're aware, takes great pride in his photography and offered her lessons. Perhaps you can guess at his true intentions, which she did not. (Oh, shit.) In the course of their lessons, he convinced her, a minor, to model for him. (Oh, *shit.*)

I found out by accident. Georgiana had been too terrified to tell me. I'm sure you can imagine how I felt. When I confronted him, he told me he planned to exhibit them (Disgusting.) at a gallery showing in a few months. He wanted to use her to make his name as an artist. Despite her age, he didn't violate any laws where the French were concerned, and he planned to go ahead with it, no matter what. Without any recourse from the French authorities and concerned for her reputation and her future, I paid him whatever he asked for the pictures and negatives. I can barely describe how unbearable I found the ordeal, so you can imagine how much worse it was for Georgiana. (Always the daughters and never the sons.) She almost ended her own life. (God!)

I can only assume extortion was his plan from the start, and getting his revenge on me a bonus. You'll forgive me if I wasn't in the right state of mind to share this that night. If you need to verify anything that I've said, you can check with Cas. As a named executor to my father's estate, he's witnessed most of this directly. If you can't find it in you to believe me, I hope that you can believe him.

I wish you nothing but happiness. Be well.

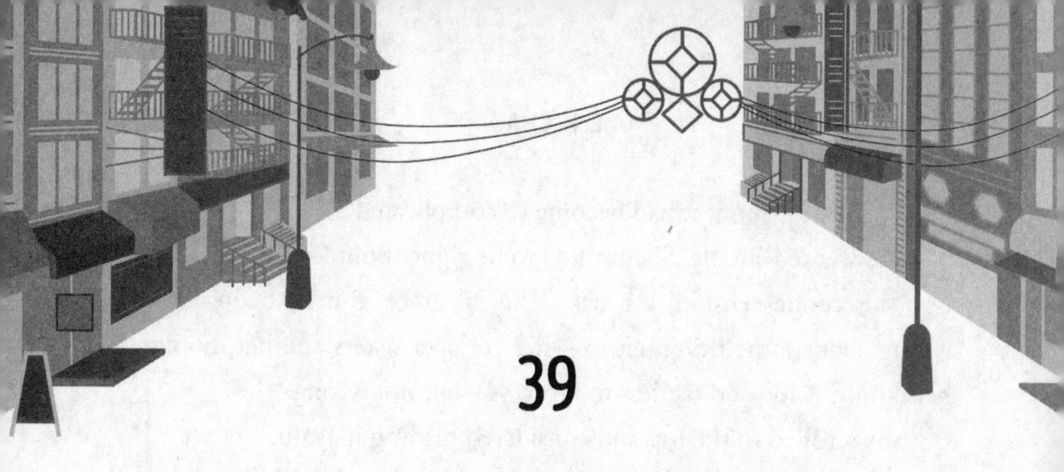

39

She scrolled up and read it again. And again. Read it a third time. She picked apart the sentences. She analyzed each word and the possible meaning of each arrangement. She scrutinized each punctuation mark, each aside, each claim he made, and succeeded only in giving herself a pounding headache. Yesterday, she would have counted Darcy among the blood enemies of her life, the incident a humiliating misstep in her journey of adulthood. Yesterday, she would have fought him on every point—his superiority, his judgment, his side of the story. Yesterday, black was black and white was white, and now all she had was a slurry of doubts.

She couldn't make heads or tails of it; it was one man's word against the other. But the more she considered it, the less Ray's story made sense. The fact that not a single aunty had heard a thing about him around the neighborhood; the ease with which he shared his story despite being terrified of anyone finding out; his sudden disappearance when it came time to confronting Darcy directly. Why hadn't any of it seemed weird? Why had she always given him the benefit of the doubt? Why couldn't Darcy try being less . . . Darcy?

Everything about it had become so complicated.

She wanted simple. She wanted to be right about Darcy—his coldness, his condescension, his lack of social grace. But he hadn't been wrong about some things either—her younger sisters and her mother, her family. Rude and tactless to say it, yes, but not wrong.

She scrolled to the top and considered reading it again.

Ping!—an instant message popped up in the center of her screen.

hey its ray u back?

She slammed the computer shut.

What she really needed was a break. A walk to clear her head. No distractions.

* * *

The sting of chemical fumes did the trick.

Sammy looked up from perusing an unmentionable magazine at the counter, mumbling around a wad of a cigar in his mouth. "Thought you weren't coming in today."

"I'm not," she said, pushing past the dingy red curtain into the back.

He spat into a small trash can beside the register. "Hiding out from your bookie, Chen?"

She ignored him and stepped into the darkroom, shutting the door behind her.

What passed for a darkroom in Sammy's was nothing more than an expanded supply closet with an industrial sink, but it did the job. Strands of negatives hung from clothespins stretching across one side of the room, bottles of solution lined up along the sink beside little ceramic Buddha statues and a bottle of dish soap.

Those first few moments in the dark were like magic.

Waiting for her eyes to adjust, breathing the sharp tang of developer solution in the air, she could feel everything slow to stillness, the world reducing to the noise of the paper sliding in the solution, to the feel of wet negatives slippery between her fingers.

Turning on the safe light, she scanned through the negatives hanging on the line and removed a strip—snapshots of their time on the roof: there was one of Kitty alone in the corner, watching the sky; Jane and Brendan close in conversation; Lydia goofing off with a fish-mouth pucker and rolled eyes.

The pace and ritual of it soothed her restlessness: the weight of the machinery as she adjusted the focus and chose her print, the smell of the solution, the gentle movement of the paper from one bath to another. But nothing compared to seeing the final image emerge into clarity like waking up from a dream.

Slipping the photo into the development solution, she carefully moved it back and forth with a pair of tongs and waited for the faces to come into focus. There was Caroline midlaugh, eyes crinkling at the corners, Brendan and Jane leaning against each other, Lydia's open-mouthed pout. And in the background, Darcy, subtle as a shadow.

She fought a smile at the sight of him, straitlaced in his suit, hands flexed at his sides. He looked the way she remembered, puffed with impatience and self-importance. Except, as she continued to prod the print around in the solution, he didn't seem to look impatient at all. There was a trace of tenderness in his expression, a gentle curiosity as he watched the scene in front of him.

So Mr. Monopoly didn't have a money clip where a heart ought to be.

The more she worked the photo in the water bath, the more details she noticed. The clean line of his jaw, the slight wrinkle of a smile at the corner of his mouth, the angle of his eyes.

Pulling the print out of the bath, she clipped it to the line to dry. Her gaze lingered on the corner of space he'd staked out.

She supposed he'd been looking at the group, watching over his friends from afar rather than joining in the conversation.

She was wrong.

While she'd been setting up the right shot to squeeze everybody into frame, he'd been watching her. Maybe it'd been a passing glance, a quick satisfaction of curiosity. Or maybe not.

Maybe she didn't have a right to know.

* * *

After finishing the last frames, she headed out of the darkroom and into the light—blinking weakly against the harsh fluorescents that lit the main floor.

A sting of cologne hit her first.

"Liza. How'd I know you were going to be here?"

She winced as she tried to open her eyes. She could already picture his teasing smirk, the flirtatious wrinkles at the corners of his eyes. A few weeks ago, she would have thought it charming—his easy familiarity, the casual closeness, the flattery. The sheen looked slicker now.

"I'm not," she said. "I'm on my way out."

He stayed her with a hand on her arm. "Can we talk?" he said. "I feel like I haven't seen you in weeks."

She shrugged, too aware of Sammy leaning in to listen with the focus of an aunty tuning in to a drama. "Let's walk."

He slid his hand against her back. "I missed you, you know."

She passed onto the street, cutting wide to allow another couple to pass. "I was out of town for a while. Visiting Char."

"Yeah? How's she doing?"

She quickened her pace. The faster she made it home, the faster she could leave him behind. "Good. She likes the work, I think. She keeps trying to get me in with the Rosings crowd."

Ray made a gagging noise. "Those are the last people you would ever want to work with."

"I think I ran into some people you know when I was out there."

A slow raise of the eyebrows. "Oh?" he said. "You know, I don't really know a lot of people."

"Someone who said he knew you," she lied.

She tried to sound casual. Nothing more casual than trying to pump someone for information.

"His name was something weird," she said. "Like Casper or something."

His expression darkened to a scowl. "Caspian. Darcy's cousin," he said. "You guys saw each other a lot?"

She nodded. "There wasn't a lot to do."

"What'd you think?" he said. "Not so bad as the others."

"He makes a better first impression. But I think Darcy changes once you get to know him."

Ray got very still. "You think he's changed?"

"No," Elizabeth replied, stealing a quick glance at his face. "I think he's about the same kind of person he always was. Just like you."

He shrunk back with a rueful smile. "I missed your cute little slogans, Lizzie," he said. "I just hope you know what you're doing. You know he won't hesitate to throw you under the bus if it suits him."

She was starting to think he wasn't the only one.

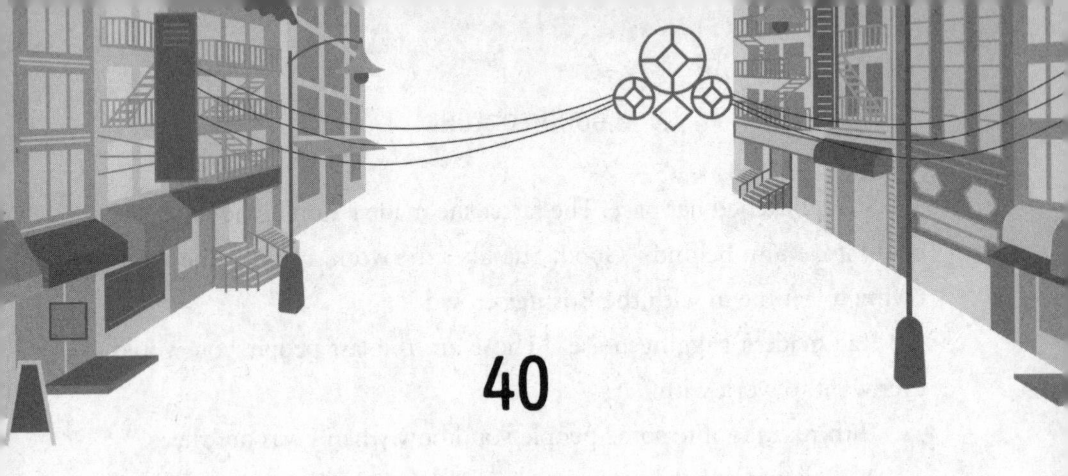

40

Nothing gave a better bang for the buck than Canal Street—especially where distractions were concerned. Always mildly inconvenient, overcrowded, and overwhelming, the street had no shortage of light, sound, or things for sale. It was the artery that ran through their neighborhoods, that linked them to Little Italy and the Lower East Side. It was where she scrounged loose change for cheap egg waffles, where she shopped for knickknacks and accessories, where her parents haggled for groceries before and after work. It was how she found her way home.

She made a stop at Lulu's, Vincent nearly crying as she walked through the door. Sure, he had four other girls; sure, he loved all his children equally—but while he appreciated the others for their ridiculousness, only his LB could be respected for her sense.

He could barely restrain himself from a show of emotion. "Ai ya, LB, home already?" he said. "Couldn't find a rich husband?"

"No," she said. "And no job either."

He patted her shoulder in sympathy, and regaled her with stories of what life had been like in her absence. In short, impossible. The problems, it turned out, hadn't been at Lulu's but at home. Kitty and Lydia fighting all the time with little refereeing; Mary screeching scales at all hours of the day and night; Lydia prattling on and on about the vacations she wanted to take, pinning up torn magazine and calendar photos of places with white sand beaches and hammocks and white people in Bermuda shorts. And Jade? Forget about it. These were not the places that they could afford to go, but did that matter? No. Did it matter that he'd been working all day and wanted a little quiet? Definitely not. Did anybody respect his time or his peace of mind? Didn't even need to ask. They just showed up with hands out, asking for money.

Thank god she was back.

And to celebrate her return, a list of errands to run and things to collect, and could she be quick about it?

The warmest welcome anyone might hope for.

Jane met her at the corner of their usual produce stall, picking through piles of bitter melon and trying to haggle with the vendor. Except Jane being Jane, her face and voice didn't show any of the necessary irritation and aggression to prove she was serious about ticking off that extra dollar per pound. She was getting fleeced.

Elizabeth could recognize a lost cause when she saw one. Fishing the bills out of her pocket, she paid for their pounds of bitter melon.

"I could have gotten her down," Jane said.

Elizabeth took the bag from the vendor with a quick thank-you and headed down the street. "No, you couldn't have. Please." She tapped Jane's bag. "What's next?"

Jane lifted the bit of scrap paper. "Watch batteries."

They dodged and avoided ornery seniors playing bumper cars with laundry carts and tall stacks of black garbage bags on their way to one of the galleria malls. When they were younger, this had been the time for anything they couldn't discuss at home—real grades, secret boyfriends, or bad habits—and Elizabeth wanted nothing more than Jane's take on everything that had happened. If only she knew how to bring it up without inducing some kind of cardiac event.

"I need to tell you something," Elizabeth said. "And I need your advice, but I need you to not be so Jane about it."

Jane walked into the watch repair shop. "Okay, what does that mean?"

"Don't get excited, don't get soft," she said. "Try to be practical."

Jane affected a grumpy expression. It made her look like a Muppet. "This *does* sound serious. What happened? Did Lydia ruin your favorite skirt or something?"

Elizabeth jabbed her in the shoulder. "If you know that Lydia ruined something of mine, you better tell me," she said.

Jane slid the handful of watches onto the counter and pushed them towards the repairman. He took them in hand and disappeared to the opposite side of his booth. "Out with it, LB."

She winced. "Darcy told me he has feelings for me."

Jane screeched, drawing the eyes of the other customers in the shop.

"What happened to not getting excited?"

"Darcy Wong?" Jane hissed. "Darcy *Wong* told you he has feelings for you?"

How many Chinese Darcys could a girl know?

"If I hadn't been there when it happened, I wouldn't have believed it either."

"What did you say?" Her eyes widened. "Oh my god, you don't like him back, do you?"

Elizabeth punched her in the shoulder. "*Please*," she said. "Do you think I've lost what's left of my mind?"

Jane shrugged. "I mean, it's not impossible . . ."

"He actually told me all of the things he hated about me first, but since that couldn't change his mind, by process of elimination . . ."

"That's kind of romantic in a—"

Elizabeth shoved her hard. "No, it's not," she cried. "Please. Whose side are you on here?"

The repairman returned with their watches, ticking and polished.

"LB," Jane said, paying. "Imagine how he feels after putting himself out there like that and being so rudely rejected."

"Hey!" Elizabeth said as they pushed back out onto the street. "I wasn't rude."

Jane gave her a knowing look.

"Anyway, there are plenty of women who would fall all over themselves for him and his money. I'm sure he'll get over it fast."

Jane cooed. "All of those beautiful women, LB, and he still wants you. That's romantic."

"I shouldn't have told you anything."

Jane giggled, singing dramatically, "It must have been love, but it's over now . . ."

Elizabeth rolled her eyes. "Shut up."

Jane ruffled her hair. "Come on. I'll buy you some egg waffles, and you can tell me in excruciating detail how you broke his heart."

For a dollar and the trouble of fending off packs of pigeons and vicious teens, they split a bag of egg waffles and sat on the steps in Forsyth Plaza, trying to hear each other over the traffic. She sketched out the major points: Ray lying about his finances, a breakdown of a friendship, potential blackmail, potential betrayal—by one or the other, or both. Whatever was the truth, it turned out they both knew each other years ago, and neither thought to mention it to her until they wanted to get her on their side.

Jane's jaw dropped, and a bubble of a waffle dropped all the way to the ground.

"Remember how weird they were when they ran into each other by the parking garage?" Elizabeth said.

Jane couldn't believe it—of one or the other, or both. There had to have been a mistake or a misunderstanding, blown all out of proportion. No one who seemed so generous and sweet could do anything like what he'd been accused of.

"You mean Darcy, or Ray?"

Jane spluttered. "Both!"

In most instances, Jane made for the perfect audience—eager, sympathetic, unfailingly kind—but there would be no way to see both sides of this situation. Someone had to be the bad guy.

Jane shook her head. "Who do you believe?"

Elizabeth chewed on her lip. "I don't know. That's the trouble."

Jane winced. "Do you really think Ray's capable of something like that?"

Men armed with charming smiles and slippery personalities could do a lot of things. Elizabeth couldn't remember how many sob stories she'd heard from girlfriends or acquaintances about men who laid emotional wreckage without even trying and, at worst, did much more.

Jane popped another waffle into her mouth with dismay. "He just seemed like such a good guy."

"That's the problem."

Jane pointed the bag in her direction, and Elizabeth snatched another waffle. "Are you okay?"

Elizabeth felt a childish urge to crawl into her sister's arms. Talking to Jane didn't change the situation, but it felt like something loosened its grip on her throat.

"I thought I was sticking up for someone who needed it, and now I think maybe I was wrong."

"If you thought you were doing the right thing, then it couldn't have been wrong," Jane said, ever the chipper cartoon chipmunk. For once, Elizabeth wished she could have her own pair of Jane-colored glasses to view the world.

Elizabeth left Jane the rest of the bag of waffles. "Enough about my bullshit. How are you doing?"

Some people were natural-born actors. Jane, on the best of days, could barely stay on script with kids about Santa Claus. Her smile wilted on the vine.

Elizabeth had never known her sister to fall often or fast; she fell hard if she fell at all. And this time, she'd fallen hard enough to hit the ground and shatter.

"Don't look at me like that," Jane said. "I'm fine."

Maybe so, but fine still wasn't anything near normal for Jane. And she wouldn't be back to normal until Elizabeth could hear her laugh again.

Elizabeth glanced down at their shoes, suddenly sheepish. "It's not that," she said. "There's something else. About Brendan."

Jane popped another waffle into her mouth and shook her head. "Whatever it is that you heard or found out, it doesn't matter," she said.

"How can you say that? Don't you want to know?" Elizabeth said. "If it was me . . ."

"I know everything I need to know," Jane replied. "If he wanted to call, he would call. If he wanted to talk to me, he would. Nothing that you could say would change that."

Elizabeth leaned her head on Jane's shoulder.

The last thing she wanted was to break her sister's heart all over again—especially when it was finally starting to mend.

Jane handed her a waffle. "I'm okay, I promise. You know it takes a lot more than that to knock me down."

The least Elizabeth owed her was the benefit of the doubt.

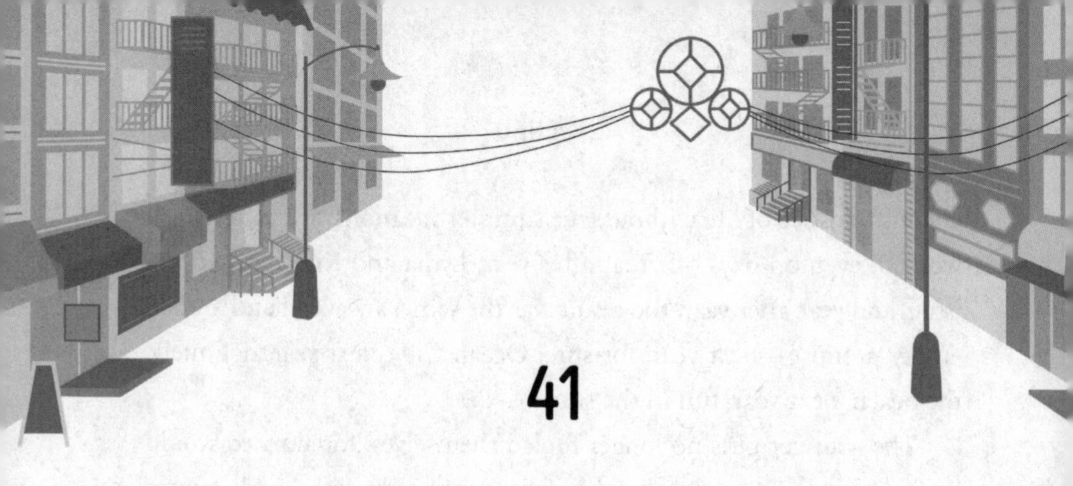

41

A summer in the city—humid, sticky, stinky, and generally unpleasant—usually meant anywhere but here for those who could afford it. Goodbye to piles of liquefying garbage on the streets, hot subway cars and other people's sweat on hot subway cars, and the trapped heat ping-ponging between glass and asphalt and sky; hello, beach. The Hamptons for the fashionable and the elite, New Jersey for most everyone else—and those who had the unfortunate luck of being left behind usually stuck their heads in their freezers and ate as much flavored ice as their stomachs could handle.

Memorial Day triggered the annual pilgrimage—shoebox apartment for the pantomime of village living, small beach towns masquerading as the coastal European *ville*. The Chens, absent money, first or second homes, and time, indulged in simpler pleasures—the roving siren song of Mister Softee, the frigid darkness of the movie theater, and a city largely emptied of people. But the city summer was brutal. Fire hydrants jimmied loose did their best to drench the streets with cooling water, the stench of fish putrefied in the heat, and still they were expected to show up for their shifts. The daughters lamented the endless injustice of life without true summer vacations; the parents still worked, even on days off. Year after year, Lydia and Kitty pressed the issue, and year after year, the result was the same: a waved hand and an empty promise—next year, for sure, Ocean City; next year, definitely, the beach; next year, fun in the sun.

The younger girls no longer fooled themselves; forewarned would be forearmed. This year, they hunted new friends with beach houses with strategic precision, hoping to coax invites for weekend stays or longer, looking to stage photos that showed their lives as full of luxury and drama as an episode of *The Hills*. But as May trickled into June and wasted away into July without an invite, they resorted to the usual tactics. Begging, bribing, kowtowing, and guilting Vincent. For once, couldn't they be normal Americans and go on vacation? For once, couldn't they *try* to pretend they knew what fun was?

Vincent could only shrug, extending his hand to ask for their normal American money. Had Coney Island been obliterated from the Earth? Weren't there still museums and parks and beaches here, all reachable for the price of a MetroCard swipe? Couldn't they find other ways to entertain themselves? How about Washington Square Park, or Jacob Riis? In short, no. Vincent could not be swayed. The restaurant could not stand to sit closed, their rent could not go unpaid, and they would all have to find some other, cheaper way of spending their time and hard-earned money in the summer than on overpriced hot dogs on the boardwalk. What did New Jersey have anyway, aaaaa? Weren't they the ones clogging up the bridges and tunnels into the city every late night and weekend? Maybe, Vincent had the gall to suggest, they could even go to the library and study their summer reading. The horror.

But Lydia could never say die. She cajoled, she seduced, she set her sights on easier targets—a young Realtor acquaintance of Jade's by the name of Bridget. They became quick friends, the kind to tie up the phone for hours every day, who became BFFs almost immediately. Between her sweet-talking and Bridget's generosity, Lydia's tactics soon bore fruit.

That week, a message blinked in wait on their answering machine—*Hi, Aunty Jade, it's Bridget. Simon and I have taken a house for the summer, and I know Lydia has been dying to go. We have a few other friends coming with us—three other girls!—and we'd love to invite Lydia along. Please let me know!*

Lydia dialed back immediately. Yes, she announced. Yes, she would absolutely join them on their trip to Seaside Heights for the month. Yes, her parents had no problem with it. Yes, yes, yes. Of course she had asked her parents. (She planned to, anyway.)

When they found out, Jade welcomed it as a gift, and it didn't matter then what Vincent said. Jade had *already promised*, Bridget *already told*, the arrangements *already made*, and it would be too late to make any changes to the plans. Please, Daddy, please, please, please—it went on for days, and even a man with a heart of stone had only so much patience before the flood wore him through entirely. And if it hadn't, one of them would surely have resorted to murder. Only one heart was broken by the news. Kitty pleaded—Could she tag along? Couldn't Jade ask Bridget since she was basically, like, her elder?—but Lydia would not be made to share her spoils.

"She didn't ask *you*, you loser," she cried. "She asked *me* and *only* me so you're going to have to stay here with the others while I live it up in their *beautiful* beach house! But I'll take tons of pictures for you."

Kitty responded as maturely as she could, first with heavy sobs that subsided into a cold rage and tantrums, then with a trail of debris to express the depth of her displeasure. "It's so unfair," she whined. "Why should *she* get to be asked to go when *I'm* two years older and I haven't gone fucking anywhere?"

Elizabeth patted her shoulder. "Kitty, trust me," she said. "New Jersey is not worth crying about."

Kitty howled. "It's *not fair*," she sobbed. "Nothing good ever happens to me in this family!"

She unleashed a torrent of complaints: the hand-me-downs, the humiliations, the hierarchy. Nothing she did mattered because someone had always done it better or first, and no one even remembered her name or what she liked because why would they need to? She couldn't even be seen as Kitty—only as one of the Chens, doomed to an eternity inside a *suffocating* and *tiny* apartment without the glories of a summer at the shore.

"If it bothers you that much, we can get some ice cream and see *Grease* at Bryant Park," Elizabeth said. "Isn't that your favorite?"

Lydia grinned. "Yes," she said, with a hiss. "Those *suh-huh-mmer ni-i-ights*."

Kitty cried harder.

"That's not helping," Elizabeth replied.

"Who cares about helping?" Lydia said. "*I* get to go to the shore."

Elizabeth rolled her eyes. "I wouldn't count on that yet," she said. "Ba can always change his mind."

The more Elizabeth tried to referee, placating one younger demon for the sake of the other, the more Darcy's words rang in the back of her head. Her baby sisters didn't care about what their parents did or about the restaurant or the rest of their lives, no matter what they were scolded or reminded or told; what they wanted was to be as free as the kids who *had*, who thought and dreamed in toys and must-haves. Elizabeth could live off Canal Street knockoffs for the rest of her life, but Lydia had ambition. What was a trip from China compared to a Chanel bag?

Someday she might change her mind, but for now? All that was worth considering was the pursuit of her own happiness. It was her American right of selfishness.

All Elizabeth could do was try to stop her from going too far. A sixteen-year-old girl left to her own devices and someone else's money rarely acted well in the best of times; an unsupervised sixteen-year-old girl in a party town in the height of the summer couldn't be trusted at all.

Vincent wouldn't hear of it. "LB, your sister is hardheaded, and she's not going to stop until she gets exactly what she wants. At least this way we don't have to pay for it and we don't have to trouble ourselves to get her there."

Elizabeth sagged. "You *can't* let her go off alone," she said. "Without any of us there, you know that Lydia won't stop until she makes a complete ass of herself."

"That's her goal," he said. "She won't be happy until she does it."

Elizabeth huffed in protest. "I'm serious," Elizabeth said. "It's cute now, but it isn't going to be cute forever. And who knows what else she'll get up to without us?"

Vincent pulled her close to him with a hum of understanding. "Don't worry, la," he said. "Nothing that Lydia does—or Kitty or Mary—will ever reflect on you. But you know Lydia won't give us any peace if she doesn't go, so let her go. There'll be people watching her, she won't starve or be left on the side of the road, and no one will look at her twice. She'll figure out she isn't the center of the universe and come home crying."

"Ba, please."

"LB, aa," he said, shaking his head. "It's done. Stop thinking about her future, and think about your own."

In the latest and greatest heartbreak in the string of short-term relationships that was turning out to be her employment history, she'd taken a full-time, paying job (at last!) processing housing applications where the company hadn't lasted as long as her probationary period. After a heady, glorious six-week run of fifteen-minute smoke breaks and riveting data entry, they'd run out of money, leaving her with a filing box she'd barely started to fill and a week's pay for severance.

Back to the drawing board, and better luck next time.

"You don't know what could happen if she goes," she warned.

He sighed. "I know what happens if she doesn't go. A lot of trouble."

So the Chens were settled.

Lydia would be going to New Jersey.

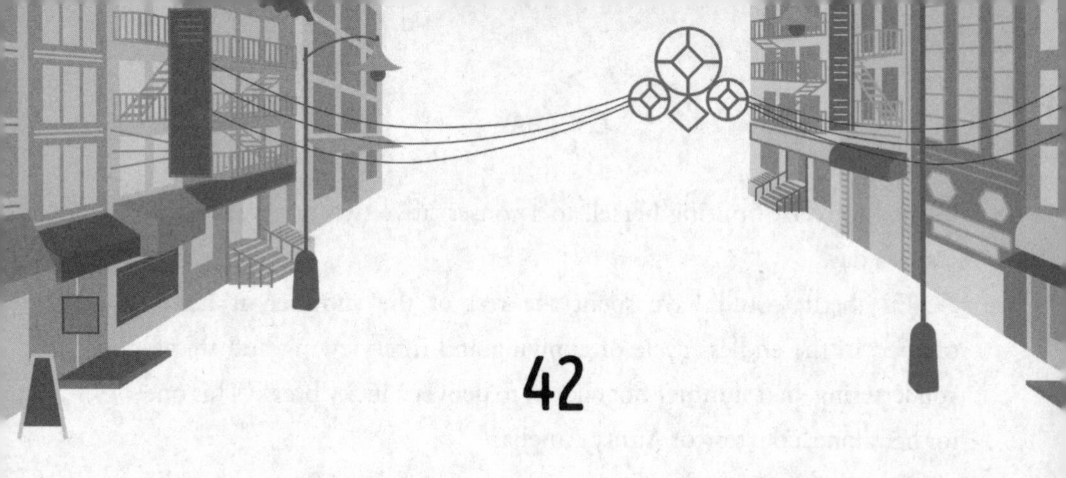

42

If absence made the heart grow fonder, somebody forgot to tell Lydia. She called as promised and as obligated, although the longer she stayed away, the shorter and shorter the calls were until they became five second bursts on the answering machine. "Went to the beach today, didn't burn, see you soon!" it usually went, punctuated by a giggle or a raucous cheer from behind her, sometimes female but mostly male. At least they could say they had proof of life.

Lydia was doing as Lydia had set out to do—to make a spectacle of herself in a town where making a spectacle was the only thing that you could do—and she would do so mightily. Only Jade seemed to miss her antics at home, lamenting the lack of excitement and news in the neighborhood; the rest of them welcomed a reprieve from the chaos.

For the first time in a long while, the Chens slipped into a relative peace. With no one to fight with or compete against, Kitty resigned herself to finding things to do, even daring to venture to the park on her own; Mary, left to her own devices, snacked and read for hours in the comfort of a bed; and Jane and Elizabeth found breathing room from having to mediate or intervene to focus on their own lives. Even Jade learned to relax, limiting herself to a conservative two or three health scares a day.

Elizabeth would have spent the rest of the summer at home, trapped in the endless cycle of applying and interviewing and thank-you-lettering, had summer not chosen to deliver a lucky break. This one for her alone, courtesy of Aunty Amelia.

After learning of a local mentorship program near Boston, Amelia had taken the liberty and the initiative to arrange for an informational interview for her favorite niece—all the better for Elizabeth to meet the right kinds of people and say the right kinds of things that would garner her the right kind of job, perhaps one very near her favorite aunt. By pure coincidence, it happened to be one of Amelia's favorite sights in the city, which she rarely had a chance to visit.

"It's beautiful," Amelia said. "I think you'll love it."

She even insisted on booking them a tour—overpriced, Elizabeth thought, given the small size and lack of notoriety around the place, which seemed little more than a dressed-up town house—but Amelia would take any opportunity for a day out and a gift shop. Anything for education. The rest of their itinerary was appropriately aggressive: museum and lighthouse visits, wandering around the North End and Boston Common, tourist trap after tourist trap, and even some candlepin bowling.

It wasn't a question but a most-expenses-paid demand—and Amelia wouldn't take no for an answer.

Come hell or high water, Elizabeth would be going to Pemberley.

* * *

She expected a second-rate museum turned tourist attraction, a Frankenstein's monster of historical details sutured onto new glass and steel. Yet, as they walked up the block, she couldn't pick it out. There was no heavy signage, no ten-foot-tall painted statues of George Washington, nothing to distinguish it as the kind of place that might be listed in a Rick Steves guidebook or a historic register. At least she wouldn't have to try to make small talk with Paul Revere.

And then Amelia stopped in the middle of the block, clasping her hands together with her best Pollyanna grin. "Isn't it beautiful?"

Even she had to admit it.

Pemberley House looked like it belonged in a picture book. The front courtyard and lawn led up a set of stone steps to a wraparound porch with wrought-iron balustrades; narrow-arched windows peered out from dark red brick; intricate metalwork adorned the steep, angled roof, dotted with ornate cornices around the facade. Despite Amelia's gushing, it didn't seem any more impressive than any of the other Victorians on the block—until they crossed the threshold.

She could almost hear the choir of angels.

Gold light poured in through large windows at the rear of the house, looking out at a sprawling yard and the other buildings in the complex. Long, wooden, barnlike structures—offices and community space, Amelia explained—ringed an open lawn with walking trails. Flowers bloomed, bees buzzed, bunnies and squirrels frolicked; Elizabeth could even hear the noise of rowdy children in the distance—the creak of swings, the crack of baseball bats, shrill laughter. Somebody call Walt Disney. It wasn't anything like what she'd expected from the street; it radiated with joy and vitality.

Their tour led them through the parlor and up floor by floor through the house, walking them through history in artifacts. From the candlesticks supposedly smuggled from the British in the Revolutionary War to a phonograph purportedly gifted by the Bell family, everything touched some legacy of history to justify its display. Even the silver spoons. It was like guesting on *Antiques Roadshow*, except without the cash prize.

Amelia *ooh*ed and *aah*ed, trailed her fingers along the cases, marveled at the upholstered furniture and the wallpaper details, and inspected every trinket the museum offered. Fingerprints on display cases—this was the extent of her interaction with history.

No thanks to Amelia's endless chatter, they finally made it to the top floor after two hours, walking the museum's small and eclectic collection of Chinese and Japanese art. Glazed ceramics and woven textiles sat alongside painted paper fans and scrolls, each with a small card explaining its origins.

"This isn't part of the original collection but part of our work here at the Foundation," the guide said. "The family trust has a great interest in curating and restoring East Asian artifacts from private collections."

Elizabeth tried to imagine these private collectors—the bygone carpet barons and steamboat executives—who felt called to hoard these relics in their homes. It wasn't love or appreciation, only empty style. What they prized, they kept, and what they kept, they felt they owned.

Elizabeth wandered past a display case full of small bowls, each one riven with gold cracks. *To celebrate and emphasize the act of restoration*, she read. A little scarred, but still holding together. A little worse for wear, but all the stronger for it.

She could relate.

After a short loop of the rest of the floor, Elizabeth couldn't wait for her aunt any longer. Desperate times called for desperate measures. In her best Lydia impression, she whimpered and pleaded to be set free while Amelia finished looking at everything.

And what kind of aunt could deny her beloved niece?

"All right," Amelia said. "Leave your aunty behind, then."

It took all of her willpower not to run down the stairs.

Outside, she couldn't deny that it was beautiful—the yard shaded by blossoming trees, the rustic red brick of the house softening to the lighter wood of the office buildings on either side, the romantic twirls of vine curling against the back of the house like something out of a J.Crew catalogue. But that was the thrill of places like this, wasn't it? The romance and the fantasy, the exclusivity. Not everyone could get in.

Elizabeth continued down one of the dirt trails, peeking through the large, paneled glass windows to the offices inside. Inside, harried, clipboard-wielding people rushed back and forth with notebooks or BlackBerrys in hand, pecking away at their emails and messages.

If Jade had her way, Elizabeth would have been one of them.

She continued past the offices, watching as the cultivated beauty of the garden quieted to something closer to nature. The lawn continued on beyond the office buildings, unmarked by anything except the occasional water fountain and park bench, worn thin in patches from the trample of feet. Farther out, she spotted a row of basketball courts beside a playground. She could imagine a place like this on a busy weekend, packed with picnicking families and teenagers with nothing better to do—the kind of place that became tradition because it would always be available.

"LB!" Aunt Amelia cried.

Standing with the tour guide at the rear of one of the office buildings, Amelia waved.

Elizabeth jogged back to meet them, sliding into the conversation just as Amelia laid her trap.

"You know, my niece Elizabeth has a lot of experience in community work."

Jade would have been proud.

The guide gave a placating smile. "I don't have anything to do with hiring," she said. "But I can get you a business card or something, if you like."

"Oh yes, please! And is there anything you can tell us about what they're working on?" Amelia said.

"The Wong Family Land Trust is very involved in the community," the guide said. "And I can tell you they're choosy about the projects they take on."

Elizabeth's heart jumped into her throat. "The Wong Family Land Trust?"

Amelia tapped the guide on the arm. "I told you my niece knows about these kinds of things."

"Yes, it's all run by the same family. Randolph Wong spearheaded it, but since he passed away, his son, Darcy, has run it."

She'd never been great at math, but even she could figure those odds.

Elizabeth wasn't a worrier by nature, but run-ins with exes, mutual or not, never turned out well. And the two of them were—was there a name for it?—*something* enough that she didn't want to suffer through any more awkwardness than she had at their last breakfast. "He's not here *now*, is he?"

The guide shook her head. "Unfortunately not," she said. "But he's due in a few days for the board meeting."

Elizabeth nearly breathed an audible sigh of relief. So she would miss him after all.

"I guess you don't see them much when they're not in session?"

"Oh, they're very hands-on. Georgiana Wong is one of our community relations ambassadors, and she's always reviewing our upcoming programming."

"Programming?" Elizabeth said.

Pemberley House, it turned out, was not just another nonprofit intended to educate passing tourists on the height of trends in the early nineteenth century as a means of becoming a tax shelter for passive income. They engineered after-school programs, summer activity sessions, and block parties, as well as a substantial ongoing mentorship program for lower-income youth.

Amelia whistled. "They must take their work seriously."

"How is it working with him?" Elizabeth blurted.

Amelia nodded. "We've heard he can be a bit overbearing."

The guide shrugged. "I haven't worked with him much myself. But the staff find him really supportive, and he's become much more involved with the house lately, especially with our mentorship programs."

"Hmmm," Amelia said, raising her eyebrows.

"He started a couple months ago, and the boys have really taken to him. But the women in the development offices can tell you more. They love working with him."

This was going too far. Kind and generous, maybe, in the spirit of charity. But Darcy turning out to be considerate? Thoughtful? *Beloved*? It didn't make sense.

From the yard, the guide led them into the complex, crossing through the breezeway to the building opposite. An upright piano stood in the corner of the main atrium, surrounded by poster-size photos of the events they'd hosted in the past. This didn't look right. She expected Death Star decorations, a shrine to himself and his good deeds, anything other than a regular-looking office building.

The least he owed her was to be insufferable.

Amelia hit an off-key note on the piano as they passed. "Needs a little tuning."

They breezed further along. "That's Georgiana's," the guide said. "She likes to play and she encourages her mentees to play, so Darcy had it sent."

"Wow," Amelia said. "LB, I don't think your sisters would do that for you."

"Probably not."

Elizabeth studied the display cases as she made her way down the hall. Bright, young faces grinned at her from group photos, brimming with excitement and promise. Handwritten letters from former mentees sat pinned inside display cases, heralding successful new roles or touting the achievements of the program.

Near the hallway sat a recent glossy poster of the last major fundraiser they hosted at the house. She recognized too many faces in it: Catherine's dour pucker, Geoffrey swimming in an ill-fitting suit jacket, Caroline and Louisa towering like birches in stilettos, Brendan trapped between them. Darcy and Georgiana stood off-center in the frame, leaning against each other. Georgiana looked like a slim, delicate girl of around seventeen, hair piled in an updo of curls on top of her head, hiding behind the shoulder of her brother. And he—well, he photographed well.

He looked relaxed, at ease, mouth curving with a smile the way that she'd sometimes seen in New York. She'd always supposed it to be a cruel kind of laughter, smug in judging himself better than those around him; now she read it as warmth. Who knew what was the truth?

Photos couldn't be trusted; she knew that better than anyone.

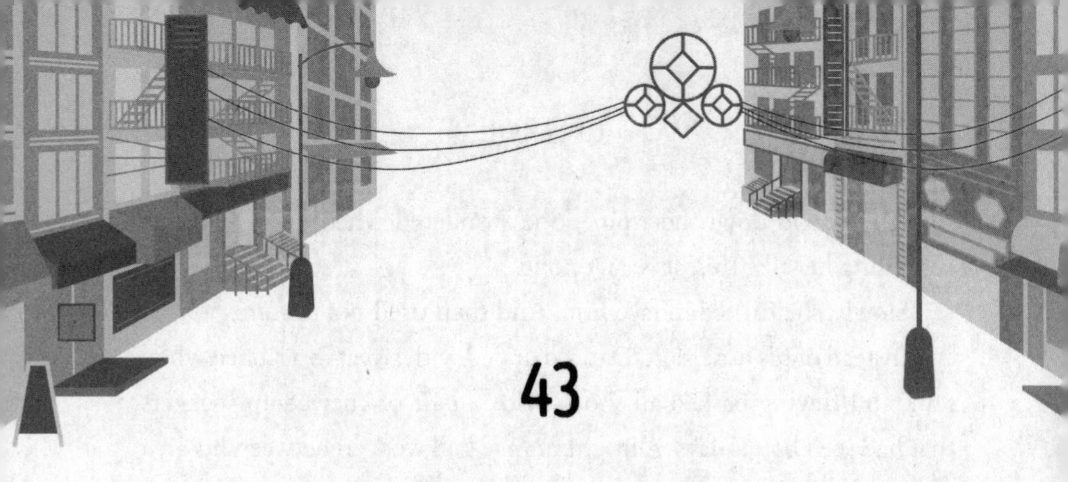

43

Coming here had been a bad idea.

She wasn't prepared to see him. Even there, inert in the photo like an insect in amber, smiling from a year agos. She couldn't see his face without hearing his voice as she last heard it, warm and low with emotion, telling her everything that counted against her in her life, without feeling the grip of his arms as he pressed her against the wall in Charlotte's dim kitchen. Without remembering—well, nothing that she could tell her aunt.

Ducking outside, she took the first trail around the edge of the building towards the far lawn, hoping to quiet her mind.

Her aunt called out behind her, "LB, where are you going?"

Elizabeth slowed but didn't stop. She followed the footpath down a sloping hill, the path narrowing as it rounded a copse of trees. Two shadows jutted out from the other side of the path as another party passed the opposite way.

She stepped aside to let them pass.

Gravel scratched behind her.

"Elizabeth."

A chill slid down her spine. She wondered when he would stop surprising her like this. It wasn't polite.

Slowly, she turned to face him. And then tried not to stare.

Instead of his usual suit, Darcy dripped with sweat in a ribbed white tank and fraying basketball shorts with a pair of chewed-up sneakers that had seen better days. A bright orange ball wedged between his arm and his side. She could almost mistake him for one of the neighborhood boys, fresh off of a pickup game, all muscle and attitude.

Now she knew she was losing her mind.

"Hi," he said.

A young man about Lydia's age squinted against the sunlight at her.

She lifted her hand in a wave. "We were told that you wouldn't be here," she said. "Not that I'm not—not that it isn't—I mean, it's nice to see you."

The last time Elizabeth struggled so hard to make conversation, she had been trying to avoid publicly humiliating herself in front of Tony Rivera, the eighth grader all of the sixth and seventh graders fought over, and an audience of middle schoolers.

This felt worse.

"How are you?" he said, slicking his hair back with a wince. "How's your family?"

The muscles in his arm rippled with the motion.

She hadn't realized he'd even had them.

Or that she'd been staring. Like his friend was currently and openly doing at her.

"Good," she stammered. "I, um, we're all good. We're . . . good."

"Good," he said. "That's good."

If they were any better, they might not have had so many things to talk about.

"I didn't know you would be here."

"How long have you been in town?" he said at the same time.

"I just got here," she said. "I came for a—to visit some family. And I didn't know that this was your—that you would be here."

"Family?" he said. "How long are you staying?"

She could feel herself tripping over her own tongue. It was like dancing with Geoffrey all over again—the steps at the wrong time in the wrong order, landing on someone else's toes, the sting of public embarrassment.

"I don't know," she said. "I mean, not long."

He nodded. "That's good," he said. "That's good."

It was bad and getting worse, and all she could do was grin and bear it like a beauty pageant contestant. The things she wanted to say were the things she couldn't mention, the questions she couldn't ask; but she'd always been the kid who liked to push on a bruise to see how it was healing. She should ask him what he thought about world peace.

If he knew what she was thinking, he didn't show it.

She once imagined she could read the way he looked at her—always critical, always scrutinizing, paring her down to her faults. It was too tempting now to try to find other things in it—something to convince her that she hadn't ruined whatever it was they had been or would have been.

She knew it was over. It hadn't ever started. She knew it as well as she knew the words of his last email. But it was hard to remember that when she looked at him, when she felt that kick of hope in her chest again.

Maybe a small part of her wanted something to work out this time. Didn't she deserve that?

The person beside him coughed loudly.

Darcy shook himself out of his thoughts. "Oh, pardon me. This is

Marcus. Marcus and I have been mentoring each other for the last few months, and I came early to surprise him."

"Seems like he surprised you too!" Marcus said with a small laugh.

She colored and shook his hand. "Nice to meet you."

"This is Elizabeth," Darcy said.

Marcus glanced between them with a knowing smile. He was sixteen at the oldest, more muscular than Darcy and nearly a head taller. He looked in better shape than either of them. "Darcy's not great at keeping surprises to himself," Marcus said. "Although I guess he's doing better at keeping secrets than I would have guessed."

Darcy nudged him with his elbow. "Watch yourself."

Marcus huffed. "I didn't say anything."

And then, silence.

The *Jeopardy!* theme song chimed in the back of her head with a faint thrum of panic.

"We should head inside and attend to some . . . business. Sorry, I didn't realize you would be coming . . ."

She shook her head, eager to show how little inconvenienced she was. "That's fine," she squeaked. "That's great. Great! You should go and do what you need to do. We were on our way out anyway."

"My best to your family," he said as they passed.

She watched them disappear in the direction of the building.

Whatever she had expected—yelling, screaming, being escorted off the premises by mall security guards—she hadn't thought to consider politeness and small talk. When had he ever cared about being polite?

Infuriating that he couldn't even piss her off now when she counted on it.

With sudden shame, she realized that she hadn't even *asked* about Marcus. Well, at least it would give him one more thing to hate about her.

Amelia came up behind her with an annoyed grunt. "I thought you were waiting for me."

"Sorry," she said. She'd blacked out and temporarily left her body.

Amelia panted. "Did you see him?"

"Who?"

"Darcy, aa," she said. "He passed me on the way here. I don't think Jocelyn was right about him at all. I tried to say hi, but he just kept walking."

"Oh," Elizabeth said. "No. I didn't see him."

Amelia tapped her arm. "You didn't hear me calling you either?" she said. "It's not nice to leave an old woman behind like that, you know."

Elizabeth snorted. "Aunty," she crooned, dropping her head on her shoulder. "Still very young, aa."

Amelia pulled her by the arm back the way they came. "Don't try to flatter me now," she laughed. "Rude girl."

They looped back, Amelia chattering on about the rest of the day, about the sight of boats on the water and the beautiful weather, about a thousand other things that Elizabeth didn't care about and couldn't remember. Her mind stayed in that courtyard, that awkward conversation, stuck on the memory of who they had just missed.

As they made their way down the block to the intersection, someone called out her name.

Darcy sprinted towards them, having changed into a fresh T-shirt, his hair finger-combed neat.

He rubbed at the back of his neck as he slowed to a stop in front of them. "I'm sorry," he said. "I don't mean to intrude."

Jeans, she thought, vacantly. He changed into blue jeans.

She hadn't expected him to know what denim was, much less own a pair himself.

He wiped his hands against the front of his pants. "I didn't know—I wasn't prepared to receive guests," he continued, to Elizabeth. "Earlier, I mean."

Amelia watched them with wide eyes. Elizabeth's mind whirred and rang with questions and calculations, spitting out conclusions like a quarter-slot jackpot.

"I mean, you didn't know we were coming," she said. "*I* didn't know we were coming."

His brow wrinkled with confusion. "You didn't know you'd be . . ."

"It seems like you're doing good work," she said, waving her hands frantically. The international sign for *I'm drowning, please save me*. Not that Amelia noticed. "That's why I'm here, actually."

She nearly winced as soon as it left her mouth. It reminded her of a Jade Chen windup, a softball of a pitch towards a pulled string.

Amelia finally threw a lifesaver. "I heard about the mentorship program," she said. "I thought LB would be interested."

He nodded. "This is our third year doing it. We've seen good results so far, but we're always trying to optimize."

Amelia cleared her throat. "I'm Amelia, Elizabeth's aunt."

"Oh!"

He hadn't learned to hide his surprise. Wonder of wonders—a relative of Elizabeth's with volume control, a sense of good manners, and something that might be called poise? Who would have believed it possible?

She bit down a grin. "Darcy, this is my aunt Amelia. Aunty Amelia, this is Darcy Wong. We met at Alexa and Bryan's wedding, and he's working with Mother on the community center."

The reveal didn't faze him for long.

Especially when Amelia troubled him with questions about the neighborhood, Pemberley House and the work they did, how he and Elizabeth knew each other, and other details of his stay. And did he turn brooding and standoffish as he had the other times she'd run into him? No, not this Darcy—the new and improved, version 2.0 Darcy.

This Darcy somehow answered every question with a handful of his own. Had they tried this bakery, or that noodle house? He'd be happy to see if he could connect them with a last-minute reservation. He made recommendations for the rest of their stay, asked about the sites they were visiting, and apologized for crashing their tour. He was warm and personable, attentive and flattering.

Would the real Darcy Wong please stand up?

"I don't come around here often," Amelia demurred. "Would you mind walking us to the bridge?"

He would be happy to do it.

Happy! To do something for *her* family!

She glanced up, looking for any other harbinger of doom. Surely the world would soon be coming to an end. But there was nothing besides the sun behind scratches of thin, white clouds.

They kept their pace in relative silence, taking the width of the whole sidewalk like the nightmare tourists they were. Amelia couldn't stop staring at the two of them as if they were some thousand-piece puzzle to be solved, and Darcy could barely meet her eyes. Sometimes she felt his eyes land on her in passing when he imagined she wasn't looking. Or maybe she only hoped he did. What she saw and what actually happened were turning out to be much further apart than she once thought.

Dear god, she was turning into her mother.

Darcy caught her arm, pulling her to a stop. "We should wait."

She glanced behind them and saw Amelia pulling up the rear, almost a yard behind them.

Amelia urged them on, walking towards them with a sudden-onset limp. "Your aunty's old, LB," she croaked. "Don't worry about me."

Not so old that she hadn't piggybacked some of Aunty Pippa's kids around last Christmas, but too old now to keep their glacial pace down the block.

"I'll be right behind you. Don't make a fuss, la."

Darcy deferred to Elizabeth with an expectant look. Elizabeth tried not to look like she wanted to murder her aunt.

They continued then at half speed, power-walking seniors in fluorescent windbreakers and fanny packs passing them at a clip.

Without Amelia, they could talk about anything on their minds—so best to avoid saying anything at all. She wondered if he might be thinking of all the things they could say to each other, all the things they'd once said to each other.

She wondered if he was waiting for her to say something first.

He looked at her cautiously, the momentary hesitation before pulling the trigger.

"You're wearing jeans," she said, in case he wasn't aware.

He stared at her, then looked down in confusion at his pants. "Yes?"

Bad things happened to her whenever she left New York, and here was the proof.

She stopped and tried again.

"I didn't know you were going to be here," she said.

He fought a smile. "So you said," he said. "There were a few things I wanted to do ahead of the meeting so I came early."

"Marcus?"

Darcy nodded. "I haven't been as involved a mentor this year as I want to be."

"He seems like a great kid."

They weaved along the middle of the sidewalk, narrowing the distance between them until she felt the ghost of his arm against her sleeve.

"He wants to go into development, so we're trying to find him a placement."

A thick crowd of students and parents in university gear rushed down the sidewalk, forcing them off to the side. His hand floated against her back as he steered her to safety.

"We expect most of the board to be in tomorrow. Brendan, Caroline, Henry, and some others."

"Are you going to tell them that I'm here?"

The crosswalk flashed a warning sign.

Some might have taken that as an omen—but not Elizabeth Chen. The Chens ignored omens as a rule and flouted them as principle.

"You can tell them yourself, if you like," he said. "We're hosting a little celebration for our mentees tonight. They'll all be there. You should come."

Nothing would make the Lees more miserable. It was a strong point in his favor.

"I mean, you can come and learn more about the program," he said. "They'll be presenting some of their work from the last few months."

Another point—it would be a step for possible career development.

What would Jade say if she let such an opportunity pass her by?

He cleared his throat. "And there's someone else who wants to meet you," he said. "If you—if there's no objection, my sister—"

"If we can," she said.

"We can send a car." He slipped his hands into his pockets, looking pleased. Quieter, he added, "I know they'd like to see you."

Whether he meant the Lees or his sister, she wasn't sure—though she wouldn't believe it. Whether he meant himself, she couldn't allow herself to wonder.

"The pictures came out," she said. At his raised eyebrow, she added, "From the roof."

"Ah," he said. "And?"

"Lydia's look insane, but at least she had a good time," she said. "I could have brought some of the ones I took for you if I'd known . . ."

He chuckled. "I don't really like to look at myself."

"I figured. But you should still have them anyway."

"Did you bring your camera with you?"

"Not today," she said. "I left it at my aunt's."

"Is that where you're staying?"

She nodded. "They're in Somerville. After a small pause, she added, "My uncle works at Tufts."

"That's a good school."

"Yeah, that's what I hear."

Like a pair of monkeys, they mirrored each other, trying to convince each other they were on the same side. Almost talking, but not quite. Nearly touching, but not quite.

Somehow keeping balanced on a knife's edge between what they were and what they once could have been.

At last, Amelia met them with a weary smile. "My legs aren't what they used to be," she said. "But I appreciate you waiting."

"How are you feeling?" Darcy asked.

Sally Field, she was not. "Oh, fine. It just takes me a little while to catch my breath." With a perky smile, she added, "Would you like to join us for lunch?"

Elizabeth elbowed her aunt. "I'm sure you have a lot of work that you have to do," she said. "For your board meeting."

Amelia protested, "What man is too busy for his friends, hmm?"

"I'm afraid she's right," he said. "There are a lot of arrangements to finalize. I'm sorry."

Amelia shrugged. "Next time then."

His hand grazed her shoulder. "Don't forget about tonight," he said. "Bring your family."

Elizabeth ignored the increasingly cartoonish expressions Amelia flashed her way. "We should let you go."

He held her gaze for a moment before stepping close and wrapping his arms around her in a short hug. So they were the kind of acquaintances—friends? enemies? *neighbors?*—to hug now. That was good to know.

She settled her hand against his back.

He stepped back with a small cough. "I should be getting back. But it was very nice to see you both."

Amelia waved at him as he ran back over the bridge.

"*Well!*" Amelia trilled, as he cleared the intersection. There were too many meanings in that one sound to pull apart. "He seems *perfectly* charming. He carries himself a little seriously, but it's nothing *too* bad. Things get so exaggerated these days."

"He isn't usually so . . . comfortable."

Amelia took her hand as they walked on. "Some people are like that, you know," she said. "It takes the right kind of person to break them out of their shell."

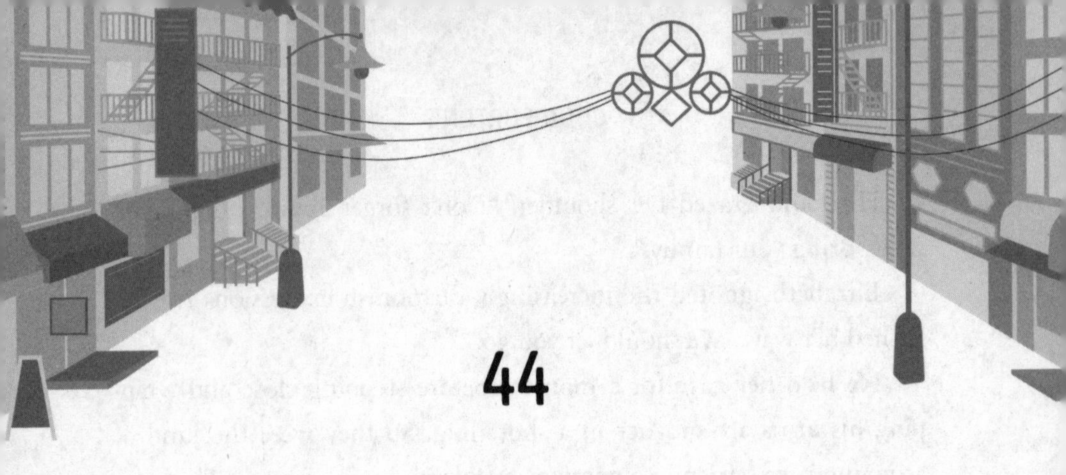

44

If this was going to be the last time they ever saw each other, she planned to make it count. She wanted to leave looking smart, educated, respectable, all of the things that he once doubted she could be. She wanted him to feel something like regret. To know that there was more to them—to her—than what he'd seen at Alexa Hu's wedding that night, than what he'd expected. To prove that she could be more than enough—in fact, much too good—for him in the first place.

The dress was one from the back of Amelia's closet, a black velvet slip dress that clung a little too tightly to her larger frame. It clashed with her shoes and rode higher on her than her petite aunt, but there was no changing it. It would be this or the same old jeans and T-shirt and barefoot like Jewel.

As promised, a Lincoln Town Car pulled up outside the house at exactly seven. Randall and Amelia seemed surprised by the care and the expense, wondering again how exactly their niece seemed to know her friend. Not that she could have explained it if she tried. Not even to herself.

The rear passenger door opened and let out a young woman, shivering in a loose wrap. She looked as delicate as a china figurine and not nearly so old as seventeen, all skin and bone waiting for muscle. Her hair gathered wispy and loose around her shoulders, curling mildly in the heat. A thin silver charm bracelet circled her small wrist, covering a raised white scar, thin as a fingernail. Her brother followed her out soon after, dressed neatly in slacks and a merino sweater.

Elizabeth came down to meet them, feeling suddenly exposed with her bare shoulders and the thinness of her dress. It felt faintly, terrifyingly, like prom all over again. She only hoped this night didn't end with her throwing up Cherry Coke and vodka all over someone's shoes.

He greeted her with a short hug, smelling clean like salt. So they hugged now—definitely.

"This is Georgiana, my sister. Geo, this is Elizabeth, my . . . friend."

Georgiana seemed even more startled by the introduction than Elizabeth, her eyes darting between her brother and Amelia and Randall on the porch.

Elizabeth hugged her in greeting. "It's nice to finally meet you," she said, warmly.

Georgiana could barely lift her eyes to meet her. "You too. I've heard so much about you." She sounded like a cartoon mouse, voice high and thin with nerves.

What others read as aloofness and snobbery turned out to be nothing more than stage fright.

Darcy bumped Georgiana's shoulder in warning, and she giggled.

She had expected him to be overprotective, a strict and serious older brother to a much younger sister, but it was the opposite. Around each other, they loosened up until they were almost normal people, teasing and cracking jokes.

With five, there could never be enough space, enough difference, enough distance; two could have their own little world.

"What have you heard about me?" Elizabeth said. "Good things, I hope."

There was a glimmer of humor in Georgiana's smile. "Mostly."

Elizabeth grinned, pulling her close. "Well, now you have to tell me everything."

"You too!" Georgiana said, breathlessly. "He didn't tell me *anything* about New York. I've always wanted to see it."

Elizabeth started with surprise. "You haven't been?"

A girl like her, with her looks and her money? They usually crossed oceans between meals.

Georgiana blushed, a deep red that spread across the bottom half of her face. "I don't go out very much."

"Most younger sisters I know would be desperate to get away."

A shadow passed over her face. "He doesn't like me to travel alone."

Elizabeth smiled. "Well, now you can say you know someone if you ever come to New York. Don't let him push you around just because he likes to do things his way."

Darcy scoffed. "If anyone's being pushed around, it isn't Geo. Trust me."

Georgiana leaned in close to whisper. "Will you tell me what he was like when he was there?"

"I'll tell you everything you want to know. And maybe more."

Darcy opened the rear door, eyeing them with apprehension. "I have a feeling I'm going to regret introducing you."

* * *

When Darcy mentioned a gala to celebrate the programs at Pemberley House, Elizabeth had pictured something like Caroline's stuffy, fussy affair at the Rainbow Room. This time, they pulled up outside an unassuming red brick building with a single banner announcing *Congratulations Pemberley Peer Fellows* by the doorway.

Inside were more surprises—no place cards, no centerpieces, no special menus and seating. The tablecloths were checkered, the decor full of framed photos of long-dead celebrities she didn't recognize, the sauce very, very red. Posters stood along the walls leading to the reception room in the rear, spotlighting the projects of the latest class of mentees and their recent accomplishments. And the smell—all butter and garlic, and melted mozzarella cheese.

It was enough to make a girl weak in the knees.

They'd barely passed the front door when Elizabeth heard someone shouting her name.

Brendan, already a few drinks in, charged towards them with a raucous yell. "LB!" he cried, crushing her in a hug. "You're here!"

So this was the horrible monster who broke her sister's heart.

"Gigi!"

Brendan picked her up, swinging her in a wide circle as she shrieked.

"Someone's having a very good night," Elizabeth said.

Brendan let Georgiana back down with a sheepish shrug. "It's just good to be back," he said. "To see you again."

The last time the Lees visited Boston, they'd broken Jane's heart—and she hoped she might repay the favor. If Brendan could be so unbothered, the least she could do was remind him of the damage he left behind. "I'm surprised you remembered," she said. "It's been such a long time since we've heard from you."

He answered with a careful smile, his friendly attention sharpened with anxiety. "I can always make time for friends."

"As long as it's convenient," she said. "But out of sight, out of mind, right?"

"Elizabeth . . ." he said, expression all puppy-dog, apologetic and bashful and confused. It might have worked on her mother or her sister, but she was neither.

It pissed her off.

What he wanted was to make a mess without having to clean it up, to be everything to everyone without ever having to be responsible for someone else's feelings. He'd been likable for so long he didn't know how to be disliked.

But he'd learn.

Elizabeth took Georgiana's hand in hers. "Should we head inside?"

Georgiana glanced back at the doorway where Darcy played host, greeting the families coming in and taking coats.

He looked almost natural, chatting with mentees and their parents as they entered the room in their Fashion Bug best.

She'd never been happier to borrow a dress; she never would have lived it down if she'd shown up in the same outfit as one of the teenage fellows.

"It's so easy for him," Georgiana said. "Doing this kind of thing. Talking to people." Her free hand scratched at her throat. "I always feel like I'm doing something wrong—like they're all looking at me. And after last year . . ."

Elizabeth squeezed her hand. "The first time I met Darcy, he didn't say anything to anyone," Elizabeth said. "You have nothing to worry about. We just need to warm you up."

Georgiana shot her a skeptical look; it apparently ran in the family. "Really?"

"And you're not walking in there alone. You have me," she said. "Whatever happens, if you think you're doing the wrong thing, I promise I'm probably doing something worse."

Georgiana gave a shaky exhale. "Even if you did, I don't think it would bother you," she said as they inched their way towards the back room. "When I feel everyone looking at me, it feels like I can't even breathe."

Elizabeth led them on into the back. "I'll tell you a secret," she said. "I learned really early to make it look like it doesn't bother me . . . even when it does. You need to when you have as many little sisters as I do."

And as ridiculous a family as she did.

In the rear room, Caroline and Louisa splayed against the bench seating with drinks in hand, watching the doorway. At the sight of Georgiana, they sprang to their feet, greeting her with pecks on the cheek and exaggerated coos of affection. *It's been so long! Such a grown girl! How nice to run into each other again!* They preened over her dress and her hair, asked after her studies, and deigned to ask Elizabeth one or two questions about her life.

Caroline lamented having to leave New York in such a hurry—"But Brendan can never make up his mind, la! Always coming and going!"—but they never thought about anything else besides their good friends. They didn't *mind* the city, but there were other jobs to inspect, other places to visit—and, really, didn't the noise and the dirtiness bother her after a while? It must have been so nice for her to finally get a breath of fresh air!

Elizabeth could only be grateful Jane missed the show. She deserved better than these snakeskin handbags.

Brendan joined them then, handing Georgiana and Elizabeth each a glass of wine.

Georgiana tested a sip, puckering at the taste. Like her brother, she couldn't hide a single thought passing through that delicate face. "It's interesting . . ."

"So, Gigi, how's everything?" Brendan said. "You still on a break from school?"

She played with the small charms on her bracelet, stammering. Elizabeth bumped her lightly in the shoulder.

"I, um, just started going back this term," she said. "I'm still trying to catch up, but I think it's been going all right."

"I heard that you're quite the musician," Elizabeth said. "My aunt and I went by Pemberley House for a tour today."

Georgiana lit up, gulping down another splash of wine with jittery excitement. "You went? How did you like it? What did you think?" she cried. "Darcy let me work on some of the program ideas when I was . . . off from school, and it was incredible. I have so many ideas for what Pemberley can do and how we can grow."

Brendan groaned. "What's wrong with you Wongs? No shop talk."

Elizabeth smiled. "It's great what you're giving back to the community. I hear you're the one to thank for it."

"D mentioned that you would say something like that," she said. "He said that's what you care about. Community building."

Elizabeth took a long sip of her wine and tried not to wonder what else *D* had said about her. "Do you know all the projects here then?"

Georgiana nodded. "Most of them." She pointed at one of the posters near the hall. This was no amateur job—no thin streaks of Magic Marker, no construction paper cutouts—but a slick diorama worthy of a lower-level conference room. "Marcus's is one of my favorites. He has this whole proposal for increasing green space with these urban garden co-ops. I hope they can make it happen."

Elizabeth nudged her with her elbow. "Come on, then."

Georgiana paled. "What?"

"Let's go say hi," she said. "And you can tell him yourself."

"Elizabeth, *no*," Georgiana hissed, but Elizabeth gently led her towards the direction of the poster.

It was hard to believe the person in front of her was the same one she'd run into on the trail at Pemberley. Marcus stood tall in a navy suit with a thin tie, his dark curly hair unruly in spite of the product in it.

"Surprise!" Elizabeth chirped.

Marcus laughed. "I thought that was you over there," he said. He extended a hand towards Georgiana. "I'm Marcus."

She gave it a light shake. "Georgiana."

"I know," Marcus said, quickly. "Your brother talks about you a lot."

"Congratulations, by the way," Elizabeth said, waving towards the posterboard. "It sounds like you did an incredible job."

He squirmed with the praise like she was a real adult. "It's just a proposal."

With her usual subtlety and grace, Elizabeth nudged Georgiana again. From there, she and Marcus fell into halting conversation, chatting about the program and about Darcy, about the challenge of funding to get something off the ground and finding possible sites for the farms.

Elizabeth watched for a moment before slowly tiptoeing back into the crowd.

A hand landed on her shoulder. "There you are," Brendan said. "I've been trying to catch up with you all night."

She sipped at her wine. "I thought you'd have other people you'd want to talk to first."

Brendan's smile slipped. "LB—Elizabeth, I know it's been a long time," he said. "Longer than I wanted . . . but it's been hard to find the time to go back."

"Or the excuse not to?" she said.

He rubbed at the back of his neck with a sigh. She hadn't noticed how exhausted he looked, but it was impossible to ignore the deep shadows under his eyes, the slight tremor in his hands. When he spoke, it was barely above a whisper. "How's she doing?" he said. "I haven't heard from her since I—since the gala."

She crossed her arms over her chest. "Whose fault is that?"

He hung his head. "It's been—there's been a lot going on," he said. "We've had to deal with my father and I've been flying back and forth . . ."

"You could have picked up the phone," she said. "Or left a message. Or done anything else besides going silent for months."

"It isn't that simple."

"It can be," she said. "You call someone if you want to call them. If you don't want to call them, you tell them that."

He drained the rest of his wine, sliding the glass onto a nearby table. "If I call her, will she even pick up?"

Elizabeth lightly shoved his shoulder. "Don't ask *me*. Ask *her*," she said. "Brendan, at some point, you have to figure out what you want to do. You can't wait for other people to tell you."

He gave a weak chuckle. "Isn't that you telling me?"

Well, who'd ever gone wrong for listening to her?

"It doesn't change the fact that I'm right."

He sniffed. "And home is . . . all right?" he said. "Everyone's doing fine?"

She slapped him hard on the back. "If you want to know how Jane's doing, you're going to have to talk to her yourself."

A sharp whine of microphone feedback interrupted them, jolting the room into a hush.

Standing on a dining chair, Darcy waved his arm in the air, trying to summon everyone's attention. "Hello," he murmured into the mic with a puff of air. "I'm not much for speeches, so this will be very short. Thank you, everyone, for coming to celebrate this year's fellows."

Whistles and loud applause rang through the space.

"This is our third year of the program, and each year has been more successful and gratifying than the last. As we keep building, we hope to launch more peer fellows into the community to continue the work that they start while they're with us," he said. He raised his drink, his eyes sweeping around the room and landing on her. "Where we come from is as important as where we want to go, so thank you all for taking part in that journey."

He smiled, and she found herself smiling back, lifting her glass in toast.

The room erupted in cheers and clinking glasses.

Elizabeth retreated to the bar, watching as groups of parents and other mentees mobbed Darcy with gratitude and questions. He shook hands and smiled for pictures, and didn't wince or frown once. This couldn't be the same Darcy she met at Alexa's wedding; he laughed too easily, smiled too wide, and wrinkled his pants. This Darcy seemed at home.

Surrounded by Marcus and Georgiana, he leaned against the wall with a highball of scotch, laughing through whatever they were telling him. He answered with a story of his own, his hands cutting wide through the air, sending Georgiana into a fit of giggles.

She couldn't remember ever seeing this Darcy before.

Georgiana threw her a shy wave.

He turned to her then and just looked—his eyes nothing but dark, his smile a slick promise, skin flushed from the alcohol.

This Darcy, she didn't know what to do with at all.

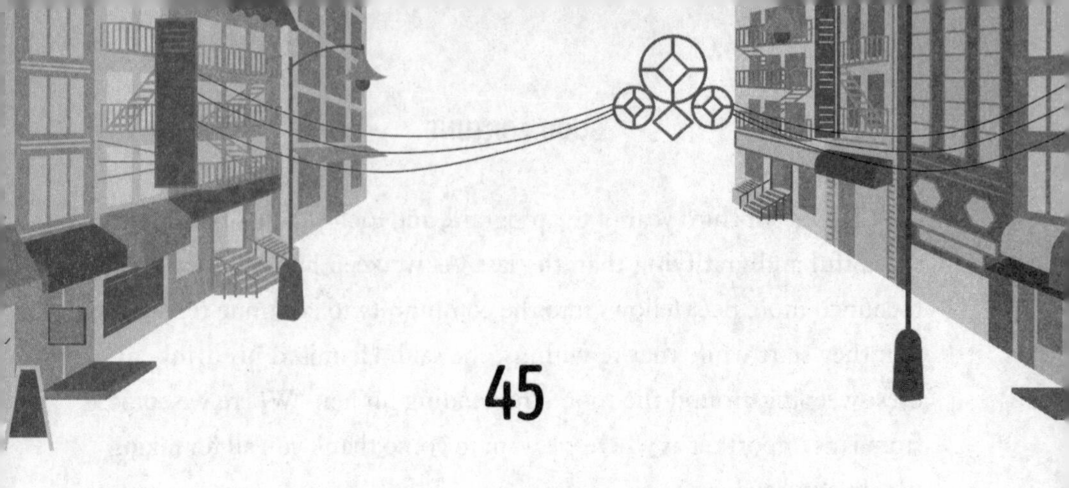

45

Something might have happened to Lydia, the message went. *Don't freak out.*

Not exactly the best introduction. But Jane had a tendency to deliver even the best of news like a chain letter: *IF YOU DON'T DO THIS IN THE NEXT 10 SECONDS, EVERYONE YOU LOVE WILL DIE!!!* No matter how many times Elizabeth faced the false alarms, she never reacted with anything short of breathless panic. A chain letter, she could resist; a sister was much harder.

Jane continued: Lydia hadn't returned last night to the beach house she was staying at with friends. By itself, this might be cause for alarm, but she hadn't been alone. There'd been a group of them, Bridget included, and she'd probably had too much to drink or gotten lost and slept it off somewhere. Worse came to worst, Elizabeth figured, she might be in a jail cell, facing a ticket for public drunkenness and vagrancy.

Everyone's on the lookout, and Bridget says she called last night and was okay so I wouldn't freak too much. I'll call as soon as I have any news. Don't worry. You know Lydia.

She did. No matter how thoughtless and distracted she might be, she had the benefit of blood and breeding on her side: a Chen and a lifetime New Yorker, inclined to scrap on instinct. But no matter how tough she was, she was still sixteen and unattended, impulsive and inattentive, and too desperate for a good time. Lydia *was* smart—but smart for sixteen, and not half as smart as she liked to think. But there was no point in worrying without any information.

No, the only thing she needed to worry about was brunch.

A send-off for Georgiana before her return to school, with a who's who of the Wongs' and Lees' inner circle and a handful of the Pemberley House board. In other words, the whole snake pit.

Elizabeth wouldn't have agreed to go if Georgiana hadn't personally invited her.

The place she had chosen made Martha Stewart look like amateur hour. All wicker and neutrals and creams, light woods and exposed lighting, white wine spritzers and WASPs; the only color around was in their party. As they arrived, there was next to no chatter in the dining room, women's voices wary of rising above the noise of the vintage wooden ceiling fans barely turning overhead.

The others at the table were dressed for the occasion in maxi sundresses, gingham prints, and wide-brim straw hats. In their cargo pants and T-shirts, Elizabeth and Amelia clashed with everyone.

"Nice to see you, Caroline," Elizabeth said, taking her seat. "Georgiana."

Caroline pursed her mouth by way of greeting.

Georgiana, playing hostess, sat at the center of the long table, twisting the chain of her charm bracelet around and around her wrist.

Only one other woman at the table looked as if she hadn't received the dress code. A broad-shouldered woman in jean shorts with a farmer's tan and sprays of freckles uneven across her face, she sat beside

Georgiana. Tight brown curls reached near her chin, fuzzing in the humidity, and she twirled a fork in her hand as she looked them over. "You're new."

Elizabeth laughed, surprising herself. "Yes," she said. "We are."

The woman lifted her fork hand and waved the tines back and forth in a wave, introducing herself as Andrea. Like Elizabeth and Amelia, she also worked for a living—as a kind of au pair to Georgiana during school holidays. They would be traveling to England together.

"Elizabeth met Darcy in New York," Georgiana said, by way of introduction.

"Oh, Gigi," Caroline cooed, leaning close. "You wouldn't like New York at all, la. Dirty, and really noisy. Anywhere we went, people *shouting*, and the cars—*ba baaaa baaaa*—honking like that all day, aa!"

And that had only been Madison Ave.

"Wait until the fireworks go off," Elizabeth added.

"I don't know," Georgiana said, breathlessly. "It sounds like such an exciting place."

Elizabeth smiled. "There's room in the city for all types. You can always find your people there."

Caroline glanced at her nails. "But what *people*."

Georgiana gave a small smile. "I'd definitely like to visit sometime."

"If you do, I'm happy to take you around," Elizabeth said.

Caroline interrupted with a loud clearing of her throat. "I can't *imagine* where the waitress is," she said. "Gigi, you picked a wonderful place, but the *staff*."

Caroline never did think much about where her words landed once she fired them off. Anything for another moment in the spotlight, no matter who else got caught in its glare.

Georgiana perked up with faint alarm, reddening up to her ears.

"Oh no, I'm sorry," she breathed. Her eyes darted around the dining room, searching for a passing waitress.

Her thin fingers reached for the charm bracelet, spinning it in quick flicks around her wrist. Gone was the ease of the girl at the gala last night. Georgiana fought for composure in the wake of all those eyes on her, looking almost near tears.

If Caroline noticed the impact her words had on her friend, she didn't say anything.

"Don't worry about it, Georgiana," Elizabeth said. "It just gives us more time to talk."

"Yes," Caroline chimed. "How *is* your family, Elizabeth?"

"Fine, thank you."

Georgiana lifted her hand up weakly from the table. If she were drowning, it wouldn't have been enough to save her.

"Oh, Gigi," Caroline whimpered. "Are you trying . . ."

Andrea waved her off. "You can do it, G. Come on."

Georgiana inched her hand even higher into the air. Her face pinked and reddened, foot tapping in quick beats against the floor as she waited and waited and waited to be noticed. After an agonizing minute, a waiter made his way over with a carafe of water in hand.

When Georgiana spoke, her voice squeaked thin enough to crack. "We're ready to order, please."

Elizabeth strained to hear her from across the width of the table. She couldn't imagine how the waiter did. But he nodded, and one by one, they went around the table with their breakfast orders. Coffee and orange juice. Half a grapefruit and Equal on the side (and if they didn't have Equal, then brown sugar, but no Splenda and no Sweet'N Low, please). Lemon-ricotta pancakes. French toast. Steak and eggs. Country breakfast.

With the waiter gone and their orders placed, they returned to their breezy chatter. Georgiana focused on the blank circle of her white starter plate, her hands folding and unfolding the napkin draped in her lap.

"Did you get a chance to talk to Darcy about that urban garden proposal?" Elizabeth tried. "I know you thought it was really promising."

Georgiana shot her a helpless look, glancing around the table as the other women leaned in and waited for her answer.

What she needed was encouragement, a little warmth to coax the hermit crab out of its shell. Instead, she was surrounded by vultures, waiting to pick each other apart for morsels of secrets and rumors.

"I think it's an interesting idea," Elizabeth prompted.

"Oh yes," Georgiana breathed. "Pemberley's always trying to build on its programs . . ."

And then, chaos.

A murmur of excitement buzzed around the table as a late addition to their party crossed the room. Cups clinked against saucers, dishes rattling, chairs scraping as everyone tried to crane for a look. Georgiana leapt to her feet, almost overturning a cup of coffee into her lap, saved only by Andrea's quick hands.

A hand slid against the back of Elizabeth's chair as their guest pecked Georgiana on the cheek in greeting.

The smell of his soap tipped her off before she even turned her head. It was recognizable, comfortable—familiar, she realized with a flash of horror.

Caroline nearly jumped out of her seat. "Join us, Darcy!" she said. "Please! We can call for an extra chair."

"Yes, please, D," Georgiana said. "It would be great to have you here."

His mouth twitched. "One man among all of you ladies? I'd be honored."

Elizabeth clicked her tongue. "Usually when a group of women get together without men, it's because they're talking about them."

He angled his head to catch her eye. "I'll be on my best behavior then."

He said it low, as if he'd only meant for her to hear it.

A shiver trailed up the length of her back, warm and tingling.

Caroline tittered a laugh. "We weren't talking about anything, and definitely not about *you*, Darcy."

If he was comforted by her assurances, he didn't show it.

The waiter delivered an extra chair and place setting, and the party shifted to make space. "So what do you want to do before you go back, G?" he said.

"Tell him to take you shopping," Caroline said.

"Or sailing," another woman suggested.

"Georgiana's more into poetry and dance," Darcy said with a light smile. "Isn't that right?"

"You make me sound *so* boring," Georgiana said. "I like to watch movies . . ."

"You watch cartoons."

Georgiana slid lower in her seat. "*Please* don't embarrass me, D."

"Like what?" Elizabeth said.

Darcy wrinkled his brow in mock concentration. "Like anything with talking cats," he said. "Anthropomorphic houses. Magic and Japanese animation."

Georgiana blushed, shrinking back in her seat.

Elizabeth softened. Growing up with a mother like Jade and four sisters to compete with for time, space, and attention couldn't be called easy, but at least it had taught her early to talk back and defend herself. Georgiana was a greenhouse orchid, raised under the shadow of her brother, too careful of strangers and too eager to please. Elizabeth wanted her to embrace it—to be proud of the things she wanted and liked, the little embarrassments. Let people say and think whatever they wanted; they would anyway, no matter how hard Georgiana tried.

It was impossible to think she and Lydia were the same age. Lydia chased being adult and landed somewhere in the disco ball years of the early twenties. No one would believe the age scribbled onto her fake laminated ID, but the way she carried herself stretched beyond high school. Georgiana reminded her of Kitty at thirteen, shrinking into bed with her older sister whenever she'd had a bad dream. One foot in girlhood and one foot out, and trying to make up for the difference with dedicated practice. It brought out the older sister in her.

They were interrupted by the appearance of the food. It was the kind of place with oversize white plates and miniature-size food, where the eyes ate better than the stomach and guests left hungrier than they came. Negative space with a side of silver dollar pancakes.

Caroline jabbed the metal edge of her spoon into her yogurt parfait with force. "Elizabeth, you must be glad to get away from home for a while."

Elizabeth poured a drizzle of syrup over her plate. "I don't know what you mean."

Caroline snuck a lick of yogurt. "I mean it must give you a relaxing break from the *agony* of the job search, aa," she said. "And from all those sisters of yours."

Amelia bristled beside her.

"Though your parents must be having such a hard time without you there at the restaurant . . ."

Elizabeth furiously sawed off a piece of pancake. "They do all right without me."

The women at the table murmured with sympathy. Imagine working in all that heat and grease in the summer, imagine the strain and wear on the hands. Imagine having to work like that for months! Years!

Elizabeth wondered if they wouldn't collapse at the idea of her working for most of her life.

"It's too much, la!" Caroline said. "I do hope you can find something else soon."

The sooner they could stop pretending to enjoy this conversation, the better her day.

"Thank you, Caroline," Elizabeth forced out.

Caroline draped her hand over Georgiana's arm. "It's important that you study and *apply* yourself, Gigi," she said. "To get where you want to go in life."

The other women echoed their agreement.

"You don't want to be stuck in a place like *that* for the rest of your life," she said, exaggerating a shudder. "Think of what that would do to your skin."

Elizabeth took a big gulp of coffee. "Some people don't have any choice."

Caroline pressed a hand to her heart. "If that was what I had to do for the rest of my life, I'd kill myself."

As always, Caroline aimed for the heart—and hit the wrong person.

Georgiana paled, flicking the thin chain of her bracelet around and around, around and around.

Amelia carefully slid the butter knife out of Elizabeth's reach.

"I don't mind working for a living," Elizabeth snapped, impaling a piece of pancake on the end of her fork. "It keeps me from being a burden to other people."

Caroline smiled flatly. "Whatever rocks your boat."

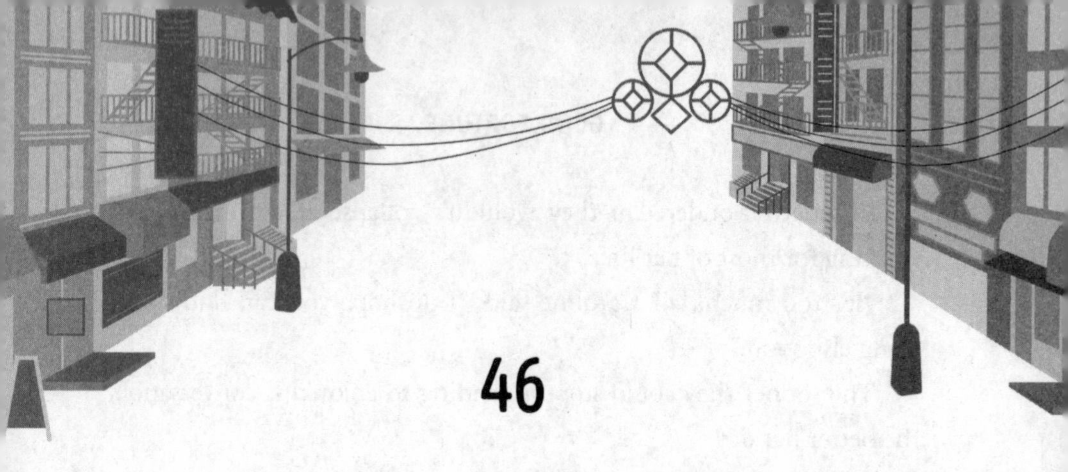

46

They muddled through the rest of their meal in stilted silence. Caroline blamed Elizabeth, Elizabeth blamed Caroline, and Georgiana blamed her hosting—but the rest of the party was grateful to wrap it up without any further theatrics.

Amelia leaned back with a groan. "There's so much food left," she whined, looking at what seemed like slim pickings to Elizabeth. "What do you think? Should we take any of it home? I don't want it to go to waste . . ."

Elizabeth watched Darcy at the hostess desk, handling the bill for the table. "Maybe," she said. "Hold on a second."

Amelia tried to follow her line of sight. "What are you doing?"

"Saying thank you."

Elizabeth followed him out as he passed into the lobby, lining up at the coat check. He was impossible to miss. He stood perfectly straight, methodically sorting the small red tickets in his hand into order. Usually the sight would send her into intense irritation, a reminder of his high-mindedness and how valuable he considered his own time; to her annoyance, now it didn't provoke anything but warmth.

Tiptoeing up beside him, she tapped him on the shoulder.

"What's—hi—is anything the matter? Did Caroline . . ."

"No, no, I wanted to . . . catch you."

"Okay," he said, slowly.

"I know she didn't have the easiest time in there. Georgiana, I mean."

He nodded, turning back towards the tickets. "She finds it difficult to engage socially sometimes. Especially after what happened."

"Yeah," she said. "I hope I didn't make it worse."

He shook his head, his thumb tracing the top edge of the coat-check tickets, back and forth and back and forth. "I don't think you did," he said. "She was—*we* were both glad to see you."

The service bell at coat check rang, and they stepped up to the counter together. With an apologetic shrug, Darcy counted out their eight tickets and lined them up in order.

With a judgmental crack of her chewing gum, the attendant brushed all the tickets in hand and walked off to retrieve their jackets.

"You don't have to wait with me," he said. "I think I can handle it."

"It's a lot of jackets for one man."

He scoffed. "You're not serious."

Months ago, she would have taken that for a slight, a flex of his superiority complex. But meeting him now felt like meeting him for the first time, glimpsing a new side of the person she once imagined she knew. It unsettled her, how little she could trust that her impression of him would stay true to the versions she met later.

She wondered if he thought the same about her.

"Is something the matter?" he said, hand sliding along her arm.

He was all warmth, and she leaned into his touch, catching the cuff of his sleeve with her finger.

"After everything that happened . . ." she began.

He shook his head. "I really don't want to talk about that."

"You didn't have to do all this," she said. "Show us around, invite us to the gala—I feel like I should thank you."

He sounded almost affronted. "Elizabeth, please. You don't have to thank me."

She laughed. "Shut up, I'm *trying* to apologize," she said. "And you should know how rare that is. I made some assumptions about you that were completely off base, and I'm sorry."

It all seemed so serious before—his crimes, as she had described them to Charlotte; his defects; his resistance to changing his mind—and now they were nothing more than shades of his personality. It was like looking back at an old yearbook after a long break; the heartbreaks turned into funny stories, the hurts faded with enough time. Everything could stand to be laughed at a little.

Maybe he hadn't tried to get on her good side, believing that he didn't need to, but she hadn't given him any chance to make up for it after either. It was the privilege of strong convictions—every belief a mission, every desire a demand. They'd been chasing opposite ends of the same thread, only to find they'd been chasing each other.

"I should be sorry," he said. "I was an ass."

"You were, but so was I," she said. "And the work that you're doing at Pemberley is incredible."

"High praise from the community rabble-rouser."

"I mean it," she said. "That's the kind of thing that the rec should be doing. All it would take is a couple facilitators to handle the programming. Some people from around the neighborhood, or one of the volunteer liaisons."

He groaned. "Are you seriously pitching me right now?"

She squeezed his hand. "If you did it before, you can do it again."

The attendant finally returned, tossing a large pile of jackets onto the counter with a scowl.

Elizabeth poked through to yank loose her aunt's windbreaker and her own leather jacket. "Let me help you."

"I think I can handle some light jackets."

"Don't be stubborn."

"That's the pot calling the kettle black, don't you think?"

She rolled her eyes, taking half of the pile into her arms and retreating to a curtained alcove beside the entryway to wait as he paid.

He met her with the remaining jackets in his arms.

"You could have held it against me," she said. "What I said about you."

His voice was quiet, suddenly serious. "No. Not against you."

She looked up into his eyes and felt a kick of nerves in her stomach. There were suddenly so many possibilities, so much potential in the air around them. Even here, in the buzz of a restaurant lobby.

His hand grazed her back.

She tilted her face up towards him, and he bent his down to meet hers. Close enough for her to smell his soap and the coffee that he drank at breakfast.

Close enough to kiss—

"Elizabeth, aaaaaaa!"

She was going to kill her aunt.

Amelia marched towards them in her Birkenstocks, her cell phone in hand. "Jane," she said. "She says it's an emergency."

Elizabeth took the phone from her aunt's hand, nearly jamming the antenna up Darcy's nose, and handed her the pile of jackets.

"Try not to talk too long, okay?" Amelia said. "Out of minutes!"

With a nod, Elizabeth ran outside.

Amid the noise of the parking lot, she couldn't hear much at first. She chalked it up to the chirp of the car alarms and the distracting chatter of other patrons. It wasn't until the first minute passed that she realized the silence came from the other end.

Jane wailed, worthy of a Chinese operatic aria, "I didn't want to ruin your vacation."

Elizabeth collapsed to sit on the curb. "What happened?"

She tried to ignore the sharp spike of fear in her chest. Nobody was in the hospital, she assured herself. Nobody was dead. Everything was going to be fine.

"It's Lydia. We think—we don't know what we think," Jane said. "She knows better . . ."

She scratched a hand through her hair. "Jane."

"Lydia isn't with Bridget. She left them."

"Left?" Elizabeth said. "Left where?"

Jane answered with another sharp jag of tears.

"Jane!" Elizabeth snapped. "Focus."

"When Lydia didn't come home, they thought what we all did. She fell asleep on the beach, or lost her key, got arrested, whatever. But the next day, Daniel—one of Bryan's friends—said that he heard from Ray about where she was."

"Ray?" Elizabeth yelped, jumping to her feet. "What the hell does Ray have to do with this?"

A heavy breath. "They think they went off together."

The fear sharpened into white-hot panic. She paced in front of the building, heart pounding in her chest, watching the drivers do loops around the lot searching for spots. "Went off *where*? To do what?"

"LB," she said, voice cracking. "Daniel said Ray's been . . . talking girls on the beach into posing for him. Into doing . . . other things." She let the insinuation sink in. "You know Lydia's been talking about her portfolio all year."

Spots dotted her vision, the world narrowing to a pinpoint. "And what—he got Lydia to . . ."

"I don't know," Jane said. "Bryan said they didn't find anything. We don't have any *proof.* All we know is that's what he was telling people . . ."

"And that our sixteen-year-old sister went missing and he was the last person to see her."

"And he's gone," Jane said. "He apparently took money from everyone before he went, and all the numbers they had for him are disconnected."

"Jesus, Jane," she said. "Where do you think he took her? Where could she be? What could he be thinking? She's *sixteen.*" Her mind spun through the possibilities, each bleaker than the last.

"They're not thinking," Jane said. "Maybe he panicked. Maybe he came to his senses and he's figuring out how to bring her back."

She felt the weight of the news sink heavily in her stomach. "Or he's waiting to see if he can sell the pictures."

"LB!"

"I'm sorry. I shouldn't have said it." She chewed on the edge of her thumbnail. "Did they call the cops?"

"Bridget said they wouldn't listen to her," Jane said. "They think Lydia's just out partying. They said they've got bigger problems than chasing after some Asian girl who drank too much and ran off with her boyfriend for a weekend."

"They mean they don't give a shit."

She sank back down on the curb, watching the brightness of the sky with a sudden bitterness. She'd spent more time worrying about someone else's sister than minding her own. She'd spent more time thinking about her own life than the emergency brewing at home. And now Lydia was god knows where with a man whose intentions were worth less than his promises, too eager to ruin a future for the cost of a dream. Why didn't she chain herself to the car to keep Lydia from going? Why didn't she fight with Vincent until he saw her side? Why hadn't she tried?

She could have been the older sister that her parents wanted her to be—the good influence, the troop leader, the substitute teacher—but she wasn't because she had her own life to live, because it had been entertaining, because she hadn't wanted to intervene. Because it had been far easier to let Lydia be Lydia for the sake of a little peace. Easier to let her baby sisters run wild, to doom themselves to their own bad choices instead of trying to change them.

It was her fault as much as it was anyone else's.

"The boys are trying to track them down now. They followed them to some motel by the beach, but that's all we've heard so far."

"Jesus," Elizabeth breathed. "Lydia can't even *drive*. What the fuck was Bridget *doing*? They were supposed to be watching her!"

"Everything you're saying, I've heard," Jane whispered. "Nonstop. For the last two days. I know you're just finding out, but please, LB. I can't."

"Fuck, Jane," Elizabeth whispered. "What is their plan here? She can't possibly be so stupid . . ."

"We don't know anything."

"Jane."

"We don't! Lydia's smart, LB. She's careless, but she's still . . . smart."

"This is all my fault, and I can't even fucking help."

"Stop it," Jane said. "This is not *your* fault."

The morning's meal churned in her belly, threatening to come up.

She felt sharp in her own body, frantic with nerves and nausea, and powerless to do anything at all. "How are Mom and Dad?"

Jane exhaled sharply. "Mother's in bed, and Dad—I've never seen him like this. Ever. Kitty is losing it. You have to come home."

"Yeah," Elizabeth said. "Tonight, if I can."

"Dad wants to go look for her. I don't know what he thinks he'll be able to do, but I guess it feels better than waiting at home. But he wants to know if you can get Great Uncle to come."

"I'll tell him," Elizabeth said.

"You and I can cover Lulu's as soon as you get here."

Elizabeth dropped her head in her hands.

"Try not to freak out. Lydia's been through worse."

If only she could believe it.

Why hadn't she seen it coming? All the signs of his character had been there, if she'd tried to look for them. The rich girl he'd had on the side, the bridges he'd tried to build with every gallery they passed, his status chasing and desperate ambition—she should have seen enough to make her doubt what he told her.

It was sickening to think how she'd once admired him for making opportunities out of nothing and bending the world to meet him. After hearing what he'd been through, who could have blamed him for that? Not her. Not when they became partners on the same side of a larger fight.

And if he leaned too much on his charm, if he talked his way in rather than working for it, she had excused it as a consequence of trying to break in without connections. She had written it off as thoughtlessness, the casual way he hurt people, but it wasn't that; he took what he could and left before anyone could blame him for the mess. He'd been using her as much as anyone else—to get to the Wongs and the Lees, or to get to Lydia, or to find another opportunity for money, for attention, anything to keep him going until the next fix. And, just like him, she wouldn't be the one to pay the price. She'd left that bill with her baby sister.

God, Lydia—

She jogged a lap around the building, hoping to settle her stomach and the racing thoughts in her head. She passed the families in the parking lot, the busboys smoking by the dumpster behind the building, the abandoned shopping carts dragged from the supermarket on the opposite plaza.

She almost ran right into him.

Darcy caught her arm as she stopped short, tripping into him. "Hey, your aunt told me to look for you."

She burst into tears.

Families heading for the restaurant steered a wide berth around them, rubbernecking or pretending not to look.

"Elizabeth, what's the matter? Are you feeling all right?"

She sank onto the curb again. "I'm fine!" she wailed.

Once she started, it seemed it wouldn't stop. Her vision blurred with the onslaught of tears, chest trembling with sobs. Some people considered crying cathartic. Those people were deranged.

He looked deeply concerned. "Should I get your aunt?"

"I'm okay," she gasped.

"You don't seem okay."

"I'm fine."

"You're hyperventilating." He sat beside her on the curb, rubbing circles against her back to calm her. She thought with faint humor that he'd probably done this thousands of times before with a younger sister of his own. "Try and breathe."

He might be the only person in the world who understood what she was going through, and the first to tell her, *I told you so*. Hadn't he told her exactly what kind of person Ray was? And hadn't she been so sure that Ray wasn't what he claimed?

"It's Lydia," she offered after another minute, lifting the cell phone. "Lydia's run away. Well, she's disappeared . . . with Ray, we think."

Except for the slight uptick of his eyebrows, nothing betrayed his surprise. He looked as stoic as ever, implacable and untouchable in a way that she couldn't be.

"She was staying with friends, and she's—I mean, she's sixteen. She doesn't know anything. She doesn't have any money. And there's—I don't know, there might have been . . . pictures."

His hand dropped from her back. "Are you sure?"

The tears stung hot against her eyes. "I knew," she hissed. "I knew and I didn't tell anyone, and—"

"Elizabeth," he said. "I'm so sorry."

Yes, he would be—sorry about what happened, sorry she hadn't taken his advice, sorry for what this meant for Lydia's future. He knew better than anyone the cost of trying to clear his sister's name after what Ray had done, and they were far worse off—in no position to negotiate, with no way to bail Lydia out if they needed. What was their pittance of savings compared to a career-making show? Compared to revenge? Who knew what Ray wanted? As if motives would matter if Lydia's photos ended up—god, online or in some trashy magazine, to be sold or downloaded by any pervert with an internet connection, where it could follow her for the rest of her life.

"Please tell your sister I'm sorry, but we have to leave right away."

"Of course."

She pressed at her eyes with closed fists. "God, how could I be so stupid?"

He touched his hand to her shoulder quickly. "You should go," he said. "Before you waste any more time."

He was right. Nothing could be done crying in Massachusetts. They would either find her in New Jersey or—no, nothing else would be acceptable. Nothing good came of imagining worst-case scenarios.

She dusted herself off and hoped she didn't look as shaky as she felt.

He barely looked at her. "I hope you find her soon."

She bit her lip hard, but the tears fell anyway.

"If I could say or do anything that could help, trust me . . ." he began. With a shake of his head, he interrupted himself. "You don't need this. I'll get your aunt."

With that, he disappeared.

And, with him, any chance of a reconciliation. Of anything at all.

With the rec out of his hands, he would be free to pretend they'd never known each other at all. It was his right.

But she didn't want it to end like this. She didn't want him to link her with what happened to her sister, with what happened to *his* sister. She wasn't ready to let it go. She wanted to keep them as they were, as they'd come to be in the last few days, all promise and potential. She wanted to remember everything as part of their story, if they ever had a story at all.

She had almost started to believe that they did.

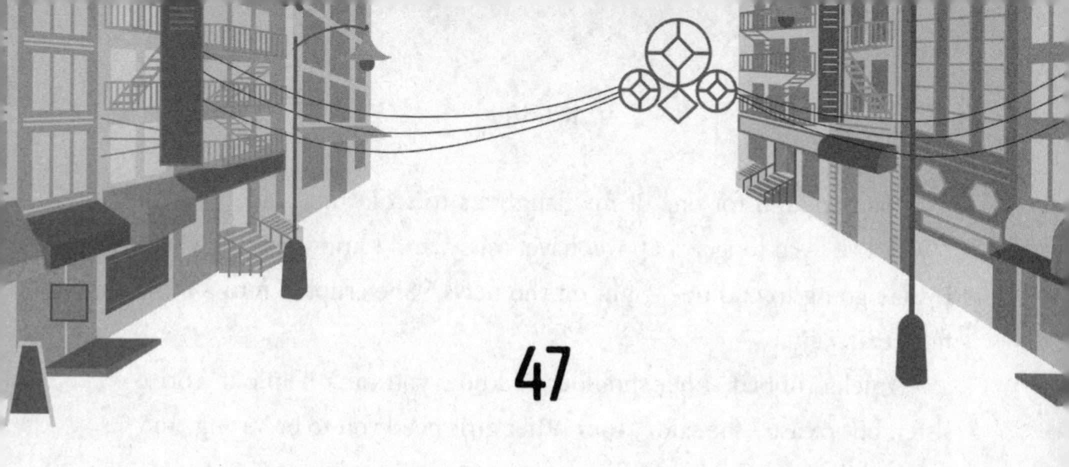

47

Jane had no update. Nothing had been seen or heard of Lydia or Ray since the news broke, and nothing had come of Vincent's search in New Jersey. Until a body washed up, the police considered it a family problem; Bryan and his friends were still looking; and the rest of them sat around desperate for news.

Jade busied herself with compiling a list of all the people she considered responsible, from whom she would seek future damages, emotional, material, and otherwise, leaving Jane to take care of the apartment and everyone else. She had been the lone voice against the plan from the very beginning, and now she was the one to suffer—stomach pains and spleen aches, indigestion and insomnia, shortness of breath and chronic fatigue. "If they had listened to me," Jade complained, "this never would have happened. We could have watched over her. We could have taken care of her. I mean, where was Bridget? Where was Bryan? I always thought that Alexa was no good, but nobody listened to me. Nobody ever does. Wait until my baby shows up dead on the milk!"

"Mother, *please*," Elizabeth said. "Things are bad enough."

"Bad enough for one of my daughters to scold me!" Jade scoffed. "Well, I've lived longer than *you* have, missy, and I know exactly where Lydia's going to end up—right on the news." She erupted into a fresh fit of tears.

Amelia rubbed at her shoulder. "I know you can't help but worry, sister, but please," she said. "Your other girls need you to be strong, and we don't know anything at all."

Jade reached for her hand. "At least both of you are here. You know, I don't care about anything as long as she comes home in one piece," Jade said. "Big brother, you tell her that we're all worried about her, and that we want her home safe. Tell her that she can have whatever she wants if she'll come home."

Mary poked her head out from their bedroom. "Mother, there's no need to lose your head."

No one answered her.

Mary tried again. "As horrible as this is for Lydia *personally*, at least we can all take comfort in the idea that *our* lives, right now, are still okay."

Kitty chucked a slipper at her from across the room. "Ai ya, Mary, the only thing you could do that would give comfort to this family is to shut up."

* * *

No news spread like bad news, and bad news spread like lice in an elementary school. Aunties from three, six streets over brought dishes of food to share, peeking politely around the doorframe as they dropped theirs off. "Lydia's a good girl, aa. We're praying for you." Though it was a terrible thing that happened, what could be expected from a girl so wild, from a family so undisciplined? Goes to show, they clucked, just goes to show.

Goes to show that nobody knew how to mind their own business. Elizabeth closed the curtains, screened their calls, and stayed away from anyone that might look to interrogate her for details. She couldn't even speak about it to Charlotte, who called with sympathies and a listening ear and didn't have much else to say beyond that. What could she say? A sister wasn't an easy thing to lose in the middle of the night like errant luggage. She was a person. She was blood.

Elizabeth lost track of the days. She mindlessly opened and closed Lulu's each day, sometimes with Jane, sometimes without, waiting desperately for Vincent's daily report from the shore. All she could do was sit in the kitchen and watch the storm of her mother's anxiety fixate on something else—the cleanliness of the kitchen, the noise of the TV, the way Kitty spoke or did the dishes. Nothing seen, nothing heard, nothing further.

At least there was still work. Every night, she and Jane stayed late to do the receipts, lock up, and close, only to come home and sit in the dim kitchen until two or three in the morning, scanning through the evening news, the paper, and search engines for morbid headlines neither of them were ready to read. Girls missing, girls dead, girls sold. No matter how much they wanted to talk about their thoughts and their fears, they couldn't—not even to each other.

Every night they were forced to wait for word felt like the last night of their lives.

Until it came.

A week later, 2:03 a.m., one short trill on the phone.

Jane's reflexes bested hers as she fumbled the cordless off of its base, switching it on and barking a greeting into the phone. One long moment passed before she exhaled and hissed, "Lydia, where *are* you? Everyone's looking for you!"

Over the phone, Lydia laughed and shouted, her slurred words hidden beneath a cacophony of bells and whistles, rings and hollers, and jingling coins. Atlantic City, baby.

Elizabeth shoved her head by the phone, Jane angling the receiver until they could both hear.

"You'll never *guess* what happened to me!"

She could have kissed her sister. And after that, ripped every single hair out of her head. "You're right," Elizabeth said. "We can't. Where are you exactly?"

"LB, you wouldn't want me to ruin the *surprise*, would you?" Lydia said. "Besides, it doesn't matter where I am but who I'm with! Don't you want to know who?" Over the line came a crackle of static. "Your *friend*!"

"Lydia," Elizabeth said. "Everyone is worried sick about you."

Lydia snorted. "Well, that's dumb. I *told* Bridget what was going on. We're meeting with a big-time talent scout, flying in from LA and everything," Lydia said. "Ray set it up. So you can tell Bryan to stop making those crank calls. Nobody believes him, anyway."

"Lydia," Elizabeth said. "Do *not* sign or do anything before you hear from us."

Lydia sighed. "I should have known you would be like this," she groaned. "You should be happy for me! Wait until you catch me on MTV or something."

"I'm not kidding. Mother's out of her mind, and Dad and Great Uncle have been trying to find you."

"We're glad you're okay," Jane added. "But you need to come home right now."

Lydia clicked her tongue. "You guys are so *serious*. I knew you would be freaking out, but come on."

"Lydia, put Ray on the phone," Jane said.

"No," Lydia laughed. "I'm calling to say I'm okay, stop being so crazy, and I'll be home soon. Love you, okay? Toodles!"

Jane clicked off the phone and set it on the kitchen table, dropping her head into her hands with a forceful sigh. "At least she's okay."

"God, if I wasn't so happy to hear she's alive, I'd kill her myself."

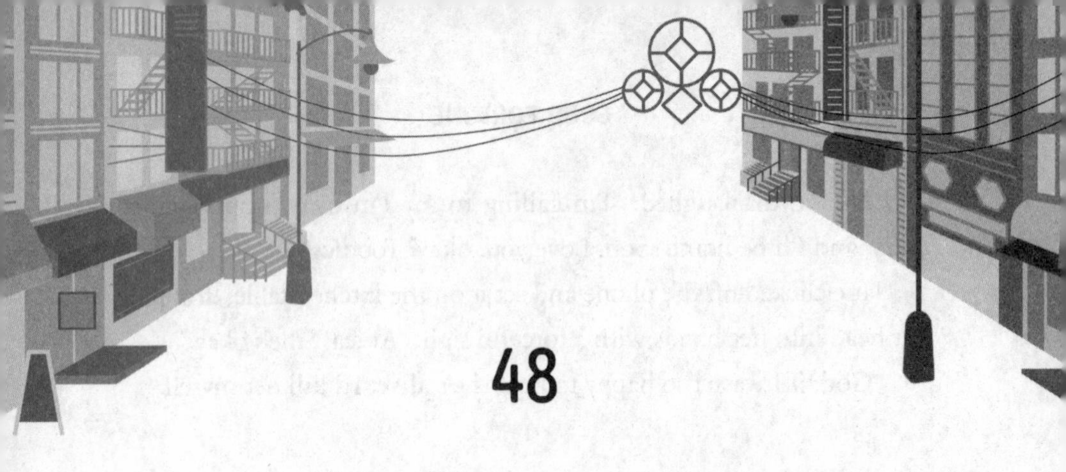

48

Confirmation followed in the morning: Lydia found, scolded, threatened, retrieved.

"It's over," Jade screamed, shaking the phone in her hand with such force that the plastic seemed to crack under her grip.

Elizabeth wrested the phone from her mother's hands—as Jade continued to howl reminders, platitudes, and agonies at Randall—and strained to listen. Static crackled, her uncle's voice tinny over the line, which she blamed on the connection as much as the exhaustion.

"It's done," he sighed, and she could hear the rise and fall of Vincent's voice raging in the background. "Close enough, anyway. There's some kind of contract she signed that we need to look at."

Elizabeth dodged her mother's quick hands and her sisters' nosiness on her way into the bathroom, kicking the door shut behind her and sitting on the edge of the tub. "What kind of contract?"

"That's what we're trying to find out."

The producer meeting, it turned out, was real enough, though the man was less connected, less powerful, and less familiar with Ray than he had promised. Lydia admitted as much to taking the photos—

"Which she said are very tasteful, whatever that's worth . . ."—and Ray to their existence, so the question was of their ownership.

"The only way we can keep Lydia safe is to make sure those photos stay in our possession," Randall sighed.

"Have you seen them?" Elizabeth asked.

"LB, I don't want to see that."

"What are you going to do?"

"If they're Ray's, we'll see how much he wants for them. If they're the producer's, we'll see if there's any room in the contract to void it. She's under eighteen, so anything she signed shouldn't count. But I don't know what I'm doing, LB. Your dad doesn't either. We probably need to hire a lawyer."

She groaned. "We can't afford one. You know that."

"It's that or . . ."

The bathroom door squealed open, revealing Jane and Amelia in the doorway.

She nodded at them to come inside.

"Anyway, we're going to see what can be done and then we'll be back. Don't wait up for us, and please don't worry."

"Thank you, Great Uncle," Elizabeth said. "I don't know what we would do without you."

He sighed. "Tell your mother to calm down," he said. "We'll let you know more when we have it."

Lydia alive! Lydia safe and unharmed! Lydia left to sort out the consequences of a bad contract with an even worse man, with nothing to show for it but nude photos.

"Thank god she's all right," Amelia cried.

No matter how relieved she felt, Elizabeth couldn't feel as satisfied as everyone else seemed to be. All she could consider was how it could have been worse.

Amelia turned to look into the hallway where Kitty lurked, chewing on a nail. "Come on. You girls might as well try to eat something. What do you say to some soy-sauce noodles?"

Kitty lifted her head. "God, yes, please."

Walking into the kitchen, Amelia unpacked their oven of all of its pots and pans and rummaged for a wide-bottomed pot. "Whatever happens, your uncle and I will do our best to help. We'll help to pay, even if it means moving some money around. This is an emergency."

"Aunty, no," Elizabeth insisted. "The two of you have done more than enough."

Jade thumped her hand hard on the tabletop. "And why not! Isn't Lydia my older brother's niece? Isn't it right that he should care what happens to her?"

Elizabeth pulled another pot from the oven and gathered water to boil the noodles. "Ma! We can't take their money."

Jade hip-checked her from the sink, snatching the handle of the pot from her. "Of course we can. Give me that, la," she cried. "You're going to burn the bottom of the pot."

Elizabeth rolled her eyes.

Water ran noisily into the pot. "It's the same as if he had to take care of me. And you know he hasn't ever taken any serious interest in you girls apart from some little gifts now and again . . ."

"Mother, please," Elizabeth said.

Jade harrumphed and switched the burner on, shoving the pot on top of the lit flame. "Elizabeth, did we ask? Did we show up with our hands out and beg for him to pay? Or did he *offer*?"

To Jade, it was only good and right and proper that her own family should do anything it could to save Lydia from a humiliating future and them from public embarrassment, never mind how unlikely it would be that they'd ever return the gesture.

But at least it was done.

And now that it was next to impossible that she and Darcy would ever have anything to do with each other again, she could admit the truth. Maybe she *had* wanted something more. Maybe they'd had a chance before any of this happened. Maybe it wouldn't have been so bad.

But now she'd never know.

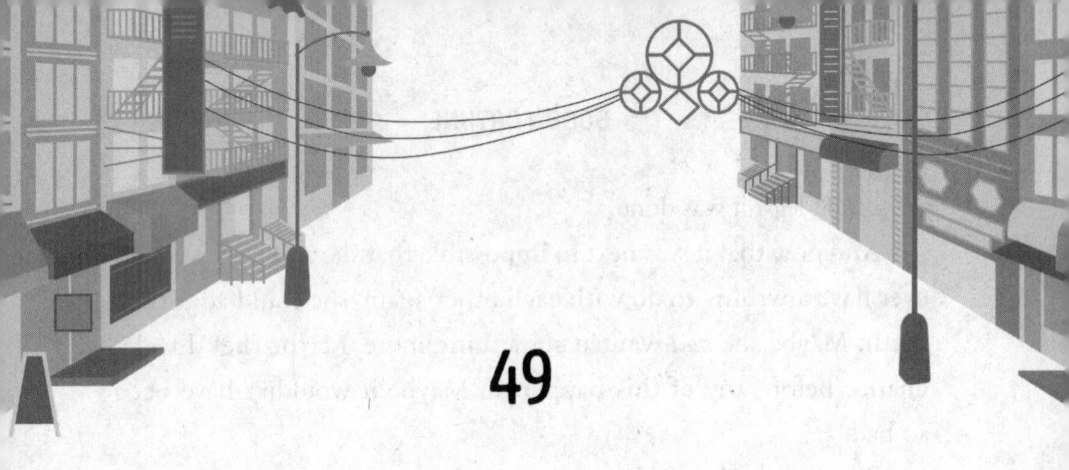

49

They prepared for a homecoming, and expected an episode of *Jerry Springer*—crying and screaming, name-calling, furniture-throwing, chaos. They were sorely disappointed on all fronts. Lydia returned to the apartment without handcuffs, dramatics, or tears, marshaled on one side by Vincent and on the other by Randall. It was Lydia who stayed the same, as unbothered as she'd been the day she left. Tanned and well rested, she twirled into the apartment in a slinky dress with a broad-brimmed sun hat and greeted them all with chic kisses against their cheeks. "Wasn't it awful here without me?"

Elizabeth resisted the impulse to chuck a pillow at her face.

And if the apartment seemed sterner, quieter, and more somber than usual, Lydia didn't notice. Lydia was her own hype man and game show host. She crowed over her victories and her adventures, unpacking unwanted gifts onto the kitchen table. None were chosen for quality or with care. She bought them whenever she happened to remember, and her memory wasn't very good. Paper-thin flip-flops and boardwalk sarongs, slap bracelets and superballs, and a novelty T-shirt for Dad—wasn't that thoughtful? Wasn't she a wonderful sister, a delightful daughter?

"I wish you all could have been there," she sighed. "But it's probably better you weren't. You wouldn't have let me try *half* the things that I got to do!"

She didn't know the half of it.

She thought it an exciting detour, her brief touch of imagined fame and grandeur—a Hollywood producer, being discovered on the beach, a very adult photo shoot—and wasn't it only natural that everyone lived to hear every detail? What else did they have going on? There were so many *amazing* things that she'd done and seen, so many *crazy people* on the boardwalk, and she didn't know where to start.

Randall excused himself with a claim of feeling unwell, Jane sank into a seat on the sofa without a word, and Vincent, usually so calm, usually so easygoing, paced the small square of the kitchen with his hands in his pockets, looking the most furious Elizabeth could ever remember.

And the more Lydia talked, the stormier his expression.

Lydia squealed. "Wait until Alexa sees *me* on Canal Street. She's going to be *sick*!"

Elizabeth knew how she felt.

Lydia couldn't see past what she did or what she wanted, and as long as she believed that she'd gotten the upper hand out of the situation, she wouldn't see anything wrong with it either. She might with a little more time, Elizabeth hoped, or distance, but not now. And until then, it was impossible to escape her endless gloating—and what achievements she had! An interrupted modeling career, an undisclosed sum of money paid to make sure that she still had a life to reclaim when she came back, a panicked set of parents and sisters.

Lydia strutted through the kitchen to pull a can of soda from the fridge. "Don't hate, girls," she cooed. "After I make my first millions, I'll make sure you guys get a little something out of it."

"Now, Lydia," Jade clucked. "Don't pick on your sisters."

Lydia rolled her eyes. "They're the ones who are still going to be stuck at home when I'm rich and famous and traveling the world. Once that producer lines me up with an agent . . ."

Vincent filled a glass of water at the sink. "You're not going to do any such thing." His voice turned steely with suppressed rage. "You're going to stop thinking about these ridiculous things and pay attention to your schoolbooks for a change."

Lydia scoffed. "Come on, Dad. All I really need is my GED."

He slammed the glass down hard against the counter, rattling the cabinet doors. Lydia jumped, Jade froze, and the rest of them slunk into the safety of the living room, watching the scene from behind the sofa.

"Careless, stupid girl! Use your head!" Vincent thundered. "Where do you think those pictures would have ended up? What do you think would have happened to you?"

Kitty slid from the sofa to the floor, wincing at every word.

Lydia's smile didn't reach her eyes.

"Husband, aa," Jade said, scooping Lydia into her arms.

"The *only* thing that saved you was your uncle. Without him, you would have signed your whole life away."

"Husband, try to be understanding, la," Jade said. "Lydia's so young, and she didn't know what she was doing . . ."

Lydia tucked her head against Jade's shoulder.

"Understanding," he clucked. "We've been too understanding already. Too much freedom. And all she's learned is how to take advantage."

"Come on, Ba," Lydia said.

He shook his head and snatched his apartment keys. "No more 'come on,'" he said. "If you take one more step out of line, I will have nothing to do with you. You can find someplace else to live and somebody else to bother—and then you'll see exactly how good you can do on your own." He marched out the front door, letting it slam shut behind him.

For a moment, Lydia looked stricken, as if aware for the first time of what her own mistakes might have cost her.

Jade looked stunned. "Now, Vincent, you can't mean that," she called, running after him into the hallway. "This is your baby!"

Lydia took a hard breath, slowly shaking off the last of what Vincent had said to her. "He'll come around," she said. "He always does."

Except this time, she didn't sound so sure.

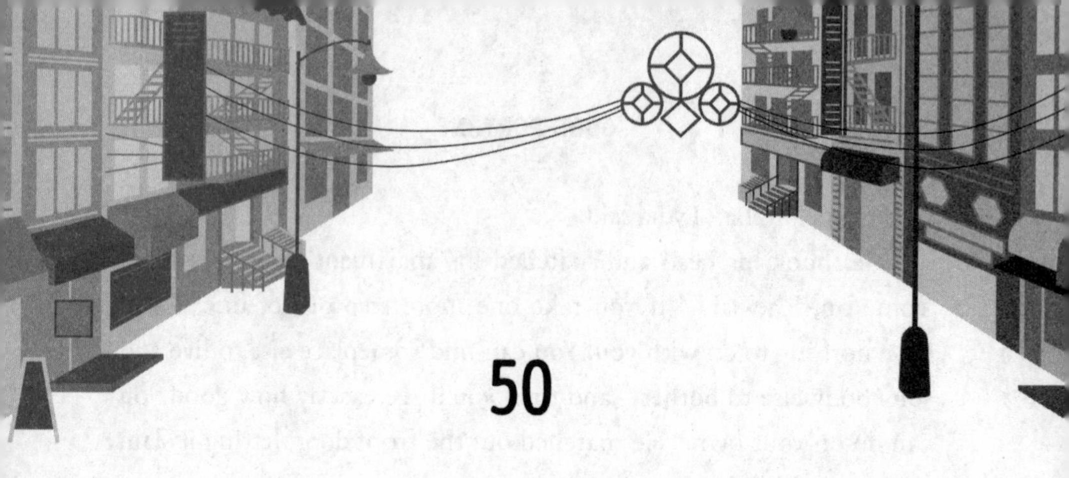

50

Lydia still insisted on celebrating. To take the sting out of what happened earlier that day, maybe, or to honor her homecoming and her accomplishments (such as they were). She insisted, she begged, she pleaded. After all, what good was having older sisters if they didn't take your side at a time like this? Didn't they think that Vincent was being too rigid, too uptight, too unfair? Didn't they think she had a right to make her own decisions? Didn't they think she deserved it?

Fine. If they didn't want to appreciate her, she would go and find people who would.

Lydia did as Lydia would do, and stormed all the way out.

Elizabeth waited out the rest of the evening on the roof, hoping the air and a smoke would clear her head—and leave her enough space to avoid all human contact until it had. On a muggy summer night, there weren't many others who preferred the still air and a haze of smog to air-conditioned comfort. Only a handful of teenage boys gathered on the opposite side of the roof, hidden by a large cloud of smoke, blasting the Beastie Boys.

They'd been cooped up together so long the last few days, the five of them, that it felt almost alien to hear her own thoughts.

It didn't last long.

The fire escape shook as someone thundered onto the roof. "LB!"

Lydia skipped over to join her, pink-faced and beaming. Wherever she'd gone, she'd certainly managed to have a good enough time.

Lydia lifted a small set of colored gel bracelets. "You forgot your present," she said, softly. Sinking onto her knees beside Elizabeth, Lydia pushed a handful of them past her wrist. Circling her arms around Elizabeth's middle, she pressed her hot mouth to her neck. "You didn't even tell me congratulations."

She smelled like sweet alcohol and cotton candy.

Elizabeth scratched her head. "You're unbelievable. Congratulations for what?"

Lydia snuggled tighter against her side. "You don't want to hear about it?" she said, quietly. "How I was discovered?"

Elizabeth brushed Lydia's hair, fingers tracing the base of her neck like she'd done for her thousands of bedtimes before. "No, Lyd," Elizabeth said. "I don't want to hear about it."

For all that Lydia fought to be seen as grown up, she could still be such a kid. All she ever wanted was to be told that things would be okay, that they could work out. Love, by any other name, might be called reassurance.

Lydia splayed her legs out wide. "God, it was so funny. I wish you could have been there."

"I don't think anything about what happened would be funny."

"Oh, LB, you don't even know. Great Uncle and Dad charged in like the FBI," she said, snorting on a laugh. "It was like something out of TVB. Ray wasn't even *there* so they were freaking out, yelling, and trying not to look like they were losing it. I told them I'd planned to call them after it was over, but they didn't want to hear it."

"You're right. That sounds hilarious," Elizabeth deadpanned.

Lydia nudged Elizabeth's jaw with her head in protest. "Dad looked like he was going to throw a chair or something."

"Funny."

"They said they were going to take us out to lunch, but all they did was talk about paperwork for hours. *So* boring. And, you know, they didn't say a *single* nice thing to me while we were there?" she said, rolling her eyes. "I was worried they'd ruin the whole thing after all my hard work, but nobody wanted to talk to me about it. *Be quiet, Lydia. Stay in the hotel room, Lydia*—which, please, it was a Holiday Inn—*and don't go anywhere*. Like, where would I go? They didn't even leave me a key! It was like being in jail."

"I don't think jail is like being at a Holiday Inn."

Lydia rolled onto her back to peer up at the sky. The city never shone with stars, but sometimes they could mistake a passing helicopter for a shooting star. It was the thought that counted.

"Such a big deal about nothing," Lydia whispered. "I already signed everything, which I *told* them, and we were figuring out the details. All they did was argue, and it didn't even fucking matter anyway because Darcy showed up. What a waste of time."

Elizabeth choked. "Darcy!"

Lydia brayed a laugh. "You should have seen his face. He looked like he was going to challenge Ray to a duel or something, but—oh, shit. I don't think I was supposed to say anything."

Lydia's big mouth, for once, was a blessing.

"What was he even doing there?"

Trying to imagine Darcy in Atlantic City tested the limits of her imagination. Trying to imagine him in a *Holiday Inn* tested the limits of reality.

Lydia shrugged. "Don't ask me. They made me leave the room as soon as they started talking."

What Lydia knew didn't amount to much, and still proved too much for her to understand.

"Well, don't tell anyone, okay? Promise."

"I promise," she said. "I won't say anything."

Lydia leaned against her shoulder, blinking at her through a haze of alcohol and exhaustion. "LB?"

Her voice hadn't sounded so small in years.

"Yeah?"

"You're not mad at me too, are you?"

She wrapped an arm around her sister's shoulders. "You did something really stupid, and you should have known better," she said. "We were all really worried about you."

"You think that because you can't see the bigger picture."

Elizabeth studied her. "What's the big picture, Lyd?"

"I did it for me but I also did it for us. You get that, don't you?"

She didn't. But that didn't matter to Lydia. It didn't matter what their father and uncle had done to rescue her. It didn't matter that she barely understood the risk she'd brought on her own future, because it was over—and they could finally go back to the tedium of their own lives. It didn't matter at all, except that she was dying to find out how it all happened.

* * *

By the time they crawled back into their apartment, most of the others had gone to sleep. Randall and Amelia, in the "guest room" of their sofa bed, and the others in their beds.

Lydia collapsed immediately into the lower bunk beside Mary, who tried to kick and elbow her off.

Only Elizabeth was too wired to sleep.

Her mind scrambled for answers in the world's worst game of Clue. So it had been Darcy Wong in New Jersey with the candlestick. But how had they found themselves in the same room together? How did Darcy find himself in New Jersey at all?

Elizabeth tiptoed to the kitchen for water and found her father still awake, paging through a newspaper with a steaming cup of tea beside him. The anger had faded into his usual tired resignation—but here he was, not sleeping. Like father, like favorite daughter.

"You should be asleep," Vincent said.

Elizabeth took a seat beside him at the table. "So should you."

Vincent pushed his mug of tea towards her.

While she (mostly) loved her mother, Elizabeth never felt more herself than when she spent time with Vincent. When she was younger, she'd been happy to sit with him for hours at Lulu's, watching him read the newspaper or crack little observations about the customers that passed in and out throughout the day. It was his quickness and humor that she had inherited and relied on to navigate the chaos of their little world, and it was him that she most admired.

"Are you going to say 'I told you so'?" he said, turning the page of his newspaper.

She tried a sip of his tea, bitter with something that looked like tree bark, and choked it down. "This is disgusting."

Vincent smiled. "Good for your system."

If that's what it took to keep her system running, she'd learn to embrace the sludge.

"Try not to be so mad," she said. "Lydia . . . doesn't know how to say it, but she knows that she messed up."

He shook his head and sighed. "She isn't going to learn until we stop trying to clean things up for her," he said. "You can't run after your sister for the rest of your life, LB."

"I can't let anything happen to her either."

"She's almost an adult," he said. "She needs to learn how to be one."

Elizabeth shrugged. "But she's still my baby sister."

Vincent stole his mug back, drinking another sip of his tea. "So what are you doing up?" he said. "Can't sleep?"

Mary answered with a gurgle of a snore.

"Too many things on my mind," Elizabeth said. "What happened in Jersey?"

Vincent removed his glasses and leveled his gaze at her. His foot kicked hers under the table. "Your sister has your mom's big mouth."

"So he was there?" Elizabeth said. "Darcy?"

Vincent leaned his chin against his hand, studying her. "So you don't know? He didn't tell you?"

"No!" she said. "Why would he tell me?"

"Your aunty has your sister's big mouth too."

She ducked her head, hoping it hid the blush that spread over her cheeks. "We're just . . . friendly."

"Well," Vincent drawled, "when your friendly Darcy told us not to tell anyone, I didn't know that meant you too."

"Ba, please," she said. "You're killing me."

"We tried to find them by retracing their steps. That's how we ran into your boyfriend. He was already there, asking the same questions."

"He's not my boyfriend," she replied, easily. "What was he doing there?"

Vincent folded up his newspaper and laid it aside. Whatever else might happen, she'd interfered with his plan to read any more of his paper that night. "He'd been to Atlantic City before, and thought he knew where to find her. We didn't want to burden him, but I don't think we could have stopped him if we wanted to."

"So what happened?"

He answered her with an impatient glare. “Darcy said that he felt responsible for what happened so he did most of the negotiating. Don’t ask me why.”

She nodded.

“The contract your sister signed was worthless since she wasn’t eighteen,” he said. “And as soon as the producer learned that Ray had lied to him, he left. But there were still the pictures and the negatives.”

Elizabeth fought a shudder. “Ray had them?”

“Darcy talked to him about getting them back. Alone. He wouldn’t let me get involved.”

She sagged against the table in a stupor. To think of all the things they could have had to talk about, and they spent it talking about Lydia. “You think he paid him off?”

“Must have,” Vincent replied. “And Ray doesn’t strike me as particularly stupid or cheap.”

He reached inside his jacket and removed a thick envelope, setting it down beside her with a nod.

She didn’t need to look inside.

Vincent lowered his voice to a whisper. “I think it had to be at least six figures.”

She almost knocked the mug onto the floor. “You’re kidding.”

Vincent shook his head.

“Ba, we can’t accept that!”

Vincent rolled his eyes. “Don’t tell me that,” he replied. “Tell *him* that.”

“A hundred thousand dollars,” she repeated, feeling dizzy. “Jesus.”

“At least.”

“Oh my god.”

“That’s all I know, LB. I promise,” Vincent said, rising from his seat at the table. “For all the other details, you need to ask friendly, aa.”

He drained the rest of his medicinal tea and rinsed the mug out in the sink.

"I'm going to bed," he said. "You figure out what to do with those."

She nodded faintly, half hearing him. "Good night, Ba."

A hundred thousand dollars. They owed him *a hundred thousand dollars*, at least! And for Darcy to do something like that without a repayment plan or a word to anyone else? They owed him Lydia's future and their eternal gratitude. They owed him a biblical debt. She could work for the rest of her life and not manage to save up that amount of money, and he paid it without credit, without expectation, without standing to gain anything at all.

And for what? For Lydia?

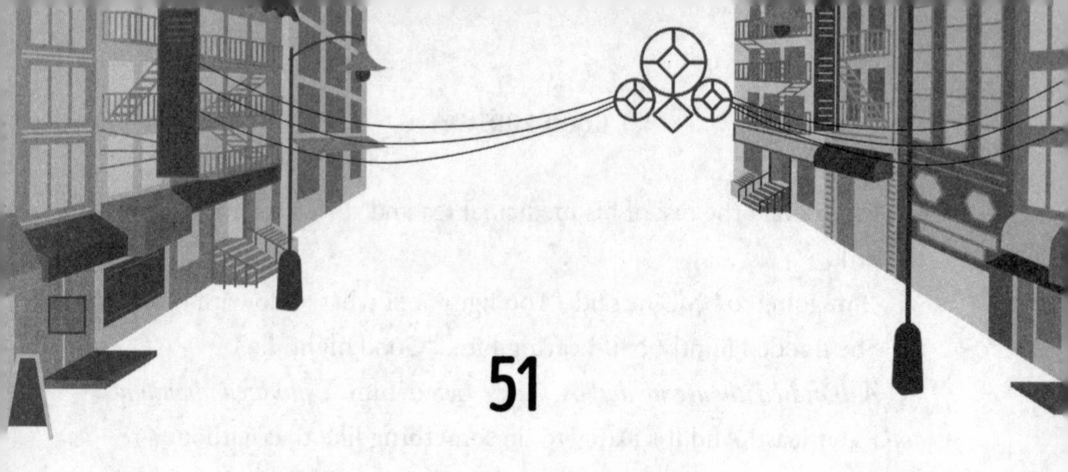

51

Presenting The Greater Chinatown Neighborhood Youth Recreational Center, the remake, the sequel, the continuing story—still under construction. Those who knew it before might have rolled their eyes at its being called *the modern heart of ancient Chinatown*, whatever that meant, but they couldn't deny the upgrade. By New York standards, six months behind was as close as anything came to being on time, and it was a vision: the exterior and the surrounding sidewalks power-washed to sparkling, the old industrial doors and windows replaced with newer models, and fresh coats of paint and plaster to cover any flaws. That was New York—a work in progress and always in process, if overrun with vermin. Come to love it, or leave.

For days, a neighborhood that talked of nothing but Lydia's disappearance and Lydia's return finally sank its teeth into fresh meat. Once construction finished, who knew what else they might do to the rest of the block or the neighborhood? Who knew if Chinatown would still look like Chinatown in a few years? Ai ya, who could depend on anything in this city these days? But for now, they could look forward to celebrating a reopening—and any excuse to roast a whole pig was worth celebrating indeed.

Besides, the aunties hissed, the official business of the opening would mean a return of the prodigal son. After all, a man didn't just leave an investment like that unattended—whether a building or a budding relationship. Brendan was a smart enough boy, la, and if other people could be just as smart, they might earn themselves a commission and a future son-in-law when he rolled around.

Jade wouldn't hear of it. "He can come and go wherever he pleases, whatever he likes. It has nothing to do with us. You know these kids say one thing and do another. So who cares if he's coming *if* he is coming?"

Jane—or so thought the neighborhood.

But Jane protested. No one could be more neutral to rumors of the Lees returning to town. There were far more important things to worry about—like her studies, for one, or Lulu's—and she'd moved on. She didn't think much about them at all. So what if she rang up two orders for the wrong amount, and nearly mixed up the takeout and the pickup orders? So what if she couldn't concentrate much on anything beyond the same page she'd been reading all day? It didn't mean a thing.

"Stare all you want," Jane said as Elizabeth refilled the napkin holders. "I'm fine."

"It's okay if you're not, you know."

"I know what everyone thinks, but it's been a long time," she said. "And he's got better things to do than come back around here."

Naturally, he came at the worst possible time.

In the crush of a busy Friday night, as Jane slid between juggling three calls to staple Styrofoam boxes of beef and broccoli shut while

Elizabeth packed their backed-up delivery orders. "Just a second!" she cried as the doorbell rang.

"Hi, Jane."

Jane nearly dropped the phone into the fryer. "Oh! Brendan!"

In the flesh.

Elizabeth snatched the receiver safely out of Jane's hand, hip-checking her sister aside. "Lulu's, what can I get you?" she rattled into the phone.

She scribbled an order down on a ticket and hung up the phone.

Jane stayed where she stood, pencil still in hand to jot down an order. "Can I get you something?"

"Hi," Brendan said. "Can we talk?"

Placing a firm hand on her sister's back, Elizabeth steered Jane towards the direction of the door. Whatever the two of them needed to say to each other, she didn't need to hear it.

It was like watching middle schoolers at a dance. The two of them moved in inches, keeping their distance while wanting nothing more than to close it.

"Stop blocking the door," Elizabeth called.

With a sheepish look, Brendan waved at her in greeting before slipping back out onto the street.

Jane looked at her, eyes wide with panic. "What do I do?"

Brendan watched them through the front window.

"Why are you asking me?" Elizabeth cried.

Vincent stepped out from the kitchen, a Chinese cleaver in one hand and a plate of roast pork in the other, and all out of patience. "What's going on, aaaa?" he said. "Can't you hear the phone ringing?"

"I got it," Elizabeth said. To Jane, she added, "You handle your own thing."

With a sigh, Jane tightened her ponytail and headed outside.

Jane remained more gracious than Elizabeth could ever be. She didn't flip him the bird, curse him out, or storm off, but stood and listened as he tried to plead his case. This was as cold as Jane could be, Elizabeth thought—her sister's arms crossed over her chest, her lips tight with skepticism, but without a trace of the drama or the heartbreak the neighborhood hoped they might see.

Vincent clanged his metal spatula against the side of the wok. "LB, aaa, we need more of that chicken for the General Tso's."

She pulled bags of breaded chicken from the fridge and slit them open, dumping them into the fry basket. They sank in the oil with a quiet sizzle.

"Sweet and sour up."

Elizabeth ladled thick sweet-and-sour sauce into a small container and snapped the lids on.

Returning to the fryer, she hoisted the basket up, shaking the excess oil off as she inspected the pieces of chicken for doneness.

The door jangled.

"Be right with you!" she said, dumping the chicken into a metal bowl.

"Elizabeth."

She froze, fry basket in hand.

Darcy stepped towards the counter. "Hi."

"Hi."

"LB, hurry up, laaaa!" Vincent cried, sliding her three steaming containers of vegetables in sauce.

She handed her father the bowl of chicken from the fryer, and turned back to the register.

She would have thought that he couldn't get far enough away from her family and all of their problems after what he did, but here he was—sweating in the heat of the fryer in a three-piece suit.

"How's your family?"

She colored. "Good. Better now, anyway, that Lydia's home," she said. "And Georgiana?"

"She's back at school," he said. "She sends her regards."

So they were back to regards.

The bell jangled as Jane walked in, Brendan following behind her.

"Sit down," Elizabeth said. "We can bring you something."

Brendan slid into a seat at one of the empty tables, but Darcy stepped off to the side and stayed standing.

Jane ducked behind the counter with a mumbled apology, but Elizabeth could see a soft glow in her cheeks. Whatever they had talked about looked like it went well.

Brendan looked at Jane, Jane looked at Brendan, Elizabeth looked at Darcy, and Darcy stared at the opposite wall, straight at the grease-splattered calendar showing an outdated month. All they could hear was the clang and scrape of the wok.

Elizabeth rang up another order. "How long are you guys in town?"

Brendan leaned back in his seat. "A few weeks," he said. "At least. We're set to meet with some engineers about the roof."

Vincent walked out from the kitchen, wiping his hands on an old rag. He eyed their two new guests with interest, bumping Elizabeth in the side as he passed. "Well, this is unexpected," he said. "Don't let my wife see you if you want to make it out alive."

Brendan chuckled. "Hello, Uncle."

"Want something to eat?"

Darcy and Brendan shook their heads. "We were just stopping by to . . . say hello," Brendan said.

Vincent glanced at Elizabeth. "Just being friendly. I understand." He pushed her out from behind the counter. "Sit down, girls. Catch up. Your dad will make you something to eat."

Elizabeth took a seat at the table, propping her feet up on the chair beside her. "You don't want to sit?"

Darcy shook his head.

"Typical," she said. With a careful glance at his face, she said, "How are you doing?"

"I'm all right," he said. "It's good to see you. You look good."

She arched a brow. "I look good?"

There was that look of exasperation she'd so missed.

She pulled a few napkins out of the holder and wiped off her hands. After a moment, she said, "You look good too."

He righted a fallen napkin holder on the table.

"I passed the center on my way here. It's really coming along," Elizabeth said.

He pulled at the chair beside her, eyeing the ripped upholstery of the seat. After a minute, he dared to sit.

His frown deepened.

"We hope we can keep it close to what it was, even with the new additions," he said. "We don't want to lose what made it special to the community."

Elizabeth's hand grazed his arm. "It's always going to have a home here," she said. "Even if it turns out to be something different."

His hand caught hers. "And is that something you can live with? The difference?"

A platter clattered down between them, sauce splashing on the table.

Darcy jumped, drawing back into his full height like a spooked cat, tension rippling along his shoulders and neck.

"Happy Family," Vincent said.

Darcy looked as if Vincent had started speaking in tongues. "What?" he stammered.

Elizabeth pointed to the plate. "*That*," she laughed, "is a Happy Family."

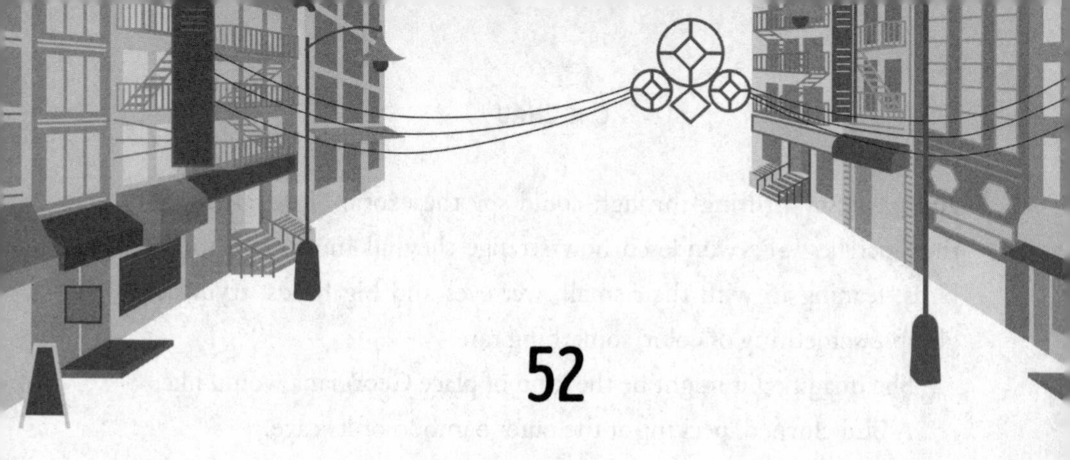

52

In the days that followed, Brendan set out to make up for lost time. No matter where they went or what they were doing, he made a habit of running into them, saying his hellos, and disappearing with Jane for chunks of time. At least it saved Elizabeth the trouble of playing third wheel.

After another morning of being surprised with a bag of bagels and Brendan cluttering up their cramped kitchen, Elizabeth snagged a bagel, her camera, and some time outside. She made her way along Forsyth Street, peeking into the small squares of courtyard and plaza that dotted the area. Too many memories of Ray stirred as she walked, but she tried to shake him off as she went.

She tracked along the handball courts, listening for the sounds of the ball ricocheting off of the walls, the shouts and jeers of spectators. She looked for the tai chi grandparents in their soft sweats and postured poses, for the children clambering on old playground equipment. She condensed the world into focus, cherry-picking her angles.

On Delancey, she ducked into the bird garden. Bamboo cages hung and swayed from hooks, crooks, and stands of all kinds where visitors and passersby drifting through could spy the exotic birds resting on their perches. She wondered how strange they all must seem to the birds, leaning in with their small, wet eyes and big heads, trying to glimpse something of color, something rare.

She imagined it might be the kind of place Georgiana would like.

A bird chirped, pecking at the outer bamboo of its cage.

When it whistled a low note, she whistled a little note back and fired a quick shot.

No matter how hard she tried to get it just right, to create perfect conditions, sometimes a picture just wouldn't turn out. After years of messing around with photography, all she'd ever learned was patience and process. Give it a shot and see if it turns out. Try again if it doesn't. Lather, rinse, and repeat.

That was all they could hope for—Brendan and Jane, her and Darcy—not to relive the mistakes of the past but to thumb through the frames they'd wasted and figure out where they'd gone wrong. How they might do better. Jane deserved nothing less than the world. What Elizabeth deserved, she didn't want to think about.

What Elizabeth deserved, she probably got.

Whatever she had once been to Darcy, there was no guarantee that he might ever see her that way again.

She tried the shutter again, but the button locked.

She'd run out of film.

On her way back into the apartment, she startled Jane and Brendan, cozy against the kitchen counter in a close embrace.

At the noise of the door, they sprang apart.

"Oh, it's you," Jane said.

Elizabeth made a show of covering her eyes as she ran into the bedroom, rummaging for a fresh roll. "Sorry," she shouted. "I forgot something."

"Don't apologize, LB," Brendan said.

"You're right, 'don't apologize,'" Elizabeth replied. "Are you trying to give Mother a heart attack? Go to the roof like normal people."

When she came back out, they had already separated, Brendan slipping into his shoes by the door. "But I'll see you later?" he said.

Elizabeth glanced through her camera, testing a shot of the two of them saying their goodbyes at the entryway.

Brendan propped the door open and waved at her. "Thanks for the advice, LB!"

Once the door shut behind him, Elizabeth raced across the room for the debrief. "What happened? Are you okay?"

Jane pressed her hands to her cheeks as if to dampen her smile. It didn't work. "I think so."

Together, they staggered their way towards the sofa, collapsing onto it in a heap.

"Are you together?" Elizabeth said. "Is he leaving again?"

In short: yes to the first, no to the second.

After weeks mulling over his own choices and some harsh advice, he'd turned himself into Lulu's to apologize. He'd listened to the wrong people, believed the wrong things, and pushed away the only thing that had made him happy.

"I didn't want to hear it," Jane said. "You know, it took me so long, but I really felt like I was over him."

After what she'd just witnessed, if it had been over, it didn't look like it would stick.

But nobody committed to an apology like Brendan. He wanted to know what it would take to make it right, no matter how long it took.

"I told him I needed him to be honest with me. About how he felt, about what his plans were, about everything."

"And what?" Elizabeth said. "Did he promise he'd change?"

Jane knew better than to fall for a line like that, no matter who was giving it.

Jane knocked her shoulder against her chest. "He said *somebody* gave him some hard advice that he'd needed. He's always been someone people go to when they're looking for a good time, and he wasn't sure if that's all I wanted, all I felt . . ."

Elizabeth raised her eyebrows. "No one who looked at you could believe that you didn't have feelings for him."

"I thought he didn't care about me," Jane said. "After everything. And I think he thought the same."

Elizabeth elbowed her sister. "*And?*"

Jane giggled. "We're . . . figuring it out. Giving it a try," she said. "It could still turn out to be nothing."

For once, Elizabeth could be the one to wear the Jane-colored glasses.

"After everything, Jane, I think you get to be happy."

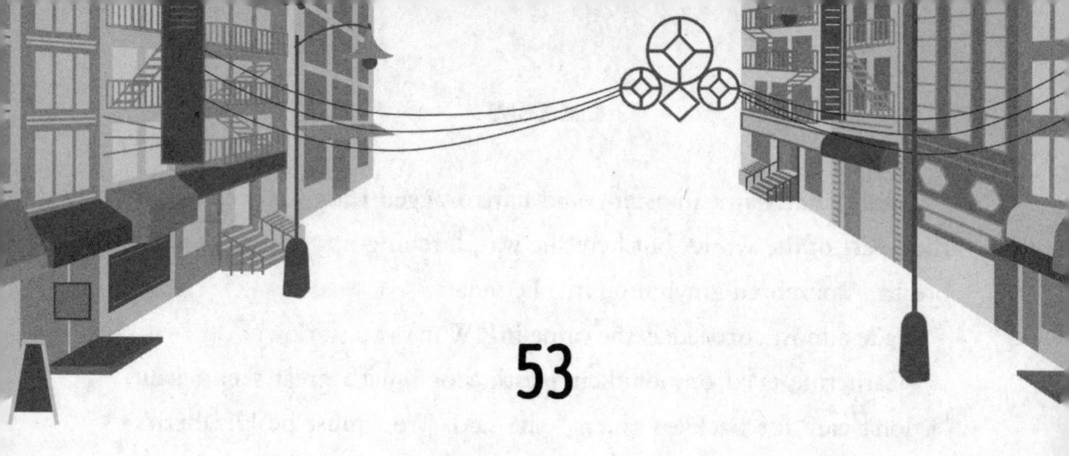

53

With every stroke of good fortune came an equal and opposite misfortune. With Lydia safely returned and not much worse for the wear, Brendan and Jane reunited and making a fresh start, and the household holding in a kind of peace, it seemed they were more than due. One of the fryers at Lulu's went down, leaving them scrambling to handle a torrent of backed-up orders. A new neighbor down the hall started complaining about cooking smells from their apartment. Brendan—always sweet, always attentive, always quick with gifts—quickly morphed into the scourge of a New York apartment: the visiting boyfriend.

Nothing would have prepared them for what followed.

The intercom, crackling with static in the pre-dim-sum weekend morning hours: "Catherine Cheung, if you please."

They did not please.

Kitty buzzed her up, already trembling with terror as the rest of them rearranged themselves on the sofa and at the kitchen table.

Jade paced, fretting the lack of any appropriate food, the state of the living room, the absence of preparation. Nothing would have made her happier than a palpitation.

Only cataclysmic disaster could have dragged Lady Catherine into their part of the world, but here she was, lurching up the stairs out of breath. A purebred greyhound in a PetSmart.

Jade almost curtsied as she came in. "Won't you sit down?"

Catherine eyed one of their plastic stools with great skepticism. "I don't care for backless chairs," she said. "You must be Elizabeth's mother, then?"

"I am," Jade said.

"And you two are the sisters?" she said, waving at Kitty and Mary.

"Some of them," Elizabeth answered.

Catherine tore through the entryway, her heeled shoes clicking against their floors. Despite her disdainful glance at the pile of ratty Vans and Keds tumbled together in the doorway, she hadn't asked or offered to remove her own shoes. "This apartment seems perfectly adequate for the four of you."

"It's typical for the neighborhood, square-footage-wise," Jade added. "Lots of sun exposure. South-facing, you know."

Catherine sniffed, scuffing the toe of her shoe against the floor. "I'm sure."

Jade raced to a kitchen drawer to produce a laminated business card, waving it in Lady Catherine's direction. "I'm an expert on the real estate in the neighborhood, if you're looking for more properties for your portfolio," Jade said, "and very nearly licensed too."

Catherine didn't take the bait.

"I managed everything—well, almost everything—for the owner, the *old* owner, of the neighborhood recreational center."

Catherine surveyed the apartment with open contempt. "No," she said. "I've come for Elizabeth."

The only things that ever came for Elizabeth were bad news and summer colds.

The last time they spoke, Lady Catherine had made it clear what she thought of Elizabeth's future (bleak) and sense (bad). Anything that warranted a personal visit was either catastrophic or crazy.

Jade could smell the blood in the water. "Let's leave the two of you to discuss your business!"

"We're going on a drive," Catherine said. The tone of her voice brooked no argument.

Jade smiled and nodded, saintlike and serene, eager to push Elizabeth straight into the tiger enclosure. "Don't forget to ask for a reference!" she hissed.

Her car and driver idled outside the building, as if expecting the need for a quick getaway. The car's interiors were spacious, the air-conditioning blasting to chill. As Elizabeth shut the door behind her, the locks clicked into place. She wondered if she hadn't consented to her own kidnapping.

Catherine knocked on the partition window twice, and they pulled into traffic. "You must know why I'm here."

"I have no idea why you're here. Is Charlotte okay?"

Catherine shifted in her seat, nostrils flaring like a menopausal bull. This apparently hadn't been the right answer. Everything Catherine asked had a right answer. "This isn't about Charlotte."

With a scowl, she reached into her handbag and tossed a small envelope on the seat between them.

Elizabeth lifted the flap.

Inside were about a half dozen photos from the Pemberley reception. Her and Darcy, close together in conversation. Laughing with Marcus and Georgiana. Nearly arm in arm as they stood reviewing one of the project posters. Even one of his less-than-sober speeches with her in the background, watching him. In the photos, he didn't care to hide anything—not the tenderness and want in his eyes, not the slight bend of his body towards her. When they looked at each other, it was as if there was nothing else in the world.

She lingered on a photo of them crowded around a display, her finger pointing at something out of frame. It caught him in profile, his head angling towards her, a smile pulling at his mouth.

He looked happy.

And in almost all of them, she realized, flipping through, he wasn't looking anywhere else but at her.

"Are you following me?" she said, straining to keep her voice flat.

"Follow you!" Catherine cried. "Elizabeth, it was a company event, not a secret spy meeting."

A company event with photographers, it turned out.

"My nephew, as you know, is a significant person," she said with a sneering curl of the lip. "He handles a great deal of responsibility—with his family, with his company, with the public. He can't afford to be distracted. Certain scrupulous persons have taken care to alert me about this little . . . situation. And, as I am exceedingly fair, I'd like to give you the opportunity to explain yourself, and tell me that this can't be what it looks like."

She wondered if those scrupulous persons hoped they might have a better chance with him without her in the picture. "What does it look like?"

Catherine huffed. "No need to be smart."

"Well, if you think it couldn't possibly be what it looks like, why do you need me to tell you?"

"I want to know what you're after."

She thumbed through the photos, fingers trailing over the sight of their faces. How different they looked in them. How happy. "I don't know what you mean."

Catherine scoffed. "Come, my dear. You clearly want something," Catherine cried. "Money, status, *employment*?"

Now she understood. They thought gold digging ran in the family. They thought they could scare her off like they had Jane.

Why was it that the rich and powerful imagined everybody wanted exactly what they had? They could keep their money, their attention, their pristine reputations; she'd take a greasy day at Lulu's shooting the shit. After all the time she'd spent with them, she'd heard enough to be grateful that she owned her own life; she wasn't sure any of them could say the same.

"Well? Answer the question."

With a chorus of angry horns, they rumbled through another light, speeding past Fourteenth Street.

Elizabeth realized she hadn't even asked where they were headed.

"I don't want to answer your questions."

"You are not so cute," Catherine said. "What are your intentions?"

Elizabeth scoffed. "Whatever I do or don't do with your nephew isn't any of your business. He's a grown man."

"So it's true."

"You said that was impossible."

"It should be impossible if he had any sense. But men can be profoundly stupid, especially when there's a woman involved."

Elizabeth bit back an insult.

"And don't think I haven't heard about this matter with your sister," she howled. "Desperately undressing herself for anyone willing to . . ."

Elizabeth jerked at the door handle, but the child-safe locks held fast. "Don't say anything about my sister," she said. "Keep my family out of your mouth."

Catherine's mouth wrinkled with humor. "Or what? You'll assault me in my own car?"

"Or you could stop and let me out."

A chorus of shrill honks sounded from outside. They inched forward through traffic. "Elizabeth, since you're having so much difficulty, I will say it again. Darcy *cannot* have anything to do with you. His life depends upon it. His *future* depends upon it. He needs someone *far* more appropriate than some girl with no greater plans than to deep-fry poultry for the rest of her life, who runs around with petty criminals and vandals."

Elizabeth huffed.

"There are bigger plans for Darcy than anything you could imagine," she said. "Do you want to be the one to get in the way of that?"

"Nothing's getting in the way of those plans if he feels the way that you think he does," Elizabeth said. "If I'm what he wants, then it has nothing to do with you."

"If you think that you can get out of this with a piece of his money, you're mistaken. You won't see a penny."

"There are worse things in the world than having to work for a living," Elizabeth said.

Not that they would know it.

"Think about what you're doing. Would you drag him away from his family? His friends? Everything he knows?"

"I'm not dragging him away from anything!" Elizabeth said.

They slowed in their approach to the next light, and Elizabeth tried the door again. All it would take was another run of bad traffic, and her taking her chance against the street. Minor injuries would be a better fate than staying in the car.

"Before you leap into traffic from a moving vehicle, Miss Elizabeth, let me ask you one thing," Catherine said. "If you really cared about Darcy, why would you want to take him away from the people that love him? From the life that he's spent so much time building for himself?"

Elizabeth chewed hard on her lip, watching the blur of buildings through the window.

"Is he to be condemned forever to a life of crab rangoon?"

Elizabeth banged her fist hard against the window. "Pull over!" she shouted through the partition.

Catherine sighed, waving her fingers in assent.

As they pulled off towards the side of the road, Elizabeth tried the door repeatedly until the driver reset the locks, glaring at her in the mirror as if she were an unruly child.

She opened the door into oncoming traffic.

"So you're determined to ruin his life," Catherine harrumphed, and Elizabeth relished in slamming the car door in her face.

The tinted windows of the car lowered as Catherine leaned her head through the gap.

"I send no regards to your mother or your family," Catherine replied.

The window slid up a few inches, and then down again.

"You are a very unmannered girl."

There could be no higher praise.

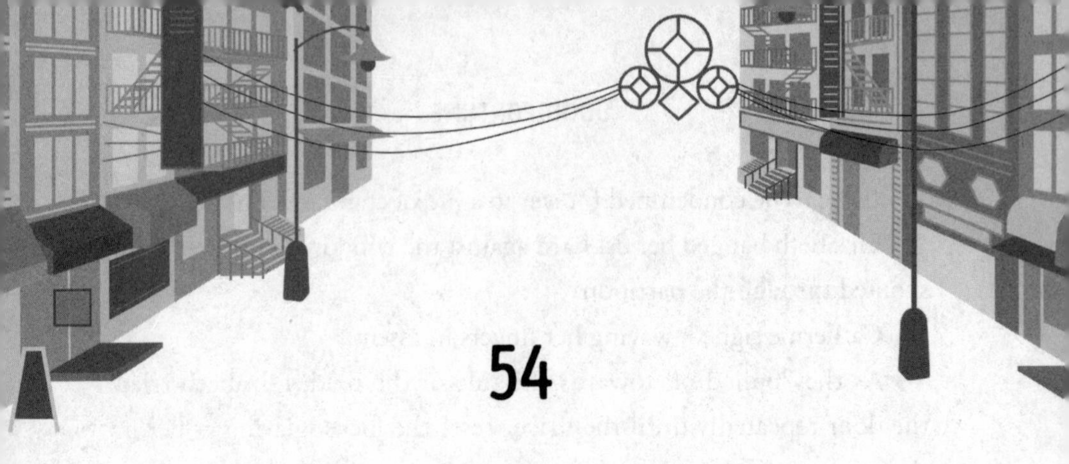

54

She rose out of the subway at East Broadway like a reincarnated soul, nursing the dregs of her bad temper. The only cure would be something sweet, anything to wash the taste of the last conversation out of her mouth. She went to the first café she passed on the corner. Ambient chatter and the dragon's hiss of the espresso machines greeted her as she joined the line.

As the first customer finished paying for his order, he trickled down to the pickup end of the counter. She glimpsed the strong line of his shoulder as he moved.

And then he turned.

She yelped.

The bike messenger waiting in line in front of her glanced at her with a wry look of amusement.

"Darcy!"

He froze, eyes wide and petrified, and gave the slightest wave.

"He looks real excited to see you," a man behind her quipped.

"Shut the fuck up."

The line inched forward.

Darcy took a position at the standing counter by the window, leaning his elbow against it as he watched her in line.

She ordered a plain drip, sliding a mass of crumpled bills from her pocket onto the counter. The barista grunted with irritation, all earnest twenties and college student, and didn't even bother waving her down. She poured the coffee into the thin paper cup and set it on the counter.

Elizabeth took her drink and joined Darcy. "What are you doing here?" *In my neighborhood*, she wanted to add.

"You might want to put the lid on before you spill it all over yourself," he said. "It looks rather hot."

She snorted, blowing lightly before stealing a sip and scalding herself immediately.

He looked at her with faint amusement. "You lose all feeling in your tongue?"

"It's burnt," she said. "I like it that way."

He chuckled.

"Are you still waiting for yours?"

His embarrassed look answered her well enough.

It took three other drink orders before the barista delivered his, a complicated multi-espresso, special-milk, temperature-designated frothy affectation that she didn't want to hear about. Into it he added two (and only two) quick dashes of cinnamon and a single Splenda.

"You didn't tell me what you're doing here."

He snapped the plastic lid on his cup.

"Will you walk with me?"

He studied her for a moment. "Are you going back to the apartment?"

"Yeah," she said, snapping the lid on her own cup. "But I'm not in a hurry."

He held the door for her as she passed, dodging the stream of sidewalk traffic to loiter by the entrance.

The crosswalk flashed a blinking red hand. Surely a good omen.

They crossed when the light changed and tracked along the outer curve of Seward Park, slowing to a crawl on the pavement. He seemed to wait for her to talk, watching her out of the corner of his eye as he dodged speedy kids zooming around the sidewalk.

"This isn't easy for me," she said. "Especially after everything that you and I have—after everything that happened, but for what you did for my sister, for my family, I have to thank you. Personally."

He inhaled sharply. "Elizabeth, no. You weren't even supposed to find out. *How* did you find out?"

She took his hand.

He stilled, his fingers lightly curling around hers.

"No, hear me out," she said. "If my family knew anything about what you did, I wouldn't be the only person thanking you either."

"I didn't want you to think—I'm sorry you found out."

"Is that why you did it?" she said. "Because you thought I wouldn't find out?"

He scoffed. "No," he said. "But if you're going to thank me, then thank me because *you* want to thank me. Not for anything or anyone else."

She squeezed his hand. "I am thanking you because I want to."

His voice dropped to a near whisper. "I did it for you."

She tugged at the cuff of his sleeve. "Let's go in the park for a bit," she said. At his skeptical look, she added, "For a little while."

"This isn't much of a park," he said. "It isn't very green."

"It's green enough for us," she replied, jerking at his sleeve with more force. "Come on."

They followed one of the small rambles inside, circling the playgrounds towards the trees. Children's laughter echoed around the empty space.

"You did it for me?" she said.

He shot her a look, an exasperated smile pulling at his mouth. "Yes," he said, matter-of-factly. A hint of resignation hung on his words. "Are you happy now?"

Elizabeth smiled. Like the first sight of green poking up underneath the February snows, something had grown while she hadn't been looking, while she despaired of winter ever ending. "Maybe."

They banked another curve and paused by the planted gardens. Trees thin of foliage bowed overhead, arms bent in embrace over the tops of their heads.

He led her off to the side, his fingers playing with the hem of her jacket. "I don't think you're the kind to play with someone else's feelings because you can," he said. His hand dared to creep onto her waist. "If your feelings are the same as they were the last time I—the last time we talked about this, I need you to tell me."

Jagged panic flickered on his face, cut with a look of open want. He was fighting to keep calm. "All you have to do is say the word, and it's over."

She stretched up on her toes and kissed him, a small peck of a kiss.

He might have surprised her with their first kiss, but she refused to let this one pass without her proper attention. His lips were soft against hers, coaxing her mouth to open, his arms bracing against her back.

She swayed, feeling the world tilt and open, cracking like a candy shell. Darcy kissed her, and she kissed him back. Darcy kissed her—lips, tongue, hands, and all—with calculated intent, as if he could make up for the last few months in the care that he showed her now. The slow slip of his tongue against hers, the pressure of his fingers against her skin, the light bitterness of his coffee almost sweet in her mouth.

He pulled away and beamed at her. The motherfucker.

She could feel herself smiling back. Lowering herself onto her heels, she tried not to give him any more reason to gloat. "You look pretty proud of yourself."

He pulled her against him. "I'm feeling pretty proud."

He was as smug as she remembered, and all she wanted to do was kiss the look off his face.

She wanted to touch him again. She wanted to never stop touching him. She wanted to make up for lost time, for the errors of their first go-around.

She kissed him again, flinging her arms around him and splashing coffee down the front of his jacket.

He groaned, stepping away to assess the damage. A large brown splotch ran halfway down his chest.

It was a nice chest.

"Elizabeth," he said. "I *told* you . . ."

She bit back a laugh. "What did you tell me?"

"Full coffee cups are a bad idea."

"Lighten up, Wong," she said. "It'll come out in the wash."

They claimed an empty park bench, draining the rest of their drinks as she tried to blot him with an old Duane Reade receipt from her pocket.

"This isn't very absorbent."

"Shh," she replied. "I have questions."

"Of course you do."

"What made you change your mind? After I . . ." She paused, her cheeks coloring.

"Told me what you really thought about me?" he said. He draped his arm over her shoulders. She considered climbing into his lap. "You didn't say anything I didn't deserve. The way I behaved—the way I treated people—it was inexcusable, but I'd never given it any thought before. And when I think about how I acted, I . . ."

She waved his comment aside, nesting her empty cup inside his. "I don't think either of us were on our best behavior. We're getting better."

He shook his head. "I couldn't stop thinking about how you called me out. It took me a long time to hear it, but when I did . . ."

"Better late than never," she said. "And I wasn't thinking when I said half of that anyway. I'm sure it could have been less . . ."

"Insulting?" he offered.

"Passionate."

He laughed, the sound rich and full. She didn't know if she'd ever heard him laugh like that before. "Probably," he said. "You thought that I didn't have any feelings."

"You're not the only one who's embarrassed."

"When I wrote that email, I thought it would make you hate me. Well, more than you *did*."

She nudged him with her shoulder. "Learn to let things go," she said. "The person you were when you wrote it and the person I was when I read it—we aren't those people anymore."

"I should be thanking you, you know," he said, quietly. At her protest, he continued. "You were right about me. I was taught to stand for my principles, and allowed to be selfish and judgmental when it suited me. Because of you, I learned the hardest lesson of my life. What don't I owe you?"

Tears filled her eyes. "If you make me cry, I'm going to punch you."

He kissed her temple.

"I'm almost afraid to ask what you thought when we ran into each other in Boston. Did you blame me for coming?"

"No!" he cried. "I was surprised, that's all."

"Me too," she said. "I didn't think you would be so . . . polite . . . after all that."

"I didn't want you to think of me that way," he said. "Mean and bitter."

She waved her hands—a magician's gesture of sorcery. "Presto," she said. "Blank slate."

"That's how it works?"

"Here?" she said. "Yes. City magic. What are you even doing here anyway?"

"Working up the courage, I guess," he said. "To come and see you."

She touched her mouth against his in a searching kiss. She'd look forward to more opportunities to explore that side of him—how he touched, how he liked to be touched, who he was when they might be alone together.

"Hey," she murmured. "Promise me something?"

He gave her a sidelong look. "Anything."

A funny quiver kicked her low in the belly. It was a dangerous thing, that smile. Bad for her resolve. "I can still bother you about the rec?"

He laughed. "You can bother me about anything."

She pulled him by the hand down the street. "Good. Now come on. I want to show you the roof."

He stumbled after her. "Lead the way."

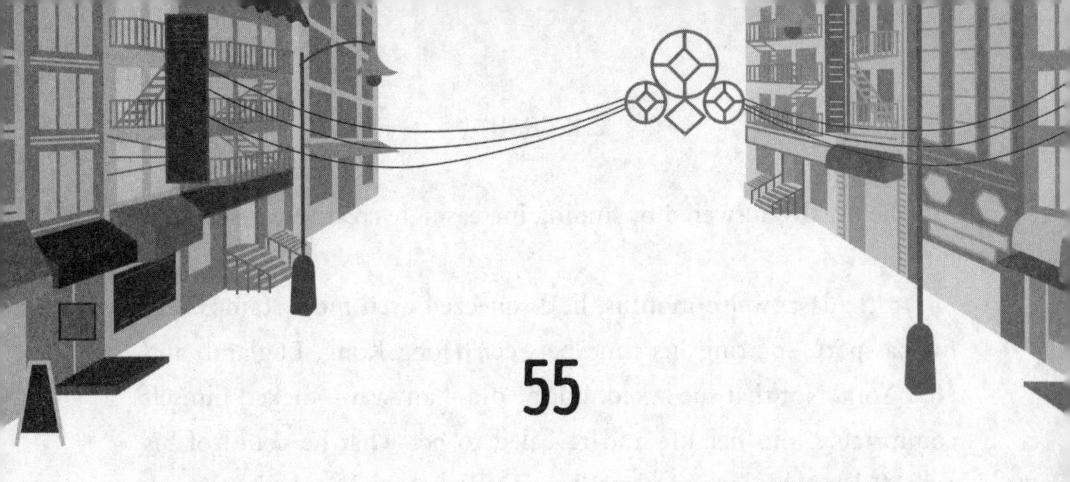

55

For the trouble of dating a flesh-and-blood derivative asset of the Wong Family Land Trust, Elizabeth earned herself an official invitation to the reopening gala for the Fortunata Community Center of Greater Chinatown a year later. What a difference a year could make. In those last twelve months, she'd taken great liberties to remind Darcy of the advantages a community liaison could offer for neighborhood relations, resorting to bribery only when appropriate.

Darcy called it annoying.

She preferred to think of it as direct action.

Jade would have been proud—if still aggravated in Elizabeth's continued failure to promote herself into a better opportunity. But even she couldn't deny Elizabeth's addition to the ranks of the fully employed. A job with the Lower Manhattan Housing Alliance couldn't be called glamorous, but it paid—over the table, no less—and exploited her exceptional skill at infuriating those higher up the chain.

Darcy thought so highly of her skills that he expected them to let her go within the year—when he hoped to hire her on at the trust instead. Quite a vote of confidence.

She usually answered by finding increasingly creative ways to shut him up.

In the last twelve months, he'd squeezed even more stamps into his passport, splitting his time between Hong Kong, England, and New York. Not that she asked. But he did it anyway—tucked himself comfortably into her life and revealed to her what he could of his own. What they carried, they shared; what they shared, they faced. Together.

And while she might never be the right kind of person to fit into his polo and lacrosse circles, he'd decided that she was the only person that fit him—and who was she to argue with sound logic like that?

Even Lady Catherine had started to thaw—with Georgiana's and Caspian's help—after a sullen and silent six months. "I assumed it was an act of protest," she admitted, "but you're still here. I suppose that must count for something." A ringing endorsement.

Tonight, Jane and Elizabeth showed up in their finest, having tucked their very expensive price tags against the bodices of their dresses to ensure they might be returned later and packing practical flats inside their bags. Darcy and Brendan met them in matching tuxedos and grins, prepared to lead them inside where donors, developers, neighbors, skeptics, and press of all kinds mingled and drank, making small talk and stealing canapés.

Despite her mother's many warnings, Elizabeth also smuggled in her camera, hoping to steal candids later in the evening when everyone might be too drunk to notice or care.

Jane and Brendan, MySpace-official and officially obnoxious, headed directly inside while Elizabeth loitered, watching the light reflect off of the new front windows.

"You're scheming again," Darcy said.

She pulled the camera from her bag, lifted it to her face, and snapped a quick portrait of him. Flash on.

He staggered with exaggerated dizziness, shaking his head. *Corny*, she thought, though she couldn't help but smile.

"I thought you were threatened with Napoleonic exile if you brought your camera."

"If *someone* knows how to keep his mouth shut, I'll be fine," she said. "What she doesn't know won't hurt her."

He wrapped an arm around her and steered her inside the main atrium, the air cool enough to trigger goosebumps. "You should consider slowing down a little," he said. "Try to enjoy the moment."

She rolled her eyes. "Pot, meet kettle."

"Hey," Brendan called, bumping his shoulder from behind. "People can see you, you know."

Darcy pushed him off. "You, of all people, are absolutely in no position to judge." The boys embraced each other with a laugh.

Elizabeth looped her arm around Jane's and headed in the direction of the shrimp cocktails. Love meant never having to apologize for what one did on an empty stomach.

With one quick movement, she swiped a handful from a passing serving tray.

Jane elbowed her lightly in the side. "It wasn't as bad as you thought, was it?"

She mumbled around a mouthful of shrimp. "Tastes fine."

Jane smiled, looking around the room. "The rec."

No, it wasn't as bad as she thought. There were still overpriced apartments with oversensitive neighbors to appease, but there were also a number of school and summer programs and open hours for the local kids and families to drop in. There was new playground equipment and outdoor space. There was power and heat and running water, and a chance to do some good.

Best of all, there was a Charlotte Luo, an expert in the neighborhood, to oversee programming operations.

Charlotte rushed the two of them from behind. "I saw that, LB," she said, holding her hand out for a shrimp. "Price for my silence."

Elizabeth smashed a piece of shrimp against her cheek. "There you go."

Charlotte pinched her arm.

"You're supposed to be setting an example," Jane laughed. "You're as bad as the kids."

It felt like old times.

Except now they were older and taller, and falling into the gravity of their own lives. Between Jane's residency and Elizabeth's new job, they'd seen less and less of each other, squeezing in time on nights and weekends and passing shifts at Lulu's. When Jane finally finished moving into her new apartment with Brendan at the end of the month, it would mark the end of an era.

Charlotte stole one last piece of shrimp. "Don't get soft on me, Chen," she said, waving some complicated hand signal at another volunteer across the room. "I can see it in your eyes."

"Who's going soft?"

Darcy and Brendan rejoined them with champagne flutes in hand, handing them each a drink.

Elizabeth stole a sip with a grateful look.

It was always the little things that surprised her—how much he thought of her, how aware he was of her presence, how much he wanted her around. To touch, to see, to make her laugh. She couldn't believe she had once thought him cold. Not this Darcy, smiling back at her over his own champagne glass.

Not this Darcy, who invested so much of himself into loving the people that he did.

How lucky she was to be one of them.

Ugh—talk about going soft. And she wasn't even buzzed yet.

He made a face at her expression. "What's the matter with you?"

She'd become one of those horrible women who were happy in relationships, and she would never live it down.

She shook her head. "You're ruining my reputation," she said. "People are supposed to think that I've got no heart at all."

He rested his hand against her back as he steered her to a quieter corner of the lobby. "You have a heart."

"Allegedly."

"That's what people said about me."

She grinned. "Not me, though."

He pecked a kiss against the corner of her mouth.

"I have a present for you," she said.

Rummaging inside her bag, she produced a large envelope with a flourish.

He gave it a light shake. "Is this a lawsuit?"

Inside was a large, glossy, black-and-white photo from the roof. Like the best of all school photos, it could only be called candid—a little blurry, a little awkward, and definitely catching the wrong expression. Last year's model frowned into the camera.

"A picture of *myself*?" he said. "LB, what am I supposed to do with this?"

"Didn't I do a great job?"

"I wanted a picture of you."

"You could give it to Geo. She's always asking for more pictures of you." She pointed at the crease in the center of his forehead. "I think it really captures your essence. Look at how annoyed you are!"

He snorted. "I wasn't annoyed with you. More with myself."

She leaned her forehead against his shoulder. "Was that when it happened?" she said.

His voice pitched in faint suspicion. "When what happened?"

"When you fell for me?" she said. "Truly, madly, deeply . . ."

He cupped her face in his hand, fingers light against her neck. "I can't tell you when, where, what, or how. I was already in the middle before I knew I even started."

She pulled him in for a kiss, tinting his mouth with the rouge of her lipstick.

"LB," he groaned. "You promised."

"Okay, but that was your fault for saying all that," she said. Reaching for a napkin, she dabbed at his mouth. A lingering pink stained his top lip. "What started it all?"

He shrugged. "I liked your honesty."

"You were sick of people being nice to you," she translated. "You didn't want someone who *pretended* to be impressed with you. That's what happened."

"Oh," he laughed. "Is that what happened?"

"I think it makes a lot of sense as a theory. Don't you?"

"I think it was after your graceful turn cleaning the windows."

She laughed loudly, attracting the glares of several couples around them. "God, that stupid accident with the ladder," she said.

"One of your finest moments."

"Feel free to leave out the detail about my bleeding teeth when you tell that story. As my boyfriend, you've got to exaggerate my good qualities as much as possible."

His nose slid along the plane of her neck. "Your boyfriend, hmm?"

A shiver trickled down her spine. Actually going weak in the knees. Reprehensible.

"At some point, LB, we're going to have to introduce ourselves to other people," he said. "This is a party."

"This is *your* party," she replied, sipping at her champagne. "I'm a plus-one."

He gave a rueful chuckle. "That's the *last* thing you are."

"Why didn't you act like a normal human being if you liked me back then?" she said. "Drop a hint or something."

He shook his head. "I would have if I didn't like you so much."

She took his hand and pulled him back towards the entrance.

"LB," he said, exasperated. "What did I just say?"

"Five minutes. Come on. Do something nice for your girlfriend."

They crept out to the street, passing down the block to the nearby stoop of a closed boutique. She pulled her camera free, uncapped the lens, and snapped his profile against the late afternoon light. She squinted through the viewfinder, centering him in the frame. "Do you remember what you said to me one of the first times we met?" she said. "About me framing you?"

"About you *choosing* to see and hear what you want?"

She fired the shutter. "Something like that."

He turned towards the camera, and she waved him back into position. Dangerous, how much she liked him. "Yes?" he said. "Where's this going?"

She slipped the camera strap from around her neck and held the camera out to him.

"What are you doing?" he said, sounding faintly panicked.

"I'm holding an expensive object out to you," she said. "Take it."

He followed her instructions.

She set her hands on her hips and arched her back, shrugging a shoulder and pouting at the camera. She stuck her tongue out and flashed a *kawaii* pose.

"You look delirious," he said.

"So that's how you see me."

He fired a few shots, and handed the camera back.

"Well?" she said, looping the strap back around her neck. "How do you find me?"

"Beautiful," he said.

"Liar."

"LB, come work with me."

She fumbled the lens cap and it clattered to the pavement. "I'm sorry?"

He stooped and picked up the cap. "Come and work for the trust," he said. "You know as much about the developers in there as anyone else, and you'd do a damn good job."

"That's nepotism," she said.

"It's a . . . reference."

She shook her head. "It's nepotism. And I have a job."

He pressed the lens cap into her palm. "I'm poaching you."

"I have my ethics, you know."

His arms wrapped around her, pulling her into a light hug. "You wouldn't be working for *me*," he said. "I mean, you are, but you aren't."

She rolled her eyes. "So what would I do?"

"Bully people," he said. "Fuck around in Excel."

"Woo a girl," she said. "Make me an offer."

He gave her a dubious look. "What happened to your ethics?"

She felt his mouth graze the top of her head.

"Can I have your camera, please?" he said.

"Are you going to break it in a nefarious plot to get me to join LuthorCorp?"

"I don't know what you're talking about."

She handed it over.

He jogged down the sidewalk, stopping a passerby to ask for a photo. A woman with a tiny Kate Spade handbag frowned but obliged.

Elizabeth grinned as he pulled her back into his arms. She never wanted to leave.

The stranger raised the viewfinder to her face.

They smiled into the lens, the flash firing twice.

Darcy took the camera back and tucked it into her bag.

"I didn't know you were so sentimental," she said.

He scoffed. "I just need a new picture for my office," he said. "Instead of that absurd nine-by-thirteen mug shot of myself you gave me."

She kissed him, and he kissed her back. Sometimes life could be so simple.

She looked out at the city that she loved so much, and he looked at her, and she considered herself, however briefly, however wrongly, one of the luckiest women in the world. Start spreading the news. For a once unremarkable girl from an unremarkable family, she wasn't doing too badly for herself after all.

ACKNOWLEDGMENTS

Debts of gratitude, both large and medium:

Isabel Kaufman (and the Fox Literary team), for your keen insights, corrections, and depth of understanding of (in no order): writing, art, the market, the industry, and what I was trying to do here; for your generous patience throughout the process, and for enthusiastically believing in this and me from the beginning. I've felt extraordinarily blessed to have you as a champion, guide, and friend.

Tara Parsons, for being the ultimate fairy godmother of this book. Your edits, insights, and encouragement were invaluable, and your painstaking work helped transform the vision of this book into reality, improving it immeasurably along the way. I wouldn't have made it to the ball without you. And to everyone at HarperVia, especially Judith Curr, Juan Mila, Paul Olsewski, and Alexa Frank—I'm thrilled this book could find such a loving home.

The Family—but especially Dad, Kevin, Aunty, Tina, and the Sisters—there are too many of you to name. Thank you for the contradictory family mythologies, and for mildly encouraging a very expensive reading and writing habit. Thank you for bringing me here in the first place. I never appreciated those trips from Chinatown to Chinatown at the time, but hindsight is 20/20.

Isobel Woodger, for your saintly patience, your bolstering, and your suggestions on early drafts to help me along. JoAnn Yao, for being the best sister a girl could ask for and for your infinite wisdom, clarity, and willingness to throw down—in writing, in work, and in life. Michele Balsam, for being the first to the party and unwavering always in your encouragement; you can say I told you so. Anna Prendella, for always pushing me (creatively and otherwise) and for all the joy and celebration. Somaya Daud, for inspiring me, teaching me, and cracking me up.

For enthusiastic and unflagging support (and occasional cheerleading), in no order: Thanks to Pamela, Austin, Cat, Meg, Hannah, Elisabeth, Sarvat, Ari, Anya, Dana, Sarah, Heather, Remy, Jordan, and Tam. For the Austen crew (Rachna, Lex, Tasnia, Carrie), I anxiously await your judgments. Grace H., for helping to fix the first twenty-five pages. Professor Perera and Gabrielle, for once telling me you thought I could write a book; I've held on to that. For the ones who came before, I'm still learning from you.

Last, but never least, Jane—I hope you aren't rolling in your grave.

A NOTE ON THE COVER

It was a joy to work on the cover design for C. K. Chau's *Good Fortune.* I took a nice trip down memory lane, looking at old photos of Chinatown streets for reference. Having grown up in NYC's Chinatown in the '90s, this novel brought me so much nostalgia. It's such an honor to have the opportunity to design the cover for this novel that I relate to in so many ways.

—Sandra Chiu

Here ends C. K. Chau's
Good Fortune.

The first edition of this book was printed and
bound at Lakeside Book Company
in Harrisonburg, Virginia, June 2023.

A NOTE ON THE TYPE

The text of this novel was set in Sabon Next LT, which was designed by Jean François Porchez. A revival of a revival, Porchez tried to simultaneously discern Jan Tschichold's own schema for the original Sabon typeface, while interpreting the complexity of a design made for two different typecasting systems. Like the original typeface, it drew inspiration from the elegant and highly legible designs of the famed sixteenth-century Parisian typographer and publisher Claude Garamond, and is named after Jacques Sabon, one of Garamond's close collaborators. Sabon Next LT has remained a popular typeface in book design for its clean look and versatility.

An imprint dedicated to publishing international voices,
offering readers a chance to encounter other lives and other
points of view via the language of the imagination.